EBURY PRESS

THE SLAYING SWORD

Kalki Ramaswamy Krishnamurthy (1899–1954) was a pioneer of modern Tamil literature whose active involvement with India's freedom struggle inducted him into journalism. A liberal humanist and true-blue Gandhian, he had a passion for his mother tongue and took pride in his pan-Indian heritage. Krishnamurthy was a fiery, often controversial, crusader for political freedom, social reform and cultural revival. He adopted the pseudonym 'Kalki' after the apocalyptic avatar with the avowed intention of destroying repressive regimes and creating a new era with radical writings. Kalki's prolific output includes essays, fiction, travel writing, art critiques, songs, poems and even a screenplay or two. He is lauded for his mesmerizing storytelling, conversational style, lyricism, wit and trademark humour. The serialized historical romances that made Kalki a cult figure appeared in the eponymous nationalist weekly he founded in 1944. His magnum opus *Ponniyin Selvan* remains a bestseller in the Tamil-speaking world.

Gowri Ramnarayan is a writer, translator, journalist, playwright, theatre director and educator. Formerly deputy editor of *The Hindu* and vocal accompanist to the legendary Carnatic musician M.S. Subbulakshmi, she has authored children's books, a biography of M.S. Subbulakshmi and profiles of iconic Indian artists. The 2017 collection *Dark Horse* anthologizes her original plays. Gowri has translated Kalki's short stories, his award-winning novel *Alai Osai* (The Sound of Waves), a two-volume biography by M.R.M. Sundaram titled *Kalki Krishnamurthy: His Life and Times*, as well as two plays by Marathi playwright Vijay Tendulkar. She is the chairperson of the Rukmini Devi Arundale Trust, senior associate editor at *Sruti* magazine and adjunct faculty at the Asian College of Journalism. Gowri has served as a jury member of the International Federation of Film Critics (FIPRESCI) at film festivals and holds a PhD in comparative aesthetics from the University of Madras.

THE SLAYING SWORD

PONNIYIN SELVAN 3

KALKI

Translated from the Tamil by Gowri Ramnarayan

EBURY PRESS

An imprint of Penguin Random House

EBURY PRESS

Ebury Press is an imprint of the Penguin Random House group of companies whose addresses can be found at global.penguinrandomhouse.com

Published by Penguin Random House India Pvt. Ltd
4th Floor, Capital Tower 1, MG Road,
Gurugram 122 002, Haryana, India

Penguin Random House India

First published in Tamil as a series *Ponniyin Selvan* in *Kalki* magazine 1950–54
Published in Ebury Press by Penguin Random House India 2024

10 9 8 7 6 5 4 3 2 1

ISBN 9780670099948

Typeset in Goudy Old Style by Manipal Technologies Limited, Manipal
Printed at Thomson Press India Ltd, New Delhi

www.penguin.co.in

1

In Kodikkarai

The cyclone hit the seas and entered the coastal regions of Tamizh Nadu on its headlong progression, leaving doom and destruction in its wake. The repercussions of the devastating games of the wind god could be seen from Kodikkarai to Poompuhar. Broken branches lay everywhere. The whirlwind had swept all the rooftops away to great distances and left them shattered to shards. Huts were reduced to splintered walls. Kodikkarai seemed to be awash with floods, as though the sea had taken over the land. Only the sandy strips between land and sea had escaped, and even there the quagmires were filled with water. Now they could easily swallow whole elephants. If a man or beast were to step on them, they would be entombed alive.

Two days after the cyclone, Periya Pazhuvettaraiyar and his retinue arrived in Kodikkarai. The palanquin followed them, with the young queen Nandini Devi in it. Pazhuvettaraiyar had enthusiastically agreed to Nandini's suggestion that there was no need to take Madhurantakan this time. Besides, the palanquin would come in useful for Madhurantakan's journeys only if Nandini too used it now and then. Blinded by lust, was it not natural for the old man to be eager to take the most beautiful girl in the world along with him?

They had reached Nagaipattinam before the cyclone struck, which enabled Pazhuvettaraiyar to complete his official duties there.

Nagaipattinam was one of the most important ports in Tamizh Nadu at that time. Innumerable goods brought by the ships were carried to the shore by little boats. The same boats took the bartered goods from the land to those freighters. There were several immigration officers to supervise these imports and exports. Was it not the responsibility of the Supreme Income Tax Commissioner to monitor the performance of their duties?

Once that task was completed, Pazhuvettaraiyar visited Chudamani Viharam, the city's famous Buddha shrine. The monks welcomed him with due honours. The Chancellor of the Exchequer inquired if their monastery or shrine had any requirements. The monks assured him that they had none and expressed their gratitude to the Chozha king.

A few days before this, two monks from the Chudamani Viharam had visited the emperor in Tanjavur on behalf of the Buddha association, to convey their good wishes for his quick recovery. They also expressed their appreciation of all the services rendered by Prince Arulmozhi Varman to Buddhism in Ilankai. They informed the emperor that the monks of the Buddhist association in Ilankai were delighted that the damaged Buddha shrines on the island were being renovated at the prince's command. They added, 'Your Majesty! We hear some good news. A large majority of the monks wish to offer the ancient throne of Ilankai to your son and crown him king of the island. Do we need any more evidence to proclaim the prince's glory?'

As he heard them speak, Pazhuvettaraiyar's mind came up with a bizarre idea. When the monks left, he shared it with the emperor.

'O lord who rules the three worlds! Your authority extends everywhere. There is none to disobey your command in this whole wide world, with the exception of your two sons. They are ill-advised by men who hold high posts in the Chozha empire. Aditta Karikalan refuses to come here. Instead, he sends messages inviting you to Kanchi. The man who gives him such improper advice is none other than Tirukovilur Malayaman, your father-in-law. Many times have you asked for your younger son to be summoned from Ilankai. I am tired of sending messengers for that purpose. Kodumbalur Periya Velar ensures that our men do not meet the prince. If it were not so, why would your dear son delay his visit for so long even after knowing that it is your wish? I have come up with an idea to deal with this situation. With your permission, I will share it with you.'

When the emperor gave his permission, the Chancellor of the Exchequer said, 'Let us send an order to arrest the prince and bring him here, accusing him of conspiring to seize the throne of Ilankai. Bhooti Vikramakesari cannot stop such a decree. Besides, if the order is delivered to the prince, he will obey at once.'

Sundara Chozha smiled. It was a bizarre idea, but why not try it out? The king was longing to see Ponniyin Selvan. Instinct told him that his end was near. Therefore, he wished to confide in his younger son. If he knew that the king wished to hand over the empire to Madhurantakan, Arulmozhi Varman would agree at once and without protest. Then, it would be easier to convince Aditta Karikalan through him.

It was with this thought that the emperor gave his consent to Pazhuvettaraiyar. The shipmaster was given strict orders to ensure that no harm befell the young prince.

Pazhuvettaraiyar was assailed by anxiety when the ships left for Ilankai with the order. He realized that if anything were to happen to the prince, he would have to face the blame. This was the reason why he wanted to go to the Nagaipattinam port to welcome the prince with all due formality and take him to Tanjavur under his personal supervision.

There were some corollaries impacting this decision. Neither Sembiyan Mahadevi nor Princess Kundavai should be allowed to meet the prince before he came to meet the emperor in Tanjavur. Both women had tremendous influence over the prince. Both disliked the Pazhuvettaraiyars. Their counsel would make the prince change his mind. This could challenge the status quo and upend the mission before the right moment—the death of Sundara Chozha.

Moreover, from the day the guard had been attacked and killed in the treasury vault, Periya Pazhuvettaraiyar was preyed by unwonted suspicions. Could someone have been hiding in the treasury? If so, who could it be? The Vaanan warrior who had escaped from the guards? In that case, could he not have learnt many more secrets?

Was there any connection between this incident and the sorcerer Ravidasan who made frequent visits to Nandini, as Chinna Pazhuvettaraiyar insisted? He had to look into it.

Periya Pazhuvettaraiyar was badly shaken by the news that it was Kundavai Devi who had sent Vandiyatevan with a missive to Prince Arulmozhi Varman. What kind of information would she have sent? Did she know that he, Sambuvaraiyar and others had taken a decision about the Chozha throne and written about it to the prince?

In any event, it was best for him to meet the prince as soon as he landed in the Chozha country. He should meet Vandiyatevan too, since there were orders to arrest him as well. He must discover how much the man knew.

These thoughts prompted Pazhuvettaraiyar to go to Nagaipattinam. Nandini had stronger reasons to accompany him. She was keen to see Vandiyatevan again and find out what Kundavai had said in the missive entrusted to him. She was also eager to know if Ravidasan had succeeded in his mission. This made her tell Pazhuvettaraiyar that she wished to accompany him. The old man agreed at once and began to fantasize about their pleasure cruise together. He hoped that it would assuage the fires consuming his body and soul.

The cyclone broke out when Pazhuvettaraiyar and Nandini were stationed in Nagaipattinam. Nandini enjoyed watching the vicious antics of the whirlwind and the waves rising above the coconut trees. However, Pazhuvettaraiyar's dream of a pleasure cruise remained unfulfilled.

Once the cyclone abated, Pazhuvettaraiyar inquired about how the boats and ships had fared, and learnt that widespread awareness of the cyclone threat had prevented extensive damage. But a few fishermen said that from their catamarans they had sighted two ships being buffeted by the cyclone in mid-sea between Kodikkarai and Ilankai. One of them had caught fire and capsized. This aroused great trepidation in Pazhuvettaraiyar. Could they be the ships he had sent to take the prince into custody? If anything had happened to the prince, he would have to shoulder great blame. How could he face the people of the Chozha realm who had boundless love for Arulmozhi Varman? What could he say to the emperor? He became obsessed with getting the news confirmed. He thought that he may learn more in Kodikkarai. Those who actually saw the drowning ship could still be there. Moreover, those who managed to escape from it might have reached the shore. Yes. He would have to go to Kodikkarai at once.

Nandini agreed with him. She said, 'I have heard that Kodikkarai is beautiful. This would be an opportunity for me to see a place I have never seen before.'

There were two routes to Kodikkarai from Nagaipattinam—by land and stream. They took the former as Pazhuvettaraiyar had a large retinue. Moreover, Nandini did not like the waterway. One of her reasons was the fear of Pazhuvettaraiyar launching into lovemaking if they took the boat. But if they went by the land route, it would be possible to question the fishermen who had returned to the shore about the burning ship in the middle of the sea.

As soon as they reached Kodikkarai, Tyagavitanka Karaiyar, the lighthouse keeper, offered his modest house to the Pazhuvettaraiyar couple. Kodikkarai had no other buildings or mansions. Yet, Nandini rejected the offer. She declared that she preferred tents.

These were put up accordingly. Further away, more tents were put up for the retinue.

As soon as they were up, a big ship was sighted on the sea. It sailed as close to the land as it could and stopped.

Pazhuvettaraiyar's agitation mounted when he saw it. From its tattered sails, it could be surmised that the ship had been caught in the cyclone. Who could be on it? The prince perhaps? It was not surprising that the tiger flag was missing. It could have been ripped away by the whirlwinds.

Pazhuvettaraiyar sent a boat to the ship. As if they had been waiting for it, two men got into the boat. One of them was Partibhendra Pallavan.

Partibhendran was thrown into a state of great consternation when the prince jumped off to save Vandiyatevan but did not return. When the day broke and the wind calmed down, he searched for the prince in several directions. One of the two men who had accompanied the prince was found, half-dead. He told them about the extraordinary bravery with which the prince had rescued Vandiyatevan and the fate that overtook the boat subsequently. This served to increase Partibhendran's grief. But he held on to the hope that the prince might have been washed ashore in Kodikkarai.

He decided to go to Kodikkarai and make enquiries. It was when he got into the boat sent by Pazhuvettaraiyar that he learnt that the old warrior and his young queen were on the Kodikkarai shore. This infuriated him.

He recalled what Aditta Karikalan had told him about the young queen of Pazhuvur. And then, quite suddenly, a sneaky wish began to rise in the inmost recesses of his heart. He simply *had* to see the ravishing siren who had stolen the mighty hero's heart and turned him mad. This secret hope flamed within and began to overwhelm him. In fact, he began to worry about whether he would not be able to see her after all.

This anxiety did not last long. As soon as he got off the boat, Partibhendran was taken straight to Pazhuvettaraiyar's tent. Pazhuvettaraiyar appeared at the entrance in all his majesty. What folly it was to think of that tall, hefty warrior as an old man, Partibhendran thought. A lion among men, his sinewy figure and strength of mind surpassed what he had seen in many young men.

As these thoughts were passing through his mind, a young girl came out of the tent like a streak of lightning shooting through the clouds. She came to stand in front of Pazhuvettaraiyar like a flowering creeper spreading over an imposing teak tree.

Casting a piercing glance at the Pallava prince, she asked, 'lord, who is this gallant warrior? I have not seen him before.' Partibhendran was bewitched by her beauty. Her voice made him reel, as though inebriated by drinking wine from a golden chalice.

2

The Web of Seduction

Old men who marry young girls live in a delusional world of suspicion. They feel a natural antipathy towards strangers. And now there was a palpable reason for Pazhuvettaraiyar to feel this repugnance. He did not like Nandini's entry at that juncture, nor her joining in the conversation. At the same time, he was unable to reprimand her.

Therefore, he got a grip on himself and said, 'Queen, the world has any number of people we do not know. Nor is it possible for us to know them all. It is no loss to us.'

Partibhendran said, '*Ayya*,* there is certainly no loss to the royal consort of the lord of the treasury in not knowing me. The loss is all mine. Devi, my name is Partibhendran.'

'Oh! I have heard of you.'

'Partibhendra, why did you leave out all your titles? Since when did you acquire such modesty and humility? Nandini!

* Sir.

He is not merely Partibhendran, but Partibhendra Pallavan, who conquered the Vengi and Kalinga kingdoms, and cut off Veerapandiyan's head,' Pazhuvettaraiyar told her.

For an instant, Nandini's face darkened like a storm looming in the sky. Lightning flashed in her eyes but disappeared at once. She broke into a peal of laughter.

'Ayya! So many people claiming the honour of cutting off Veerapandiyan's head! Can they be counted at all?'

'Devi, the Chancellor of the Exchequer has said this out of his regard for me. I have no right to that honour. It belongs to Prince Aditta Karikalan alone.'

'Why do you say that? Shouldn't you get some credit for flogging a dead snake?' said Pazhuvettaraiyar, with a sneering chuckle.

'No, lord, no. Aditta Karikalan did not kill a dead snake. When he raised his sword, Veerapandiyan was a live snake all right. Had *I* raised that sword, I would have thrown it away and Veerapandiyan would have survived.' Partibhendran addressed Pazhuvettaraiyar, but his eyes were fixed on Nandini's face.

Nandini realized that the conversation was taking a dangerous turn.

Turning to Pazhuvettaraiyar, she asked, 'Why bring up that old story again? Should we not enquire about what brought him here?'

Pazhuvettaraiyar said at once, '*Tambi!*[*] Forget the old story. Tell me *your* story. When did you leave Kanchi? Where did you go? What is the reason for you to disembark here?'

---

[*] Younger brother.

Partibhendran had lost his head upon seeing Nandini. Now he pulled himself together. 'Ayya, you must forgive me for rambling on and on. I have come with extremely important news; news that could plunge the entire Chozha realm into sorrow. Prince Arulmozhi Varman, who left Ilankai with me on my ship, jumped into the sea when the cyclone was raging. What happened to him after that remains unknown. I came to check if he had reached the shore here,' he said.

Before he could finish, Pazhuvettaraiyar bellowed, 'What did you say?' and crashed to the ground like a massive tree uprooted by a cyclone.

Partibhendran leapt to catch him. Nandini came between them, caught his hands and pushed him away. Then she sat down and took Pazhuvettaraiyar's head on her lap, shouting, 'Water!'

The maid brought water from the tent. A few other soldiers, the lighthouse keeper and his family members came running. Nandini regally waved them all away. 'Lord! Lord!' she said caressingly as she sprinkled water on his face. In a few minutes, the old man's eyes opened. He regained consciousness and sat up with a jerk.

'Nandini! What I heard a few moments ago, was it really true? What did this Pallavan say? Didn't he say that Ponniyin Selvan was drowned in the sea? When he was a child, with these very hands had I joyfully taken up the little prince on my shoulders! With the very same hands, did I stamp the seal on the order of his arrest. *Ayyo!*[*] What will this country think of me?' he groaned and began to beat his head with his hands.

[*] Exclamation signifying deep disturbance.

Until then, neither Nandini, nor anyone else, had ever seen that man of steel wailing in such heartbroken despair.

'Dear one! Don't be so agitated. He has not given us all the news yet. Would it not be better to hear him out and decide on the steps to be taken?' Nandini said.

'Yes, you are right. Partibhendra! Be quick. Did you not say that Ponniyin Selvan died by drowning in the sea? Is it true? Or did you invent it all with some vicious motive? Beware! Don't play with fire!' the old man roared, his eyes blazing.

'Ayya! Pardon me. I did not say that the prince is dead. I cannot believe that this Tamizh realm would have suffered such a terrible loss. All I said was that when the cyclone was raging at its height, the prince jumped from my ship into the sea. By god's grace, he might have survived. He could have been washed ashore right here. It was with that hope that I came here to check if it was so.'

'Why did he jump into the sea when the cyclone was raging? For what purpose? Why did he get into your ship at all? What were you doing when he jumped?' the Pazhuvur lord demanded convulsively.

Nandini interjected, 'Ayya! Let him explain in detail, starting from why he went to Ilankai in the first place.'

'Yes, tell me the exact truth. Otherwise, you cannot escape with your life,' said Pazhuvettaraiyar and ground his teeth.

'Lord! I am not in the habit of speaking anything but the truth. Even if I wish to do so, my tongue will not utter falsehood. Listen! The news reached Kanchi that you, Sambuvaraiyar and several other feudal chieftains were engaged in a conspiracy against the Chozha race.'

'A lie! Lie! A complete lie!'

'The news may have been false. That is my hope too. I am only repeating the information that reached Kanchi. It made Tirukovilur Malayaman and Aditta Karikalan send me to Ilankai to bring Arulmozhi Varman back to Kanchi with me.'

With this prelude, Partibhendran recounted everything that happened in Ilankai from the time he reached the island.

When he finished, Pazhuvettaraiyar said, 'O god! A catastrophe has befallen the Chozha land. And all because of me. Am I not the wretch who ordered the prince's arrest? Was it not I who sent the ships?'

'Lord! It is not your fault. Even if you had not ordered it, the prince would have left for Kanchi on this man's ship. Don't blame yourself unnecessarily. Destiny overrides all our actions. Moreover . . .' Nandini stopped and whispered something to Pazhuvettaraiyar.

Pazhuvettaraiyar's face brightened a little. 'Yes, yes. It did not strike me . . .' he said. Then, looking at Partibhendran, he added, 'Pallava! I am going to your ship and will subject it to a thorough search. You shall remain here until then. Don't try to escape. I am going to order my soldiers to hurl a spear at you if you take to your heels. Beware! Don't die with a wound on your back. You belong to the lineage of the brave!'

'My salutations, ayya. I have absolutely no intention of running away. But if I did, none of your soldiers could stop me. Nor do I have any intention of getting wounded on the back,' Partibhendran said.

'Lord, don't worry about him. I will see to him. If he tries to escape, this dagger will pierce his chest. Be at your ease as you go and search the ship. Question the sailors to check if he has spoken the truth.' Nandini drew out a small dagger from her waist as she spoke.

'Queen, why should you take on this responsibility? Go into the tent. Or go to Tyagavitanka Karaiyar's house. Our soldiers will take care of him. Or I can take him with me to the ship.'

'I will not accompany you, ayya. If I do, you will start suspecting that the sailors are influenced by me in their testimony. I will not move from here. You may go without any anxiety.'

'Dear one! I am not moving an inch till you return. I will be looking at you all the time from here,' Nandini said and added in his ear, 'Who knows whether he is here to gather intelligence? Moreover, no one should come to know the news about the prince until you return.'

Pazhuvettaraiyar nodded and got into the boat. The boat moved towards the ship.

Nandini kept looking at the boat for some time. All the while, she was aware that Partibhendran was staring at her face. Swiftly, she turned towards him. She expected him to hang his head in embarrassment. But will the bee turn away from the honeyed flower?

Displaying once again her small sharp dagger, Nandini said, 'Ayya, don't you try to escape.'

'Devi, why flash the dagger and try to scare me? Escape? Run? Once caught, can a fish escape from the net? Trapped in your spreading net, I—'

Nandini cut in to say, '—What are you saying, ayya? Are you calling me a fisherwoman? If the Pazhuvur lord were to hear you!'

'I don't care! Nor did I mean a fishing net. I am talking about the net of ravishment cast by your eyes.'

'*Chee! Chee!*[*] How dare you? Being called a fisherwoman is bad enough, but are you calling me a whore who entraps men?'

'Pardon me, I meant no such insult. Does a spider spin its web to catch flies? It weaves a web for its dwelling place. Flies fall into it of their own accord.'

'Spider, did you say? Do I look so hideous?'

'A mistake! I should have said lamp instead. A lamp burns to cast an aura of light around itself, but believing it to be a fruit, silly wasps fall into it and die.'

'A lamp can be extinguished by a puff of wind. Or blown out by a breath. That is all the power it has.'

'A lamp may be blown out. But who can extinguish the full moon? The full moon rises according to the laws of nature. It spreads its cool luminescence to delight the earth and sky. But look at how stupid the sea can be! Why should the sea throw itself into a tumult when it sees the full moon? Why should it yearn for the unattainable?'

'I have heard much about the powerful imagination of the Pallava kings and their aesthetic sensibility. Now I realize that it is all true.'

'Until yesterday, I had not believed what I had read in legends and epics. Today I do.'

'What do you mean?'

'I have heard that some women have the power to bring the sky and the earth under their feet. The demons who

* An exclamation of disgust.

churned the ocean of milk to extract the nectar of immortality forgot all about it when they were deceived by a seductress. The mighty demons Sunda and Upasunda killed each other as they fought over a woman. Sage Viswamitra's penance was shattered by Menaka, the celestial nymph. Kovalan was enthralled by Madhavi. For the sake of Kaikeyi, Dasaratha exiled Rama to the forest. The queen of Egypt caused the destruction of the Roman empire–'

'Stop! Stop! Why do you mention these women?'

'Don't you know, Devi? Don't you really know why?'

'You could not be more mistaken if you had me in your mind while you speak of them.'

'No. What you possess is no less powerful.'

'Your own words contradict your statement.'

'How?'

'I sent the Pazhuvur lord to the ship on purpose, just to ask you about something.'

'It was because I understood your purpose that I stayed back.'

'Did you not say that a woman tried to save Veerapandiyan and Aditta Karikalan disregarded her?'

'Yes, I did.'

'Do you know that naïve young girl who tried to save him?'

'The young queen Nandini Devi who lights up the Pazhuvur palace now.'

'If I had truly possessed the kind of power you attributed to me a while ago, would I not have succeeded in preserving the life of the man I wanted to save? Why was it impossible for me to do so?'

'It is true that in his frenzy of bloodletting, Aditta Karikalan did not fulfil your desire at that time. But I know the torments he has been enduring for the last three years.'

'How do you know, ayya? Did he tell you?'

'For three years, he suffered in silence. I knew only that some sorrow was eating into him. He opened his heart to me just ten days ago, that is, the day before I left for Ilankai. Since then . . .'

'Since then what?'

'The desire to see the young queen of Pazhuvur entered my heart.'

'Do you remember saying that if you had been Aditta Karikalan, you would have left Veerapandiyan alive at my request?'

'Very well.'

'Is it true?'

'I swear it. Devi, you can test me.'

'Ayya, I have a doubt. May I share it?'

'Whatever you say in your golden voice is bound to delight my ears and overwhelm my heart.'

'I suspect that all this banter is intended to test me. You talk about my web of seduction in order to cast your own net, trying to discover what lies deep within me.'

Partibhendran was startled out of his wits. It was true that he had begun with that intention. But all duplicity was forgotten as he had been lured into a state of enthralment. He was now embarrassed about his initial thoughts. Without admitting it, he said, 'Devi! Let a thunderbolt strike my head if I had tried to test you or spy on you.'

'Ayyo! Don't say that!' Nandini screamed.

'Why, Devi? Why?'

'The man who came from your master, the older prince . . . What is his name?'

'You mean Vandiyatevan?'

'Yes. He tried to extract intelligence from me very cunningly. From what you say, it looks as though a thunderbolt *did* strike him!'

'Unfortunately, the thunderbolt did not strike him, but the ship on which he was found. The danger he faced affected the young prince as well.'

'I feel sorry when I think of the princess of Pazhaiyarai. Poor thing! The two persons whom she loved most died at one and the same time. What a misfortune!'

'Devi, who are the *two* persons?'

'The princess has a special love for her younger brother, doesn't she?'

'The whole world knows it. Who is the second person who claims her love?'

'Why, the envoy sent by the older prince.'

'You mean, Vandiyatevan?'

'Yes.'

'Chee! Chee! Princess Kundavai who has the power to control the entire Chozha empire, and this cheapskate, this bumptious braggart . . .'

'Yes, she became infatuated with him. That is why she sent him to Ilankai with a letter so that he may escape from Pazhuvettaraiyar's punishment. This poor old man is devastated to think that he is the cause of this calamity. But in reality, it is Princess Kundavai who is responsible for it. If only she had not sent that letter . . .'

'True! True! This disaster would not have occurred.'

'When my husband returns from the ship, you must point out this truth to him. You will earn my gratitude if you do.'

'Devi! Is this the only way to earn your gratitude? Are there no other tasks that you could give me?'

'Ayya! There are a hundred ways in which the gratitude of a helpless woman may be earned.'

'Please tell me. Aditta Karikalan obtained one such opportunity. He let it slip from his hands and has been agonizing over it ever since. I will not make that mistake.'

'Is this true, ayya? Are you the kind of man who would do anything to fulfil a woman's wish?'

'It depends on the woman, Devi! Until yesterday, I would not have done anything to satisfy any woman I had met. In fact, I would have laughed at the very idea. Not today. Try me! If I had a hundred lives, I would surrender them all to fulfil your wish. If I had a thousand kingdoms, I would give them up at your bidding. If I am asked to sacrifice everything forever, both in this world and the next, I will be ready to do so. At a word from you, I will forgive brutal enemies. I would cut off the heads of my dearest friends and place them at your feet.'

This outburst of frenzy set Partibhendran's entire body trembling. His words spilled out in a muddle. His lips quivered. His teeth ground themselves. His hair stood on its end. His breath emerged like the hissing of bellows in a smithy.

Readers will be astounded by this transformation. Why, just the day before, if he had been told that he would undergo such a change, Partibhendran himself would have refused to believe it. And in later years, its recollection would certainly shock him.

Such sea changes are not unique, or confined to Partibhendra Pallavan alone; they are intrinsic to human nature. How can the secrets of the human mind be grasped when the secrets of the human body have not been fully discovered? Hardened criminals suddenly morph into men of stoical strength and purity—they dance and sing in an ecstasy of devotion, become worthy of divine grace, and perform incomparable service to human society. In contrast, all of a sudden, men of unblemished virtue slide into a bottomless abyss.

After listening to Partibhendran's hysterical outpourings, Nandini said, 'Enough, ayya! Enough! I will never ask you to perform such terrible deeds. Rather, I am going to tell you something that will please and delight both you and me.'

3

The Owl's Hoot

Nandini looked at the sea. Pazhuvettaraiyar's boat was nearing Partibhendran's ship.

She heaved a big sigh of relief. It turned into a gale in Partibhendran's mind. 'Devi! Tell me. Tell me what I must do. No need to make any distinctions here—what pleases you, pleases me,' the Pallava warrior said.

Bizarre ideas came into his mind. He had no doubt that the girl was suffering like a caged parrot trapped by the cruel old man. Why not free her from that tomcat? Let her give the word. He would imprison the old man in that very ship and drop him in some unknown land far away. Blackguard! How dare he take a girl young enough to be his daughter, or even his granddaughter, to be his wife?

Nandini was still looking at Pazhuvettaraiyar, who was climbing into the ship now.

'Thank goodness! He got in safely. Valiant as he is, he is old after all. I was worried that he would stumble as he got into the ship,' she said.

Partibhendran was disappointed. He thought, 'Why should she care about the old man? What if he does fall from the boat and die? Good for the country, freedom for her. Why should she be so concerned?'

Meanwhile, Nandini continued, 'Only today did I fully realize his love for the Chozha clan. How agitated he was to hear of the prince in danger! Ayya, the prince could have survived, couldn't he? Is it absolutely certain that he is dead?'

'No, not a certainty. But it is impossible for someone who jumped into the sea during such a cyclone to have survived. What can we do about the winds of destiny?'

'Not destiny, but the greed of that Pazhaiyarai demoness. That is the reason for this mishap. Do you know, Kundavai Devi has great faith in astrology and palmistry? Having examined her younger brother's horoscope and the lines on his palms, she was convinced that he would become the king of the three worlds. Ayyo! Poor thing! How shattered she would be when she learns about the fate that has overtaken him. I wish I could be with her and console her,' said Nandini, in a voice that sounded jubilant. For a moment, Partibhendran was taken aback. Then he decided that his ears were to blame.

'Queen, why should you console her? After all, this disaster was caused by her ambition. She will have to suffer for it.'

'How can you say that, ayya? There are thousand, ten thousand people in this Chozha country who would be devastated if they saw a single teardrop in her eyes. She is the daughter of the Chozha emperor, the peerless beauty of the three worlds!'

'Once, I too had believed that. That was before seeing you . . .'

'And after seeing me?'

'I think that the sum of all her beauty cannot compare with the beauty of your little toe.'

'That's what you say now. If you see her tomorrow, you will forget all about my existence.'

'Never. Am I not asking you to test me? Give me your command, right now.'

'I don't have the right to command, ayya, all I make is a request. Some people say that dissension and chaos have been generated in the Chozha kingdom after my marriage to Pazhuvettaraiyar. I seek your help to prove them wrong.'

Partibhendran was rather disappointed. He had believed that Nandini would give him some arduous task over a personal matter, and he would delight her by carrying it out. But she was talking about matters of state!

'Tell me, queen, tell me your wish,' he said.

'Ayya, it is Princess Kundavai who has been preventing peace from prevailing in the Chozha country. It was her arrogance that enraged the feudal lords and high-ranking officials. Her ambition is to somehow place her younger brother Arulmozhi Varman on the Chozha throne. That is why she was blocking all possibilities of settlement. That reason exists no longer. Now it would be easy to reach an accord. Listen, ayya, you have already said that the feudal lords and high-ranking authorities of the Chozha kingdom wish for Madhurantakan to succeed Sundara Chozha. The emperor too has agreed.'

'Is that so?'

'Yes, ayya. If not, would he have ordered the arrest of the prince? But I still feel that it is not the right solution. There is room for a cordial solution acceptable to both sides. Why not divide the kingdom to allot the region beyond the Vellaru to Aditta Karikalan, and the region below to Madhurantakan? Weren't the Pallava kings, your ancestors, content to rule over Tondaimandalam alone? Didn't the Chozha kings of the past remain satisfied to rule over the region between the two rivers?

'Why are you telling me all this? How do the fortunes of any kingdom matter to me? What do I care about who rules and in what region?'

'Ayya, I thought that you were a true and loyal friend to Aditta Karikalan!'

'So far, I have spent all my time in remaining loyal to others, fighting for their glory, working for their welfare. But now, I want to live for myself. Queen, listen to me! I have often pondered why I was born in this world, why I continue to exist. The Pallava kings, my forefathers, ruled over large empires. They created dream worlds of sculptures like Mamallapuram. I believed that I might have been born to re-establish their glory. But my mind was not in it. I felt no enthusiasm for building kingdoms. I was content to work for the greatness of the Chozha race. I rejoiced in Aditta Karikalan's friendship. I had thought of spending my whole lifetime in this manner. But my eyes were opened today. Just a few minutes ago, I realized why I had been born. There!

The voice of the sea echoes the voice of my heart. The birds in the woods call out in agreement. Devi! Don't talk to me about dividing the Chozha kingdom. Speak of other things! Tell me to bring invaluable corals from islands across the ocean. Ask me to bring pearls from the depths of the sea. Ask me to climb to the pinnacle of the Meru mountains to fetch the sanjivini herbs. Tell me to soar over empyrean heights above the clouds, pluck the stars and string them together to adorn your neck. Tell me to bring the full moon to serve as your mirror.'

'Enough, ayya! Enough! As it is, the Pazhaiyarai princess has been calling me mad. Don't make me lose my wits altogether.'

Partibhendran felt sheepish. 'It is I who is mad. Forgive me. Please tell me what you wish for,' he said.

'I seek your help to clear my name that has been defamed all over the Chozha country, and in all the Tamizh realm. The people say that disaster threatens the Chozha clan because I married this old man. They say that it was I who made Madhurantakan crave to be king. They say that it was I who made the feudal lords take his side. I don't want to die with this slander attached to my name.'

'Why do you talk of dying? To torment me?'

'Pallava prince! Do you know anything about palmistry? Do you have any faith in it?'

Without giving a direct reply, Partibhendran said, 'Show me your hand.'

Nandini extended her right hand. Partibhendran stared at it for some time and said, 'Amazing! It is rare to see such lines. Show me the other hand too.'

Nandini extended her other hand. Partibhendran looked at it and said, 'Devi! Has anyone seen these lines, and made any predictions?'

'Yes, the Pazhaiyarai princess once looked at my hands and said . . .'

'What did she say?'

'She said that I would die young.'

'That is true,' said Partibhendran.

'Ayya! You agree?'

'But it is clear that her knowledge on this subject is half-baked. It is true that one of the lines indicates a short life. But another says that the threat will be overcome and a new life will begin. It also says that following that rebirth, there will be a long and joyful life that even kings and emperors cannot attain. It is also clear that this is obtained after a chance meeting with a young man by the seashore. The lines state very clearly that he will sacrifice his entire life to satisfy your least wish.'

Saying this, Partibhendran suddenly grabbed both her outstretched hands and placed them over his eyes.

Snatching her hands away, Nandini said, 'Chee! Chee! What have you done?'

'Forgive me. I forgot that they were your hands. I thought they were two lotus flowers.'

'If Pazhuvettaraiyar had seen this, he would have impaled you on the stake.'

'Devi! I am sad to think that I have only one life to give you.'

'Why give up that single life this way? Guard it well to help this orphaned girl.'

'Tell me what I should do.'

'The Chozha empire must be saved from disintegration by fratricidal discord. You must help this cause.'

'How?'

'Bring your friend Aditta Karikalan to Sambuvaraiyar's palace in Kadambur. Sambuvaraiyar has a daughter. My ambition will be fulfilled if she is wedded to Aditta Karikalan.'

'All this preamble for such a trifle? I will definitely bring Aditta Karikalan to Kadambur. What else?'

'If Sambuvaraiyar's daughter is married to Aditta Karikalan, half the conflict will be over. The other half will be settled if the Chozha kingdom is divided into two segments, north and south, and handed over to Aditta Karikalan and Madhurantakan.'

'After that?'

'My name will be cleared. Then I will fulfil my own destiny. I will jump into the deep sea and give up my life.'

'I will follow you and save you. Our new life will begin. We will cross the seas and go to distant lands where I will establish a huge kingdom.'

'Ayya! Please do not talk in this manner. I belong to the tribe of the virtuous women of Tamizh Nadu. I am the lawfully wedded wife of Periya Pazhuvettaraiyar.'

'Devi, tell me the truth. Why did you marry this old man? Do you love him? Or were you forced to do so?'

Nandini heaved a long sigh. Her eyes looked upwards, as though she had taken flight into the sorrows of the past.

'Poor thing! No need to blame the old man. I married him of my own free will, with my wholehearted consent.'

'Why? What for? What did you find in him?'

'I didn't find anything in him. I married him because I wanted the comforts and powers of living in the palace.'

'I cannot believe it.'

'It is difficult to believe. From my days of childhood, someone taunted me for being poor and orphaned. She even said that I had no right to play with children of the royal family. I made this mistake because I could not bear her scorn.'

'Devi, who was the woman who treated you with such contempt?'

'Don't you see? Can't you guess?'

'It must be Princess Kundavai?'

'Yes.'

'One day, I will certainly teach her a lesson.'

'God himself has punished her. Her dear brother and dearest lover lost in a single stroke. When I think of her plight, I cannot help but be moved to sympathy.'

'This punishment is hardly enough for that arrogant woman.'

'Her punishment will be complete if you help me in the matter I mentioned just a while ago. Her ambition to become the sole despot of the Chozha realm will be reduced to dust.'

'I will fulfil your wish. How will you reward me?'

'I will give you anything you ask for. Anything that does not go against the honour of Tamizh womanhood.'

'Queen! A new faith has been established in the western lands. It has spread across Arabia, Persia, the region of Baghdad . . . According to that faith, married couples may separate if they so wish. There is a ritual ceremony for that separation. Women can marry again . . .'

'Yes, I too have heard of it.'

'Let us go to those lands. Convert to that faith.'

'I have daydreamed of such things . . . at times. But is it a practical step to take?'

'Why not? Of course it is. If you agree, it can certainly happen. I will go across the seas with you. I will establish a great kingdom with the power of the sword I hold in my hand. I will put you on a throne studded with the nine gems. I will place a dazzling crown on your head. I was born to do this. That is why I escaped death in the many battles I fought.'

'Ayya! There! My husband is returning, Calm yourself. Let us talk about these things later.'

'When is "later"?'

'Come to Tanjavur with us. If not as an invited guest, as a prisoner in custody.'

'Your invitation is more than enough for me.'

The boat carrying Pazhuvettaraiyar reached the shore. The old man got off and came striding up to them as though he were the embodiment of fury.

Nandini and Partibhendran stood up. Pazhuvettaraiyar looked at them with flaming eyes. Poor man! Just to think of the two of them talking together made him wrathful. But there was no way he could find an outlet for that wrath. This made him seethe all the more.

'Lord! Did you inspect the ship thoroughly? Did you interrogate the sailors fully? Is what this man said really true?'

Her voice calmed the Pazhuvur lord a little.

'Yes, queen. What he said has been proved to be true. The adored son of the Chozha land, the cherished scion of the Chozha clan, the invaluable treasure of the Tamizh realm—is gone!' said he and turned to Partibhendran. 'And all because of this murderous criminal, this blackguard who is standing here!' he roared.

'Ayya! I am not responsible for this; don't blame me for it. It is the bewitching ghoul controlling the entire Chozha realm who is responsible for the prince getting drowned.'

Misreading this as a reference to Nandini, the old man's flooding rage broke through the dam.

'Blackguard! What did you say?' he shouted as he seized the spear lying on the ground and aimed it at Partibhendran.

Nandini gripped his arm to stop him. 'Lord! What are you doing? Your great spear has killed so many enemies. Should it be stained by the blood of a guest?'

'Queen! He? A guest? Did you not hear what he said about you just now?' the old man stuttered in rage.

'Hear him out. Was he talking about me? If that were so, I would not trouble you, but take my revenge with this dagger of mine.'

'Ayya! Am I insane? Why would I say such a thing about the young queen of Pazhuvur? Did I not mean the siren in Pazhaiyarai? Princess Kundavai sent a secret missive to the prince through a young man. Didn't the prince jump into the sea to save that ruffian, despite all my attempts to stop him? That is why I said that Kundavai was the cause of the prince's death.'

Pazhuvettaraiyar felt a little ashamed of his unseemly haste but did not give himself away. He said, 'Don't try to cover it up! You are also responsible for the prince's untimely death. How did you consent to his jumping off the ship in the midst of such an appalling cyclone? Get lost! Don't let me see you again!'

Nandini interposed to say, 'lord! Is it not better to take him to Tanjavur with us? Would it not be good if he were to personally explain to the emperor exactly what occurred? Otherwise, those who are waiting to blame us will add this to their list. Without any qualms, they would declare that we were the ones who deliberately drowned the prince in the sea.'

'Let them say what they will. I don't fear them. I will issue an order to cut off the tongues of those who say such things. But his accompanying us may be good in a way. Partibhendra! Why are you looking around you? Do you think you can run away?' said he, and clapped his hands to call the soldiers standing by. Four men approached swiftly.

'Bind him!' he ordered them.

The four men approached Partibhendran. Waiting until they were quite close to him, Partibhendran demonstrated his skills in a flash. The four men fell in four different directions.

'If I am to be bound, don't depute others to do it. I am ready to be bound by Pazhuvettaraiyar alone, the warrior of warriors, who bears sixty-four battle scars from fifty-six battles. I will not allow anyone else to touch me.'

Pazhuvettaraiyar's face brightened a little. 'You are undoubtedly a brave warrior of the Pallava race. Tell me if you are ready to come to Tanjavur with us. There is no need to bind you.'

'That is my wish too. I want to see the emperor and tell him exactly what occurred. I too don't wish to incur unnecessary blame,' Partibhendran answered.

'All right, let us leave immediately.'

An owl hooted in the woods close by.

The two men did not notice the change in Nandini's expression since she had turned away to look in the direction from which it came.

Partibhendran remarked, 'There is something outlandish about these Kodikkarai woods. Owls hooting in full daylight!'

The hoots were repeated twice.

Nandini asked, 'Should we leave at once? Wouldn't it be better to stay for one more day? It is possible that the prince held onto a log and has been swept ashore.'

'Partibhendra! Did you see how sharp-witted the young Pazhuvur queen is? This thought failed to strike either of us. Yes, we must stay on for another day. That is not enough, we must post men along the coast and tell them to conduct a relentless search,' said Pazhuvettaraiyar.

'I have no objections, ayya, though I have no hope of finding the prince anymore. If you had seen the sea's turbulence during the cyclone, you too would lose hope like me,' Partibhendran said.

But the old man would not have it so. He made his guards stand all along the coast for ten miles. He too went on wandering restlessly by the shore.

4

The Screw Pine Bush

In the middle of the sea, the boat continued to sway as merrily as a cradle. It was difficult to imagine that this was where towering waves had risen as high as a palm tree just a while ago.

Prince Arulmozhi Varman, Vandiyatevan and Poonkuzhali were on the boat. Poonkuzhali held the oars but plied them slowly, intent as she was in listening to the conversation between Vandiyatevan and the prince. They were discussing what they should do once the boat reached the Kodikkarai shore. Giving many reasons for his case, Vandiyatevan insisted that the prince should not go to Tanjavur but come straight to Pazhaiyarai.

'Your sister wants to see you on some urgent business. She asked me to bring you directly to her. I must fulfil that task,' he begged.

The prince retorted angrily, 'You want me to break my father's command so that you may keep your word?'

'It is Pazhuvettaraiyar's command, not your father's,' Vandiyatevan countered. He added, 'Even if you want to see the emperor, is it better for you to go as a free man or as a prisoner of the Pazhuvettaraiyars? Listen to me, the moment the news of your arrest becomes public, the people will stand up in revolt. That's all. This country will see a bloodbath. Think about it. Will this be a good thing? God himself must have dispatched the whirlwind to stop such a catastrophe from overtaking the Chozha realm. Do you want to trigger an insurrection in the country against the will of god?'

Of all the expostulations he made, this was the one that sounded most convincing to the prince. He did know that the people held him in great regard. It was perfectly possible for riots to break out if it became known that he was taken into custody by the Pazhuvettaraiyars. He plunged into a reverie.

A little later, he asked, 'Even if I agree, how is it possible for me to do what you want? Won't the Pazhuvettaraiyars be waiting for me in Kodikkarai with their men?'

'This boatwoman will help us. She will take us into the Kodikkarai woods unseen by the crowds that may be thronging the shore. Poonkuzhali! Did you hear me? Can you do that?' Vandiyatevan asked.

Poonkuzhali was in seventh heaven. She was filled with boundless joy at having saved the prince.

She had been troubled by the thought of parting from him once they reached the shore. What greater privilege could she have than to help him even more, in any way she could?

'If we take the boat a little to the west of Kodikkarai, it would be possible to get into the channel covered on both sides by thick mangrove woods. It isn't easy for anyone to enter it,' Poonkuzhali said.

'Can you leave us there and get more information from Kodikkarai?'

'Yes. There are any number of places where the boat can be docked unseen.'

'Prince! Did you hear this?' Vandiyatevan asked.

'I did, my friend. You are asking me to sneak into my motherland and hide like a thief.'

Silence reigned for some time. Then the prince asked, 'Samudra Kumari, why have you stopped rowing?'

'Poor thing! How long can this girl go on rowing all by herself? Give me the oar, amma! I will take over for a while,' Vandiyatevan said.

The prince understood his intention and gave a little smile. 'My friend! All your strategies are wasted. I am not going to Pazhaiyarai. Nor am I going to Tanjavur. God is going to take me into his own abode,' he said.

Vandiyatevan and Poonkuzhali looked at the prince in dismay. They saw that his body had begun to shake.

Vandiyatevan went closer to the prince and then asked, 'Ayya! What's this? Why is your body trembling so badly?'

'I have the shivering fever. Don't you remember my telling you that this fever had spread in Ilankai? It is rare for those infected by it to survive.'

Vandiyatevan was more flabbergasted now than when the lightning struck the ship's mast in the middle of the ocean. The prince's words left him completely nonplussed.

The oar slipped from Poonkuzhali's hand. Her body was drained of all its stamina. Only her eyes, immovably fixed on the prince, showed that she was still alive.

The shivering increased and soon, the prince began to toss and turn.

Unnerved, Vandiyatevan asked, 'Ayya, what should I do? Tell me! My mind has gone blank. Poonkuzhali, there must be a physician in Kodikkarai . . . ?'

Poonkuzhali was struck dumb.

Suddenly, the prince jumped up. His shaking body stumbled as it failed to stand upright. His words came out in a muddle, 'Take me to my sister. Take me at once to the princess!'

Delighted as he was to hear this, Vandiyatevan simply did not know what to do.

'*Akka*!* I'm coming at once. I am coming to see you right away. I will not let anyone stop me now!' Swaying unsteadily as he shouted these words, the prince now tried to jump from the boat.

Fortunately, by then, Vandiyatevan had grasped that the prince was in a feverish delirium. He caught hold of him before he could jump into the sea. The prince was endowed with great strength. His delirious frenzy had imbued him with unexpected vigour. He tried to struggle out of Vandiyatevan's grip. Realizing that he could not control the prince, Vandiyatevan shrieked, 'Poonkuzhali! Poonkuzhali! Come, quick!'

Poonkuzhali came to life and rushed to grab the prince by the hand. All the powers of a rogue elephant that he had

* Elder sister.

acquired in his fevered condition drained out of him in an instant. He became a whimpering child, 'Akka! I will lie still, just as you say. Don't be upset with me, Akka! Where would I be without you?'

Very gently, Vandiyatevan and Poonkuzhali made the prince lie down.

Ponniyin Selvan remained still. His eyes stared into nothing. Vague, unintelligible words spilled out of his mouth.

Vandiyatevan realized that it would be useless to consult the prince. He also knew that he bore the responsibility of saving the prince from this dreadful peril. But he had an intelligent girl with him who was as eager as he was to safeguard the prince. He would also count on god's mercy, which had saved him from multiple threats before.

'Poonkuzhali, should we not go faster?' Vandiyatevan asked.

Poonkuzhali's arms regained their strength. The boat began to gain speed.

Vandiyatevan remained by the prince's side, terrified by the thought of what he should do if the fevered prince tried once again to jump into the sea. He kept a close watch while resolutely pondering on what was to be done next.

'Girl! What do you think? Should we take a chance and land in Kodikkarai? Won't your family members help to protect the prince?'

'Ayya, in these days, how can we be sure about who is to be trusted? My sister-in-law is greedy. My father receives his stipend from the Pazhuvettaraiyars,' Poonkuzhali said and added, 'Moreover, Pazhuvettaraiyars' men who came to capture you may still be hanging around in Kodikkarai. More may have joined them, expecting the prince to arrive.'

Vandiyatevan was surprised by her foresight and delighted to have her assistance in such a tight situation.

'Does it mean that you think it would be a risk to go to Kodikkarai?'

'Look!' said Poonkuzhali as she pointed to where a ship was standing with the lighthouse behind it.

'Ah! A huge ship! Whose ship could it be? Perhaps Partibhendran's . . . In that case, with the prince in this state, would it not be best to take him to Kanchi?'

'It could be Pazhuvettaraiyar's ship. Ayya, do you see anything behind the ship?'

'I see the Kodikkarai lighthouse.'

'See anything different there?'

'No, I don't.'

'I do. I think a group of men are standing on top of the lighthouse and staring hard at the sea.'

'Can they see this boat?'

'Not until we get a little closer.'

'It would be best for us to take precautions. Shall we slip into that channel to the west of Kodikkarai you mentioned earlier?'

'Yes. We can be there by nightfall. Ayya, remember the dark *mandapam*[*] where you hid all day? The channel goes up close to it. If you would wait there for some time, I will go to Kodikkarai, find out what I can and return as quickly as possible.'

'Does the channel end there?'

'It goes all the way to Nagaipattinam.'

---

[*] Pavilion.

They heard the prince talking to himself in a loud voice.

'Yes, Akka, yes. It happened just as you said. In Anuradhapuram, the Buddhist monks did offer me the throne and the crown of Ilankai. Akka, I refused them. I have no wish to rule any kingdom. I will do anything you say. But I don't want to take on the trials of ruling a kingdom. Far better to be happy, sailing a boat on the sea. Listen, Akka! In Kodikkarai, there is a girl with a boat . . .'

A thrill ran through Poonkuzhali's entire body. On the other hand, Vandiyatevan became angry. Both waited breathlessly to hear what the prince would say next. But he had regained some consciousness. He looked around with wide eyes and asked in a feeble voice, 'Haven't we reached Kodikkarai yet?'

Vandiyatevan said, 'There! You can see the shore.' But before he could think of asking the prince for advice, Ponniyin Selvan slipped back into a feverish delirium.

The prince's reference to the girl with a boat had filled Poonkuzhali with surging thoughts. She was too embarrassed to even look at the prince or Vandiyatevan. She focused her attention on the boat, which had been moving towards the ship, and changed its direction to make for the southwest.

As night fell, the boat entered the channel that dove into the land from the sea. As Poonkuzhali had said, both banks were high and thick with tall trees.

Stopping by the bank, Poonkuzhali said in a low voice, 'Ayya, mind the boat,' and jumped to the ground. She climbed a tall tree and looked around. She scrambled down very quickly to say, 'What a good thing we came here! Guards are posted across ten miles by the shore. There is a crowd around the lighthouse and a great deal of commotion.'

'Can you make out who they are?'

'No. But they must be Pazhuvettaraiyars' men. Who else can they be? But let us first go to the place I mentioned. Later in the night, I will go home and find out everything,' she said.

'Girl, what if someone sees you? We are doomed if anything happens to you now,' Vandiyatevan said.

'Ayya! Until now, I'd never cared about my safety. Today, I have started feeling extremely concerned about preserving my life. Nothing will happen to me until the prince is free from danger,' said Poonkuzhali.

The boat went slowly, with Poonkuzhali making sure that the oars made no sound at all.

Darkness enveloped the banks on both sides. The tall trees cast their black shadows, making the channel appear darker.

The stars peeped down from the sky. Like Vandiyatevan, they seemed to be watching the progress of the boat with great disquietude.

Reflected on the waters, they mirrored Vandiyatevan's mental turmoil, bobbing and stirring continually as the breezes shook the tree shadows.

After a short while that seemed like an age, Poonkuzhali made her way through the woods. It may be said that her body strode forward while her heart continued to circle the boat.

She walked fast in the enveloping darkness, unmindful of the thorny bushes, mounds, ditches and the wild creatures in the wood. She ran across the open glades, making her way straight to the Kuzhagar temple. She reached it just as the priest was locking the sanctum.

Making sure that there was no one around, she went to stand before him just as he turned away from the locked door.

The priest was a little surprised to see her at that time, even though he was familiar with her ways.

'Is it you, Poonkuzhali? I wondered who it could be. Kodikkarai is all hustle and bustle. Where were you, Amma? You haven't been seen here for quite some time. This very evening I wondered why there was no news of you despite all the hubbub,' he said.

'I was away, swami. I came to enquire about the commotion. Who are the people crowding the shore?' Poonkuzhali asked him.

'Don't you know anything? Didn't you go home?'

'I was going home but stopped when I saw the crowd. Don't you know that I don't like newcomers? Who's here?'

'Periya Pazhuvettaraiyar is here. His young queen is here. Their entourage is here. Someone called Partibhendra Pallavan from Kanchi, he is also here. Not on a casual visit, he has brought terrible news. Haven't you heard, Poonkuzhali?'

'What is that terrible news? I know nothing about it.'

'It seems Prince Arulmozhi Varman was on that bounder's ship. When the cyclone was raging, the prince jumped into the sea to save someone. He hasn't been found. Pazhuvettaraiyar's men are scouring Kodikkarai to see if by some chance the prince has been washed ashore. Pazhuvettaraiyar too is wandering around. Why, so is his young queen. She was here just now. Poonkuzhali! People say all kinds of things about the young queen of Pazhuvur. Totally false! Do you know how tormented she is by the plight that has overtaken our prince?'

'Is that so? Ayya! I am happy to hear you say so. But why did she come here?'

'She came to pray that, somehow, the prince may be found alive. Does everyone have a heart of stone like you? This terrible news about the prince has not shaken you, not in the least!'

'What is the use of getting shaken up? Haven't you yourself said several times that everything happens according to the decree of fate? Never mind. I don't want to go home when so many dignitaries are there. Please give me the food offered to the god. I will eat it here and stay in the temple.'

'You are a strange creature, Poonkuzhali! Everyone wants to meet important people and get to know them. But you dislike strangers. You are frightened of men of high rank. Why? Will they gobble you up? Why should you stay all alone in this forest?'

'Ayya! It is all right if you don't want to give me the food. Just don't scold me.'

'Siva! Siva! Why should I scold you? All I thought was that this food would not be enough to satisfy your hunger. Please take it!' said the priest, and gave her the bundle of food.

Poonkuzhali took it and opened it. 'This won't be enough to satisfy me for sure. Why are you offering so little to a god who is so great? Is it fair? Never mind. What's in the jug? Water?'

'No, amma, it is milk used for the ritual oblation. I'm taking it home for the child.'

'Let me be your child for today. Please give me the milk too. You will be blessed if you do.'

'And a fine girl you are! All right, keep the jug safe,' said the priest and handed it to Poonkuzhali.

From somewhere close by came the hoot of an owl.

Taken aback, Poonkuzhali asked, 'Ayya, what's that?'

'Don't you know, Amma? An owl is hooting. Any dearth of owls in this Kodikkarai wood?' said the priest.

The call was repeated.

'Yes, it does sound like an owl,' Poonkuzhali said.

'No owl will harm you. Lock yourself in the temple,' said the priest and left.

When the priest disappeared from view, Poonkuzhali started on her way, jug in hand, the bundle tied around her waist.

She went in the direction of the owl's hoot. After a little distance, a stream obstructed her path. On both its sides, screw pine bushes had proliferated like a dense jungle. Unmindful of their pricking thorns, she strode along, keeping close to the bank.

The screw pine flowers had bloomed in a burst of fragrance. But Poonkuzhali remained impervious to their heady scent. She went on walking with slow silent steps, her ears alert and bristling. None of the nocturnal sounds, familiar or strange, caught her attention.

So, what was she looking for . . . ?

There . . . the sound of two people talking in low tones.

One was a male voice, the other belonged to a woman.

Poonkuzhali hid herself as well as she could and sharpened her ears.

'Sorcerer! Everyone believes as you do that the prince fell into the sea and was drowned. Pazhuvettaraiyar is drowning in grief. But I don't believe it,' said the woman's voice.

5

Rakkammal

When Pazhuvettaraiyar and Partibhendran went to the seashore to reconnoitre, Nandini remained by herself, lost in a reverie as she gazed at the sea.

She turned when she heard a voice addressing her, 'Queen!'

Tyagavitanka Karaiyar's daughter-in-law stood there.

'Who are you?' Nandini asked her.

'My name is Rakkammal.'

'Why are you here?'

Instead of replying, Rakkammal stood staring at Nandini's face.

'Why are you staring at me? What do you see in my face?'

Startled, Rakkammal answered, 'Forgive me, amma! I remembered another face when I saw you. But it cannot be.'

'What are you babbling about? What cannot be?'

'There cannot be any connection between you and that dumb, delirious creature.'

'Who is that dumb creature?'

'She is in Ilankai. My father-in-law's sister. She comes here sometimes.'

'What about her and me?'

'That's what I said, there can be no connection.'

'Then why did you remember her face when you saw mine?'

'The problem is with my eyes. Your face . . .'

'Is it like hers?'

'At first I thought so.'

'Rakkammal, where is that mute woman now?'

'She rarely comes here.'

'Should she come here again, will you bring her to me?'

'Why, amma?'

'I want to see the woman who has a face like mine.'

'Queen, don't you belong to the Pandya land?'

'Yes. You?'

'I too am from the Pandya country. But the dumb woman is from Chozha country. Therefore . . .'

'Never mind that. Like you, a few others too have told me about her. Will you bring her to me? If you do, I will give you whatever reward you wish for.'

'Queen, bringing her would be like bringing the whirlwind. She never stays in one place, never listens to others. Did I not tell you she is demented?'

'All right. At least tell me why you are here now.'

'Queen, a few days ago, two men were here. They mentioned your name.'

'Why?'

'They said that they wanted to go to Ilankai quickly, for you. I sent them on a boat with my husband to row them across.'

'Has he returned?'

'No. That's what worries me. If something has happened to him . . .'

'Don't worry. Nothing will happen. If anything does, I will take care of you. Do you know anything about the men who left by that boat?'

'They are back. Didn't you hear the owl hooting just a while ago?'

'I did. So what?'

'Did you not recognize it as the sorcerer's voice?'

'How do you know? Are you associated with the sorcerer?'

'Yes, queen,' said Rakkammal, and made the sign with her hands.

Looking hard at her in surprise, Nandini asked, 'Where are they now? Do you know?'

'The sorcerer is waiting to see you.'

'Why can't he come to see me? Why wait for me?'

'He doesn't want to meet the Pallava warrior who is here. He had encountered him in Ilankai. Nor does he wish to meet your husband.'

'Did you see the sorcerer?'

'Just now when I heard the owl's call. He asked me to bring you. He is hiding near the stream close to the Kuzhagar temple. Will you come?'

'How can I go there?'

'We can say that we are going to the Kuzhagar temple.'

'Good idea. Don't we need any other protection?'

'No. If you like, we can take Sendan Amudan with us.'

'Who is he?'

'He is the son of the dumb woman in Tanjavur.'

'Siva! Siva! How many mutes!'

'This is an accursed family. Some are dumb by birth. Others are dumb despite having tongues that can speak. My husband is like that. He can talk very well. But my plan is to see that he doesn't talk much.'

'Do you know if the mute woman in Ilankai has any children?'

'Once, she gave birth to twins. No one knows what happened to them. I have been trying to find out that secret but without success.'

'Why has the Tanjavur fellow come here?'

'He has come in search of his uncle's daughter, Poonkuzhali. She is not here. That is why he is waiting.'

'Where did she go?'

'I wanted to tell you about it myself. The day after my husband took the sorcerer on the boat, two others came here. The Pazhuvur men too arrived to catch them. That very night, my sister-in-law took one of those men to Ilankai.'

'Does she know how to handle a boat?'

'That is her job. When she does not sail, she wanders around in the mangrove woods. There is no nook or corner in the woods that she is not familiar with.'

'What do you conclude from the fact that she has not returned?'

'Everyone is bewailing the death of someone in the sea. That will become a certainty only after Poonkuzhali returns.'

'She too could have drowned.'

'Not she! The sea is her cradle. Moreover, I was looking at the sea from the top of the lighthouse just a while ago. A boat seemed to be approaching from a great distance . . .'

'Then?'

'It did not come to the shore.'

'What could have happened?'

'Seeing the crowd assembled here, it could have been taken into the canal through the mangrove woods.'

'Is that possible?'

'Nothing is impossible for Poonkuzhali. The Tanjavur fellow was with me on the lighthouse. He too thought as I did.'

'All right. Let it be. Come, let us go to the Kuzhagar temple now.'

'Shall I ask Sendan Amudan to join us?'

'No. Let him go on searching for his uncle's daughter. Let us not stand in his way.'

Together, the two women went towards the Kuzhagar temple. Like Poonkuzhali, Rakkammal too knew all about the mud holes of Kodikkarai. She guided Nandini very skilfully.

When they reached the Kuzhagar temple, the priest was surprised to see them.

'Queen! What's this? Why have you come alone, at this time, without your attendants? Couldn't you have sent word to me? I would have been prepared to receive you.'

'Is this the time for formalities? What a calamity for the Chozha realm! They say that the sea has taken the precious son of the Chozha land. I came to beg and plead with the lord to save the prince.'

'No such mishap will ever take place, amma! Don't worry. Our prince will not face any danger from the sea king.'

'How do you say this with such conviction?'

'Because of the time of his birth and its ascendant star. Can the sea take the man who was born to rule the world? Don't grieve. Pray to Kuzhagar. He will surely save the prince.'

Saying this, the priest circled the deity with the flame and gave her the sacred ash. He added, 'Amma! I am so happy that you have reached such a high position.'

'Did you know me before?'

'Yes, queen! I have seen you in the temple at Pazhaiyarai, and also in the temple by the banks of the river Vaikai. What is your brother Tirumalai doing now?'

'He wanders from place to place singing azhvar hymns. It has been a long time since I saw him.'

'He is sorry about that, amma. He regrets that you never met him after becoming the queen of Pazhuvur.'

'What can I do, ayya? Everyone in the household I married into is a devout *Saiva*.* He is a staunch *Vaishnava*.† Moreover, he goes around fighting with Saivas everywhere. How can I have anything to do with him? Should I not ensure that the people in the family I have married into don't get upset?'

'True, amma, true! What is important is never to cause any distress to your husband. Let Azhvarkadiyan go his way!'

The women took leave of the priest and began to walk away.

The priest said, 'But you are going by yourselves! If you wait just a little, I will join you.'

---

* Follower of Siva.

† Followes of Vishnu.

'No, there is no need for you to make haste. This woman knows the area very well. Besides, Kodikkarai is so bustling now that there is nothing to fear,' Nandini said.

The women came out of the temple. The moment the priest was out of sight, Rakkammal led Nandini by the hand to the back of the temple. In a little while, they reached the stream thick with screw pine bushes. They walked beside it under the light of the stars.

6

Poonkuzhali's Terror

Poonkuzhali held her breath as she stood behind the screw pine bush. Though they spoke softly, she could hear most of the conversation between Nandini and the sorcerer.

When Nandini told him that she did not believe the prince was drowned, the sorcerer said, 'Queen! You never believe anything I say. But why do you disbelieve me now?'

'Haven't you heard about the prince's horoscope and what it predicts? The priest at the Kuzhagar temple spoke about it just now . . .'

'Madness! The power of my mantras is stronger than the influence of the stars and planets. Do you know how I chanted mantras to bring a cyclone over the calm sea? At first, even that spy from Kanchi did not believe it. But he would have certainly believed it when he lost his life in the sea.'

'Did you see him drown in the sea?'

'How does it matter? I saw his ship catch fire and sink.'

'It seems the prince jumped in to save him from the burning ship.'

'Did he return?'

'He did not return to the Pallavan's ship.'

'Then what are you worried about? I left Vandiyatevan alive so that both enemies could be sacrificed at the same time.'

'Whatever you may say, my mind refuses to believe it. Something tells me that both are alive. Do you know Poonkuzhali?'

'Very well. She was a problem for us in Ilankai. She too could have been lost in the cyclone.'

'That is just not true. From the top of the lighthouse, Rakkammal saw a boat in the distance. It disappeared suddenly. She thought there were two people on that boat.'

'In that case, take the old man and leave immediately. I will stay back and look into it before I go.'

'Why shouldn't we stay here?'

'If the old man remains here, he will want to take the prince back with all the panoply of royalty. Our task will be ruined.'

'I too would like to ask, why is it necessary for those two men to die? If everyone agrees to crown Madhurantakan . . . ?'

'Lady! Don't lapse into feminine waywardness now. The Kanchi spy knows all our secrets. He would have definitely told the prince. Get going before dawn breaks. Rakkammal! If Poonkuzhali brought them here, where would she hide them?'

'There is a mandapam covered by thickets, her hideaway. I discovered it after she kept the Kanchi spy hidden there for a whole day.'

'Good. I know where it is. I will go and wait there. Queen! How is the emperor? Any news?'

'Which emperor do you mean?'

'My tongue will never call the ailing Sundara Chozha "emperor". I am asking you about *our* emperor.'

'I had news of his being safe and well ten days ago. Ah! How many days have passed since I last saw him!'

'All right. Go quickly. What is that fool of a Pallavan going to do?'

'We are taking him to Tanjavur.'

'Be wary of him.'

'Don't worry about him. He is willing to do anything for me.'

'Still, it is better to be careful. Were you not somewhat fooled by that Kanchi spy?'

'True. That is why I want to see him alive.'

'Get rid of any such wish, totally.'

They were still talking as they started to walk. Poonkuzhali hid herself even more carefully. Fortunately, they walked away from her.

What she had overheard by chance filled Poonkuzhali with terror. She shuddered as she thought of all the perils surrounding Ponniyin Selvan. Her throat ran dry, her mind was befuddled. Her dominant instinct was to get back. She began to walk quickly.

The prince was afflicted by a vile and poisonous fever. Pazhuvettaraiyar was waiting to take him into custody. Assassins were preparing to kill him. This siren in the form of a woman was ready to assist them. Partibhendran too had fallen into her web of seduction. These people knew the mandapam where she had hoped to hide the prince safely.

Poonkuzhali realized that it was her responsibility to save the prince from all these dangers. That was the reason for her bewilderment. It made her feel something she had never known before. She was afraid that she had lost her way. Was she wandering in circles? What could she do if she encountered the prince's enemies? How could she pacify them and escape?

No, no. She was on the right track. She could see the stream. She had left the boat in that corner. Poonkuzhali ran to it. The boat was not there. Her heart stopped beating. Ayyo! Where could it have gone?

Had Pazhuvettaraiyar's men found it in her absence? Taken the prince and Vandiyatevan into custody? It would be terrible but by no means the worst thing that could occur. But could anything more horrendous have taken place? Had Vandiyatevan carried the prince to the hidden mandapam? With the assassins waiting there? What a blunder she had made!

Poonkuzhali felt impelled to go to the hidden mandapam at once. She began to run, once again preyed by the same fear of having lost her way.

What was that? Footsteps? Someone following her? Who? Why? Could it be that dreadful sorcerer? Why should she fear him? She could pull out the dagger at her waist. Whoever it may be, why should she run?

No. No. She *had* to run. This was not the time to fight. Her arms lacked strength. She would miss the target. She had to keep herself safe in any way she could. What of the prince, if something were to happen to her? Vandiyatevan had already warned her. She had promised to come back with her life intact. She had to keep her word.

Poonkuzhali ran into an even thicker patch of the forest. But her pursuer kept pace with her. Screeching birds flew up from the trees as she streaked past. Wild pigs awoke from their slumber and ran helter-skelter. A leaping antelope collided with her as it sprinted away. And yet, the man who was following her did not give up. His footsteps and puffing breaths continued to be heard.

Poonkuzhali was exhausted. Then exhaustion changed to fury. She decided that she would take action against her pursuer, whoever he may be.

7

A Song in the Woods

Precisely at the moment when Poonkuzhali stopped running and turned to look behind her, a sweet song rose in the dark wood.

> Lord of the golden form
> A tiger skin at your waist
> The glistening konrai flower
> On your auburn locks . . .

Poonkuzhali recognized Sendan Amudan's voice at once. She laughed aloud. Momentarily, she even forgot that she had heard the footsteps coming from a different direction.

'Cousin, *you?*'

'Yes, Poonkuzhali.'

'Where are you? Come forward.'

'Here I am,' said Sendan Amudan as he came before her.

'You scared the living daylights out of me. Why did you come chasing me in the dark?'

'I travelled all the way from Tanjavur to see you and hear your lovely songs. I waited here for many days. Today, I followed you when I saw you by chance. Why were you running so fast . . . ? Let me hear you sing.'

'Found the right place for singing, didn't you? And the perfect occasion!'

'If you won't sing, I will. Watch me as I wake the wild creatures and set them scampering,' said Sendan Amudan and began to sing about Siva who wore the crescent moon on his head.

'Stop, cousin. Stop singing.'

'Only if you will sing instead,' said Amudan in a loud voice, followed by a whisper, 'Poonkuzhali, another man is following you. I sang at the top of my voice only to warn you. He had some secret talks with your sister-in-law. Do you know him?' He added again loudly, 'What do you say? Will you sing? Or shall I? When Siva can dance in the graveyard, can't you sing in the woods?'

'Don't get angry. I will sing right away,' said Poonkuzhali and sang:

O parrots on the wing!
O mynahs that sing!
Only may you move
The lord of Arur,
The righteous lord
To feel my pain.
Unable to forget him,

My bangles slip away
And sleep eludes me.

She finished the song and whispered, 'Amuda! How did you know I was here?'

'Poonkuzhali, I saw the boat from the top of the lighthouse. I guessed it might be you and came searching for you. A few Pazhuvur men too came here at the same time. You were not in the boat. But I saw my friend Vandiyatevan and the prince. I told Vandiyatevan about the Pazhuvur men. We carried the prince to the hidden mandapam.'

'Ayyo! What a terrible blunder!! What about the boat?'

'Thinking that if anyone saw the boat it would give rise to suspicion, we sank it in the waters,' said Amudan and raised his voice to add, 'Poonkuzhali! Why have you stopped? Go on. Sing the rest of the song.'

'I have forgotten it. Amuda, isn't there a song about lord Kuzhagar of Kodikkarai? Do you remember it?'

'Oh yes, I do,' said Amudan and began to sing.

In the wild, beside the sea
Where biting winds do sharply blow
My sinful eyes are forced to see
You standing still in solitude
Forlorn–
With none to bear you company
My lord!

When the song ended Poonkuzhali asked in a low voice, 'Cousin, has my pursuer gone or is he hiding nearby?'

'The footsteps stopped when we stopped here. He must be hiding somewhere close by. Do you know him?'

Poonkuzhali raised her voice to say, 'I do know it very well. Aren't you asking me about Sundarar's song about the owls in Kodikkarai? Listen to this–'

> Holed up
> in the spreading woods
> owls and bitterns
> screech and hoot
> on and on.
> Brutal hunters
> prowl around.
> Your lady fair
> is terrified.
> O handsome lord
> of Kodi shores,
> why choose to dwell
> in the wilds?

Aloud she said, 'See, Amuda! Owls and bitterns hooted in the poet's time just as they do now. But nowadays, *men* have started screeching like owls. I heard such a call just a while ago. Do you know who these rogues may be? Let me see if I can screech like them. See if my voice can produce an owl's call.'

And then Poonkuzhali went on to mimic the owl's cry thrice.

'You sing sublime songs in a voice sweeter than honey. Where did you learn to screech like an owl?' Amudan asked.

'I learnt it from a sorcerer. You must learn to screech like an owl for your spells to work.'

'You know witchcraft too?'

'I know some. Do you want to test the power of my mantras?'

'How?'

'Someone is hiding close by and listening to everything we are saying. If you like, you can look for him.'

Rustlings interrupted Poonkuzhali before she could finish speaking. The sorcerer Ravidasan guffawed loudly as he emerged from where he had been hiding.

'Girl! Is that so? I thought that you knew all about trickery. You are acquainted with mantras too?'

'Blackguard! So it was you!'

'Girl, do you know who I am?'

'You are the man who tried to kill the prince in Ilankai. You failed. So you cast spells to bring a cyclone into the sea, and made the prince and his friend drown.'

'How are you certain that they did drown? Did you see it?'

'Their bodies were washed ashore. I buried them in the Bhuta Isle. Traitor! May your mantras be destroyed by a thunderbolt!'

'Girl! Don't try to deceive me. Did you not cast counterspells to rejuvenate them?'

'Ayyo! How did you know that?'

'I, Ravidasan, have not only the physical eye but the inner eye. With my powers of sorcery, I can see things happening at great distances.'

'Then why are you asking me?'

'To test you. Tell me where you have hidden them. If not, I will reduce both of you to ashes.'

His eyes glowed like live coals as he intoned, '*Om hreem hraam vashat*!* Are you going to tell me? I am going to unleash the power of my mantra!'

Trembling in fear, Poonkuzhali gripped Sendan Amudan and said softly, 'Amuda! I am going to start running. Try to stop him from following.'

Then she said to the sorcerer, 'Please don't do anything to harm me. I will show you where they are. Come!' With this, Poonkuzhali began to run in the direction opposite to where the mandapam was located.

Sendan Amudan tried to hold Ravidasan back and stop him from following her.

Poonkuzhali continued to run.

The sorcerer shoved Amudan away and began to run after her.

Poonkuzhali ran like an antelope.

The sorcerer followed her like a hunter chasing the antelope. But catching her was no easy task.

Just when the sorcerer wanted to give up, Poonkuzhali too stopped as if overcome by fatigue. The sorcerer continued running after her.

Behind them, Sendan Amudan too stumbled along. He did wonder if he should go to the hidden mandapam to warn the men waiting there. But he had no heart to leave Poonkuzhali to the mercies of the sorcerer.

---

* A phrase mimicking a tantric mantra.

Poonkuzhali climbed a dune. She did not merely stand there but clapped her hands, inviting the sorcerer to come up. Puffing and panting, the sorcerer climbed up to her. Just as he decided to grab her and slap her hard on the cheek, Poonkuzhali said. 'Look! Look at my lovers!'

The sorcerer looked at where she pointed. He saw the same scene that Vandiyatevan had witnessed before.

Flames were appearing and disappearing randomly across the mangrove swamp. Ravidasan's hair stood on end even though he knew what made those ghastly forms emerge.

'O man of magic! Why don't you cast a spell to drive these fire-breathing phantoms away? They torture me beyond measure.'

Ravidasan became uncontrollably angry. 'Girl! You think you can trick me?' he roared.

'Why should I trick you?'

'Didn't you promise to take me to where Vandiyatevan and the prince are hiding?'

'You did not believe me when I said that they were dead. What else could I do?'

'Is it true that the prince is dead? Can you swear to it?'

'Why do you need oaths? Look at the sky!'

Ravidasan looked at the sky. He saw the comet.

'Don't you know that a comet appears in the sky to augur death in the royal family? Well, it has happened.'

'Girl, give me the jug. Anything left in it? Running after you has made me thirsty.'

All of a sudden, Poonkuzhali began to run again. She jumped from the dune and ran into the mangrove swamp among the fiery phantoms.

Anger blinded Ravidasan. He was possessed by the maniacal desire to grab Poonkuzhali by the neck and squeeze her to death. He ran behind her at full tilt.

After running for a while, Poonkuzhali suddenly bowed her head and jumped a few feet sideways.

The speed at which Ravidasan was pelting after her made it impossible for him to turn where she did. He had to move a few steps ahead before he could stop. He tried to swivel back and leap at her. But he could not. What had happened to his feet? Why weren't they moving? Why were they getting cold? What was this? The chill crept up from his feet.

Ravidasan bent down to see his feet sinking into the slushy mud. Inch by inch, they were disappearing into the mangrove sludge in slow motion.

Ravidasan realized the danger he was in. He tried to extricate himself from the sucking mud patch. He tried to kick his legs free, but his attempts met with failure. He felt that a monstrous spirit was pulling him down from the sludge below.

Poonkuzhali laughed aloud. 'A sorcerer trapped in the monster's mouth? Why don't you try your mantras?'

Ravidasan shook in fear and rage. 'Bitch! Is this your work?' said he.

'Didn't you want to squeeze my neck? You can squeeze your hands instead,' she said.

Controlling his temper, Ravidasan said, 'Girl, I swear to you, I won't harm you. Please give me your hand and pull me out.'

Poonkuzhali laughed uproariously. 'I cannot help you. Call all the spirits under your mantra's control.'

By this time, Ravidasan had sunk to his thighs.

His face looked hideous. His eyes burned red like blazing firewood.

He stretched his hands and grabbed the roots of the wild grass growing just outside the patch of sinking mud. He tried once again to come out, but his legs would not budge.

'Girl! Please save me! You will be blessed!' he shrieked.

Sendan Amudan reached them by this time and became aware of Ravidasan's situation. His eyes reflected pity.

Poonkuzhali said to him, 'Come, let us go.'

'No, no. Nightmares will plague me all my life if I abandon him like this. Let us get him out before we go.'

'Cousin! He wanted to grab me by the neck and squeeze me to death.'

'God will punish him for his sins. Let us save him before we leave.'

'Then give me your scarf.'

Amudan gave it to her. Poonkuzhali tied one of its ends to a bush close to the sinkhole and tossed the other end to Ravidasan.

'Hold on to this. If you yank it, the bush will be uprooted. Don't try to get out. Someone will pass by in the morning and help you out,' she said.

'Ayyo! Do I have to stay here all night? I cannot. Kill me rather than leave me like this.'

Poonkuzhali disregarded his shouts and began to run, dragging Sendan Amudan by the hand. The sorcerer's shrieks followed them until they climbed the dune and got down into the woods on the other side.

When the voice could no longer be heard, Poonkuzhali said, 'Cousin! You arrived in the nick of time. How? Why?'

'After the experience in the dungeons, I didn't want to stay in Tanjavur. The Pazhuvur queen's spies were continually turning up and troubling me. So I went to Pazhaiyarai. Kundavai Devi sent me here. She told me that there were many dangers threatening the prince. I was to tell Vandiyatevan to take the prince to the Chudamani Viharam in Nagaipattinam, leave him there and report to her. I also wanted to see you and hear you sing.'

'You found the perfect time for the singing! But the princess is right. The prince is facing unimaginable threats. Apart from the conspiracies of his adversaries, he is now affected by ague and fever.'

'Yes, I saw that. It was with great difficulty that the two of us managed to carry him to the hidden mandapam. Poonkuzhali, the monks at the Chudamani Viharam are extremely skilled in medical science. They will be able to cure the prince.'

'But how can we take him to Nagaipattinam?'

'By the canal.'

'But how? You have lost the boat!'

'The boat is under the water, we can pull it out.'

'Then we must leave this very night. But all four of us won't fit into that little boat.'

'No need, Poonkuzhali. We have discussed it and come to a decision. Vandiyatevan will go straight to Pazhaiyarai from here. You and I will have to take the prince to Nagaipattinam.'

Poonkuzhali had gooseflesh. She would be journeying with the prince once again. But no danger should threaten them along the way.

They reached the hidden mandapam. Sendan Amudan clapped loudly.

'Who is there?' came Vandiyatevan's stern voice.

'Sendan!'

'Who else?'

'My cousin.'

Vandiyatevan peeped out. 'No one but you two?' he asked.

'No. Why this doubt?'

'Lower your voice. The prince is sleeping. Someone came here some time ago. I came out thinking that it was you. But he appeared to be the sorcerer.'

'Then?'

'You two began to sing. I thought you had chosen a great time for warbling! Fortunately, the sorcerer heard it and went away. Did you see him?'

'Yes.'

'How did you deal with him?'

'I didn't do anything. It is she who has got him stuck waist-deep in the quagmire.'

'Her voice too was to be heard, a little.'

'Yes.'

'The prince regained consciousness and asked, "Who is singing?" I told him it was the boatwoman. He fell asleep listening to it.'

Poonkuzhali felt a thrill running through her again.

Amudan said, 'She didn't stop with singing. Didn't she also screech like an owl?'

'I heard that too. I thought that many wonders were happening in the forest. I also thought that you two cousins were celebrating the season of courtship.'

'Useless chatter!' Poonkuzhali remarked.

'What else can we do? We must get through the night somehow,' Vandiyatevan said.

'No, we won't be able to get away if we stay here till dawn. We must leave in the night.'

Jackals began to howl from somewhere in the distance. An owl's screech could be heard through the howls.

Sendan Amudan shuddered. He had a mental picture of the sorcerer stuck in the quagmire, surrounded by jackals who were coming closer and closer. The sorcerer was trying to drive them away by screeching like an owl.

Vandiyatevan and Sendan Amudan picked up the prince without disturbing his sleep. Poonkuzhali followed them.

The moon had appeared by the time they reached the canal.

They made the prince recline against a tree with Poonkuzhali by his side. Then, with tremendous effort, Vandiyatevan and Sendan Amudan dragged the boat out of the water and drew it to the shore.

The prince opened his eyes. In a very faint voice, he said, 'I'm thirsty.'

Poonkuzhali gave him some milk from the jar.

After a few sips, the prince said, 'Poonkuzhali, I thought a celestial nymph was pouring nectar into my mouth.'

8

'Ayyo! Ghost!'

A heavenly kalpaka tree showered its many coloured blooms on Poonkuzhali as *kinnari* instruments poured ethereal music. Poonkuzhali's nerves turned into harp strings and joined them in song.

'Prince! I am only a poor boatwoman, and what you drank was not nectar, but milk from the Kuzhagar temple,' she said.

'How can I believe that you are not from the heavens? Are you not the daughter of Varuna, god of the waters? Samudra Kumari! How many times have you saved my life? What can I ever do for you in return?' said the prince.

'You must allow me to spend another night and day with you.'

'How is it possible? I must leave for Pazhaiyarai at once.'

'No. We have received a message saying that you must be taken to Nagaipattinam.'

'From whom?'

'Princess Kundavai.'

'Who is the other man dragging the boat with Vandiyatevan?'

'My cousin Sendan Amudan. The princess sent a message through him to take you to the Chudamani Viharam in Nagaipattinam.'

'Ah! Has my sister changed her mind? Has she given up her ambition to crown me? For a long time, I have wanted to join the Buddha association and become a monk. I will travel to countries far, far away—the Malay peninsula, Burma and China . . . How lucky I am! Poonkuzhali, come, let us go!'

Poonkuzhali suspected that the prince had slipped into a delirium once again.

Just then, the sounds of wailing came from the distance.

The startled prince sat up and asked, 'Poonkuzhali! What is that?'

'An owl's cry,' she replied.

'No. A human voice. The cry of someone in grave danger shrieking for help. Let us save him before we go. Let us do something good before joining the Buddha's order,' said the prince as he tried to get up and run. The effort made him stumble and keel over. Poonkuzhali caught him as he fell.

The two men came running. With great care, they lifted the prince who had once again lost consciousness, took him to the boat and made him lie down.

The boat began to move. All three had squeezed themselves into that constricted space.

Vandiyatevan said, 'Poonkuzhali, This boat cannot hold four people. In any case, I have to take my leave. Let me get off here. It is your responsibility to keep the prince safe. I don't have to say anything more.'

His voice shook. A moonbeam touched his face. Teardrops shone in his eyes.

'Why don't you get off after we pass the mangrove wood? I have left my horse there. Remember the directions I gave you to find that spot?' Amudan asked.

'I will get down here, sleep for some time in the Kuzhagar temple and leave before dawn. Otherwise, I won't be able to travel tomorrow. Who knows how many obstacles are waiting for me along the way?' Vandiyatevan said.

Poonkuzhali gave him the food parcel she had kept firmly tied at her waist until then. 'Offerings from the Kuzhagar temple. Have it before you go to sleep,' she said.

'What about you? You too have not eaten anything.'

'Sendan or I will go and get some food from one of the many villages a few miles down the stream. That is not the case with you. Must you not reach Pazhaiyarai unseen?'

'Don't forget that the prince is on the boat.'

'Who will imagine that there's a prince in this ramshackle boat? Don't worry! It is our responsibility. No one will give this boat a second glance.'

'All right, I will get off.'

They heard the wailing again. 'Ah! What's that?' asked the prince and passed out again.

Poonkuzhali got up.

'No! If the prince comes to know of this, he will never forgive me. Amuda, stay on the boat. I will get the sorcerer out of the sludge and return,' she said and jumped out of the boat.

'I will come with you. I won't leave you alone with that scoundrel,' Amudan said.

'No, Amuda. Stay in the boat. Take good care of the prince. I will go with Poonkuzhali. I need to see the sorcerer anyway,' said Vandiyatevan and ran after Poonkuzhali.

In her mind's eye, Poonkuzhali saw the sorcerer buried up to his chest, with jackals standing around him, ready to pounce and consume him. She also saw the prince glaring at her and saying, 'Murderer!' These visions charged her feet with great speed. She reached the patch of mud where she had left the sorcerer, only to be disappointed. He was not there.

Vandiyatevan, who had followed her, said, 'You have forgotten the place. It could be somewhere else. After all, Kodikkarai has many of these mud holes.'

Poonkuzhali pointed to Sendan Amudan's scarf still hanging from the corner of the bush. Poor thing! She was struck dumb.

'Do you think he would have been swallowed by the sludge?' she asked.

'No, no. Is it so easy to kill Ravidasan? He has a hundred lives! He would have escaped,' Vandiyatevan said, as he untied the scarf and took it. Though he consoled Poonkuzhali, he did believe that Ravidasan had met his well-deserved death.

Realizing that there was no point in lingering, they started to return to the stream, which was well hidden on both sides by the foliage. Then they saw two figures, male and female, holding on to a branch and peeping through the trees.

'There!' Poonkuzhali pointed to them.

'Know them?'

'Yes. The sorcerer and my brother's wife. She must have come here before we did and saved him.'

'Good thing.'

'Not a good thing. They are staring at the boat on the stream.'

One of the figures turned around and looked in their direction. Then hid themselves in the undergrowth.

'Ayyo! They have seen us.'

'Come with me, quietly, I will think of something. Don't be surprised by anything I say. Just follow my lead,' Vandiyatevan said.

Both walked past the place where the two figures had been standing and sat down on the bank of the stream.

Vandiyatevan made sure that the hidden persons could overhear their conversation.

'Poonkuzhali, look here! Why are you worried? The sorcerer is dead and gone. A very good thing,' he said.

'Ayyo! What a gruesome death!' Poonkuzhali exclaimed.

'Why all this pity for the man you have murdered?'

'Ayyo! Was it I who murdered him?'

'Who made him fall into the sinking mud? You! Then you were suddenly overcome by remorse and wanted to save him. But the mud has swallowed him. Who knows whether you came to save him or to make sure he is dead?'

'Who asked you to follow me?'

'That's how I have learnt about the crime you have committed. Murderess!'

'I? A murderess?'

'Yes, murderess. No, I don't claim to be any better. I killed the prince by drowning him in the sea. You killed the sorcerer by plunging him into the slush. Now we are quits. Our mutual crimes have cancelled one another. If you don't talk to anyone about my crime, I too will not tell anyone about yours.'

'Was it you who killed the prince? But just now, you said you had never seen him?'

'I lied. But there is no need to lie now. So, are you with me in this matter?'

'What if I refuse?'

'I will go straight to Nandini Devi and tell her that you killed Ravidasan by pushing him into the sludge. No witnesses to my crime, but there is a witness to yours!'

'What will Nandini Devi do to me?'

'Nothing much. She will have you buried up to the neck and beheaded by an elephant's kick.'

'Ayyo! How horrible!'

'If you don't want to end up like that, you must agree to what I say.'

'What should I do?'

'There! See the boat with your cousin in it? Get into it. Both of you must go straight to Ilankai. Stay there and weep for your prince.'

'Why should I go to Ilankai? How does it matter if I continue to stay here?'

'Ah! What if you sneak to Pazhuvettaraiyar about my crime? All said and done, he has great regard for the prince. He will try to take revenge. I still have some work left to do in the world.'

'Scoundrel! At least tell me why you killed the prince.'

'Why not? I will tell you. The prince and his sister plotted against Aditta Karikalan to grab the throne from him. Aditta

Karikalan is my master. His enemy is my enemy. That is why I killed the prince. Understood?'

'You will be punished for this terrible sin.'

'You don't have to worry about that! Are you going to do what I have told you?'

'Do I have any other option? There! The boat is coming. I will get into it.'

'Look! Listen well. As soon as you get into the boat, you must go straight into the sea. You are wholly undone if you turn towards Kodikkarai. I will be watching from here. I will not leave until your boat reaches the sea.'

'All right. Stay here. Let a hundred jackals devour you.'

Vandiyatevan made a sign. Poonkuzhali left quickly and got into the boat.

The boat moved on.

Vandiyatevan remained sitting there as he had said he would.

Half an hour passed.

The boat went along the stream and disappeared.

Suddenly, hideous guffaws broke out behind Vandiyatevan.

Vandiyatevan jumped up, pretending to be startled.

The sorcerer emerged from the bushes, laughing horribly like a ghoul.

'Ayyo! A ghost!' Vandiyatevan hollered and began to run.

9

Three in a Boat

The day broke. The world slipped out of the embrace of the dark and beauteous goddess of the night. Unwilling to part, she hung back, giving the world what appeared to be the very last lingering kiss. 'We will meet again in the evening. After all, this parting is only for a few hours. Go in peace,' said the world. Night left reluctantly, casting backward glances at the world, again and again.

When the false-hearted paramour left, the world shivered in delight. 'Ah! Freedom!' sang the happy birds in their thousands. Trees and bushes burst into bloom. Bees swarmed around the flowers and sang in joy. Butterflies spread their iridescent wings and danced everywhere.

A golden sheen tinted the horizon. One by one, the stars faded away, while the crescent moon hung back as it continued to dither in the sky.

The boat moved very slowly on the stream. The chorus of birds and the splashing of oars awakened Poonkuzhali. Her eyes opened gently, like two blue buds blooming together. She saw the prince's face before her. He was still asleep. Or was it fever that kept him unconscious? She didn't know. But how lustrous his face was!

Sendan Amudan was plying the oars. 'Poonkuzhali! Why did you get up? Why don't you sleep for some more time?' he asked.

Poonkuzhali smiled. Not with her lips alone. Her whole body blossomed in that smile.

Poonkuzhali was born in the woods. And yet, birdsong and bee drone had never sounded so sweet to her.

'Cousin! Please sing a song in a morning raga,' she said.

'Would I open my mouth when you are beside me? You should sing,' said Amudan.

'You sang in the darkness of the night,' Poonkuzhali reminded him.

'I sang for a purpose. Now it is you who should sing.'

'I would like to. But it may disturb the prince.'

'Not at all. Why don't you both sing together?' said the prince.

Poonkuzhali hung her head shyly.

'Where is the boat taking us?'

'To the Chudamani Viharam in Nagaipattinam,' Poonkuzhali said.

'So what I saw and heard last night was not a dream,' said the prince.

'Yes, ayya. This is the man who brought the message from your sister.'

'Amuda, tell me what my sister said. Didn't she ask me to join the monastery?'

As Amudan hesitated to answer, both he and Poonkuzhali were startled to hear the sound of hoofbeats.

There was no change in the prince's expression. 'Where is my friend? Where is the warrior of the Vaanan clan?' he asked and closed his eyes.

In a little while, Vandiyatevan appeared on horseback. The boat stopped. Vandiyatevan dismounted and approached them.

'Not to worry, I just came to see if you were safe. There will be no more threats,' Vandiyatevan said.

'The sorcerer?' Poonkuzhali asked.

'He has absolutely no suspicion that the prince is in this boat. He fully believed what I said.'

'You saw him?'

'Yes. But I pretended that I thought he was a ghost.'

'I have never seen anyone who can lie like you.'

'Don't say "lie"; call it the power of imagination. How is the prince?'

'He wakes up now and then to say a few words. And then passes out.'

'This fever is like that.'

'How long does it last?'

'Sometimes for a whole month. Take him carefully to the Chudamani Viharam. The monks will cure him in two weeks. Beware! Poonkuzhali, I entrust the prince to you. If he sees any temple or temple spire, your cousin will start singing hymns and go away to worship the gods.'

Sendan Amudan said, 'Not after meeting you. Even my desire to serve Siva has decreased considerably.'

'Because of me? Or is it because of this girl? Tell the truth!'

Dismissing this, Sendan Amudan asked, 'Did you find the horse where I said it would be?'

'The horse found me. Is this not the horse I left in Tanjavur with you?'

'Yes.'

'It neighed as soon as it saw me in the dark forest. Amuda, being captured by the Arabs has taught me that making horses run unshod is cruelty. They must be fitted with iron shoes. I am going to get this done in the first smithy I see on the way. All right, this is no time for chatter. I don't know if I will see you and the prince again. If he wakes again, tell him I am going to Pazhaiyarai. Tell him that I will send a message from there as soon as possible. Only then will he be at peace.'

Vandiyatevan turned his horse and rode away. Soon, he disappeared from view.

The boat moved along the stream flanked by thick screw pine bushes on both sides. Their fragrance was exhilarating. Among them were punnai and kadamba trees scattering their pearly white and ruby red flowers on the stream. Poonkuzhali felt that if there was indeed any path from the earth to the heavens, it had to be the route they were following.

Whenever a village appeared on the way, Sendan went to get milk for the prince and food for Poonkuzhali.

Poonkuzhali kept her eyes away from the prince when he was awake. But when he slept, she could not take them away from him. Sometimes, she talked to Amudan. They also sang happily together.

When Sendan went in search of food, Poonkuzhali nursed the prince by stroking his forehead and running her fingers through his hair. She was in a state of bliss. Thrills coursed through her body. Her heart was overwhelmed.

She felt as though she had served him in the same way in many previous lives. Thousands of indistinct thoughts flapped their wings and crowded her mind as they flitted in and out.

Their journey lasted a day and a night. Sendan and Poonkuzhali took turns to wield the oars and take naps. When she slept, Poonkuzhali had many dreams, hazy and sweet.

The boat reached Nagaipattinam the next morning when the whole world shimmered in gold. The stream branched into a canal, which went straight to the Chudamani Viharam. They took it and stopped just behind the monastery.

It appeared as though there was some kind of furore around the Chudamani Viharam. People were shouting and making a din in front of the building. The monks were running to and fro.

Sendan Amudan said that he would find out what the rumpus was all about.

10

Chudamani Viharam

Poompuhar city had been overrun by the sea. In the course of time, it was Nagaipattinam that claimed the status of being the country's most important port city. Merchandise from the stately freighters was constantly being unloaded on its quay. Merchants from foreign countries were keen to establish a nexus of trade with the Chozha realm, enriched by the river Kaveri. Pearls, gems, diamonds and fragrant substances were traded, as were horses from Arabia.

Nagaipattinam was a many-splendoured city in the poet Sundarar's time. His verses mention its long streets and domed mansions with overhanging balconies.

And guess what the poet wanted from lord Kayarohana, the temple deity? Not gold, gems, garments and ornaments, which he had obtained in other towns. Instead, he put up a demand for a highbred horse. Seeing the Arabian steeds arriving in the port city must have triggered the poet's desire to ride one! And he got it too—a thick-maned horse, along with gold, a jewel-studded staff, gems, robes and sandals—or so says the *Periya Puranam* text.

Apart from the legends, historical records on stone tablets and copper plates provide information about the city. 'Nagaipattinam is filled with many temples, inns, water tanks, groves and streets with splendid mansions,' say the copper plates of Anaimangalam, as they go on to describe the famous Buddha monastery of those times called the Chudamani Viharam.

Back then, the Malay peninsula was renowned as the Srivijaya kingdom, with Kadaram (Kedah) as its capital. This vast empire spreading around the capital city was ruled for a long time by kings of the Sailendra dynasty. Among them, King Makaradhvaja Chudamani Varman acquired great fame. The copper plates of Anaimangalam acclaim him with wonder as, 'an expert in diplomacy, and equal to Brihaspati (the guru of the gods) in wisdom. Like a sun to the lotus was he in supporting men of learning. He was the munificent kalpaka tree to those who sought his aid.' The copper plates add that his son, Mara Vijayottunga Varman, 'built the Chudamani Viharam to equal the Meru Mountain' in stature, as a lasting memorial to his father's name.

Readers may ask, 'Why should Mara Vijayottunga Varman of Kadaram come to Nagaipattinam to build a Buddhist shrine?'

The Srivijaya kingdom was one of the foreign lands with long-term trading connections to the Tamizh country. Several subjects of that kingdom had permanently immigrated to settle in Nagaipattinam. Many others visited it frequently.

The king of Kadaram and his subjects followed the Buddha's creed. The king built the Chudamani Viharam so that his people may have a convenient place to perform their worship. He might have also been influenced by the thought that the Buddha's faith had originated in India.

The kings of the Tamizh realm believed in maintaining harmony among all creeds. Therefore, they accorded permission to build the Chudamani Viharam in Nagaipattinam. They did not stop there. They continued to donate grants and tax-free lands to the shrine now and then.

In the years that followed the period in which our story takes place, King Rajaraja Chozha gave a tax-free grant of Anaimangalam and some other villages to the Chudamani Viharam. Rajaraja's son, Rajendra Chozha of historical renown, ratified the grant by inscribing it in copper plates, each fourteen inches long and five inches wide, hung on a big copper ring, together known as the Anaimangalam copper plates. Some historians refer to them as 'the Leiden plates', as they are now displayed in the museum in Leiden in the Netherlands.

* * *

The kings of the Chozha dynasty had been staunch Siva followers from Vijayalaya Chozha's time. Kings Aditta, Parantaka and Gandaraditta built several Siva temples and gave grants for different kinds of services therein. But they had no hatred towards other creeds. They possessed the liberality to foster the different creeds followed by their subjects. Sundara Chozha went one step ahead of his ancestors in giving special grants to Buddha shrines. This made all the Buddha followers in his kingdom extremely happy. Their exhilaration was augmented by Arulmozhi Varman's renovations of the ruined Buddhist monuments in Ilankai.

With things being as they were, what was the reason for any fracas in the Chudamani shrine? Why were the flustered monks running here and there? Why all this shouting and clamour in front of the monastery?

* * *

Sendan Amudan and Poonkuzhali had taken the boat into the Chudamani Viharam by the canal. Finding no one there, Amudan faltered as he made his way to the front yard that housed the *chaityam* or the Buddha temple open to the public. On that morning, worshippers who stood holding trays of lotuses, champa flowers and other offerings, seemed to have forgotten why they were there. Monks were standing on the steps of the chaityam shrine with tears in their eyes. A man standing below was telling them something. Instead of the usual chant of 'Sadhu! Sadhu!' there were lamenting cries of 'Ah!' '*Adaada*!'* 'Ayyo!'

Sendan Amudan grasped the situation when he went close enough to hear what was being said. The man talking to the monks was a mariner from Partibhendran's ship, which had reached the Nagaipattinam port the night before. The news of the prince being taken by the sea had been shared by the sailors as soon as they disembarked and had spread across the

---

* Alas.

city. Early in the morning, the chief monk had sent for one of those sailors to enquire if the news was true. He told them what he knew. In a grief-stricken voice, he said, 'The prince did not return after jumping into the sea when the whirlwinds were raging.'

Many in the crowd broke into sobs.

Tears streamed down from the chief monk's eyes.

He walked up the steps of the chaityam in silence and entered the monastery. The other monks followed him. No one noticed that Sendan Amudan had joined them.

The chief monk looked at the others and said, 'Is this the mercy of lord Buddha? I had been building so many castles in the air! Recently, when I went to see the emperor in Tanjavur, I told him about the amazing deeds of his son Arulmozhi Varman. Princess Kundavai too was listening to me. Later, she said that she would give a grant to launch an infirmary beside this monastery. She added, "*Acharya!*[*] You would have heard all kinds of rumours floating around. The prince may have to stay for a few days as a guest in the Chudamani Viharam. Can you take care of him?" "Devi!" I said. "If we do get such an opportunity, we would care for the prince as our most precious treasure." What is the use? The prince has drowned in the sea. The hopes of all the good people in this country have drowned with him. The Chozha empire has drowned with him. How did the king of the sea dare to do something so heinous? Is there no one to question him?'

Silence reigned in that group. The other monks shed tears.

---

[*] Spiritual teacher.

Seizing that moment, Sendan Amudan tried to push through the group and approach their leader.

The others tried to stop him. 'Who is he? How did he get in?' they asked one another.

'Ayya! My name is Sendan Amudan. I belong to Tanjavur. I must speak to your master.'

Many said, 'Go on!'

Seeing him hesitate, the chief monk said, 'Speak! There is no secret that may not be shared with them.'

'Ayya! I have brought a sick man.'

'Who is he? What is his ailment? Where have you left him?' they asked.

'I have left him in the central courtyard of the monastery.'

'How did you get there?'

'By the canal. I brought him by boat. He has a shivering fever. You must come at once–'

'Good lord! It is a highly contagious fever. Why did you bring him here? And at this time!'

'Acharya, I thought Emperor Ashoka belonged to the Buddha faith. Now I know he did not.'

'Why do you say that?'

'I saw a pillar erected by Ashoka near Kanchi, where the inscription says that serving the sick is the first dharma of the Buddha's creed. But you are driving us away . . .'

The chief monk said to the others, 'Wait. I will go and take a look.' He added to Amudan, 'Come, son!' and took him along.

The master was startled to see the young man and woman in the central courtyard of the monastery. 'What have you done? Women are not allowed inside the monastery! There are separate quarters for the women renunciates.'

When he went closer and saw who the young man was, astonishment and joy momentarily robbed him of all speech.

To clear his doubt, he asked Amudan, 'Prince Arulmozhi Varman?'

The prince heard him. He said. 'No, acharya, no. I am no prince. This boy and girl are trying to drive me mad. I am a boatman. I asked this girl just now, "Will you marry me? Let us take the boat and go to countries far, far away." She talked some nonsense about my being born to rule the world! Poor fisherwoman as she was, she would not marry me. My welfare was the only thing that mattered to her. She was going to rejoice when she heard about my great victories in the future. How's that? Who is mad–she or I?'

Sendan Amudan whispered in the master's ear. But the monk had already realized that the prince was ranting because of his fever. He remembered Kundavai Devi asking him to shelter the prince.

To the other monks, he said, 'This boy has the shivering ague. Thousands will be infected if we let him go. So many people in Ilankai died of this fever. I am going to take this youth into my room and take care of him. Don't pay any attention to his feverish ravings.'

The chief monk put his arm around the prince and raised him. Sendan Amudan helped to lift him. Everyone went up the steps.

Poonkuzhali thought, 'In a few moments they will have climbed all the stairs. They will open the door and go in. The door will close. Once shut, it will remain shut. It will not be possible to see the prince again.'

It happened just as she visualized it. Once they went up the stairs, a door did open. Leaving Sendan Amudan outside, everyone went in.

The door shut itself with a bang. Poonkuzhali felt the door shutting in her heart.

She stood watching the prince disappear. It was highly improbable that she would meet him again. Would she attain that good fortune in her next birth?

11

The Forge

Vandiyatevan spurred his horse to make straight for Pazhaiyarai. He preferred to follow the route as he remembered it rather than ask for directions. He went through the forest for quite some time before realizing that the track had completely worn out his tired horse. Vandiyatevan too was overcome by fatigue. It had been many days since he'd had a good night's sleep. All he had done was to close his eyes and teeter on the verge of sleep now and then, though never in a single spot or undisturbed. Once he reached Pazhaiyarai and conveyed the news to the princess, his responsibility would be over. And then he planned to crash for days on end to make up for all the lost hours of slumber.

He thought of how happy he would be when he told her, 'I have completed the task you gave me.' A frisson of excitement shot through him when he imagined her face brightening in a radiant glow.

He remembered something else. How many lies and tall stories had he trumped up from the day he left Kanchi! Necessary, of course, and yet, when he recalled them, he cringed in body and mind. A short time with Prince Arulmozhi Varman had changed his entire outlook. He had believed that those who were involved in matters of state should be adept at political subterfuge. He had also been motivated by his ambition to regain the kingdom of his ancestors through such guile. No longer. The prince's moral uprightness and integrity had made him detest fibs and falsehood. He thought of all the lies he had told the previous night for the sorcerer's benefit, in order to save the prince. Now he became apprehensive about their consequences. What if someone had overheard him and relayed it all to Kundavai Devi? She would not believe it. But still, how potentially dangerous it was!

Vandiyatevan decided to give up all prevarications, adhere to the truth and learn to manage any difficulties that may arise from it. Let men like Azhvarkadiyan and Ravidasan resort to spying. Why should he? He would abandon tricks and wiles. He would be satisfied with victories achieved with the help of his sword, even if they ended in death.

With these thoughts to occupy him, Vandiyatevan failed to notice that his horse had lost speed. In fact, the animal had started snoozing, only to be shaken awake when it stumbled as it struggled to place one of its forelegs on the ground. He dismounted, patted the horse and examined its leg. A sharp stone had lodged itself in its hoof, but fortunately, it had not lamed the horse. He removed the stone, stroked and cheered the horse, and mounted it again. He recalled how the Arabs on the ship had jeered, 'The people of the Tamizh land are cruel. They make their horses run unshod. How long can such horses last?'

Vandiyatevan had heard of countries where shoeing horses was the norm. Soldiers wore armour to protect themselves, horses had to be shod to protect their feet. He would stop at the first smithy along the way, and if possible, get this done. Otherwise, it would be difficult to ride it as far as Pazhaiyarai. And if it stopped, how would he get another? He would have to steal a horse! Chee! Chee! The very thought made him cringe.

Deciding that come what may, he would stick to the highway, Vandiyatevan managed to find it and took it, confident that he would encounter no one who would recognize him. Pazhuvettaraiyar's men and Ravidasan posed no threat as they would be following him. Moreover, there were good chances of finding a smithy on the highway.

Vandiyatevan's expectations were not in vain. Soon, he saw a village rife with some kind of bustle. Festoons hung on streets and houses. They may have been put up to welcome Periya Pazhuvettaraiyar. But Vandiyatevan would be far away before he arrived with his retinue.

Once he entered the village, he could not guess why men and women were standing in little groups, talking anxiously. Some of them stepped forward to stop him and ask for news. Unwilling to get sidetracked, Vandiyatevan spurred on without letting anyone stop him.

Once he crossed the village, he saw a blacksmith's forge on the roadside. He didn't have the heart to go past it. He stopped and went in.

A smith was at work within. A young boy was blowing into the bellows. As he stepped in, Vandiyatevan sensed a man slipping out at the back. But it was the sword that the smith was working on that captured all his attention. It was a singular blade, just removed from the fire after being tempered, dazzling silver on one side and flaming red on the other.

'This is what one calls a sword!' he thought in wonder.

12

Throw Them into the Fire

The smith remained intent on his work. He looked up only after Vandiyatevan cleared his throat several times.

'And who may you be?' asked the smith. 'What do you want? Sword? Spear? But these days, there is no demand for sword and shield. Why would you want one?'

'Ayya, why do you say that when you hold a sword in your hands? You are working on it.'

'This is a rare job to come my way. They brought this old sword to be repaired. Some years ago, during the Pandya and the Vadapennai wars, and even when the Ilankai war began, this smithy had spears and swords stacked in heaps. But now, all I get are weapons for sale. Did you come here for such a purpose?'

'No, no. I would need my sword for some time. Once I finish the job I have undertaken, I will go on a pilgrimage, belting out hymns and banging cymbals. At that time, I will bring my weapons to you if you like.'

'Then why have you come to me?'

'I have done some hard riding and still have a long way to go. I have heard about iron shoes for horses. Can you make them?'

'Yes. They do it in Arabia. It is coming into vogue here too. I have some experience in this kind of work.'

'Will you shoe my horse?'

'It will take some time. I can take it up only after finishing the work on hand.'

Vandiyatevan thought it over. Both he and his horse were exhausted. He decided to get the horse shod before resuming his journey.

'All right, I will wait. But you will do it once you are free, won't you?'

'Oh yes.'

Vandiyatevan gazed at the tempered sword for some time.

'This sword has intricate carvings, like a weapon from a royal house. To whom does it belong?'

'Son! A river named Harischandra flows close by.'

'So?'

'I often bathe in it.'

'Good thing. Earns points for the next world.'

'Like the fabled king Harischandra, I have vowed never to lie and to speak the truth as far as possible.'

'Who asked you to lie? Not me.'

'If you don't question me about the sword, I will not have to lie.'

'Is that really so?' Vandiyatevan said to himself.

'I won't ask and you don't have to break your vow. It will be enough if you finish the work on hand and do mine as quickly as possible.'

The smith concentrated on his work in silence.

Vandiyatevan continued to stare at the sword. He was surprised to see the image of the fish carved on the blade close to the hilt. Did it have any significance? Or was it simply decorative?

The smith held the sword over the fire before hammering on the image as if to erase it.

Vandiyatevan wondered why his eyes were closing. The slumber he had been keeping at bay for many days now cast its inescapable net over him. After nodding and swaying for some time in a sitting position, he fell asleep beside the forge.

Nightmares began to plague him.

A man came to the smithy for the sword. 'How much?' he asked the smith.

'No charge. Let this be my gift to the young Pazhuvur queen,' the smith replied.

'Beware! No one should know about this. Never repeat the Pazhuvur queen's name. If you do . . .'

'Why should I mention her name at all? I won't,' said the smith.

'Why are you speaking so loudly while this youth is sleeping here?'

'He is fast asleep. Not even a thunderbolt would wake him.'

'If you feel that he has even an inkling of this matter, throw him into the forge and finish him off.'

The dream ended with the smith and the visitor throwing him into the fire.

Then Vandiyatevan was dragged into hell by the attendants of Yama, the god of death. Yama enquired about Vandiyatevan's actions on earth. Chitraguptan, his registrar, checked the records to state, 'He is an expert liar. He has told countless lies.'

'No, no. I told them all in the service of the royal family, to fulfil the tasks I undertook.'

'A lie is a lie, for whatever reason it may have been spoken. Fling him at once into the deepest pit of fire,' Yama ordered. At once, a hundred thousand voices from hell broke out in howls.

Yama's attendants dragged him to a flaming furnace and prepared to throw him in. Vandiyatevan was startled to see that their faces resembled the two Pazhuvettaraiyars. Princess Kundavai came running to say, 'He lied to carry out my mission. Throw me into the fire instead of him.'

Nandini Devi too made her entry and said, 'Throw them both in!' Vandiyatevan awoke as he was shrieking and struggling to free himself from the attendants who were trying to cast them into the fire. He sat up, relieved that it was only a dream. But his body was still shaking. He vowed never to lie again.

'Did I sleep for a long time?' he asked the smith.

'Only for about five hours,' the smith replied. 'Son, if you sleep like a log during the day, what will you do at night?

'O my god! Five hours! Have you shoed the horse?'

'Have to start now. But what is the use of shoeing the horse for a sleepyhead like you? You will let your horse be snatched away, and yourself too for that matter.'

Vandiyatevan was startled. Suspicion made him run to the front yard. The horse was not there.

'Ayyo! Where's my horse?' he hollered as his hand reached for his sword.

'Don't worry. Your horse is safe. Look in the backyard.'

Vandiyatevan found his horse standing in a thatched yard, fenced on three sides. The boy with the bellows was now feeding it with grass. Seeing its master, the horse neighed and shook itself.

'Ayya, hold your horse. I must measure its hoof,' said the boy.

Vandiyatevan went to stand beside the horse and caressed it.

As the boy took the measurements, he asked, 'Who brought it here?'

'I did.'

'Why?'

'Father told me to do it.'

'What for?'

'A little while ago, Periya Pazhuvettaraiyar and his retinue passed through this village. They would have certainly taken the horse if they had seen it.'

Vandiyatevan remembered his past experience with Pazhuvur soldiers in Veeranaryanapuram. He was ashamed of his negligence. He felt grateful to the smith and his son.

Both returned to the smithy once the measurements were taken.

The smith took a piece of iron, bent it in the shape of a horseshoe and began to hammer it.

'Thank you for saving my horse,' Vandiyatevan told him.

'It is my duty to take care of the property of those who come to me.'

'How long has it been since the Pazhuvur retinue passed by?'

'About an hour. What surprises me is that you slept through all that racket.'

'I did. But you needn't have wasted so much time. You could have started work as soon as they left.'

'How could I? Who would have the heart to do any work after hearing the news they brought? I have pulled myself together for your sake. Son, where do you come from?'

Wondering what kind of news it could be, Vandiyatevan said, 'Ilankai.'

The smith looked him up and down and asked in an undertone, 'Son, did you see Prince Arulmozhi Varman there?'

Having taken the vow to speak nothing but the truth just a while ago, Vandiyatevan said, 'Yes.'

'When did you last see him?'

'This morning.'

'Are you making fun of me, tambi?'

'No. I'm telling the truth.'

'Can you say where the prince happens to be at this moment?'

'I will, if you ask me.'

'Where is he?'

'In the Chudamani Viharam, in Nagaipattinam.'

'Son, I have seen many fibbers in my time but none like you!'

Vandiyatevan laughed to himself. It seemed that he was fated to be disbelieved when he spoke the truth.

'Tambi, when did you leave Ilankai?'

'Four days ago.'

'That is why you haven't heard the news.'

'What news?'

'Ponniyin Selvan has drowned in the sea.'

With great difficulty, Vandiyatevan made an effort to appear shocked.

'Ayyo! Who told you?'

'It has been the talk of the town since yesterday. The news was confirmed by Pazhuvettaraiyar when he came here today. Why hasn't a thunderbolt fallen on that blackguard's head?'

'Why are you cursing the old man?'

'This is all his doing. The people say that it is his plot that has caused the prince to drown in the sea. They cancelled all the welcome ceremonies they had arranged for him.'

'Are the people so fond of the prince then?'

'Do you have to ask? Everyone is sobbing. Not in this village alone. The whole Chozha realm is going to weep and wail. The emperor is already ailing. How traumatized will he be when he hears this news? Who knows what calamities may befall! The comet has been trailing in the sky. Some catastrophe is bound to occur!'

Pondering those disasters made Vandiyatevan feel relieved about the smith disbelieving his statement. He did not have to lie anymore, but the need to speak the truth about the prince had become redundant now. There had to be an important reason for Kundavai Devi wanting the prince to remain in the Chudamani Viharam. He should consult her and follow her advice.

'Tambi, what are you thinking about?'

'I too was caught in mid-sea during the cyclone. I am thanking god for his grace in saving me.'

'Is there such a thing?'

'What are you saying?'

'If there was such a thing as god's grace, would the Pazhuvettaraiyars be allowed to continue their atrocities? Would Ponniyin Selvan have drowned in the sea?'

'Ayya, the Pazhuvettaraiyars are in positions of power. Should you talk about them like this? Be a little careful,' Vandiyatevan said.

The smith replied, 'It is you who must be careful. At least I talk when I am awake. But you babble in your sleep!'

'Ayyo! What did I say?'

'You called the Pazhuvettaraiyars the envoys of Yama. You described the young Pazhuvur queen as a ghoul. What you said was absolutely true. But what would happen to you if anyone happened to overhear this? The Pazhuvur cavalcade passed while you were going on and on. I was terrified.'

'What did you do?'

I went out and shut the smithy's door. Your horse had been taken and tethered at the back before that.'

'What else did I gabble about?'

'No end to the gabbling.'

'Ayyo! What did I say?'

'You urged the prince to come to Pazhaiyarai. He said that he wanted to be taken into custody by the Pazhuvettaraiyars. Tambi! You went on to say all kinds of things about Kundavai Devi. Beware, my son! Beware!'

Vandiyatevan hung his head in shame. He was scared that he might have said something inopportune about the princess. He should never go to sleep without locking himself into a room, he thought. Or in a forest, desert or mountain cave, uninhabited by human beings.

'Tambi, how did you get caught in the cyclone? How did you escape?'

'My ship was struck by lightning and capsized. I held on to the broken mast and floated for a long time. A boatwoman helped me to reach the shore.'

'The prince too could have survived in the same way.'

'If it was god's will, yes.'

'Where did you stay last night?'

'In Kodikkarai. It was crowded with Pazhuvettaraiyar's entourage. So I slept in the temple and left before dawn.'

'That is why you missed hearing the news about the prince.'

'Thank you for letting me know. Ayya! I must go to Pazhaiyarai quickly and without getting embroiled in Pazhuvettaraiyar's company. What would be the best route?'

'Pazhuvettaraiyar is taking the highway. You can follow the path beside the river Mullai.'

'It would be good if you could hurry up with the horseshoe.'

'Here!' said the smith and began to hammer the piece of iron bent and tempered in the forge.

For each stroke, he called out a name. 'For Periya Pazhuvettaraiyar! This is for Chinna Pazhuvettaraiyar! Sambuvaraiyar! Mazhavaraiyar!' Vandiyatevan came to understand the people's anger towards these chieftains.

The horse was shod. Vandiyatevan tried to pay the smith for his labour, but he refused to accept it. 'I did this because you are a good fellow, not for money,' he said.

Vandiyatevan thanked the smith once again and took leave of him.

As he was leaving, the smith asked, 'Tambi, why are you going to Pazhaiyarai?'

Vandiyatevan answered, 'Ayya, if you don't ask me, I won't have to lie.'

The smith laughed and said, 'My son! You are getting smarter by the minute! Be just as smart when you are asleep.'

It was sunset when Vandiyatevan resumed his journey. If he could reach the river Mullai before twilight faded to dusk, all he would have to do was follow the path by the riverbank. He wouldn't have to ask anyone for directions.

It was the early phase of the night but a thousand million stars sparkled in the sky. The river was bordered by bushes, not trees tall and thick. Therefore, the path remained visible under a starlit sky.

Thousands of fireflies rivalled the stars as they frolicked over those bushes.

Vandiyatevan's heart rejoiced. There were many reasons for his elation. When the whole country was sunk in despair over the prince's fate, he alone knew that the prince was alive and safe. He had come to understand the immense love the people of the land had for Ponniyin Selvan. He was delighted to recall having deceived Ravidasan. What excited him most of all was the thought that, very soon, he was going to meet Princess Kundavai.

He was not just going to meet her, but meet her after having completed the task she had assigned to him. He felt proud of having overcome all the challenges that had impeded him in carrying out that mission. The mere thought that he would see the princess by this time tomorrow was enough to make his heart tingle.

Vandiyatevan was enthralled by the stars twinkling in the sky, the fireflies hovering on the earth, the susurrating sound of the flowing river, the caressing touch of the cool, gentle breezes. Sky and earth were steeped in bliss. He remembered an old love song. It was the perfect place to sing it. No human presence anywhere. Why, even the birds had returned to their nests. There was nothing to stop him from breaking into song. And who was he thinking of when he addressed the girl in his song?

> O doe-eyed beauty!
> Enthralled by you
> The stars in the sky
> Quiver in wonder.
> Your honeyed voice,
> Like balmy breeze
> Your soothing words
> Your gleaming eyes . . .
> Why am I reeling
> And losing my mind?

The moment Vandiyatevan ended his song, jackals set up their howling as though to compete with him.

At the same time, he heard a human voice breaking into laughter.

Taken aback, Vandiyatevan looked around. His hand went to his sword.

A figure emerged from the dark shadows of a punnai tree.

'Tambi, your song was fabulous! The jackal chorus was even more fabulous!' said Tevaralan and laughed again.

13

The Poisoned Arrow

To see Tevaralan at that hour gave Vandiyatevan a jolt. He remembered the man's frenzied dance and fearsome prophecies at the Kadambur palace. He also recalled the information that Tevaralan and Ravidasan had shared with him when the cyclone was raging. It would be difficult to sift truth from concoctions, but it was certain that they were involved in some hideous and mysterious act of conspiracy. And now he was caught by this man, in a place devoid of any human presence. He looked around to see if he should spur his horse and gallop away.

A fire was burning in the distance. It had to be a cremation ground. A human body, made of the earth, was being consumed by fire. What hopes and passions would have simmered and seethed in that corporeal figure when it was alive? How many joys and sorrows would it have undergone? All to be reduced to ash in half an hour's time. Such was the inevitable plight of every single human being born in the world, from the king of kings to paupers and beggars. All to be devoured by flames and end in a fistful of cinders . . .

Fear left him as quickly as it had struck him. He thought, 'Why should I be frightened of this vile imposter? Obviously, he has come to say something. Why not hear him out? Perhaps it was he who disappeared from the back when I entered the smithy. That extraordinary sword could be his—didn't it have the image of the fish etched on it? Talking to him could bring some new information to light.'

Vandiyatevan slowed down. Anyway, his horse seemed to be having some difficulty in adjusting to its new shoes and he was loath to overtax it.

'How did you manage to spring up here out of the blue?' he asked.

'It is I who should ask this question. We left you bound to the mast in mid-sea. How did you escape?' Tevaralan asked him.

'So you think you are the only mantra expert going around! I know some too.'

'I am happy to know that you have come to believe in mantras. My powerful mantras told me that you were journeying here, alone. That is why I came ahead and waited for you.'

'Why? What do you expect from me?'

'Think! Or use your mantras to find out.'

'You have shared your secrets with me in the middle of the sea. I don't know how much of it is true and how much is invented. I have decided to forget them all. I am not going to share them with anyone.'

'That doesn't worry me. Your tongue will be cut off the moment you think of spilling them.'

Vandiyatevan shivered. He remembered the mute women he had met in Tanjavur and Ilankai. He went on riding in silence. Why was this rascal following him? How to get away from him? How useful it would be to have a quagmire here, as in Kodikkarai! Should he push the man into the river? It would be useless, the river was shallow. As a last resort, he could use his sword.

'Tambi! I know what you are thinking. It's useless. Don't try it.'

Vandiyatevan wanted to change the subject. He needed time to plan his escape. He had to keep the man talking until then.

'Where is your crony, Ravidasan?

Tevaralan laughed like a ghost. 'It is you who should know. Where is Ravidasan?'

Vandiyatevan was disconcerted. He had blundered in mentioning Ravidasan. Had the man met Ravidasan or was he simply fishing for information?

'Tambi, why don't you speak? You won't tell me? Never mind. At least tell me where that boatwoman Poonkuzhali may be.'

Vandiyatevan panicked as though he had stepped on a snake. He was afraid to say anything more.

'All right, so you won't say anything about her either. There may be a sound reason for you to try to protect her. Tambi, just now, were you thinking of her when you sang that love song?'

'No, certainly not!' said Vandiyatevan in a flustered voice.

'Why are you so perturbed? Why are you so vexed?'

'All right. No time for discussions. Why are you holding my reins? Let go. I need to be off. My work has to be done quickly.'

'You haven't asked me why I came here.'

'Well, why don't you tell me?'

'The river Mullai has an amazing power. Any wish made on its banks will be attained at once.'

'I made no wish.'

'That's a lie. The woman you thought of when you sang the love song wishes to see you. You can meet her if you like.'

'When?'

'This very night.'

'What a tall tale that is!'

'Not at all. Look there!' said Tevaralan and pointed. Vandiyatevan stared until he perceived a curtained palanquin in the distance.

Ah! A palanquin. Where had he seen it before? Why, it was the Pazhuvur queen's palanquin. Perhaps . . . with Nandini inside? He could not suppress his curiosity to see if he was right.

He rode up to the palanquin and stopped. He saw the curtain with the image of the palm tree. It seemed to be moving.

Tevaralan emitted a strange sound. Vandiyatevan jumped down from the horse.

From behind the bushes close by, ten or twelve men came running to pounce on him. Holding him in an immobilizing grip, they bound his eyes, hands and feet. Another snatched his sword. Then they threw him into the palanquin. The rest marched before and behind the palanquin now being carried briskly along by the bearers. One of the men led Vandiyatevan's horse. Tevaralan went ahead to show the way.

It had all happened in the blink of an eye. Stunned by the unexpected and combined attack, Vandiyatevan found himself being carried away before he could understand what was happening.

As the palanquin began to move, slowly, his mind cleared. The binding over his eyes slipped off. Pushing the curtain aside with his bound hands, Vandiyatevan saw that the palanquin was leaving the riverbank and taking a crosscut to some unknown destination.

It would have been possible to free himself and jump out. The horse was trotting behind them. It would not be an impossible task to repulse those men, mount the horse and gallop away. But something prevented him from adopting those measures. A singular scent pervaded the palanquin. At first, it stimulated him. He did not have the heart to get away from its alluring fragrance. Where would the palanquin take him? There were many reasons to suggest that it would take him to Nandini. The lurking desire to see her manifested itself—feebly at first—only to grow into an all-consuming obsession superseding every objection. What on earth could she do to him? Moreover, he would discover why she had him brought to her. He would gain whatever information he could from her. If she had plots of her own, would it be so impossible to come up with counterplots? It was doubtful if he would ever get the chance to meet her again. There was no need for him to visit Tanjavur again. Such a visit would be dangerous. It would be far easier to see her along the way. Why not see her just once more?

There was another important reason for him to see Nandini.

The mute queen in Ilankai! Was he right in thinking that she resembled Nandini? Should he not learn more?

Vandiyatevan was suddenly overcome by sleep. No, no, this was no sleep. He had slept long during the day. This was some kind of stupor, induced by the suffused fragrance. Ayyo! How dreadful! He should jump out of the palanquin.

Vandiyatevan tried to untie the knots at his wrists. His hands refused to move. He tried to get up. He could not. He tried to kick his legs free, but they were frozen. His eyelids dropped. His wits dimmed. He passed out completely.

When Vandiyatevan emerged from the blackout, he was impelled by his last memory to jump down from the palanquin. But the wonder was that he now found himself in a large, brightly lit chamber. This room too was fragrant, but not with the scent that had blurred his mind—it was more like an incense that cleared his thoughts. The door was open. He sat up and looked around. His curiosity was aroused.

Nandini entered through the open door. He gazed at her unblinkingly. He had many reasons to be wonderstruck. First, her unparalleled beauty, and second, the unexpectedness of the encounter. A third was the comparison he made between the older woman he had seen in Ilankai and the young woman before him. Did they merely resemble each other? Or was the woman before him the same older lady now clad in splendid garments and jewels?

Nandini remarked in a tinkling voice, 'Ayya! You are a very good man.'

'Thank you,' said Vandiyatevan.

'The sign of a good man is not to inform anyone when he departs. You left the Tanjavur palace without telling me.'

Vandiyatevan laughed.

'I helped you enter the Tanjavur fort. From my own finger, I took the ring with the palm tree insignia and gave it to you. Should you not have returned it before you left?'

Vandiyatevan hung his head in silence.

'Where is it? Can you return it now? You won't need it anymore. After all, you have no intention of returning to the Tanjavur Fort,' said Nandini and extended her flowerlike hand.

'Devi, Bhooti Vikramakesari seized the ring in Ilankai. Pardon me, I am unable to return it,' Vandiyatevan said.

'You are a man with a great sense of gratitude. Have you not given my ring to my worst enemy?'

'It was taken from me by force.'

'The warrior of warriors, born in the valiant Vaanan clan, allowed himself to be overcome by force? I cannot believe it.'

'Devi! Have I not been brought here by force? Your men . . .'

'Tell me the truth, ayya, reflect well before you speak. Was it force that brought you here? Not your willingness? Was there no opportunity along the way to escape from the palanquin?' Nandini's questions pierced Vandiyatevan like sharp arrows.

'Yes, I did wish to come.'

'Why?'

'Why did you have me brought here?'

'To ask for my ring to be returned.'

'Is that the only reason?'

'There is one more. On that night, were you not inside the treasury vault that is under my husband's charge?'

Vandiyatevan was startled.

'You think I didn't know? Well! If I hadn't known, could you have escaped on that night?'

'Devi . . .'

'Yes. I knew. So did Periya Pazhuvettaraiyar. Pazhuvettaraiyar ordered the guard to kill you there and then. As soon as he left, I changed the order. That is why you were able to survive. Instead, your dear friend became the casualty. If not, your bones would still be lying in the vault, beside the heaps of pearls.'

Vandiyatevan was astounded. He could not believe everything she said. But if it was untrue, how did she know that he was inside the vault? Believing that he should respond with customary expressions of gratitude he began with, 'Devi . . .'

'No. Why do you want to speak words that don't come from the heart? Don't try to thank me.'

'No, Devi.'

'Do you know why I mentioned saving your life that day? Not because I expect you to profess gratitude but only to warn you not to use that subterranean passage again. It is now guarded very strongly. Understood?'

'I have no intention of going there again.'

'Why should you? You don't have the habit of remembering those who helped you. Your friend was exposed to danger because of you. I brought him to my palace, had him treated and healed before sending him away. Are you happy about that? Or is it that you have an inborn propensity to betray friends just as you betray trust?'

Every single word spoken by Nandini went through his heart like poisoned darts and left him in torment.

'You had the physician's son who accompanied you to Kodikkarai captured instead of you. Did you ever try to enquire about what happened to him?'

'I was going to ask you.'

'I will tell you about him if you tell me what happened to Prince Arulmozhi Varman who left Ilankai with you.'

Vandiyatevan was completely shaken. He wondered if Nandini was tormenting him just to extract information about the prince. He decided that he would not be duped.

'Queen! Please don't ask me.'

'Yes. I knew you would say that. You will resist being questioned about it. Can you at least tell me about the girl you love? How is she doing?'

Fire flamed in Vandiyatevan's eyes. 'Whom do you mean? Watch your words,' he said.

'Ah! I do watch my words! Don't imagine that I am talking about that great princess of Pazhaiyarai. She won't even bother to waste a glance at you. To her, you are nothing but dust under her feet. I asked you about the girl who brought you back from Ilankai. Isn't Poonkuzhali your lover?'

'No. Not at all. She herself showed me her lovers at midnight—the fire-breathing phantoms of the mangrove mudflats. She said that they were her lovers.'

'She is fortunate! Her lovers have forms of light. My lovers are shaped in darkness. Their forms cannot be known. Have you ever slept in a ruined pavilion shrouded in the darkness of the night? Have you seen bats and owls flapping their noisy wings as they flit through it as nebulous shapes? Those shapes wander in my mind endlessly. They flap their wings. They strike my heart. They brush my cheeks as they fly past. Where do those dark shadows come from? Where do they go? Why do they circle me? Do you know?' Nandini stopped and stared around aimlessly with frenzied eyes.

Vandiyatevan's iron heart was shaken. Pity and an unidentifiable dread filled his mind. 'No, Devi! Calm down,' he said.

'Who are you to ask me to calm down?'

'I am a young man belonging to the Vaanan clan. Devi! Who are you?'

'Who am I? I don't know. That is what I am trying to discover. Who am I? Are you asking me if I am human? Or a ghost? A ghoul?'

'No. You could be a celestial woman who has fallen from the heavens due to some god's curse.'

'Yes, there is a curse upon me. But I don't know what it can be. I don't know who I am or why I was born. But now, god has given me a sign. Look!' said Nandini as she picked up the sword beside her and raised it. Under the light of the lamp, the newly burnished sword shone with a dazzling brilliance.

One look at the sword was enough for Vandiyatevan to recognize it as the one he had seen in the smithy. Until then, Nandini's words had traumatized him like poisoned arrows. But his strength returned the moment he saw the weapon of steel. He was accustomed to sword and spear; he had bonded with them from the time he was born. He was no longer afraid. He realized he would not be afraid even if Nandini were to use that sword against him.

'Devi, I see! An intricately carved sword. A sword to be claimed by a royal clan. A sword to be held by a valiant hero. How did it come into your delicate hands? What sign has god given you through this sword?' he asked.

14

The Flying Horse

Nandini lovingly clasped the brilliant sword to her bosom. A red lotus kissed the burning flame when she held the sword against her face and lips. The next moment saw a bloody cloud passing across the full moon. Nandini's face morphed into the horrendous beauty of the divine Kali of the Kapalika cult,* the goddess who demanded blood sacrifice.

She put the sword down. Her face regained its magnetic allure.

'Yes, this sword is a divine token vouchsafed to me. I have still not understood what it intimates. I frequently send it to the smithy to be cleaned, polished, sharpened. I guard it as a tigress guards her cub. The cub should not be trapped by the wild antlered stags before it reaches the right age. I nurture it as the Arabs cherish their horses. I serve this sword as Queen

---

* A tantric cult of Siva originating in medieval India. Kapalika or 'skull men', derived from the Sanskrit word kapala, or skull.

Vanamadevi serves her ailing husband Sundara Chozha. God has not yet proclaimed what I should do with it. My hands have been trained to string flowers. Would god command these hands to plunge this sword into a villain's heart? Is it god's will that I should thrust this sword into my heart and die with my splendidly adorned body drenched in blood? The god who bestowed this weapon on me will let me know what I should do with it at the opportune moment. Since I don't know when that may be, I keep myself in a state of readiness at all times. The whole country knows that the Pazhuvur queen, famous for her beauty, is enamoured of adorning herself gorgeously. I do keep myself beautified and bejewelled, by day and by night. Poor Pazhuvettaraiyar believes that I do this to delight him and to maintain his status. He knows nothing of the fire that blazes in my heart.'

Dazed by this outburst, Vandiyatevan forced himself to regain his wits enough to ask, 'Where is Periya Pazhuvettaraiyar?'

'Why? Are you afraid to face him?' Nandini asked.

'No. When I am not afraid of facing you, why should I be afraid of Pazhuvettaraiyar?' Vandiyatevan countered.

'Ah! This is why I like you. For some reason, everyone is afraid of me. Pazhuvettaraiyar–the great veteran warrior, the bearer of sixty-four battle scars–is afraid of me. Chinna Pazhuvettaraiyar, reputed to strike terror into the god of death, trembles when he approaches me. Madhurantakan, who wants to be the sole emperor of the Chozha realm, fears me. Emperor Sundara Chozha, who is approaching the world of death, shudders and swoons every time he sees me. I had heard so much about Aditta Karikalan's best friend, the lion-hearted Partibhendra Pallavan. Half an hour with me was enough to reduce this newcomer to meek submission. Forgetting his duty to return to his master, he is following me, ready to perform any menial task that I may give him. But he trembles when he comes anywhere near me. As a child, I was fascinated by fire. I would stretch my finger to touch the flame but withdraw it at the last minute. I remember this when I see Partibhendran's approach and retreat. Not just Partibhendran, but his master Aditta Karikalan–whose envoy you were when you left Kanchi and came to Tanjavur–why, he too feared me despite his boundless love for me. How it transformed my life! Ayya! When you meet your master again, will you convey to him this message from me? Will you tell him that I have forgotten the past? Today, my relationship with him is that of a grandmother. He need not be afraid of me. I won't gobble him up.'

'Devi, it is by no means certain that I would return with my life intact and meet Aditta Karikalan again. And if I do, I will have much to tell him. Please forgive me if I cannot promise to convey your message.'

'Yes. You are the only man of courage among all the people I have met. You don't conceal what is in your heart. That is the reason why I like you. O warrior of the Vaanan clan! I don't meet too many people. I don't travel by chariot like the Pazhaiyarai princess but in a curtained palanquin. I see only those by whom I have some work to be done. Most of them happen to be cowards. They do not dare to speak frankly. You say what you think without any attempt at concealment.'

'I know that it would be useless. Queen! There can be no secret in any man's heart that your piercing eyes cannot discover.'

'It may be true. However, I am unable to understand what is in *your* mind. Let it go. You asked me about Pazhuvettaraiyar. Partibhendran and he have gone to the neighbouring village, where a play on Kannaki and the dance of Murugan are to be performed. They want to see if they can get some prophecies about the young prince when the dancer goes into a trance. They are mad! They have gone to question the wrong man. They will return late. That is why I had you brought here. Ayya! I ask you again. You know the truth about the prince, don't you? But you will not tell me . . .'

'No, Devi. Just today I decided I would always speak the truth and never resort to falsehood. That is why I cannot talk about the prince. I had forgotten my decision a little while ago. Forgive me,' said Vandiyatevan as he unrolled the sash around his waist and took out the ring with the palm tree image.

'Devi, here it is. Bhooti Vikramakesari's men did indeed seize it from me in Ilankai. But the general returned it. I entrust it to you. Please accept it graciously.'

Nandini saw that it was the ring she had given him.

'Ayya, I am not in the habit of taking back things I have given away. I merely wanted to test your honesty. You have passed the test. You have spared me the job of having my men subject you to a security check. You may keep the ring as a way to remember me by.'

'Devi! Consider it well. I may have to use it again.'

'It is all right. Use it as you will. I am now going to order you to be taken away in the palanquin with your eyes bound, back to where they seized you.'

'If I refuse?'

'You will not be able to find your way out of this ruined palace or fort. You will keep returning to it.'

'Devi! This ruined fort . . . palace . . .'

'Some people call it the Pallava Fort, not without reason. Once, when these Chozha lands were under Pallava rule, the Pallava kings built this palace and fort. Then the Chozha country was seized by the Pandyas and the Pandya kings lived here. The fort and palace were devastated during the great war in Vijayalaya Chozha's time. We are in the portion that was not completely destroyed. But only those who know the way can enter and exit from this place. What do you say? Shall I tell my men to take you? Or will you make your own way?'

'No, Devi. I don't have the time to find the way. Let those who brought me take me back. But . . . before I leave . . . Is there no other reason for bringing me here? Is there no other assistance that I may render? Please let me know.'

'Well, I will tell you because you have made this offer. I want a flying horse. If you can get hold of one, you may bring it to me.'

'What? Did you say a *flying horse*?'

'Yes. A flying horse.'

'Do you mean an Arabian horse so fleet of foot that it appears to fly?'

'No, *no*! I cannot mount such a horse. I don't mean a horse that runs with its hoofs on the ground. I mean a horse that spreads its wings like a bird in its flight. I have heard of such miraculous horses in fiction. I want that winged horse.'

'Why? To fly into paradise?'

'Do I look like someone who has earned her ascent to paradise? I have no good deeds to my credit. I have committed terrible sins.'

'Do those who reach paradise perform nothing but good deeds? They commit sins too. They come back to the earth to atone for those sins before they return to paradise.'

'No. I have no wish to go there. There is a desert in the Pandya country. It has bare rocks where nothing green can grow. But they have caves where holy men of the Jaina faith performed their penances. Now they are inhabited by snakes and jackals. Those rocks in the Pandya land are dearer to me than the heavenly city.'

'Devi! That is an outlandish wish.'

'If I have a flying horse, I will go to that desert. From there, I will fly to the Ilankai island with its sky-scraping mountains shrouded by huge forests, where elephants roam as herds of buffaloes do in the Chozha realm. I have heard of mountains at the centre of the earth whose peaks have been snow-clad from the day they were formed, glowing silver at sunrise. Mounted on my flying horse, I want to soar over those silver mountains. Beyond them, they say are wastelands, a wilderness of spreading sands, a thousand times more vast than the Pandya desert. To be there during the day would be like standing in the fires. I want to go there. And even farther, where they say the climate is so glacial that animals and human beings walk across the frozen seas. I want to take my flying horse to see those marvels.'

'Devi! I cannot bring you a flying horse. But there are easier ways of travelling to some of the places you have mentioned.

A good boat will take you to Ilankai in half a day. Boarding a ship–'

'–Ayya! I know that. But I am afraid of the sea. I am terrified of ships. I get scared even when I am on a boat that pitches and sways on the river. Your suggestions are useless to me. You may go,' said Nandini as she stood up.

'Devi, is there nothing else that you would say to me?'

'No. But it looks as though *you* wish to say something to me.'

'I wish to ask a question. Please answer it. Were you not in Ilankai a few days ago? Were you not standing on the streets of Anuradhapuram under the dark shadows, alone?'

'Not at all. I have never stepped outside Pazhuvettaraiyar's palace or his protection. Why did you have this doubt?'

'Devi, I saw you in Ilankai a few days ago. Or I saw an apparition like you. You talked about a flying horse. I wondered if you possessed one and had flown to Ilankai on it. But you were not decked in silks and ornaments as you are now. You wore a simple garment and no jewellery, your tresses were hanging unbound.'

'No, ayya, it was not I. Did the woman you mentioned speak at all?'

'No. She spoke through gestures. But you are acquainted with sorcerers. Perhaps the power of mantras may have brought your astral form there.'

'If it was neither me nor my astral form . . . ?'

'It has to be a mute woman who resembles you closely.'

Nandini's glance was fixed on something far away. She heaved a long sigh.

'Ayya, did you not say just now that you wished to help me in some way?'

'Yes.'

'Were you sincere about it?'

'Of course.'

'Then listen to me. If you happen to see that lady any time in the future, please bring her to me, somehow. If that is not possible, take me to her,' Nandini said.

In half an hour, Vandiyatevan was by the river Mullai with his horse beside him. Those who brought him there vanished in a trice. Tevaralan was nowhere to be seen.

Vandiyatevan rode his horse alongside the river all night long.

In the third phase of the night, the comet could be seen trailing across the sky in its fullest form. He contemplated whether the comet that aroused so much fear in the populace was truly the harbinger of some catastrophe. Or whether the belief was nothing but a blind superstition. He also recalled Nandini's words, words which had become deeply embedded in his heart. The repulsion he had felt when he saw her for the first time in Tanjavur was now replaced by sympathy. And yet, since her intentions and ambitions remained unknown to him, and the truth about her life a mystery, he also felt anger towards her. Her inimitable beauty was accompanied by powers of seduction. It would be best not to have anything to do with her. It would have been better for him if she had taken her ring back. But she had refused it. He could throw it into the river . . . but he had no heart to do it. It could come in useful in these times of danger. Why throw it away?

He could get rid of it once he reached Pazhaiyarai and conveyed the news to the princess. After that, he would never take up such troublesome tasks.

In the fourth phase of the night, the crescent moon rose in the east. Vandiyatevan had been told not to face the crescent while riding. He tethered his horse to a tree and went to sleep under the shadows.

15

The Kalamukha Ascetics

Vandiyatevan was awakened by the morning sun's crimson rays directed sharply at his face. But he did not have the heart to get up just yet. He opened his eyes and saw two fearful-looking ascetics walking at a little distance from him. Their matted locks, the trident in one hand and a pot of fire in the other, told him that they were Saivas of the Kalamukha sect. Regretting the absence of Azhvarkadiyan to engage them in a debate, he decided to feign sleep until they passed him by.

He did not open his eyes even when he sensed their presence beside him, nor when one of them cleared his throat.

'*Sivoham!*[*] The boy is sleeping like a log,' he said.

'Sivoham! How good would it be to have such a boy in our ranks,' said the other.

---

[*] 'I am Siva', a reminder of the individual soul's oneness with transcendent reality.

'Sivoham! You say that because he looks bright. But he will be of no use to us. Danger looms over him,' the first man said.

Vandiyatevan began to feel suffocated as he maintained the act. But if he opened his eyes, the sham would be discovered. Moreover, he would not be able to overhear them if they continued to talk about the threat hanging over him.

To his disappointment, they moved on, with one of the Kalamukhas remarking, 'Sivoham! Each to his fate! Come, let us go.'

Vandiyatevan got up after giving them time to move away. The words 'danger hangs over him' lingered in his ears.

Kalamukhas were descended from the older Kapalika sect. They followed all the traditions of the Kapalikas except for the rite of human sacrifice. Many believed that the Kalamukhas acquired the powers of clairvoyance by performing rigorous penances in the cremation ground. The common folk thought they had the power to inflict curses. Therefore, any number of people were ready to give them respect and honour. Many feudal lords had made grants for regular offerings of food to the Kalamukhas in several temples. However, until then, no king of the Chozha dynasty had extended his favours to them.

Vandiyatevan, who knew this, emboldened himself by dismissing the Kalamukhas. 'Let them talk their nonsense. What new danger am I going to face now!' And yet, he could not entirely overcome his curiosity to learn about the future.

When Vandiyatevan got up, he saw the Kalamukhas walking by an old mandapam. There was an artificial mound beside it with a cave, whose entrance was shaped like a lion's head with its mouth open. The Kalamukhas had taken over the caves that had been occupied by Digambara Jaina monks in the past.

Vandiyatevan felt compelled to approach them and engage them in conversation. He left the horse tethered and went to the mound. As he went closer, he heard the Kalamukhas talking on the other side of the cave, somewhat faintly.

One of them said, 'That boy was not feigning it, he was truly asleep.'

'How are you so sure?' asked the other.

'I have never seen anyone who did not want to know more when he heard about approaching danger.'

'The boy appears to be valiant. It would be good to have him with us. What do you say?'

'Why bother with youths like him? Soon, the man who is to ascend the Chozha throne is going to join the Kalamukha faith.'

'Whom do you mean?'

'Who but Madhurantakan? Don't you know this?'

'How can it be? What about the other two?'

'One drowned in the sea. The other's life is getting short.'

Vandiyatevan did not wish to hear or talk to the Kalamukha ascetics any more.

He wanted to reach Pazhaiyarai quickly, deliver his message to the princess and go to Kanchi. Was it not Aditta Karikalan to whom he owed his greatest allegiance? And it was true that the prince was surrounded by dangers. Partibhendran had fallen into the Pazhuvur queen's snare. No guessing when Aditta Karikalan, who always plunged into action with frantic improvidence, would be imperilled. Vandiyatevan's primary duty was to guard him. He should go to him at once; it was a crime to linger.

Vandiyatevan moved silently to his horse, mounted it and let it canter. As he passed the cave, he saw the Kalamukhas staring at him. One of those faces seemed familiar. But he rode on without any wish to stop and learn more.

He passed through densely populated villages and saw that the news about Ponniyin Selvan had not reached them. The people were quietly going about their business. So far, so good. He should be in Pazhaiyarai and inform the princess before the news became public. Terrible things could happen if the wrong news reached her first. Kundavai Devi may hesitate to believe it but that Kodumbalur princess would give up her life. This thought perturbed Vandiyatevan, but his horse could not understand his agitation. Having been newly shod, it struggled to maintain its usual pace. Finally, at the hour before sunset, Vandiyatevan was able to see the walls of the Pazhaiyarai fort.

He could see the Durga temple beside the portals. Many ideas about getting into the fort swooped into his mind at lightning speed. But none seemed practical. The palm tree insignia was of no use here. Anyway, the sentinels would have been warned about it in advance. The moment they saw the ring, they would arrest him without further ado and send him to Chinna Pazhuvettaraiyar. He did not want to be captured before he met Princess Kundavai.

Still pondering, he slowed his horse down to a trot and noticed a cavalcade approaching from another direction. It comprised spear-holding soldiers, insignias, horse riders with a golden chariot shaped like a lotus in their midst. Ah! Who was seated on the chariot? Not Prince Madhurantaka Tevar? The prince he had seen in the Kadambur palace and the Tanjavur treasury vault! Vandiyatevan became fired up at once, as an idea flashed through his mind.

'I have never seen anyone who did not want to know more when he heard about approaching danger.' This comment made by the Kalamukha ascetic had imprinted itself on Vandiyatevan's mind. Had he not almost succumbed to it? He would have to see if he could put it to use now.

Vandiyatevan drove his tired horse speedily towards the golden, lotus-shaped chariot.

No one in Madhurantakan's retinue had ever imagined that anyone could act so brashly. The horse went right up close to the chariot before anyone could stop it. Vandiyatevan raised himself and shouted 'Oh! Danger!' and tumbled down from the horse. The horse stepped aside and came to a halt.

All this took place in a few seconds. Some of the men had drawn their swords while others raised their spears. But they were relieved to see the transgressor tumble to the ground.

Everyone laughed at the man who had tumbled down. Madhurantakan laughed too. The chariot had stopped by then. At his signal, two soldiers came to raise Vandiyatevan, but he had raised himself to a sitting position. Then he jumped up without their help and stood staring at Madhurantakan as though unaware of having fallen to the ground.

'Bring him here,' Madhurantakan ordered his men. Two soldiers took Vandiyatevan to the chariot. His eyes were still fixed on Madhurantakan's face.

'Fellow, who are you?' the prince asked.

'Me? I am me! Your majesty! Don't you know me?' Vandiyatevan said.

'What are you blabbering?' asked the prince and said to his men, 'Stand aside.' The men obeyed.

'Who did you think I was?' Madhurantakan asked again.

'Forgive me, your highness! I was wrong. You are . . . you are . . .' Vandiyatevan stuttered.

'Have you seen me before?' the prince enquired.

'Yes . . . no . . .'

'Yes or no? Tell me the truth.'

'Since yesterday, I have decided to speak nothing but the truth. That is why I am unable to be sure . . .'

'Is that so? Speaking the truth since yesterday! This is crazy!' laughed the prince and spoke again, 'But why does it make you uncertain?'

'These days, what can anyone say with any certitude? One man looks like another. He who was in a palanquin one day is seated on a chariot . . .'

'What did you say?' asked Madhurantakan, taken aback.

'I said that I could not be sure because one man resembles another.'

'Whom do I resemble?'

'I have seen you twice. Or, at least, someone like you. I was doubtful about whether it was you. It was to ascertain . . . that . . . I . . . a little while ago . . .'

'Tried to raise yourself on the horse and stare at me?'

'Yes, ayya!'

'What did you learn?'

'That you may or may not be the man I had seen . . .'

Madhurantakan's voice reflected his rising anger. 'You are a rogue. I will . . . '

'Prince! Please don't be angry. I will tell you where I saw you—or someone who looked like you . . . After that, you can decide . . . '

'Out with it, quick!'

'A huge fort. High ramparts on all four sides. A gathering of great men. Midnight. A huge lamp hangs on the wall. Its light is obscured by smoke. There are warriors . . . talking furiously, questioning their leader. He gets angry and goes to the palanquin placed in a corner by the wall. He draws its curtain aside. A beauteous man emerges from the palanquin. As soon as they see him, the warriors shout, "Hail! Hail!" Some call out, "Hail Crown Prince!" I recall some others shouting, "Victory to the emperor!" Ayya, the face of the man who emerged from the palanquin resembled yours. Please forgive me if I have said anything wrong.'

Madhurantakan had been listening to this without interrupting. Now, there were beads of sweat on his forehead. His face showed traces of fear.

'You who have been speaking the truth since yesterday, were you part of that group?' he asked.

'No, ayya, absolutely not.'

'Then how do you speak as though you had been an eyewitness?'

'I cannot be sure whether what I saw was real or part of a dream. Here's another scene. A dark subterranean passage winding down and up again. Three men are walking in it. A man holding the flare goes first, a guard follows behind, a handsome man walks between them. Gold and precious gems seem to be shining in the nooks and corners when the torchlight falls on them. Monstrous figures are carved on the pillars. The handsome face of the man walking between the three in that underground tunnel seemed to be yours. Whether it was true or not is something that you will have to say.'

In a tone steeped in fear, Prince Madhurantakan said, 'Enough. Stop!'

Vandiyatevan remained still.

'Are you an interpreter of omens and portents?'

'No, ayya! It is not my profession. But I can speak of what has happened and what will happen.'

Madhurantakan reflected a little before asking, 'What was it that you shouted out when you tried to hoist yourself up on the horse?'

'Danger, I shouted.'

'Danger to whom?'

'To you.'

'What danger?'

'You are surrounded by several threats. Similarly, top-ranking positions are waiting for you. These things must be explained at leisure. Your soldiers have taken my sword. If you take me into the fort with you . . .'

'All right. Come with me. Let us talk at leisure.'

Madhurantaka Tevar signalled to the leader of his entourage and ordered him to bring Vandiyatevan into the fort with the company. The order did not please the leader, but he obeyed and took Vandiyatevan along.

Shortly, the portals of the Pazhaiyarai fort opened.

Madhurantakan and his retinue entered the fort with Vandiyatevan.

16

Madhurantaka Tevar

We met Madhurantaka Tevar, an important character in our narrative, in the Kadambur palace at the very beginning of our story. We saw him again at midnight when he returned to his own palace through Pazhuvettaraiyar's subterranean passage. At those times, we were unable to give our readers a suitable introduction to the renowned prince who was to take the Tanjavur throne one day as Parakesari Uttama Chozha. Now we wish to make amends for this lapse.

We should remind our readers about Madhurantakan's lineage before we come to him.

Before Sundara Chozha became king, the Chozha empire had long been under the rule of his uncle Gandaraditta. Gandaraditta and his wife, Sembiyan Mahadevi, were devout worshippers of Siva who spent their entire lives renovating Siva temples.

Gandaraditta had a great desire to collect all the *tevaram* hymns scattered across Tamizh Nadu—an ambition that was not fulfilled in his lifetime. But he did compile some and wrote his own verses in the tevaram mode. Among them, the verses he composed on Chidambaram and the temple therein continue to be part of the anthology of hymns named *Tiruvisappa.*

In his verses, Gandaraditta mentions his father, Emperor Parantaka, roofing the Chidambaram temple in gold, and his conquest of Ilankai and the Pandya country. Inscribing his own name in the last verse, he also names Tanjavur the capital of the Chozhas in his time.

The mighty-sceptred
Chozha king
who did bring
the Pandya tyrant,
and the Lanka Isle,
under his rule
In Tanjavur.
He roofed in gold
the Tillai* shrine,
where bangled girls
dance and sing.
When will I find
my lord divine
in Tillai shrine?

The rumbling clouds
circle the groves

* Chidambaram.

of Gandaraditta,
the Chozha king.
Those who sing
his string of songs
(in Tamil sweet,
whose honeyed taste
can never pall)
on the dancing lord
on the golden stage
in the shrine renowned
in Tillai town
in the Chozha realm
will proudly claim
joy divine
and lasting bliss.

Gandaraditta did not believe in waging battles and expanding the kingdom. Since he was distressed by the sufferings of humanity engendered by wars, he tried to avoid them as best he could. This led to the shrinking of the Chozha empire during his reign.

At a ripe age, Gandaraditta married the daughter of the Mazhavaraiyar clan. Madhurantakan was their son.

Foes were sprouting up all around the empire. Gandaraditta's younger brother Arinjaya was fatally wounded on the battlefield and awaited death. Arinjaya's son Sundara Chozha was a young man who had already proved victorious in several wars and earned a name for his military prowess. This made Gandaraditta decide that Sundara Chozha should be king after him and announce this decision to his subjects. To prevent family conflicts over the succession issue, he also proclaimed that Sundara Chozha's progeny had the right to ascend the throne after their father. He had told his wife, Sembiyan Mahadevi, that she should raise their son Madhurantakan as a devout Saiva, committed to the service of the faith.

These were matters well-known across the realm.

Sembiyan Mahadevi kept her promise to her husband and raised their son to adore the lord and detach himself from worldly pleasures.

Until he was twenty, Madhurantakan showed no interest in matters of state. To him, his mother's word was law. The thought that the Chozha throne belonged to him did not even enter his head.

That mindset began to change when he married Chinna Pazhuvettaraiyar's daughter two years ago. Fuelled by the Pazhuvur queen's counsels, the initial spark of temptation grew until it became a wild forest fire. Impelled as they were by diverse motivations, the feudal rulers and high-ranking officers of the Chozha empire began their machinations in support of Madhurantakan. They were waiting for Sundara Chozha's death to put Madhurantakan on the throne. But Madhurantakan did not wish to wait any longer. He had begun to think that Sundara Chozha had no right to the throne that he should have inherited. And now that Sundara Chozha was bedridden and unable to administer the kingdom, why shouldn't he ascend the throne straightaway and take that responsibility on himself?

Controlling his craze for power became the Pazhuvettaraiyars' responsibility now. They did not want to aggravate the situation with undue haste. Sundara Chozha's sons were mighty warriors. They had endeared themselves to the people by their upstanding qualities and valiant deeds. Two great leaders–Tirukovilur Malayaman and Kodumbalur Velar–stood staunchly by their side. Most of the army favoured Sundara Chozha's sons. Therefore, the Pazhuvettaraiyars decided to be patient until the death of the emperor. They had also learnt that the emperor's mind, too, had changed a little. There would be no problem at all if he himself declared that the throne belonged to Madhurantakan after him. Objections to such a proclamation would be raised only by Sembiyan Mahadevi and Kundavai Devi. Kundavai's schemes could be quashed by counter-schemes. But it would not be easy to oppose Sembiyan Mahadevi, who was revered throughout the country as someone graced with divinity. It was well known that the lady did not want her son to be crowned. How would the people accept the son taking the throne against his mother's wishes? She must either follow her husband to the other world or change her mind. And who would have greater power to change his mother's mind than the son himself?

Therefore, the Pazhuvettaraiyars had been frequently advising the son to persuade his mother. But Madhurantakan was not keen to do it. His desire to rule had become a mania. however, he avoided discussing it with his mother. He did not even want to meet her.

But Sembiyan Mahadevi sent word to Tanjavur saying that she was going to fulfil one of her husband's dearest wishes and wanted to have her son beside her on that occasion. Chinna Pazhuvettaraiyar urged him to go and try to change his mother's mind about his right to the Tanjavur throne.

17

Nambi, the Saintly Youth of Tirunaraiyur

Madhurantaka Tevar entered Pazhaiyarai with Vandiyatevan and his entourage. The procession moved through the military colonies into the streets where the people lived, the marketplaces, temples and the lanes around them. Here and there, a few people stood in their front yards to watch the procession. Vandiyatevan saw that there was no enthusiasm among the populace. The city had been full of bustle and clamour the first time he had entered it. Now the streets were deserted. It was obvious that the people had no regard for Madhurantaka Tevar. This was an advantage to Vandiyatevan.

As they approached the old Chozha palace, they saw a huge cavalcade coming from another direction. At its centre was an open palanquin with an unknown boy who appeared to be a devotee of Siva. The crowd was thickest around him, with many men playing the cymbals and singing hymns.

'Hail Chidambaram!'

'Hail Tirunaraiyur Nambi!'

'Hail the blessed devotee of Ganesha!'

'Hara Hara Mahadeva!'

Madhurantakan looked at the procession with envy. The attendant replied to his query, 'The palanquin carries the boy, Nambi, from Tirunaraiyur.'

Madhurantakan said, 'What a rumpus! No one to cast a second glance at us but such a fuss over this boy!'

The procession passed them in the distance. Among those who were walking beside the palanquin, Vandiyatevan thought that he saw the Saiva who had fought with Azhvarkadiyan on the boat when they were crossing the river Kollidam.

Madhurantaka Tevar and his company reached Sembiyan Mahadevi's palace. The queen was standing at the entrance as though waiting in welcome. Madhurantakan got down and greeted his mother. Kissing his forehead, the queen told him, 'Son! You have arrived at the right time. Nambi of Tirunaraiyur is approaching. Go and refresh yourself and come to the court hall as soon as you can.'

Vandiyatevan noticed the light draining from Madhurantakan's face. Poor man! He must have thought that the queen had been waiting to greet him. What a disappointment! Was it not natural for the man who wanted to sit on the Chozha throne to be cast down when he realized that she had been waiting to welcome the Siva devotee in the approaching procession?

They went to the rooms allotted to Madhurantaka Tevar. The prince took his own time to change and freshen up. He did not seem too keen on going to the assembly hall. His mother was sending attendants one after another to call him. Finally, he asked, 'Where is the interpreter of signs?'

Vandiyatevan, who had been desperate to accompany him to the court, came forward to say, 'Here I am.' Madhurantakan took him and a few other attendants and went to the hall.

An assembly was being held there. Sembiyan Mahadevi, Princess Kundavai and several women from the palace were seated on one side. At the very centre of the hall sat a youth of tender years. Bright of face, he was smeared with sacred ash and wore the holy *rudraksha* beads. Palm leaf scrolls were scattered before him. He had one in his hands. An older man, similarly attired, stood beside him with an expression of rapture. There were many more crowding the hall. Vandiyatevan saw that the youth was the boy on the palanquin, and the man was the Saiva he had encountered on the boat. His gaze circled the hall until it came to rest on Kundavai Devi's glowing face. Kundavai's eyes registered surprise when they first saw Vandiyatevan, after which they ignored him altogether. He began to doubt whether she had recognized him at all.

When Madhurantakan entered the court, everyone except the women rose to honour him. They sat down again after he took his seat.

Sembiyan Mahadevi said to him, 'Son! This young boy, Nambi, belongs to Tirunaraiyur town where he has received the grace of lord Ganesha. He has found some tevaram hymns hitherto unknown. Once long ago, Mangaiyarkarasi, a daughter of the Chozha clan, became the queen of the Pandya realm. At her invitation, the poet Sambandar went to the Pandya capital Madurai and was victorious in his debate with men of the Jaina faith. This youth has acquired some of the verses that Sambandar had sung at that time, where he has also mentioned the lady of our Chozha clan. I am overwhelmed when I hear them. Had he been alive, your father would have also been thrilled. Please listen.'

Madhurantakan replied, 'Yes mother, I will. Let the reading begin.' But his face showed no interest. His mind was elsewhere. Even though he was displeased to see a common youth wearing ash and holy beads on a splendid seat in the middle of the assembly with so much fanfare, he put up with it to satisfy his mother.

Tirunaraiyur Nambi, blessed by lord Ganesha, began to read from the palm leaf in his hands. He sang the verses where Sambandar first sees Madurai city and asks, 'Is this not the sacred centre where Mangaiyarkarasi, who excels in her devotion to Siva, lives?' The verses went on to say:

Aalavai, this very town, where
Dwelling with his dear spouse
(The lady with the lovely eyes)
The lord imparts the scriptures four
Discoursing on their sense and gist.
The lord aglow in blazing red,
Is served always with zeal and care
By this queen among women,
Daughter of the Chozha king,
Consort of the Pandya king,

Lady with the bangled wrists,
Chaste and pure, she brings to mind
The goddess on the lotus bloom.

Daughter of the Chozha king
Whose upright rule is world renowned;
This is she, the Pandya queen,
whose voice is soft and sweetly tuned;
who never fails to pray and serve
the lord supreme and infinite
Measureless, beyond our ken
Whose head and feet cannot be found
Even by the gods themselves.

This very town is Aalavai,
where the lord finds perfect joy
in dwelling with his wife divine.

As she listened to the verses being read aloud, tears of bliss rained from Sembiyan Mahadevi's eyes. She exulted again and again in her great good fortune of having been married into the clan in which the Pandya queen Mangaiyarkarasi was born, and living in that Chozha land as a queen.

The only line that imprinted itself on Madhurantakan was the description of the Chozha king as 'world-renowned'. He was infuriated by the thought that the Chozha crown of antique fame—which should have graced his head—had been snatched by another.

Sambandar goes to see Mangaiyarkarasi. The Pandya queen takes one look at him and is overcome by anxiety. 'Ayyo!

He is just a boy. The Jainas are great monsters. How can this child win a debate against them?' Realizing this, Sambandar reassures her–

Doe-eyed lady, hear me out,
Consort of the Pandya king,
Don't see me as a naïve child
Or sigh over my tender age.
With the lord standing by me
The lord of Aalavai city
Easy prey I will not be
To evil men of shameful deeds
Hailing from the Elephant Hills
And many other regions too,
Who harm and hurt the populace.

As Tirunaraiyur Nambi sang this verse, Sembiyan Mahadevi forgot all about the terrestrial world in her ecstasy. She saw herself as Queen Mangaiyarkarasi, with Nambi as the young poet Sambandar.

Madhurantakan thought, 'Yes, I am young like the poet Sambandar. But I will not fear Tirukovilur Malayaman and Kodumbalur Velar, or the sons of Sundara Chozha who enjoy their support. Just as Sambandar had the grace of god, I too have the assistance of the Pazhuvettaraiyars.'

No word or note fell on Vandiyatevan's ears. His eyes and thoughts were completely engrossed in Kundavai Devi. He wondered whether the princess had not recognized him, or if she was deliberately ignoring him. Was she perhaps angry because he had not come straight to her after completing his mission? He wondered how he could meet her alone, and how he was going to convey his news to her.

When the songs ended, Sembiyan Mahadevi looked at the elder who had accompanied Nambi and said, 'Ayya! This boy seems to be the poet Sambandar himself who has taken birth again. Take him on a journey across the Tamizh realm. Collect all the hymns you may find in different places. The verses of the poets Appar, Sambandar and Sundarar must be compiled in individual segments and recited in Siva temples every day. That was my husband's wish. I hope to accomplish it in my lifetime. I will arrange for the palanquins, attendants and other necessities for you to undertake such a journey. I will send word to the emperor through my son to grant permission.' The jubilant roar that reverberated in the assembly after this announcement was nothing but sheer cacophony to Madhurantakan's ears.

18

The Interpreter of Signs

When the assembly convened to honour Nambi of Tirunaraiyur was about to disperse, Sembiyan Mahadevi said to her beloved son, 'Let me go up to the doorway to bid them goodbye. Go to your chambers, relax and return. I have something important to tell you.'

'All right, mother,' said Madhurantakan and left for his chambers. His mind blazed in jealousy and rage. Such flamboyant ceremonies to honour a vagabond, a pauper! The honour of the whole royal family was being impaired by his mother's conduct. No wonder the Pazhuvettaraiyars kept complaining about her. It was enough for the queen to see anyone with ash and rudraksha beads singing a few hymns, or a man requesting funds for temple restoration. She was going to empty the state treasury by throwing the money away at such people. As if this were not enough, Princess Kundavai lavished whatever was left on building infirmaries. How could he realize his ambition if he allowed them to go on splurging as they did? How would he be able to send the Chozha armies in all directions and establish his rule over the whole world?

And now the great queen wanted to talk to her son again! God knew what esoteric subjects she would dwell on! She could start with yoga and meditation! Perhaps elucidate the technique of focusing the eye on the tip of the nose to arouse the *kundalini*[*] power to master all the sixty-four arts without studying them! Or go on and on about the inner significance of Nataraja's dance, the implications of his matted locks and crescent. Such expositions had already made him half-crazy and a laughing stock to everyone. He should not give room for those talks anymore. And if she insisted, he should not allow himself to listen.

All right. He would talk to the interpreter of portents before his mother sent for him again. How did the man know about those two incidents that no one could know? Amazing! He must have some miraculous power. Would he predict the future the way he described the past? Best to ask him straightaway.

Madhurantakan noticed the interpreter of signs casting about in uncertainty. With a wave, he ordered the man to follow him. Vandiyatevan was eager to catch Kundavai Devi's eye and convey his message with a glance. But the princess left with the queen and without a backward look.

What was this? Had the princess forgotten him completely? She met innumerable people every day. How would she

---

[*] Kundalini, which translates from Sanskrit to 'coiled snake', describes the energy that rests, often dormant, coiled at the base of the spine. When it rises or awakens, it can cause a varied number of experiences and symptoms.

remember his face, which she had seen just once or twice, he thought. How daft am I to have been thinking of the princess day and night, through dangers and disasters? Why should the princess think of me? The bee yearns for honey and circles the flower. But what does the flower care about the bee? The flower smiles at the sun. Who was that sun who could make Kundavai's face bloom?

And yet, would she not even be interested to know how he had fared with the task she had set him? Would someone have informed her about it already? How was that possible? No, no. Her face showed anxious preoccupation, perhaps because she could not recognize him. How could she identify the man who took her message to Ilankai if he returned as a member of Madhurantakan's entourage? Ah! How astonished she would be when he told her about the stratagems he had employed to gain entry into the city! But how was he to meet her? How could he send word to her?

'Interpreter of portents, why are you so lost in thought?' Vandiyatevan was startled by Madhurantakan's voice. By then, they had reached Madhurantakan's private chamber.

In those days, there were diverse categories of men to foretell the future–astrologers and diviners, readers of portents and signs. Astrologers made predictions by examining horoscopes and the configurations of the stars and planets. Diviners based their general prophecies on the words used by their clients, the time of consultation or by asking the client to choose one among a hundred and eight numbers. Palmistry remained unchanged in its methods from the past to the present.

The readers of portents were like sages who possessed the inner eye. They focused their mind to describe events from the past, present and future as if they were seeing them with their own eyes. Some of them spoke with their eyes closed in a state of trance. Others spoke of things that had happened and were about to happen as if they were seeing them in the burning flame on which their eyes were fixed intently. A few could see the past and future of their clients in their minds as soon as they caught sight of them. Apart from such clairvoyants, there were soothsayers who made their predictions based on external signs, such as the trajectory of a crow in flight.

Vandiyatevan was disconcerted to hear himself being addressed as a reader of portents. Who could guess what questions the prince would ask him? He would have to somehow manage to give satisfactory answers. God! How to escape from there, and from him? How to find the princess alone and talk to her?

'Nothing much, ayya! I was just thinking that instead of interpreting signs, if only I could have learnt a few hymns like the boy I saw in the court! What honours and bounties I would receive!'

'Who stops you? Why don't you learn a few tevaram songs and sing them too?'

'What is the use of wishful thinking? Things will happen according to the decree of destiny.'

'What do you think about the boy who sang? What's his fortune to be?'

'A great one, where the grace of Siva mingles with royal patronage. Kings and queens will honour him. His name will be associated with great souls and endure in the world for ages to come.'

Vandiyatevan's 'prediction' was both blind and rash. But it triggered tremendous mental agitation in Madhurantakan.

'Let me see what you have to say about *my* fortunes.'

Vandiyatevan needed time to reflect. So he said, 'Can't be done in haste. If I must make forecasts in detail, a lamp must be lit, incense burnt, and you should be seated behind the flame. I will then foretell the happenings of the future exactly as I see them.'

In a state of ferment, Madhurantakan called for lamp and incense to be fetched at once.

Two seats were placed before and behind the lamp. Madhurantakan took his seat, after which Vandiyatevan sat down on the opposite seat, facing the prince.

For some time, he remained in a 'state of meditation' with his eyes closed. His mouth muttered mantras.

Then he shook himself all over with great force and 'entered into a trance'. His body shuddered in a frenzy.

He opened his eyes wide and stared hard at the flame. Then he looked at Madhurantakan and said, 'Ayya! You must forgive me if I had tossed off any casual remarks about you. There is nothing ordinary about your fortune. There is absolutely no connection between you and the boy in court today. His rewards are attained by royal patronage. But yours . . . Ah! What I see in the flame dumbfounds me!'

'What do you see? Tell me! Tell me!' Madhurantakan urged him.

'Ah! How can I tell you? I cannot find the words. Kings with crowns on their heads are assembled in a formation as far as the eye can see. Ministers, councillors, officers—they are all standing in row after row. Beyond them stand the soldiers of the army like an illimitable ocean. The shining brilliance of their spears and swords, and the armour on their chests, dazzle the eye. In the distance, the terraced mansions are packed with clamouring crowds. They are shouting slogans.'

'Tell me! Tell me! What are they shouting?'

'Prince! I cannot make out the words clearly as thousands are bellowing together. I think they are shouting "Hail, The Scion of the Chozha clan!" "Hail, Emperor of the Three Worlds!" "Hail, King of kings"!'

'Then?'

'The people are advancing in crowds. Soldiers armed with swords and spears are trying to contain them. There is nothing but chaos and commotion.'

'Right! Right! Why have the crowds gathered?'

'That is what I am going to see now. The tiger standard is soaring sky-high. Flags with the emblem of the fish, bow, palm tree, lion, bull and boar are flying at a lower level below. In a court as splendid as the one built by the mythical architect Mayan, stands a golden throne encrusted with precious gems. On a seat beside it, a coruscating crown, studded with diamonds and sapphires, is shining like a million suns. Above the crown, a white state umbrella spreads itself like the moon casting its cool beams. Girls resembling nymphs stand waiting with white silken whisks in their hands. Golden pots are placed in a row, filled with sanctified waters from the holy rivers. Prince! Everything is ready for the coronation.'

'Who is being crowned? Tell me that!' said Madhurantakan.

'We will know very soon. There! The main doors of the mandapam are opened. Heralds arrive, making announcements. A brave and majestic-looking old man comes first, with another man beside him who looks like his brother. Behind them, a prince as handsome as the god of love walks in.'

'Who? Who is he?'

Once again, Vandiyatevan stared hard at Madhurantaka Tevar and turned to look at the flame.

'Ayya! He looks exactly like you. Why, it *is* you! The two men who came ahead take you to the throne. Roars of "Victory! Victory!" resound like the ocean. Hundreds of hands rain flowers, gems and yellow grain on you. There! You are now close to the throne. Ah! Ah! What is this? What is this impediment that springs up like a bad omen? A woman with dishevelled hair runs to stand between you and the throne. She tries to stop you. You push her away . . . ! Oh my god! What is this? The scene is obscured by the spreading smoke. Nothing can be seen . . . '

'Look! Look! Look hard! What happens after that?'

'Pardon me, your highness! A miasma of smoke has shrouded everything.'

'Look again, look. Have you seen that woman anywhere before?'

'Prince! The woman has disappeared. You too have disappeared. Court, throne, crown, everything has dissolved. There must be someone in this palace with tantric powers. They must have deliberately cast spells to terminate this session. Ayyo! My face is burning!'

Vandiyatevan covered his face with his hands. He remained in the same posture for some time before opening his eyes.

All the nerves in Madhurantaka Tevar's body were on edge now. Fury bubbled on his face. His eyes shone like pieces of burning coal. Vandiyatevan became somewhat afraid. He feared that he had pushed the prince's passions to their breaking point.

'Look once more. Look well and tell me what you see.'

'No use, prince! A scene that has dissolved will not appear again immediately. It will appear only after a few days. But I can look again and describe any other scene that I may see.'

'Tell me, tell me. Tell me whatever you see.'

'There is chaos in the crowd. The people are angry and grief-stricken. A messenger is giving them some news. He says that someone from the royal family has been drowned in the sea. Ayyo! Poor man! The people are going to thrash him. Prince! If any such incident takes place, please do not go anywhere near the people. If you must do so, take every precaution.'

'Did they not mention the name of the person who was drowned in the sea?'

'I missed the name in the general din and mayhem. That scene has vanished now. But I see a hideous mob of men with garlands of skulls. They look like Kapalikas . . . Like Kalamukhas . . . One of them holds a monstrous scythe in his hands. There is a sacrificial altar before him. Prince! Here too, I see a prince approaching. The Kalamukhas surround him and dance in exultation. Ayyo! Don't ever get into the middle of such a mob, not even by mistake!'

Madhurantakan began to sweat. His body shuddered.

Vandiyatevan noted this. He grasped his head with his hands and said, 'Prince! I can see no more. Please forgive me. My head is spinning. My eyes are darkening. Someone is stopping me with spells. I will continue in another place, at another time.'

A palace attendant entered to say that the dowager queen had asked him to bring the prince to her.

Madhurantakan left with him, determined to pour out all the rage boiling within him on his mother.

'Ayya, I am unable to bear this headache. Let me go out of the palace and take a turn around the city,' said Vandiyatevan and took the prince's permission to do so.

* * *

Pinakapani, the Pazhaiyarai physician's son, had found a new interest in life. Until recently, he had been content to study medical science from his father. During the Kodikkarai journey, Vandiyatevan had introduced him to the world outside. It is natural for anyone who has just fallen in love to share his new-found feelings with someone or the other. Realizing that Pinakapani was a first-rate idiot, Vandiyatevan did not stop there but began to describe the dangers of becoming besotted with women. He told Pinakapani all about his personal experience in the joys and sorrows of being smitten by love. Initially, Pinakapani did not care for this kind of talk. But gradually, his mind changed. He began to feel an inexplicable resentment towards Vandiyatevan. This rage increased when Vandiyatevan refused to disclose the identity of the woman he loved despite Pinakapani's demands. By the time they reached Kodikkarai he began to see Vandiyatevan as his enemy.

The smoking embers turned into flames when he met Poonkuzhali. She not only rejected his advances but made fun of him as well. Pinakapani's mania reached new heights when he realized that she had greater regard for Vandiyatevan than for him. This made him dare to betray Vandiyatevan to the Pazhuvur men.

Unable to capture Vandiyatevan, the Pazhuvur soldiers seized Pinakapani and took him to Tanjavur to be imprisoned in the dungeons. All this made his animosity towards Vandiyatevan grow.

He was released before Princess Kundavai went to the dungeons to free him. It was Nandini who had arranged this. She had become angry and suspicious when Vandiyatevan got away from the Tanjavur palace without taking leave of her. Her suspicions mounted when she learnt that he had gone to Pazhaiyarai, and later, escaped to Ilankai. She guessed that one day, he would certainly return and try to meet Kundavai again. She felt strongly that she should have a trusted informant in Pazhaiyarai to keep watch.

After talking to Pinakapani, she decided that he was the right man for the job. She entrusted him with this crucial responsibility.

'One day, the man who betrayed you will certainly return to Pazhaiyarai. You must remain vigilant and keep your eyes and ears wide open to see where he goes and what he does, and send me information at once. If you do, I will reward you handsomely.'

Then, Chinna Pazhuvettaraiyar summoned him and gave him an order concerning Vandiyatevan. 'If you help to catch the traitor when he turns up, I will appoint you in our intelligence agency and raise you to a high position.'

From that day, Pinakapani lost all interest in his medical profession. He roamed the Pazhaiyarai streets, building all kinds of castles in the air. He was constantly struck by suspicions. He would go up close to strangers on the street, stare at them, shake his head and go away, muttering, 'No, not him.' This made everyone conclude that the physician's son had gone mad.

But Pinakapani did not give up his efforts.

He paid no great attention to Madhurantaka Tevar and his entourage when they entered the fort. He did not expect Vandiyatevan to be in that company and had been scanning the huge crowds accompanying Tirunaraiyur Nambi. But he did see Madhurantakan and his group from a distance. Once, when the horse rider next to Madhurantakan turned to look behind him, Pinakapani was struck by doubt. But he could not clear it as the group went into the palace all too quickly.

19

Timely Rescue

Pinakapani had been unable to enter the court when Tirunaraiyur Nambi was being honoured. He stood outside with the crowd trying to peep in. Vandiyatevan's mind was elsewhere, but Pinakapani kept on staring at Vandiyatevan's face. All this was being observed by another man without anyone getting wise to it. He was none other than our old friend Azhvarkadiyan.

After casting Madhurantakan's mind in a tumult, Vandiyatevan came out of the palace. The physician's son who had been waiting there now approached him to ask, 'Fellow, who are you?'

Taken by surprise, Vandiyatevan said, 'You want to know who I am? Which "I" do you mean? This fleshly frame made of the five elements of earth, water, air, fire and ether? Do you mean the soul that supports life? Or do you mean the oversoul, the matrix of the life force animating the human soul? Son!

What kind of a question is this? There is no "I" or "You". Everything is god. The world is nothing but an illusion. Ask great savants like Tirunaraiyur Nambi to explain the mysteries of *Pati*, the oversoul, *Pasu*, the human soul, and *Pasam*, the world. Understand?' said Vandiyatevan and jumped on his horse still standing outside the palace. He made his horse canter along until he was sure that Pinakapani was not following him. Then, he slowed down to a more leisurely pace.

But was the physician's son to be duped so easily? His doubt had become a certainty. He informed the chief of the city security forces and he roamed around the streets with the two guards sent to accompany him. Just as he had anticipated, he ran into Vandiyatevan at an intersection of four roads.

'Arrest him! He is a spy!' Pinakapani shouted.

'Fellow! Are you mad?' Vandiyatevan asked.

'Whom do you call mad? This body? The soul within the body? The oversoul?' Pinakapani challenged him.

'From the nonsense you spout, it is clear that you are mad.'

'I am not mad. I am the son of the physician who accompanied you to Kodikkarai. Guards! This is the spy who got away from the Tanjavur Fort and escaped to Ilankai. Seize him at once!'

The guards approached Vandiyatevan. 'Beware! Don't listen to him. I am the reader of signs who came with Prince Madhurantakan.'

'No! No! He is a great liar! Arrest him at once!' Pinakapani shrieked.

A large crowd had gathered around them by then. Some took Vandiyatevan's side, others supported the physician's son.

One of them said, 'He doesn't look like a reader of signs.'

'Nor does he look like a spy,' said another.

'Can a fortune teller be so young?'

'Why not? Will a spy go riding nonchalantly through the open streets?'

'Why does a reader of signs wear a sword?'

'If he is a spy, whom does he spy for? What intelligence has he come to gather in Pazhaiyarai?'

But Pinakapani went on yelling, 'Arrest him! Arrest him at once. This is Pazhuvettaraiyar's order!'

The moment Pazhuvettaraiyar's name was mentioned, the men in the crowd began to sympathize with Vandiyatevan. They tried to find a loophole for him.

By this time, Azhvarkadiyan had reached the outskirts of the crowd. He shouted, 'Is the interpreter of signs who came with Prince Madhurantakan here?'

'No, he is a spy,' Pinakapani screamed.

'What's all this? If you are the sign reader who came with the prince, come with me! The princess asked me to bring you,' Azhvarkadiyan said.

Vandiyatevan's heart leapt. 'I am that reader of signs. I will come,' he said.

'Don't let him go! Don't let the spy escape!' Pinakapani hollered.

Signalling with his eyes, Azhvarkadiyan said, 'You can come with me only if you prove that you are an interpreter of signs.'

'How do you want me to prove it?' Vandiyatevan asked quickly.

'See those two horses galloping there? It looks as if the riders are bringing news of some emergency. Speak! What is the news they bring?'

Staring hard at the approaching horsemen, Vandiyatevan said, 'I will tell you. A disaster connected with the waters has overtaken someone belonging to the royal family. They are bringing this sorrowful news.'

The riders reached the crowd before he closed his mouth. Blocked by the crowd, the horses came to a halt.

'You look like messengers. What news do you bring?' Azhvarkadiyan enquired.

'Yes, we are message-bearers bringing devastating news. The ship on which Prince Arulmozhi Varman was journeying was trapped in the whirlwinds. The prince jumped into the sea to save someone and was drowned.' As soon as one of the horsemen finished speaking, cries of heart-rending grief broke out in the crowd.

How did so many people gather so quickly? Men and women, old and young, crowded around the messengers. They broke into laments and pelted them with questions.

The majority of the populace knew that the Pazhuvettaraiyars did not exactly fancy Arulmozhi Varman. The news that they had sent their men to arrest the prince in Ilankai had reached their ears. Therefore, several people began to chunter about the Pazhuvettaraiyars. Then they began to curse them openly. They said to each other, 'The Pazhuvettaraiyars must have deliberately drowned the prince.' Their chatter, wails and curses resounded like the roar of the ocean.

Caught in this tumult, the Tanjavur messengers found it impossible to make their way to the palace. Their efforts to push through met with no success. The people barred their way with their repeated questions, 'How?' 'Where?' 'When?' 'Is this certain?'

Azhvarkadiyan said to the guards accompanying Pinakapani, 'Why are you standing stock still? Take the messengers to the palace.' The guards too had been stunned. Now they came forward to push through the crowd. But their progress was slow. The people followed them relentlessly. And the crowds went on swelling, more and more.

In that vast crowd where all hearts were united in distress, and in lamenting over Arulmozhi Varman's plight, a single creature went on screaming, 'Ayyo! This is a plot! A plot to let the spy escape!' But no one heeded him. No one heard his shouts. The physician's son was pushed along like driftwood on the floods of a great river.

Vandiyatevan had dismounted as soon as the crowds began to swell. Azhvarkadiyan grabbed his hand. 'Leave the horse. We can find it later. Come with me at once,' he said.

'If your assistance had not been so perfectly timed, I don't know what my situation would have been!' Vandiyatevan said.

'This is your habit! You get into a tight spot. Someone comes to rescue you from that crisis,' Azhvarkadiyan taunted him.

Both stood aside to avoid being swept along. When the crowds moved away, Azhvarkadiyan took Vandiyatevan in another direction.

They entered the locked house in the corner of the street, went to the garden at the back and walked through paths canopied by creepers. Soon, they came to a blue stream. A boat was floating on that stream. A lady was seated on the boat. Vandiyatevan's heart gave a great leap when he saw her.

20

Mother and Son

When the attendant came to tell him that his mother was expecting him, Madhurantakan went to see Sembiyan Mahadevi, the noble lady renowned all over the land for her devotion to Siva. There was a time when Madhurantakan had been completely devoted to her. That devotion had now turned to a burning rage. 'Not even in stories have I heard of a mother who betrayed her own son. Why should it be my fate to have such a mother?' The more he thought of this, the more all the love in his heart turned to vindictiveness. His spite grew into a blaze.

This fury was somewhat quelled when he saw his mother's face, suffused with a rare quietude. He prostrated before her as he usually did. 'May your devotion to Siva grow and flourish!' said she and made him take a seat.

That blessing struck Madhurantakan like an arrow.

'Madhurantaka, is my daughter-in-law doing well? And how is everyone doing in your father-in-law's house and the household of the Chancellor of the Exchequer?' his mother asked him.

'Everyone is well. But what do you care?' the son muttered.

'Did you see the emperor before you left Tanjavur? How is he doing now?' the queen asked.

'I did see him and take leave of him before I left. The emperor's health is getting worse and worse, day by day. His mental trauma is greater than his physical suffering,' Madhurantakan said.

'What is this, child? What has happened to trouble his mind?'

'Is it not natural for those who commit acts of crime and injustice, and those who defraud others to enjoy what doesn't belong to them, to experience mental suffering?'

'What are you saying? What act of crime or injustice has the emperor committed?'

'What more does he need to do? Is it not enough that he has been usurping for so many years, the throne that belongs to me? Is it not a crime? Is it not injustice?'

'Child! How did poison seep into your pure heart? Whose evil counsel has influenced you and corrupted you?'

'None. Why do you think your son is a rank idiot? Do you believe that he is too brainless to think for himself?'

'Even wise men may be swayed by bad advice. Wasn't Kaikeyi persuaded by Manthara's evil counsel?'

'I too know that women's minds can be ruined by evil counsels.'

'Madhurantaka! Whom do you mean?'

'Mother! Why did you call me? Tell me that.'

'Were you not present at the ceremony held just a while ago?'

'Yes. You placed a callow tramp on a palanquin. You put him on a throne and honoured him. He must be swaggering with a swollen head . . . '

'Ayyo! Don't indulge in blasphemy! Child, though he is only a boy, he is someone who is ripe in knowledge and piety.'

'Let him be as great as you please. His greatness will not diminish if I slight him. I don't object to your honouring him so excessively. Tell me why you called me here.'

Sembiyan Mahadevi released a long sigh. Then she began to speak. 'I am astonished by the change in you. Even in my dreams, I never thought that your two years' stay in the Pazhuvettaraiyar mansion would transform you like this. Never mind. I must do my duty. I must try to fulfil the promise I made to your father to the best of my ability. Son, before I tell you why I called you, let me tell you my story, the story of how I came to marry your father. Please listen to me with patience.'

Madhurantakan seated himself more comfortably, signifying that he would do so.

'When you were a child, you have come once or twice to Mazhapadi, my birthplace. You have seen the Siva temple there. I have heard it said that it is one of the sixty-four temples built by your ancestor Kochengat Chozha. Your grandfather—that is, my father—was the head of a large household in Mazhapadi. Ours is an old clan. At one time, the Mazhavaraiyars were as influential as feudal lords. They had joined the Pandyas in the war against Vijayalaya Chozha. That is why, after the Chozhas achieved victory, the Mazhavaraiyars lost their power. This did not bother me at all when I was a young girl. My heart was with Nataraja, the god in the temple. An elder had told me about an incident in the past. The poet Sundarar was walking beside the Siva temple in Mazhapadi, then hidden by konrai trees in full bloom. He heard a voice calling out, "Sundaram! Have you forgotten me?" The poet asked his disciples if they heard it. They had not. Then he asked if there was any temple close by. Discovering the shrine behind the trees, the poet ran to the sanctum and sang, "O lord of the golden form! Whom do I think of but you?"

'Those lines became imprinted in my mind. I haunted the temple. I would stand in front of the deity and repeat those lines. As the days passed, the lord began to dwell in my heart. I fantasized about marrying Siva. I imagined myself to be his divine consort like Parvati or Dakshayani. Like them, I closed my eyes and meditated on attaining the lord. I was repelled by any mention of marriage. My childhood passed in this manner. My devotion increased as I attained the years of youth. The people at home and in town began to call me "crazy". I did not care. I spent all my time at the temple. I would string different kinds of flower garlands and rejoice to see the deity adorned with them. I meditated for long hours. One day, hearing a commotion, I opened my eyes and saw five or six people standing before me. My eyes were drawn to the man who stood in front. I thought that lord Siva himself had manifested himself with his retinue. I got up with folded hands, tears streaming from my eyes and bowed. He must have noticed this for a voice asked, "Who is this girl? Why is she weeping?" My father's voice answered, "She is my daughter. At this young age, she has developed a deep devotion for Siva. She is constantly here, meditating, singing hymns and shedding tears."

'When I looked up again, I saw that the man before me was not god but a member of some royal family. I could not bear my humiliation. I ran home speedily. But the man who overwhelmed me did not leave me. He came home with my father. Son, he was none other than my husband and your dear father, Gandaraditta Tevar.'

The queen paused here, her eyes moist with old memories. She wiped her eyes and continued, 'I learnt more about your father. He had recently ascended the Chozha throne. He had also undertaken a pilgrimage to visit several Siva shrines. He was then forty years old. The lady he had married when he was young had passed away. He had no thought of another marriage. In fact, he had decided not to marry again. But he had second thoughts when he met me. In my father's presence, he asked me if I would agree to his wish. I was enraptured, believing that Siva had himself appeared to redeem me. I gave my heartfelt consent. Soon, we were married. That is how your grandfather regained his influential position with the titular name "Mazhavaraiyar".

'Son! When your father and I were married, we had a heart-to-heart talk and decided that we would not have children but dedicate our lives to the service of the lord. There was an important reason for that decision. Son! I never imagined that I would have to share all these matters with you. But the necessity has arisen now. Please listen to me carefully.'

Sembiyan Mahadevi took a deep breath. Madhurantakan too began to listen to his mother with greater attention.

21

'Call Yourself a Mother?'

Sembiyan Mahadevi, who appeared to be the embodiment of piety, continued to speak.

'Son, the Chozha empire was facing an ordeal when your father Gandaraditta Tevar ascended the throne. You know how the empire stretched from Ilankai in the south to the river Krishna in the north during the reign of your grandfather, Emperor Parantaka. But in his last days, several adversities troubled the empire and the dynasty. The Rashtrakutas invaded the land with an army as huge as the mythical Ravana's battalions. Parantaka's first son, the heroic Rajaditta, went to face them. It was in Takkolam in the north that they met in a war as horrendous as the Kurukshetra war. Blood flowed like a river and thousands died. The Rashtrakuta army fled in disarray, but not before Rajaditta was sacrificed and your uncle Arinjaya, severely wounded. No information was available about the latter. Arinjaya's first son Sundara Chozha had joined the war in Ilankai. There was no news about him either. Your father Gandaraditta was the only man of the royal family who was beside your grandfather at that time.

'Your father had an aversion for matters of state from a very young age and had become devoted to lord Siva. He disliked wars. "Why should people die due to the craze for conquest?" he asked himself in distress. He argued about it with his brothers. He gave his attention to pilgrimage, worship and associating with savants. He did not even want to touch any weapon. Nor did he train himself in the military arts or war strategies. He believed that diplomacy was all about lying, scam, treachery, pretence, plots, counter-plots, slaughter and other sins. "What is the difference between a thief who steals others' belongings and a king who conquers other lands?" he asked.

'Son, fate decreed that a man with these principles should accept the burden of ruling the Chozha kingdom.

'As Emperor Parantaka awaited death, he was anguished by the setbacks in the kingdom and by the death of Rajaditta. He called your father and told him, "You must take care of the kingdom."

'Not wishing to make his father suffer more when he was on the brink of death, your father accepted the charge. Viranarayani Devi, who had married your father before me, was already dead. I had not even seen your father at that time. Therefore, your grandfather was troubled about the fate of the country after your father's lifetime. Fortunately, the search party in Ilankai located Sundara Chozha on an island and brought him back.

'Emperor Parantaka doted on Sundara Chozha. He had raised him with every indulgence and great affection.

Moreover, many wise men had foretold that the Chozha kingdom would achieve glory through the boy. Therefore, he died saying that when your father ascended the throne, Sundara Chozha should be proclaimed crown prince and his descendants should have the right to the throne after him.

'Your father was determined that nothing should prevent the fulfilment of Emperor Parantaka's dying wish. Your father was not interested in ruling the land, he had no interest in matters of state. His mind hovered at the feet of the lord. He entrusted the administration of the kingdom to his younger brother Arinjaya and Arinjaya's son Sundara Chozha, and engaged himself in serving the lord. As I said before, he had no thought of remarriage. But I proved to be a distraction. He loved and married me only because he realized that I was "crazy" in my Siva worship. I must have performed penances through several previous births to have been fortunate enough to have had him as my partner in life. Only a very few great souls have seen god. Lord Siva appeared before your father and led him away from this terrestrial world. Just as I see you now, your father saw the great lord with his own eyes. You and I are duty-bound to carry out the wishes of that noble soul.'

Sembiyan Mahadevi paused. Having listened to her with a trembling body and seething mind, Madhurantakan asked, 'How can that be, mother? My father did not tell me anything. How am I duty-bound? In what way am I duty-bound?'

'Son! Hear me out. When your father attained the feet of the lord, you were but a little child. That is why he was unable to tell you anything then. But he told me. When we got married, we decided that we would not have children. But weak as I was, I could not maintain that vow. My girlhood devotion for Siva had turned into my love for your father. As the days passed, I longed for a child to hold in my arms, against my breast, on my lap, a child to kiss and caress. Whenever I saw other women caressing the children on their lap, singing lullabies to them, my body quivered, my heart burned. I begged the god I had adored from childhood. He blessed me. He granted me a child—you! Though I was exhilarated to have you, I was also afraid that I had angered your father. The great man was not angry with me. But he did burden me with the responsibility of fulfilling his word.

'Son! I swore to your father that I would raise you without any attachment to the material world, and with devotion for the lord. Until recently, I was proud of having fulfilled my vow. But my dearest son! My precious child! It hurts to hear things to the contrary now. Won't you heal my wound by telling me that what I have heard is nothing but a lie?' Sembiyan Mahadevi begged her son.

'Mother! Your mysterious words wound my heart too. What have you heard? What do you expect from me? What is the pledge you want me to make?'

'Child! You seem to have lost the power to understand what is in my heart. You want me to spell it out. Well, I will tell you. I hear that you have slipped from the sacred Ganga into a cesspool. Your devotion to the lord has been replaced by the desire for the kingdom. You want to ascend the Chozha throne. Our enemies have sullied the purity of your heart. I will be at peace only if you tell me that all this is untrue.'

Madhurantakan got up from his seat.

'My mind has not been sullied by any enemy. Are those who wish to put me on the throne my enemies? Are those who are ready to give their lives for me my enemies? Never. Who is my worst enemy? It is *you!* You who gave birth to me,' he shrieked.

Madhurantakan forgot all about the respect he owed his mother. He forgot Chinna Pazhuvettaraiyar's injunctions to use pleasant words to persuade his mother to change her mind. His rage exploded into invectives.

'You, and no other, have been my enemy from the time I was born. Call yourself a mother? Call yourself a woman? Epics and poems show mothers putting up extraordinary struggles to protect their children's rights. I have seen it in real life too. With a nature so totally contrary to motherhood, can you be human at all? Are you a demoness in the guise of a human being? What harm have I done to you that you should betray me so abominably? Why are you bent on snatching the kingdom that belongs to me by every right, and bestowing it on another? You say that it was my father's wish. You say that you made a commitment to him. Where are the proofs? I don't believe you. You say that someone has influenced me adversely. Not at all. On the contrary, someone has influenced *you* with evil counsels, blighted your heart, turned you into your own son's enemy. I will never give up my claim to the Chozha kingdom. It is mine by right. Not at your bidding. Not even if my father were to return from the other world to bid me. This Chozha empire is *mine.* This ancient throne is *mine.* The crown worn by the ancient King Karikal Valavan is *mine.* I will certainly take them. You gave me the rudraksha beads I wear around my neck. I wore them all these days out of respect for you as a mother. This rudraksha chain has made me impotent, the laughing stock of the entire country. I am throwing it away. Here, keep it!'

Ranting like a madman, Madhurantakan hastily tried to break the string of rudraksha beads around his neck. But though he tugged hard, all he could do was hurt his neck; the string refused to snap.

Madhurantakan was handsome. It could be said that he was better looking than the sons of Sundara Chozha. He had the captivating allure of femininity which they did not possess. That attractive face was now rendered hideous by rage and indignation. Sembiyan Mahadevi closed her eyes, unable to endure this transformation.

Only when he stopped hollering did she open them again. In a voice filled with unabated tranquillity, she said to him, 'Son! Please be calm. Even if I am a demoness, please hear me out.'

That voice did induce Madhurantakan to subside a little. 'I will. I did not say that I would not listen to you.'

'You mentioned a mother's natural instinct. Even a wicked ogress will not betray her own child. Even wild beasts try to protect their cubs from other wild beasts. I am trying to do the same thing. Apart from what I have told you, there is another reason that makes me advise you to abandon your desire for the kingdom. This will endanger your life. Is it a crime for your mother to want you to remain alive? Your demand will turn Sundara Chozha's sons into your enemies. Karikalan and Arulmozhi Varman are mighty warriors. You have never handled weapons. The entire army will be on their side. The captains and generals will also support them. They have friends in neighbouring countries. Who are your supporters?

Whom will you rely on when you make war with them? Son! You know that a comet has appeared in the sky. The whole world knows that a comet heralds death in the royal family. I am anxious that disaster should not overtake you. Child, is it wrong for me to want my only son to remain alive? Is this my treachery towards you?'

These words allayed Madhurantakan's anger and softened his heart.

'Mother! Forgive me. Why did you not say that this was the reason for your anxiety? I would have instantly put your mind at rest. I am not bereft of support. The feudal lords and high-ranking authorities in the Chozha empire are by my side. The Pazhuvettaraiyars are with me. Sambuvaraiyar of Kadambur is with me. Mazhavaraiyar, who is your brother and my uncle, is also on my side. Neela Tangaraiyar, Irattaikudai Rajaliar and Kundratur Kizhar stand by me with all their strength. They have all taken an oath to support me.'

'Son, I don't believe in their oaths. Once, they took the oath to be true to Sundara Chozha and his descendants. But let us assume that they remain true to you. Don't you know that their troops are very small? The army in the north is led by Aditta Karikalan. The army in the south is with Kodumbalur Velar.'

'Mother! The feudal rulers who support me are capable of raising an army of ten thousand each.'

'Leaving the army aside, what about the people? Don't you know how the people of the Chozha realm adore the sons of Sundara Chozha? You yourself saw it today. What massive crowds would have gathered to welcome Aditta Karikalan or Arulmozhi Varman if one of them had entered the city?

The people of this city did have some regard for you. But they have begun to dislike you since you became kin to the Pazhuvettaraiyars.'

'Mother! I am not at all bothered about the people's regard. What is the use of their regard? They are subjects to be ruled by the king. They must be devoted to anyone who sits on the throne.'

'Son! Those who have advised you have not instructed you in the very first lesson of statecraft. No king can rule for long without the love of the people. His rule will be ineffective.'

A commotion began to resound in front of the palace as the great lady spoke these words. Wailing, cursing, raging and questioning voices rose from thousands of human throats, and reverberated like the ocean buffeted by the mighty winds.

'Son! This is the first sign of the catastrophe that could strike the Chozha empire. I will go and find out what is happening. Stay here until I return.'

22

What is that Din?

As soon as he reached the stream, Vandiyatevan ascertained that the woman seated on the boat was the princess herself. His steps faltered when Azhvarkadiyan came to a halt.

'Why are you still standing here? The princess has been waiting for you for a long time. Give her the good news as soon as you get into the boat. Tell her that the prince is safe and sound. Don't waste time bragging about your valiant deeds. I am going back. We have opened the floodgates of revolt. Let me see if what we have let loose can be captured and caged again. How many problems are unleashed by your bluster and bravado!' said Azhvarkadiyan as he left to take the same route to return.

Vandiyatevan was astounded. How did the man know all this? He had not asked for any information! Pure guesswork? Or did he know everything? Vandiyatevan recalled that there were two categories among paupers—those who turned paupers under misfortunes, and those who belonged to the 'lineage' of paupers. He became a spy due to circumstances. That was why he brought troubles upon himself all the time. This Vaishnava must be a spy by descent. That is why he went about his business with all the steadiness of a professional. But whom did he work for? Could the account he gave of himself be true?

It was with these thoughts that Vandiyatevan approached the stream. He saw the face of the princess on the boat. He forgot Azhvarkadiyan. He forgot the task that had engaged him until then. He forgot the world. He forgot himself.

Ah! This girl's face had not left him even for an instant. It had followed him in wakefulness and dream, storm and rain, in the forests and seas. And yet, why did that face seem more beautiful when seen in the flesh? Why did his throat get blocked? Why did his heart start pounding?

Overwhelmed, Vandiyatevan got down the steps and into the boat. The princess made a sign to the boatman. The boat began to move. Vandiyatevan's heart began to reel.

'Reader of signs! Do you make your predictions for princes alone? Or will you read the signs for me? How do you read them? By watching the planets and stars? Observing the movements of crows and sparrows? Studying the lines on palms? Looks as though you do it by gazing at the face. Otherwise, why would you be staring so hard at me? If this is your method, no gentlewoman would come forward to consult you.' Kundavai's words fell on Vandiyatevan's ears like the tinkling of little bells.

'Devi! It is not to read your fortune that I gaze at your face. I was trying to remember when and where I had seen you before.'

'I know! I know! I know that you are extremely forgetful. Let me remind you. Some forty days ago, you saw me in the astrologer's house in Kudantai. Then you saw me beside the Arasalaru.'

'Devi! Please stop. I cannot believe you. Was it just forty days ago that I first saw you? Not forty thousand years ago? Not a hundred thousand times in hundreds of lives? Beneath the cliffs? On the crest of the hills? Beside the mountain spring? Did I not save you in the forest as you were fleeing from the wild tiger? Did I not slay the tiger with my spear? I was a hunter then, a wanderer in the woods. I trapped beautiful parrots with wings of varying hues and brought them to you. You took them from me, threw them into the air and laughed to see them flying away. Once I was a fisherman. I went to lakes and rivers far away to catch fish gleaming in gold, silver and emerald green for you. You dropped them back into the waters and rejoiced to see them leap and swim. I dove into the depths of the distant seas and found corals and pearls for you. You ran your hands through them before calling all the children in the town and showering them into their little hands. I plucked the ilantai fruit that grows once in thirty years from a three-hundred-year-old tree and offered it to you. You enjoyed watching your pet mynah bird pick at the fruit. I drizzled the mandara and parijata flowers that I had procured from the heavens before you. You dismissed them saying, "In no way can their fragrance equal the scent of the mullai flowers blooming over the fence in my backyard." I brought his peerless ruby necklace from Indra, king of the gods. "Will I ever touch a neckpiece worn by the dissolute Indra?" you said. I spent years performing penance to the goddess Parvati and obtained her anklet for you to wear. "Sacrilege!" you said and ordered me to return it. I went to the battlefield to defeat the kings of the sixty-four kingdoms and laid their crowns at your feet. I was distressed by the thought that your flowerlike feet may get hurt as you kicked them away. Princess! Tell me, are all these things untrue? Or did I indeed meet you just forty days ago?'

Not satisfied with this outburst, he began again. 'Devi! Once, we were on a silver boat holding golden oars, and sailing on moonbeams in the empyrean sea . . . '

'Ayyo!' princess Kundavai exclaimed. 'This man has gone completely mad! We must get back to the shore.'

'No, Devi, no! Until I reached this stream, my mind was crystal clear. If not, could I have devised a ploy to enter Pazhaiyarai city? Could I have convinced Madhurantaka Tevar that I was a reader of portents and got into the palace? Or escaped so easily from the physician's son? It is only when I got into this boat and saw your face that I became intoxicated - like a man who has imbibed liquor.'

'Then don't look at my face, ayya! Look at the clear waters of the stream, the blue sky, the tall trees on the banks, the palace domes, the white lilies and red lotuses on the waters. Or keep looking at the deaf boatman and tell me if you have succeeded in your mission. Have you brought the prince with you, is he doing well, where and with whom have you left him? Tell me everything that happened from the moment you left this place and spare no detail.'

Vandiyatevan replied, 'Devi! Would I have returned to face you if I had not succeeded in completing the task you gave me? Overcoming a thousand hurdles, I have brought the prince from Ilankai. I cannot say that the prince is doing well. When I left him, he was suffering from a high fever. But I have left him in safe hands, with boatwoman Poonkuzhali and young Sendan Amudan who grows flowers. They will be ready to sacrifice their lives a thousand times for the prince.'

That was when the sound of a thousand voices howling in unison assaulted their ears. It was with fear and anxiety that Vandiyatevan and the princess turned to see where it came from. 'What is it? Sounds like the bellowing of an angry mob.'

'Yes, it does,' Vandiyatevan said.

23

Vanathi

If the poets were asked to describe the princess of Kodumbalur, they would immediately recall the charm of the twilight hour. When the day begins to fade, the mind is overcast by melancholy, but not without a soothing sense of serenity. As the sun's last rays thin and vanish, and darkness envelops all sides, the goddess of the sky lights up millions of twinkling lanterns in a trice. Unlike the blinding sun, the stars delight the eye, and all we have to do is look up at them to overcome the gloom. And then, should the full moon make its appearance, its pearly beams would thrill flesh and spirit, and indeed the whole world.

True, the lotus closes its petals at eventide. But the jasmine explodes in bloom, and the fragrance intoxicates the earth and sky. True, the merry songs of the birds end at sunset. But how mellifluous the music from temple bells and *nadasvaram* pipes! How sweet the songs of the lute and harp, played by slender fingers from the upper chambers of the mansions!

The beauty of the Kodumbalur princess had the same indiscernible blend of joy and wistfulness. Her nature was imbued with the same ambivalence. At times, she was the embodiment of the tragic heroines Chandramati and Savitri. In other instances, you thought that the celestial dancers Rambha and Urvasi must rejoice in dance and song like Vanathi herself. She could be the beauteous Madhavi exulting in Kovalan's love, only to morph into Kannaki, grief-stricken by the loss of her spouse. She could be the lovelorn Valli, whose heart was with Velan, the god who wore a flower garland. Or the exulting Devayani, wedding her beloved Velan amidst superlunary celebrations.

For days at a stretch, no smile would crease Vanathi's face. On other days, she broke into incessant peals of laughter, spreading mirth across the world.

It may be guessed that Vanathi had inherited her ingrained traits from the circumstances of her birth and upbringing. When she was in her mother's womb, her father, Siriya Velar of Kodumbalur, was involved in brutal warfare. News of his victories alternated with those of defeat, making joy and sorrow see-saw in her mother's mind. Her mother died soon after Vanathi was born. Her father raised her with every indulgence, but that did not last long. The great warrior that he was, Siriya Velar did not want to remain in the palace even for Vanathi's sake. When Veerapandiyan went into hiding, he went with the troops chasing the Ilankai forces that had come to aid the Pandyas. He lost his life on the battlefield and became part of history with the title 'Siriya Velar who fell in Ilankai'.

After this, Vanathi's life became mired in sorrow, a sorrow that could be experienced only by a motherless girl at the demise of the doting father who had raised her. Though she was surrounded by love and care in the Kodumbalur palace, no one could take her father's place. People consoled her in various ways. One of them said, 'Child! Don't grieve! Your father will return to your womb to be born as a great warrior. He will perform acts of bravery that will astonish the world.'

These words took root in Vanathi's mind. She tried to overcome the grief she felt on her father's death by fantasizing about an imaginary son—with some success.

For days on end, she dreamed of this son, the things he would do, the great deeds he would perform. She would visualize that brave son travelling to lands far, far away and winning monumental battles. She saw him returning swiftly to place at her feet all the treasures he had won in those battles. She saw him crowned and seated on the throne. She saw great kings bowing and paying tribute to him. She saw great crowds of people rising to greet him like the vast ocean billowing at the sight of the full moon. She saw him taking hundreds of warships across the seas and planting the flag of victory on those foreign lands. She heard him tell her again and again, 'Mother! Don't I owe all these glories to you?'

Sometimes, her naïveté made her run her hand over her stomach to see if that imaginary son had already entered her womb. After all, in those times, everyone in Tamizh Nadu knew the Mahabharata and the story of how Kunti Devi had her sons by divine intervention. Vanathi wondered which god would give her a similar boon. Even when she became old enough to realize that marriage was a prerequisite for child-bearing, she hardly thought about who her husband would be.

Coming to the Pazhaiyarai palace brought about a transformation in her life, her world view. Kundavai's affection brought her solace and joy. Her style and elegance, in both appearance and deportment, and her refined modes of expression, introduced Vanathi to a different world, hitherto unknown. The jealousy of the other girls, who had come to Pazhaiyarai for the same reason as she had, generated a new excitement in her life. Her heart told her that she must possess something special to arouse their envy. At the same time, her inborn sweetness and generosity of spirit made her remain good-natured and well-mannered. But none of these things stopped her dreaming about her brave son.

That was when she happened to meet Ponniyin Selvan. Then and there, her castles in the air crumbled to fragments. Until then, she had hardly given any thought to who her spouse would be. She had dismissed the whole idea though she did know that she could have a child only if she had a husband. But what could she do with her recalcitrant mind now? It had set itself on the prince idolized by the entire Chozha realm, and so illustrious that the kings of all the fifty-four kingdoms of the subcontinent would beg him to marry their daughters. Would such a man spare her even a single glance? Not even in dreams could she be fortunate enough to marry such a personage.

However, having given her heart to the prince, was it at all possible to marry anyone else? All her fantasies had to be shattered into shards. The more she thought about it, the more she felt that her heart would explode. Once again, she turned into a figure of sorrow. Guessing Vanathi's feelings, Princess Kundavai tried to encourage her as much as she could, with greater affection and support. She also hinted that it was not so wrong after all for Vanathi to set her mind on the prince, nor was her desire unattainable.

The predictions of the Kudantai astrologer about her unborn son stoked the fire in her heart. Her fantasies became more and more expansive. She could not bear the exuberance of joy any more than the angst of yearning. When excessive elation and despondency alternated quickly, fainting became nature's method of mental release and survival.

In Tanjavur, her tensions were enhanced by the play on Emperor Parantaka, the nocturnal cry for help, and the fearful scene she witnessed that night. That was when she understood the insurmountable enmity between the Kodumbalur and the Pazhuvur clans. She became aware of the extent of the influence wielded by the Pazhuvettaraiyars. Would they allow her dreams about Prince Arulmozhi Varman to be fulfilled? Even if they did, what about the women in their families? Would the young queen of Pazhuvur give her consent? Whenever she thought of Nandini, Vanathi was reminded of the bewitching cobra. The whole world knew of her power and authority. She had learnt about Nandini's animosity to Kundavai Devi. Would it not be directed towards Vanathi as well? Why, she might harm Ponniyin Selvan too! The figure that stood before the emperor at midnight—was it truly Nandini herself? What was the reason for the emperor to have screamed in fear? Why did Kundavai Devi refuse to talk about these subjects?

The princess' demeanour had undergone a change. She did not indulge in banterings with Vanathi as before. Instead, she went in search of solitude. Some great anxiety was preying on her. Perhaps it had to do with Ponniyin Selvan, which was why she refused to talk to Vanathi about it.

The princess had gone away by herself even on that day. How these girls got completely out of hand in her absence! What a racket they made! Untouched by anxiety as they were, nothing could quell their merrymaking. Vanathi had never been able to tolerate their teasing. Afflicted by desolation in the past few days, she found their empty-headed banter unbearable.

Vanathi decided to go to Sembiyan Mahadevi's palace and look for the princess. She knew that an assembly had been convened, but the court had dispersed by the time she got there. She was told that the senior queen was engaged in confidential talks with her son. For some reason, this accelerated her anxiety.

It was when she was leaving the palace that Vanathi heard the great din of the crowds outside the palace. A mounting sense of urgency made her feel that she had to see the princess at once. When she enquired about Kundavai's whereabouts, one of the maids told her that the princess had been holding a private conversation with Azhvarkadiyan and had gone towards the stream in the palace garden.

For some time now, the princess had not cared to be disturbed when she sought to be alone. As Vanathi hesitated, Varini, one of the girls in the palace, came running to proclaim the news. 'Ponnniyin Selvan has been drowned in the sea!' she shrieked and burst into sobs. The other girls began to weep loudly. Vanathi stood stock still. She was unable to react. Everyone stared at her. Their harsh eyes seemed to accuse her,

'Wretch! It is you whose misfortunes have made the prince drown in the sea!' Vanathi could bear it no longer, she ran towards the stream in the palace garden. It was only now that she understood the import of what she had heard.

But even more overpowering than the shocking news was the thought that for a few days now, she had been seeing the prince's face reflected in the waters. The face looked real but disappeared when she tried to touch it. Now she knew why. The prince had been thinking of her, he had called out to her as he was drowning in the sea. Wretch that she was, she had been watching from the shore, not knowing what he meant. What a blunder! But no use thinking about what had occurred. What was she going to do now?

'Silly girl!' Vanathi told herself. 'Do you still have to think about what you should do? The stream in the palace garden flows into the Arasalaru. The Arasalaru goes to merge into the sea. The prince is waiting for you at the bottom of the sea in a magnificent palace of corals and pearls. What prevents you from joining him? Why should you stay behind?'

Once she came to this decision, Vanathi found herself at peace. Her agitation subsided, her sorrow was gone, her anxiety was over.

Going straight to the stream, she descended the marble steps and looked around. A boat was approaching the shore. The princess was in it. Vanathi wondered, 'Who is the young man with her . . . ? He is the man we saw in the Kudantai astrologer's house . . . who had taken the scroll to Ilankai . . . he must have brought the news about the prince. The princess has taken him aside to get all the details. She has left me behind to avoid making me suffer. Once she returns, I cannot carry out my wish. She will try to pacify me, console me. She will certainly stop me from joining the prince. And yet, is it fair to go without a last goodbye? Orphaned as I am, she gave me so much love. Should I not convey my gratitude to her? No. I cannot wait any more. Not a moment more. There! I see his face in the water. His whole form appears now. He is calling me. He is inviting me with a glowing smile. "All barriers to our union have been removed. Come!" Why tarry? Ah! Why does my head spin? Am I going to faint? No matter. It is enough if I fall into the water.'

Vanathi's wish was fulfilled. She did fall into the stream. Her burning body became cool as it went down, down, down. It was impossible to know for how long and how deep she fell. A few seconds? For several ages?

Vanathi was now in a wonderful world under the sea. Such beautiful mansions, so many storeys high that their pinnacles could not be seen. The light had turned cool and pleasant as it penetrated the waters. But what was the source of that light? The walls of the mansions! No surprise. Made of pearls, diamonds, sapphires, and rubies from the heads of serpents, it was natural for them to refract this cool luminescence.

Who are those people in the approaching crowd? How their bodies glow! Such an aura around their faces! They appear to be celestial beings. Had she reached paradise instead of the netherworld of serpents?

The scenes began to shift with great rapidity, like a dream within a dream.

Vanathi was led to a splendid hall, ornamented and festooned. Ponniyin Selvan stood at the centre of the hall, welcoming her with a radiant face. The heavenly *dundubhi* drums played, gems and flowers rained down. Auspicious greetings resounded as the prince exchanged garlands with her and they were married. Vanathi swooned in ecstasy. She remained unconscious for a long time. Then, she felt the touch of hands. At first, Vanathi thought it was Ponniyin Selvan who had raised her and placed her head on his lap. But there were bangles on those wrists. It was a woman's voice that said, 'Vanathi! Vanathi! How could you do this?'

Making a huge effort, Vanathi opened her eyes and saw Kundavai's face. She murmured, 'Akka! Akka! Did you attend the wedding? I didn't see you.'

24

Consciousness Regained

Vanathi's eyes closed themselves as she lost consciousness once again. Then, little by little, her mind began to regain its faculties. She realized that her marriage to the prince in the upper or the nether world was a hallucination. She recollected hearing the excruciating news about the prince, standing beside the stream and falling into the waters. This brought her immeasurable disappointment and heart-rending agony. She could not open her eyes.

Who pulled her out of the waters? It had to be Kundavai Devi, whose boat had been approaching the shore. 'Why did she save me?' Vanathi moaned to herself. 'Why could she not have let me drown once and for all? I must take issue with her over this as soon as I open my eyes. Is this all the love she has for her brother?'

The princess was speaking . . . to whom . . . ?

'She is babbling in a daze. Thank goodness she has survived! I'm terrified when I think of what could have happened if our boat had been farther away?'

'In a way, it would have been a good thing. She would have met a pleasant end. Now that you have saved her, the Kodumbalur princess will have to undergo untold misery.'

Vanathi thought, 'Ah! Who speaks with so much empathy? It is the young man we saw at the astrologer's house. He must have brought the news of the prince's drowning. But let me hear more. My ears are functioning though my eyes are closed.'

'How can you be so pitiless? Do all men have hearts of stone?' That was the voice of the princess.

'What have I said to be deemed stony-hearted?'

'Is it not enough to have said that this girl is better off dead? Do you know the pains I have taken to nurture her?'

'Did you hear what she babbled about?'

'What did you make of it?'

'She said something about marrying the prince.'

'Her desire has become so deep-rooted that she murmurs about him even when she is unconscious.'

'Not good for her. It will only bring her distress and chagrin.'

'Why do you say that? Is there any girl from any other noble family who would make a better match for the prince? Don't you know that the warrior clan of Kodumbalur belongs to an ancient line?'

'I know it very well. But what I think and what you say are two different things. Old as her clan may be, her dream will not come true.'

'Certainly, it will. For it is not merely her fancy. It is my ambition, a decision I have taken.'

'In this particular case, your decision too may not be carried out.'

'Why do you say this again and again? Is it not true that Arulmozhi Varman is safe in the Chudamani Viharam in Nagaipattinam?'

'Ah! What joyful tidings!' thought Vanathi. 'The prince is safe! In Chudamani Viharam. How lucky I am to hear this! How wonderful that I did not drown in the stream. One more reason to be grateful to the princess to whom I am already so deeply indebted. But ayyo! Why is he pouring burning oil into my ears?'

Vandiyatevan was saying, 'Devi, it is true that the prince is safe and sound. But does it guarantee that her wish will be fulfilled? I think the prince will not marry this girl.'

'Think as you please! But there *is* a man in this world who would never cross my will and carry out my wishes without fail–my brother Arulmozhi Varman.'

'Princess! There is another–myself.'

'Then why should I worry at all? What can hinder the fulfilment of my ambition? Would the Pazhuvettaraiyars try to stop this too?'

'I don't know about the Pazhuvettaraiyars. And I do know that the prince has boundless affection for you. He will listen to you in everything else. He has no interest at all in ruling kingdoms. He rejected the Ilankai kingdom before my eyes. And yet, at your insistence, he will agree to rule the realm. But marrying this girl . . .'

'Are you saying that he will not agree? What fault would he see in my dear companion to reject her? For that matter, what flaw do *you* see?'

'Devi, I see nothing lacking in this girl. To me, even the lowliest attendant in Princess Kundavai's palace is a celestial maiden. A bunny rabbit in her garden is nobler than the mighty elephant of the king of the gods. The prince too perceives no flaw in her. But isn't it possible that he may be drawn towards someone else . . . ?'

Vanathi thought, 'Why is this man stabbing my heart with these cruel words?'

The princess said, 'Ayya! I don't understand. Why do you slander my brother?'

'It is not slander, Devi! I am telling you what I saw with my own eyes, what I heard with my own ears.'

'Go on. I am ready to hear the worst now. '

'I had told you about Poonkuzhali, the boatwoman. It was she who helped me reach Ilankai. It was she who saved me and the prince from the sea. It is she who has taken the prince to the Chudamani Viharam. I have not entrusted the prince to Sendan Amudan's care. It was my trust in Poonkuzhali that made me leave him with them. If she had a thousand lives, she would sacrifice them all for the sake of the prince.'

'So what? A boatwoman remains a boatwoman. How can she dream of the man who was born to rule the world? Can the sparrow hopping on the ground ever hope to see the kite circling the sky?'

'Why not? The sparrow can look up to see the kite. The kite may look down at the sparrow.'

'If my brother has any such ideas, I am here to uproot them. This is not at all possible. I have saved Arulmozhi from all kinds of harm. I will extricate him from this boatwoman's net as well.'

'And is a boatwoman to be so cheaply dismissed? Are clan and ancestry so important? Is it not red blood that flows in the boatwoman's body? Doesn't her heart throb like the hearts of princesses born in the palace? If you think about it, the love of a princess may be influenced by her desire to gain status and sovereignty. But the boatwoman's love is unblemished, pure. At least, that is what the prince believes. Why should anyone bar the way? Now . . . take my case. If only I could tear my breast and show you what lies within . . .'

'No, no. It is best that it remains safe within. Affection, desire, love—these are all very well for other people. It is different for those who are born to rule a kingdom. They must not allow their minds to wander but marry within the royal clan. Failing to do so creates all kinds of problems. My own family can provide an example. When my father was young, at a time when he had no idea that he would have to take the throne, in the same way . . . with a girl raised in the wilderness . . . But why should I tell you this? The girl is regaining consciousness. Her eyelids are moving. Do you have anything else to share? Tell me about the dangers you encountered in Ilankai.'

'Yes, Devi. When we were walking on the streets of Anuradhapuram after the prince rejected the Ilankai throne, suddenly, the front part of a building broke and crashed down. Had we stayed there for just a moment more, we would have been entombed alive. But a woman appeared and made a beckoning sign to the prince. I don't know who she was, but the prince appeared to know her. Devi! No need for you to entertain any suspicions. The lady was ripe in years.'

'How old would she be?'

'Old enough to be the prince's mother. Moreover, she was deaf and mute.'

'What? *What?* Say it again!'

'She was deaf and mute from birth and some forty-five years old.'

'Ayya! Did you see the lady in Ilankai? Tell me more about her. Do you know anything about where she was born and raised?'

'She was born on an island off the coast of Ilankai.'

Princess Kundavai became extremely agitated as she said, 'Ayya! Go on. What did she look like?'

'Devi, I saw something of a miracle in her appearance. I hesitate to say it.'

'Don't stop; tell me quickly.'

'She looked exactly like a woman I had seen in the Chozha realm but older. She was unadorned, her unbound hair hung all around her. But the face and figure were exactly the same. For a moment, I was actually deceived.'

'Ayya, who is that "someone" here, resembling that lady?'

'Princess, can't you make a guess?'

'Was it I? This girl Vanathi? My mother in the Tanjavur palace?'

'No.'

'Nandini, the young queen of Pazhuvur?'

'The same.'

'God! Then my suspicions were true.'

'What did you suspect?'

'I suspected that the woman I hated as someone more vicious than the venomous cobra, was my own elder sister. From what you say, it appears to be true. Destiny can be horrendously cruel. This proves how wrong it is for persons in the royal family to marry a woman of unknown birth and ancestry.'

'Devi! I am not someone whose clan and origin are altogether unknown. My ancestors ruled this Tamizh realm for over three hundred years. They had taken the Chera, Chozha and Pandya rulers captive. Though I have no kingdom today, I have a sword in my hand, strength in my shoulders and courage in my heart.'

'Ayya! I will hear all about the glories of your clan later. But right now, there are many things to be done. I still require your assistance. You will give it to me, won't you?'

'If I have a thousand lives, I am willing to offer them all to you.'

'You seem to be boatwoman Poonkuzhali's sibling. Well, let us shelve this subject. This girl is going to open her eyes.'

By this time, Vanathi had fully regained consciousness. Many thoughts rose in her mind. She became determined to remain alive until she proved to the prince that her love was greater than the love of the boatwoman. Moreover, she recalled the nocturnal cry and the scene she had witnessed in the emperor's chamber in Tanjavur. They began to make sense to her.

As soon as she opened her eyes, the princess asked her affectionately, 'My darling! How do you feel now?'

'I am all right. Only, I am sorry to have given you so much trouble,' Vanathi replied.

Just then Azhvarkadiyan strode in and announced, 'I too am here to give you trouble, Devi. There is chaos and confusion among the crowds gathered in front of the palace. The people are enraged by the news of the prince having drowned. This could lead to devastating repercussions if you don't go immediately and pacify them.'

25

The Chief Minister Arrives

The streets of Pazhaiyarai saw pandemonium of a kind never seen before. Throng followed throng as the multitudes made their way to the sector where the royal palaces were situated. Men, women, elders, youngsters and children came in clustering groups. Saivas, Vaishnavas, Jainas and Buddhists were mingled in that procession. Even the Kalamukhas, men of austere penances, could be seen here and there. They wailed and moaned and cursed the Pazhuvettaraiyars as they marched on.

The young men banged their staves against one another. Roused by their clashing, many whispered, 'Slam the Pazhuvettaraiyars on the head!' Others repeated it loudly, the most notable being the Kalamukhas.

The royal palaces in Pazhaiyarai had crescent-shaped facades. Together, all the palaces faced a large common courtyard, vast enough for thousands of people to assemble during celebratory events. The courtyard was fenced in by a wall with three entrances, each guarded by sentinels.

The crowd came in batches to assemble in front of all three gateways and went on swelling by the minute. The sentinels allowed only the messengers and the accompanying guards into the courtyard and tried to stop the others. But not for long. Voices from different parts of the crowd began to shout, 'Go in! Go in!' Like the Kaveri flooding in full spate through a widening crack, the crowd swept the sentinels aside and burst into the courtyard.

This was the furore that Sembiyan Mahadevi heard when she was talking to Madhurantakan. She stopped debating with her son and came to the balcony in front of the palace. The noise abated the moment the multitudes saw the great lady with a divine aura around her face, standing with her hands folded in serenity.

'Mother! Where is the prince? Where is Ponniyin Selvan? Where is Prince Arulmozhi Varman who is so dear to you?' the crowd clamoured loudly.

Sembiyan Mahadevi stood still, too astonished and bewildered to grasp the situation. She realized that something had happened to Ponniyin Selvan, who had stolen the hearts of all the people in Pazhaiyarai. But what was it? How did it happen? Had the Pazhuvettaraiyars done something disastrous to defame the Chozha clan, and Madhurantakan too?

The Tanjavur messengers managed to squeeze through the hordes to come forward. One of the guards escorting them said, 'Devi! These men have brought important news from Tanjavur.'

Silencing the crowd with a gesture, Sembiyan Mahadevi asked the messengers, 'What news have you brought?'

'Mother! We are the unfortunate bearers of tragic news. Prince Arulmozhi Varman was coming from Ilankai to Kodikkarai at the emperor's command. His ship was struck by a cyclone. The accompanying ship was shattered and submerged. The prince jumped into the sea to save the men on the drowning ship. After that, he could not be found. Arrangements have been made to search the sea and coastline. The emperor and his queen, the daughter of Malayaman, are grief-stricken. The emperor has sent word asking you, Princess Kundavai and Madhurantaka Tevar to come to Tanjavur at once.'

Sembiyan Mahadevi heard the message, as did the crowding citizens. Tears began to stream down her eyes. This made the people groan in misery.

A man standing in front of the crowd yelled, 'Mother! You must not go to Tanjavur, nor Princess Kundavai, nor Madhurantaka Tevar. Bring the emperor here!'

Another said, 'It is a lie that the prince was drowned in the sea. The Pazhuvettaraiyars must have killed him.'

'Madhurantakan must not go to Tanjavur. He must always stay here,' another shouted.

Many voices hollered, 'Where is Princess Kundavai? We must see her.'

Sembiyan Mahadevi sent a maid to fetch the princess. At the same time, Azhvarkadiyan, who had been standing in the crowd, made his way to the garden and found Kundavai in an arbour, ministering to Vanathi. He heard Vandiyatevan's last words to the princess as he walked in and told her about the hullabaloo in the palace courtyard.

The princess entrusted Vanathi to the maids and left in haste.

As Kundavai joined Sembiyan Mahadevi on the palace balcony, she saw tears streaming from the queen's eyes. This brought tears to Kundavai 's too. Seeing this, the people were cast in greater despair.

The men in the crowd began to address Kundavai Devi. 'Ponniyin Selvan did not drown. He was killed by the Pazhuvettaraiyars!' 'The emperor has been imprisoned by the Pazhuvettaraiyars. He must be set free. At your command, we are willing to march at once.'

Wiping her eyes, Kundavai desperately tried to find a way to pacify the people and send them home without revealing the truth about the prince. She signalled to Azhvarkadiyan who had arrived by then with Vandiyatevan and stood right in front on the ground below.

When he came up, she spoke to him in a low voice.

Azhvarkadiyan faced the people and made a gesture asking for silence. Then, he proclaimed in a stentorian voice, 'The princess cannot believe that Ponniyin Selvan is dead. The king of the sea would have saved him just as mother Kaveri had saved him once before. The interpreter of portents has been consulted and he gives the same assurance. The princess will make proper arrangements to search for the prince and find him. Now she requests all of you to go home in peace.'

A sound ran through the crowd like a long sigh of relief.

Someone shouted, 'Where is the reader of signs? We want to hear the good news from his mouth.'

Seizing his chance, Vandiyatevan jumped up to the balcony. Standing beside Azhvarkadiyan, he announced, 'It is true that the prince faced a great threat. But there was no danger to his life. He will be found very soon.'

'How do you know?' a voice asked.

'I am a reader of signs. I learnt this by looking at the planets and stars. I know it by observing the portents.'

'A lie! What you say is a lie! You are no reader of signs. You are a spy.'

Vandiyatevan looked at the accuser. He recognized him as the physician's son.

'Madman! Are you calling me a spy? If I am one, whose spy am I?'

Pat came the answer, 'Pazhuvettaraiyars' spy.'

'What did you say?' Vandiyatevan thundered.

Vandiyatevan was standing some twelve feet above the courtyard. Without heeding this, he sprang down upon the physician's son. Their boxing match began.

Since a fight attracts everyone at all times, the people gathered in a circle around the combatants and began to watch their struggle.

Those on the balcony looked down anxiously.

Without knowing exactly what was taking place, the people began to shout more vociferously than before.

From the gateway came the sounds of conches and pipes blowing, followed by the heraldic announcement, 'Make way for Chief Minister Aniruddha Brahmarayar!'

And, at once, as if by magic, the path seemed to clear itself for the chief minister.

26

Aniruddha's Entreaty

The chief minister's palanquin cleaved its way through the multitudes packing the palace courtyard. The people on both sides saluted him with respect. Many expressed their distress over the prince. The chief minister too wore a worried expression on his face. And yet, he raised both his hands to offer his blessing and consolation as he went in. Once the palanquin was placed at the entrance of the palace, the chief minister stepped out and looked up to see the queen and the princess. Then his eyes were drawn to the spot where Vandiyatevan and Pinakapani were still fighting, quite oblivious to what was happening around them. Azhvarkadiyan had come down to say something in the chief minister's ear. Immediately, he gave the order to his men, 'Arrest these ruffians making a racket in the palace courtyard.' Azhvarkadiyan went with the guards who broke through the crowd to seize the two combatants. Having seen a sign from Azhvarkadiyan, Vandiyatevan allowed himself to be seized.

Aniruddha Brahmarayar went up to the balcony and told the people, 'I am aware of your distress and anger. Like you, the emperor and the queens too are plunged in sorrow. Don't do anything to increase their anguish. Excellent arrangements have been made to find the prince. Please return to your homes peacefully.'

A man shouted, 'We want to see the emperor; the emperor must return to Pazhaiyarai.'

Another asked, 'What of our soldiers in Ilankai?'

'The emperor is safe in the Tanjavur palace. The palace is being guarded day and night by the Velakkara soldiers. I myself will bring the emperor to this city as soon as possible. Nor is there any need for you to worry about our soldiers in Ilankai. The Ilankai war has been concluded with a thumping victory. Our soldiers will come home soon.' A joyful clamour broke out as soon as the chief minister made this announcement. The people began to disperse, hailing Aniruddha Brahmarayar.

The chief minister said to the queen, 'I have something important to discuss with you. Can we go in?' Turning to the princess, he added, 'I will come and see you later.'

Kundavai went back to her quarters, beset with worries. If at all Kundavai feared anyone in the Chozha empire, it was the eagle-eyed Aniruddha Brahmarayar. Apart from taking in all that was explicit and obvious from the outside view as it were, his eye was capable of probing the mind and discovering the secrets buried within. The princess was confused because she could never gauge just what and how much he knew.

She was enraged by his order to imprison both Pinakapani and Vandiyatevan but felt unable to disclose her feelings. She could not show her support to Vandiyatevan before the massive crowd. So, as she hastened to the women's quarters, she vowed to herself, 'He is coming to see me later, is he? I will tackle him squarely!'

Sembiyan Mahadevi commanded devotion and reverence from everyone in the Chozha empire—Chief Minister Aniruddha Brahmarayar was no exception. And yet, at that time, the noble lady received him with some trepidation. She took her seat only after he sat down.

'Ayya! I have been facing one crisis after another for some time now. Have you also brought some dire tidings? Or are you going to give me solace?' she asked him.

'Devi, pardon me. I am unable to answer your question. It all depends on how you receive the news I bring,' was the savvy minister's response.

'Is the news about Ponniyin Selvan true? Ayya, I am not able to believe it. What great hopes we had placed on him! How many times did we talk about him as one who was born to rule the whole world?'

'It is true that you told me about such predictions made by astrologers. I neither agreed nor disagreed with you.'

'Never mind. Now tell me—is it true that the sea king has stolen Ponniyin Selvan?'

'How can we say that it is true? All we can say is that such a rumour is rife throughout the land.'

'What will be its impact on this Chozha realm if it turns out to be true? What kind of calamity would follow?'

'Those calamities are not going to wait until it is proven to be true.'

'Yes, yes. Rumours are enough to trigger disasters. Until now, I have never seen the people of Pazhaiyarai so enraged as to break into the palace grounds in such multitudes.'

'Don't think that this has happened only in Pazhaiyarai. Since yesterday, Tanjavur city has been in a state of pandemonium. The Velakkara corps refused to leave the emperor's palace. The people came in hordes to surround the Pazhuvettaraiyars' mansions. Rogue elephants had to be let loose to disperse the crowds.'

'Ayyo! How terrible!'

'It was a good thing that Madhurantaka Tevar had come to Pazhaiyarai. If not, this fearful blame would have fallen on his shoulders too.'

'Ayya! You will be astonished to know how Madhurantakan has changed.'

'No, Devi. I have known this for some time.'

'And yet you made no attempts to change his mind. Please advise me now.'

'Amma, I don't think that it is necessary to change Madhurantakan's mind. I am here to support him.'

'What does that mean? I don't understand.'

'Devi, Madhurantakan thinks that the Chozha throne belongs to him. It is only fair that he should wish to succeed the emperor. It is a wish that has become deeply rooted in his mind. Trying to thwart it will not benefit the Chozha kingdom. It would be more appropriate to fulfil that wish.'

'Ayyo! What are you saying? Have you turned traitor to the Chozha kingdom? How devastating these times are turning out to be!'

'Devi! Not even in my dreams have I had any treacherous thoughts towards the emperor. I am here at the emperor's command. It is his petition that I am conveying to you. Madhurantakan wants to become king after Sundara Chozha's lifetime. The Pazhuvettaraiyars are scheming for that end. But the emperor wants to give the throne and crown to Madhurantakan right away. He has sent me to get your consent for this.'

'It may be the emperor's wish, but he will never get my consent. I will never accept this plan that goes against my husband's wishes. Chief Minister! You are a man of great understanding. How dare you ask me to do something so grievously wrong, even at the emperor's behest? Have you completely forgotten that there are some truths about the right to the Chozha throne known only to you and me?'

'Devi, I have not forgotten anything. But I happen to know some truths unknown to you. That is why I am here as the emperor's envoy.'

'Ayya! The whole world knows all about your astuteness and diplomatic skills. But don't display them to me, a woman.'

'Devi, I am not here to argue with you, nor to display my cleverness. I am here to beg and plead with you to save this Chozha land from great peril.'

'Make your appeal to lord Siva who wears the crescent, or to your cherished god, Vishnu.'

'True, Devi. If you refuse to relent, this country will have to be saved only by the gods.'

'What is this grave threat to the land that can be averted only if Madhurantakan takes the throne?'

'Listen, noble lady! The people of this city broke out in anger today. There will be uprisings tomorrow from Kanchi to Rameswaram and it will not end there. I hear that Bhooti

Vikramakesari has gathered the army and left Ilankai. When the news reaches Aditta Karikalan, he too will not be able to control himself. He will march to Tanjavur with his huge army stationed in the north. The Pazhuvettaraiyars and other feudal chieftains have already started assembling their troops. Like the war between the Pandavas and the Kauravas, a horrendous fratricidal war will break out in this country. All your kinspeople will be destroyed. Are you going to let this happen?'

'Ayya, I have no clansmen or kinsfolk. Chief Minister! You are a man of imposing intellectual sagacity. You must have heard of the great soul, Sankara. He has said *the goddess Parvati is your mother, the lord Siva is the father. Only those who are imbued with faith can be called kinsfolk.* So it is with me. I have no one else in the world who is related to me.'

'Devi! May I remind you of the fourth line in the same verse where Sankara says, *the land of your birth is all the three worlds to you.* Our motherland is everything to us. Would you sit by and watch your own country being destroyed by internecine warfare?'

'It is absolutely true that the land of my birth is dearer to me than the three worlds. But is it confined merely to this strip of land called the Chozha country? Not at all. My motherland stretches up to the Himalayas in the north. If I have no place in this Chozha land, I will go to Kasi, the holy city. I will go to Kashmiram and Kailasam. I have wanted to undertake such a pilgrimage for a long time. Help me do it.'

'Amma, I agree that the land stretching from the Trikona hills in the south to the Himalayan range in the north is our motherland. But this vast and sacred land called "Bharatam" is now facing extraordinary perils. Pathans, Turks, Mughals and Arabs have risen in large numbers and are seeking new lands to conquer. Just as the Huns and the Greeks invaded these territories in the past, these tribes following a new faith are advancing towards this land. Their strange faith has it that merit can be earned by demolishing temples and shattering idols. Devi, there are no great kings in the north to stop them now. I had dreamed that the Chozha warriors would march to the river Ganga and the Himalayas beyond to establish an empire spanning the entire subcontinent, and stop the invaders from wreaking havoc here. Please help me fulfil this dream. Please stop these fratricidal wars. Give your consent to Madhurantaka Tevar being crowned.'

Sembiyan Mahadevi became lost in her own reflections and remained silent for some time. Then she said, 'Ayya, you terrify me by talking about things that my simple mind cannot comprehend. If this sacred land of Bharatam has to face such perils, it is for the almighty to stop them. What can a helpless woman like me do? I will never forget the injunctions my husband gave me before he attained the feet of the lord. I will never do anything that would go against them.'

'In that case, I will have to share a truth that is unknown to you,' said the chief minister.

They were interrupted by Madhurantakan, who made a boisterous entry. 'Amma! What is this I hear? Has Arulmozhi Varman drowned in the sea?' he asked.

'Devi, console your dear son. I will tell you about this on another day,' said Anirudha Brahmarayar as he took his leave.

'This man is my first enemy. See how he has come to give you evil counsel even while I am here?' The chief minister heard these words of Madhurantakan very clearly as he made his exit.

27

Kundavai's Bewilderment

The chief minister reached Kundavai's palace. The princess stood up and prostrated before him.

'May you live long and attain a husband renowned for his valour and rectitude,' he blessed her.

'Ayya, is this your blessing for a time like this?' Kundavai asked him.

'It is what an old man like me is accustomed to give. What would you prefer, amma?'

'We are all worried about my father's health. The entire country is immersed in anxiety over Arulmozhi Varman.'

'But amma, I don't see any trace of anxiety on your face.'

'I was born in a brave warrior clan. Do you expect me to burst into sobs the moment "danger" is mentioned?'

'Never would I say such a thing. All I ask is for the princess to console gutless people like me.'

'Acharya! Does someone like *you* need to be consoled by *me*? Why, don't you have an iron heart that remains immovable even when the entire world turns upside down?'

'But you make me flounder, amma! Those who dwell in the women's quarters should spend their time in dance and song. But see the disastrous results when you meddle in matters of state!'

'Ayyo! What an indictment! How have I "meddled"? What kind of disaster has it brought about?'

'I left Ilankai suggesting that Ponniyin Selvan should remain on the island for some time. You sent a message at odds with my recommendation, asking him to come back at once. Who will heed this old codger's counsel against yours? Did you see its adverse consequences? The sea has swallowed the prince most dear to the people's hearts. You saw the furore in front of the palace just now. Such disruptions are happening all over the country. Amma, are you not responsible for this?'

'Why do you say that it was *my* message that made Arulmozhi leave Ilankai? Don't you know that the Pazhuvettaraiyars had sent two ships full of soldiers to arrest him and bring him here?'

'I do, amma, I do. If it had stopped there, Ponniyin Selvan's plight could be attributed to the Pazhuvettaraiyars. But both their ships have been destroyed. Who can refute them if they say that the prince left Ilankai in response to *your* letter?'

'Ayya! How did you know that I had sent a letter? How did the Pazhuvettaraiyars know it?'

'An excellent question! Amma, the whole world knows it. Your envoy was first imprisoned in Ilankai by our soldiers. Therefore, everyone in Ilankai knows about it. Through the physician's son who accompanied him to Kodikkarai, everyone in our country knows this. What you did in secret has now become public knowledge. That is why the elders said that women should not mess with state affairs.'

Kundavai stood stock still in consternation, unable to respond. The chief minister had well and truly confounded her. This made her get annoyed with the Vaanan warrior. With all his derring-do, he had ruined things by publicizing the mission and needed to be soundly reprimanded. She also recalled his having been imprisoned at the chief minister's order. Why did he make so much trouble for himself and put her in a spot? Couldn't he have simply stayed put? Why did he jump from the balcony and start a fight just because the physician's son spouted nonsense?

'Ayya, I have a request. Please grant it.'

'Devi, command me! Can anyone in this kingdom ever refuse to obey you?'

'Two men were fighting in front of the palace when you arrived. You ordered them to be imprisoned.'

'What they did was a major crime. It was extremely wrong of them to have launched a fight on the palace grounds and in the presence of the great queen. Moreover, at a time when a vast crowd was boiling in fury, it could have ignited chaos and rioting. What if the people had blindly joined the fight?'

'Yes, ayya. It was a gross misdemeanour. And yet I implore you to forgive and release one of them.'

'Who is the fortunate recipient of the princess' grace?'

'The man I sent as my envoy to Ilankai.'

'Serendipity, that's what it has turned out to be.'

'Why do you say that?'

'I had wanted to arrest that envoy. He got himself trapped here.'

'Why?'

'Amma, he is accused of a hideous crime.'

'What's that?'

'He has pushed Ponniyin Selvan into the sea and drowned him.'

'Atrocious! Who accuses him of such a crime?'

'Many do. Partibhendran, who brought the prince on his ship, says so. The Pazhuvettaraiyars tend to agree. I too have my suspicions.'

'Ayya! Beware! Do you suspect me of sending an assassin to murder my brother?'

'Not at all, amma! You sent him as your trusted envoy. But you could have been wrong to trust him. Could he not be a spy?'

'Never. Aditta Karikalan sent him to aid me with a written assurance that he could be completely trusted.'

'Couldn't Aditta Karikalan be deceived too? Or the man might have been influenced to switch his loyalty along the way? I heard the word "spy" when I arrived. The man standing below accused the man on the balcony. What was that?'

'The man above was Vandiyatevan of the Vaanan clan, the warrior sent by my brother. The man below was Pinakapani, the son of the physician. He accused Vandiyatevan of being the Pazhuvettaraiyars' spy. Imbecility!'

'Why can't it be true?'

'It can never be true. He had escaped from the Pazhuvettaraiyars, who have been sending any number of men in their relentless efforts to capture him.'

'How then did the Pazhuvur signet ring come into his possession?'

'Because it was given to him by that vicious demoness, that venomous cobra–forgive me, the young queen of Pazhuvur.'

'I am happy to see that you are aware of it because you would not have believed it if I had told you. It is true that the warrior of the Vaanan tribe is no secret agent of the Pazhuvettaraiyars. But he could be the Pazhuvur queen's spy.'

'How is that possible?'

'I will tell you how. Vandiyatevan–the trusted envoy you sent to Ilankai–met the Pazhuvur queen when she was riding in her palanquin outside the Tanjavur Fort. That was when he accepted her signet ring. Then he met her again, within the fort, in the women's quarters of the Pazhuvur palace. She hid him in the treasury vault and helped him get away from there. She knew that he was going to carry a missive from you. After his return from Ilankai, they met again in the ruined Pandya palace near the river Harischandra. Her signet ring is still in his possession. What do you think? Do you still place complete trust in your envoy?'

It was then that Kundavai found herself completely bewildered.

28

A Spy for a Spy

Looking at the princess who remained speechless, the chief minister asked, 'Amma! Why are you silent? Do you still trust Vandiyatevan?'

'Ayya! You are the minister of ministers. What can I say? It looks as though I may start doubting myself if I continue to talk to you,' said the princess.

'Well, in times like these, surrounded as we are by multiple adversaries and mystifying conspiracies, it is not so easy to decide who can or cannot be trusted,' said Chief Minister Aniruddha Brahmarayar.

'Yet, it appears that no mystery or conspiracy remains unknown to you. How did you acquire all these details about my envoy?'

'Devi, I possess a thousand eyes and two thousand ears spread across the land. I have my men in the Pazhuvur palace and an agent in the Pazhuvur queen's personal guards. There are many like Azhvarkadiyan who wander from place to place to gather intelligence. I do honestly believe that nothing can happen in the kingdom without my knowledge. And yet, who knows? There may be men who mislead me. And mysteries unknown to me.'

As he talked, Kundavai wondered if the wily minister knew that Ponniyin Selvan was in the Chudamani Viharam. She made a tremendous effort to suppress the thought.

'Ayya, what you say may be true. But I cannot believe the young Vaanan warrior to be the Pazhuvur queen's informant. Please set him free.'

'Think well, amma. That woman Nandini has some kind of magnetic power. The pious Madhurantakan fell into her web and became obsessed with the kingdom. Sambuvaraiyar's son Kandamaran has taken her letter to Aditta Karikalan. Partibhendran, the diehard enemy of the Pazhuvettaraiyars, has now become her slave. He has come forward to support a settlement between Madhurantakan and Karikalan where each would be allotted half the kingdom.'

'Outrageous! Divide the kingdom? A kingdom that our ancestors struggled so hard to establish and expand!'

'You will not wish to divide the kingdom, nor I. Amma! Ten days ago, such a proposal would have made even Partibhendran explode in rage. But now, he is in the front ranks of those who support this plan.'

'Strange! What kind of magical powers does the Pazhuvur queen possess?'

'Princess, you are asking me a question that I was going to ask you! Let it go. But how can you be so sure that Vandiyatevan will remain immune to her spells?'

'Ayya, I can only tell you what my intuition tells me. I don't know why, but my heart tells me with absolute certainty that the scion of the Vaanan clan will never betray us.'

'Then, let us put it to the test.'

'How?'

'We must send an envoy to Kanchi at once. We need to send a message to Aditta Karikalan with someone whom he trusts implicitly.'

'About what?'

'A few moments ago, you asked forgiveness for calling Nandini a venomous cobra. But in reality, she is far more dangerous than a snake can ever be. She has planned to uproot and decimate the Chozha race without a trace.'

'Appalling!' said Kundavai, her mind seething with different thoughts.

'She has instigated Sambuvaraiyar to invite Aditta Karikalan to Kadambur. She is talking about Aditta Karikalan marrying Sambuvaraiyar's daughter and a girl from the Pazhuvettaraiyar household. She is also bent on dividing the kingdom and working out a settlement between the factions. These are the ostensible points under discussion. But no one knows her hidden intentions. Despite my arrogance in believing that I know it all, I am unable to discover her motives.'

'Ayya! What should we do about it?'

'Somehow or the other, we must stop Aditta Karikalan from going to the Kadambur palace. That is why both you and I must write our letters and send them through Vandiyatevan. If Karikalan insists on going to Kadambur against our counsel, Vandiyatevan should accompany him. He must stay inseparably close to your brother, like a shadow, and guard him. He must not allow Karikalan to meet Nandini alone.'

Kundavai heaved a great sigh. She understood the grave importance of the issue that gave rise to the chief minister's suggestion. She could not guess whether he had a complete grasp of all the details or was prompted by political motivations alone.

'Ayya, why do you think it is so vital to prevent their meeting?'

'Devi, some members of Veerapandiyan's emergency squad have vowed to destroy the Chozha race completely. Freshly minted gold coins are being supplied to them from Pazhuvettaraiyar's treasury. Need I say more?'

'No,' murmured the princess. She thought of the prince lying ill in Chudamani Viharam. Dangers could beset him too.

'Ayya, it is a matter of great fortune that you happen to be our chief minister when the Chozha realm is facing disaster after disaster. What arrangements have you made concerning Ponniyin Selvan?'

'I have asked for special pujas and prayers to be offered in the temples of Siva and Vishnu across the country. The Jaina and Buddha shrines too are conducting similar forms of worship. The monks in the Chudamani Viharam in Nagaipattinam are to hold continuous prayers for forty-eight days. What else do you think can be done?'

Kundavai tried to see if there was any change of expression on the chief minister's face when he mentioned the Chudamani Viharam. She could find none.

'Ayya, this reminds me,' she said. 'I believe that, for some reason, Periya Pazhuvettaraiyar is vexed with the Chudamani Viharam. This vexation has increased with the news of the monks in Ilankai offering the throne to the prince. They may blame the monks in the Chudamai Viharam for the prince's disappearance. You must make adequate arrangements to protect them.'

'I will do it at once. With the emperor's permission, I can even send a small troupe to guard the Chudamani Viharam. What about sending Vandiyatevan to Kanchi?'

'Ayya, would it not be better to send somebody else for this crucial task?'

'If you trust him, I would like to send him. I have learnt something about his daring deeds. We must send someone who will remain undaunted by any challenge. Didn't I see this with my own eyes in the palace courtyard today when he hammered the physician's son? If I had not stopped them, the physician's son would have gone to play doctor to Yama, the god of death.'

The princess was exhilarated. And yet, she said somewhat doubtfully, 'Is it enough to have a warrior's skills? He is so impetuous. How rashly he started the fight . . .'

'In that case, why don't I send my disciple Tirumalai with him? Azhvarkadiyan is well known for his steady thinking,' Aniruddhar said.

The princess thought, 'It is doubtful whether even god knows what goes on in this man's mind! He wants to send a spy to spy on a spy!'

29

Vanathi's Transformation

Vanathi came to Kundavai just as the princess was setting out to release Vandiyatevan from prison and send him on a journey once again.

She said, 'My darling! I am sorry I had to leave you. I have some work to do. I will finish it and be with you. Stay in the garden. Don't go anywhere near the stream!'

'Akka! I will not trouble you any longer. I wish to return to Kodumbalur. Please give me leave,' said Vanathi.

'What is this, Vanathi? Why are you adding to the shocks I have already received? Why are you angry with me? Why this sudden craving for home?'

'No one can be a greater ingrate than I if I get angry with you. Nor do I have any new-found love for home. What can I call home when I have neither mother nor father? My mother died without fulfilling her vow to offer puja at the local Kali temple. Maybe I continue to have these fainting spells because this vow has not been carried out.'

'You don't have to go so far. I will send word to have that puja performed.'

'That's not all, Akka. My uncle is returning from Ilankai. He will not cross Tanjavur and come to Pazhaiyarai. I wish to be in Kodumbalur to receive him and ask him about everything that happened in Ilankai.'

'Why are you so keen on knowing about the happenings in Ilankai?'

'How can you ask me? Have you forgotten that my father died in the Ilankai war?'

'No. But he has been avenged now.'

'I don't think so, at least, not completely. Velar is returning in haste before the war has ended.'

'Are you going to ask him to return to Ilankai and continue the war? Is that why you insist on going to Kodumbalur?'

'Who am I to talk about such big issues? All I want is to learn about what happened there.'

'Ah! Now I understand you. You want to hear about Ponniyin Selvan's brave deeds from your uncle.'

'Would it be wrong, Akka?'

'No. But your insisting on leaving me at this time is a big mistake.'

'Akka! Am I leaving you all alone? You have so many companions like me, all waiting to know your mind and carry out your wishes.'

'Have you too started talking in this mode? The news about my brother has addled your wits. You need not worry too much about it.'

'How can my anxiety over your brother be greater than yours, Akka?'

'Tell me the truth. Did you faint, or fall into the stream deliberately?'

'Why should I do it deliberately? I did faint and slip into the stream. You and the Vaanan warrior saved me.'

'You don't seem to be grateful.'

'I will be grateful to you not only in this life but in the lives to come.'

'You talk as though your present life is over. Vanathi, listen to me. Don't torment yourself. I don't think Arulmozhi Varman would have succumbed to any disaster. I am telling you what I said a little while ago to the crowd in the palace courtyard. Mother Kaveri saved my brother once. The king of the sea would have saved him as well. We will get the good news very soon.'

'On what basis do you reassure me so confidently?'

'My heart tells me so. If anything had happened to my brother, I would have known it in my heart of hearts. I would not be talking normally as I am doing now.'

'I don't have much faith in what my heart says. I believe in neither the heart nor the heart of hearts.'

'How can you make such a categorical declaration?'

'I have been having hallucinations in my heart and my inmost heart–in my dreams and when I was awake.'

'About what, Vanathi?'

'Your brother's face appeared in the waters, often. It beckoned to me.'

'Why do you call it hallucination? There is a consonance between what you saw in your mind and the news we have received.'

'If you hear it all, you will know what a crazy illusion it was. When I fell into the stream I went to the world of serpents. A marriage ceremony took place . . .'

'Who got married to whom?'

'I don't wish to say. Akka, on the whole, I have no belief in what appears in the mind or a dream. I have decided to trust only what I see and what I hear.'

'Vanathi, you are completely wrong. Sometimes what the eye and the ear perceive can turn out to be false. What appears in the mind is proven to be true. I can give you many instances from stories and poems . . .'

'I will hear them at another time. Akka, now give me leave to go,' Vanathi said.

Princess Kundavai was astounded. How did the girl acquire so much confidence and obstinacy, she wondered.

'Vanathi! What's the hurry? Can't you leave after a few days? The whole country is in an uproar now. Should you not be escorted home with adequate protection?'

'What should I fear, Akka? The guards and palanquin bearers who brought me from Kodumbalur have been idling all this time without any work. They will take me back.'

'Well! You think I will send you off just like that?'

'Akka, I beg of you. I have no fears. No one in this land will dare to harm Kodumbalur Vanathi. Who doesn't know that I am the dear companion of Princess Kundavai Devi? Please give me leave for just one more thing. On the way, I wish to go to the Kudantai astrologer's house and consult him. May I?'

'I too wish to come. But you are in such a hurry!'

'No, Akka, this time I wish to consult him on my own.'

Kundavai was completely stunned. The princess could not understand how the girl had been transformed in a single day, in just a few hours, to become inflexibly stubborn. She concluded that she could not stop Vanathi's journey.

'All right, Vanathi. You can do as you please. Get ready for the journey. I will be back after meeting the warrior of the Vaanan clan and getting him released.'

30

The Two Prisons

As soon as she left Vanathi, the princess went straight to the prison house. Leaving the guards outside, she went by herself to the room where Vandiyatevan was kept in solitary confinement. He was staring at the ceiling and singing a *temmangu* folk song with gusto.

> O doe-eyed beauty!
> The stars in the sky
> are cast into raptures
> and quiver in wonder
> when they see you!

Only when she came up close and cleared her throat did he see the princess. He stood up at once and said with great courtesy, 'Welcome! Welcome! Princess, welcome! Please take your seat.'

'What seat?' asked the princess.

'This is your palace, under your sovereign rule, within your command. You may choose to sit on any of the thrones available here.'

'When your Vaanan ancestors ruled the three worlds, their palace might have resembled this place. In my town, they call it a prison house.'

'Devi, my native place has neither palace nor prison house now. The kings of many countries got together and razed palace, prison and everything else to the ground.'

'Why! Why? Why were they roused to such fury against the Vaanan palace and prison house?'

'All because of a poet.'

'Ah! How?'

'When my ancestors reigned supreme, their officers arrested the vassal kings who did not pay their tributes on time. They were confined in prison cells on both sides of the palace courtyard. Those kings would wait with great trepidation, wondering when the emperor would call for them so that they could beg forgiveness and return to their towns. But they did not have it easy. As they waited, they watched poets and scholars walking into the king's assembly. On seeing those bards return, they would exclaim, "Look at these poets, how fortunate they are! Look at the prizes they are taking away!" One cried, "That poet is carrying my white state umbrella!" Another sighed, "The poet is riding on my palanquin!" A third would wail, "Ayyo! He is making off with my royal elephant!" A fourth would happily predict, "That is my horse! One day, my horse will throw this poet off its back." The last poet on his way out heard them. He sang of the envious kings carping at the bards who were carrying off their possessions as gifts from the Vaanan emperor. That verse became popular all over the land.This brought disaster to our empire. All the kings got together to invade and destroy our palace, prison and everything else.'

'But they could not blot out the poet's song. Your clan is fortunate indeed. Its fame will last forever.'

'Well, now, here I am to tarnish their fame.'

'Ah! So you have come to accept that truth.'

'How can I not accept it? Of all kinds of slavery, slavery to a woman is the very worst. I have besmirched my family's reputation by listening to a woman's words. I was forced to run, hide and wander surreptitiously. I thought I would find an outlet for all my rage by making an end of the physician's son. But the attempt was thwarted.'

'Why are you so angry with Pinakapani?'

'I have more than enough reason to be angry with him. A fine fellow you found to send with me! He was about to wreck all my endeavours. As if that were not enough, a little while ago, he tried to have me captured by the Pazhuvettaraiyars as a spy. I barely escaped from that when he accused me of being the Pazhuvur queen's spy before thousands of people in the palace courtyard.'

'O prince of the Vaanan race! Is it not true?'

'What is not true?'

'I am asking you about Pinakapani's charge that you are the Pazhuvur queen's secret agent. Will you tell me the truth?'

'I have taken a vow never to tell the truth.'

'What kind of a vow is that? Did you take it after meeting the Pazhuvur queen beside the river Harischandra?'

'No, long before. Everyone believed me as long as I said what was *not* true. Once, when I tripped up in disclosing that the prince was safely lodged in the Chudamani Viharam, no one would believe me. In fact, they laughed at me.'

'What a grave mistake! Luckily, they did not believe you. How badly things things would have turned out to be if they had believed it.'

'Such mistakes will never occur again.'

'I thank you for taking this pledge.'

'What pledge?'

'That you would perform the given task without making mistakes.'

'Good god! I took no such pledge! Enough. Get me out of prison. I will go my way.'

'In that case, there's no release for you. You will have to remain here.'

Vandiyatevan laughed aloud.

'Why do you laugh?'

'Devi! Do you think that I cannot escape from this cell if you don't release me?'

The princess gave him a steady look and said, 'Ayya! You are a clever man, particularly in escaping from prisons. This is bound to be child's play for someone who broke free from Pazhuvettaraiyar's treasury vault.'

'In that case, open the door and set me free.'

'I may open the door. Or you may find a way to break free. But there is a prison house from which you will never be able to escape.'

'Chinna Pazhuvettaraiyar's dungeon?'

'No. That poses no problem for you. You will kill the tigers waiting outside the dungeon and clear out.'

'Then what do you mean?'

'My heart.'

'Devi! I am an orphan without hearth or home. The glory of my clan is nothing but an old tale, a poetic fantasy. But you are the cherished daughter of the emperor of the three worlds.'

'Who knows? One day, all the glory of this Chozha dynasty may become an old tale.'

'But today you are someone who has incalculable power over this land. Even the emperor, the chief minister and the Pazhuvettaraiyars would not dare to flout your wishes.'

'If this is indeed true, how can you alone flout my authority?'

'State authority is a different matter. But did you not mention the heart's authority?'

'So what's wrong with it?'

'What's wrong is our difference in status.'

'Don't you know the adage, "Can love be locked out by bolted doors"?'

'This is applicable to Ponniyin Selvan and the boatwoman too.'

'Yes. I thought my brother was born to rule the world. That is why I wished to seal his heart.'

'Having heard a great deal about the prince, I too went to meet him with great expectations. I wished to accompany him everywhere so that I could cover myself with glory by performing brave deeds on the battlefield.'

'And now that wish has left you.'

'Yes. Ponniyin Selvan prefers a peaceful life. He would rather wield a chisel to build temples than brandish a sword on the warfront.'

'But Madhurantakan has a devouring wish to rule the kingdom. The goat becomes a tiger. The tiger turns into a goat. Like the old myth in which god turns a fox into a horse and a horse into a fox . . .'

'Devi, by your grace, I too became a fox. To escape from enemies, I too had to hide myself, employ tricks and ploys, make up lies and fabrications. Devi, I can't do it anymore. Please let me go.'

'Ayyo! Vanathi, who I thought was my dearest friend, wants to leave me. Do you also wish to abandon me?'

'Devi, I don't know anything about how things stand between you and the Kodumbalur princess. Mighty kings are performing penances just to hold your precious hand. I am but a wayfarer who came to be employed, to serve . . .'

The princess extended her hand. With great hesitation, doubting whether it was really happening to him, Vandiyatevan took that flowerlike hand with both his hands and placed it over his eyes. His body and soul were suffused with rhapsodic bliss.

'O warrior of the Vaanan tribe! I am descended from an ancient royal clan of the Tamizh land with intrepid virtue as my heritage. Some of the women in our clan have joined their husbands on the funeral pyre. They jumped into the fire believing that the flames burning the body of their spouse were as cool as moonbeams.'

'I have heard of this, Devi.'

'This hand of mine, having clasped yours, will never touch another's.'

Vandiyatevan was rendered speechless, powerless. Unable to move or think, he remained transfixed, gazing at her eyes brimming with tears.

'Ayya! Think of my plight if your brash exploits should put your life in danger.'

'Devi, can the man enthroned in your heart be a coward?'

'There is a difference between cowardice and chariness. Even the chief minister has no doubts about your courage.'

'Then what is his doubt?'

'He is afraid that you may be the Pazhuvur queen's informant.'

'I am willing to answer him in the same way I answered Pinakapani. Open the prison door and tell me where the minister is to be found.'

'Pinakapani may have known something about physical combat. Aniruddha Brahmarayar's only weapon is a razor-sharp intellect.'

'Then let him begin by testing the sharpness of my sword.'

'Ayya, in this country Aniruddha Brahmarayar is second only to the emperor in the reverence he commands. Even the Pazhuvettaraiyars are reluctant to oppose him openly.'

'The Pazhuvettaraiyars have guilty hearts. They should be afraid. Why should I be afraid?'

'He has been my father's close friend from childhood. Any disrespect shown to him is disrespect shown to the emperor and myself.'

'In that case, at least tell me how I can win his trust?'

'The chief minister wishes to send a trustworthy man to Kanchi. I have guaranteed that you would be the right person.'

'Devi, don't send me to Kanchi. A voice from within has been telling me not to go there.'

'Could it be the voice of the Pazhuvur queen . . .'

'Not at all. Would I listen to that poisonous snake instead of you?'

'Ayya! At no time should you talk about the Pazhuvur queen in this manner.'

'What's this? Why this sudden change of attitude?'

'Yes. The information you have brought from Ilankai has changed my heart completely towards her.'

'Does this mean I have to show awe and respect to the Pazhuvur queen?'

'Yes.'

'Even if she gives me the sword that she devoutly worships and asks me to bring her the head of a certain person?'

Kundavai shuddered. Her voice trembled when she replied.

'Show her respect, but don't do her bidding. She may be unaware of the nature of the mission she is engaged in.'

'That is exactly what she herself told me. "I don't know why I worship this sword," she said.'

In a voice that trembled even more, Kundavai said, 'God almighty would have to save this ancient Chozha race.'

'May god use this poor man as a tool to do so,' Vandiyatevan said.

'Ayya, I too have the same hope. After returning from Kanchi, you must go to Ilankai once again. You must somehow bring the mute lady here.'

'Bringing her would be like bringing a cyclone stuffed into a pot. Someone said that . . . yes, it was Azhvarkadiyan. Perhaps he has already brought her here.'

'No, it was a task beyond him. It must be done by you.'

'Then don't send me to Kanchi, Devi!'

'Why?'

'My master is there. If he asks me, I am bound to tell him everything. He will rise up in fury if he learns about the feudal chieftains' conspiracy. If he hears about how the emperor is being kept like a prisoner, he will leave at once, with his army. If the news about Ponniyin Selvan has reached his ears, he might have started marching already.'

'That is why I want to send you. Somehow, you must prevent him from leaving Kanchi.'

'What if he leaves Kanchi before I get there?'

'Go and join him wherever he may be. There is another job that you must do that is more important than everything else.'

'Tell me.'

'We have news that Periya Pazhuvettaraiyar has started for Kadambur with the young queen.'

'Is it really the young queen or someone else in her palanquin?'

'No, it is the young queen herself. After all, my uncle is here, isn't he?'

'Why are they going to Kadambur?'

'They have invited Aditta Karikalan to Kadambur. The ostensible reason is to foster a marriage alliance. There is also talk of dividing the kingdom to achieve an amicable settlement.'

'My master will never agree.'

'I am not worried about any of those things now.'

'What are you worried about, Devi?'

'An inexplicable fear has taken hold of me. My heart beats fast. Indeterminate horrors surround me when I am half asleep. I have macabre dreams that shake me awake. After that, my body goes on trembling for a long time.'

'Why are you asking me to leave you in this situation? Whatever danger you may face, I will give my life to–'

'My fears are not for myself. They are about my elder brother and the Pazhuvur queen. I quake when I think of what may happen if they meet. You must stop them from meeting by themselves.'

'Devi, who can stop the prince when he is bent on a course of action?'

'Ayya, you must become the iron armour protecting my brother. If it becomes necessary, you must tell my brother who Nandini really is.'

'He has to believe me!'

'It is your responsibility to make him believe you. I don't know how you will do it. But it will be best if you can manage to keep them apart.'

'Devi, I will do my best. Don't blame me if I fail,' Vandiyatevan said.

'Ayya, whether you succeed or fail, there is no release for you from the prison of my heart,' the princess said.

31

The Garment of Green Silk

The next morning, Vandiyatevan was riding towards Kudantai town along the banks of the Arasalaru with Chief Minister Aniruddha Brahmarayar's letter inscribed on a palm leaf. He did not goad his horse to gallop but let it trot slowly, taking in the scenic splendours on both sides.

The thriving Chozha terrain appeared at its best at the beginning of the month of *Aippasi.** Clothed in myriad shades of silken green, the goddess of nature shone in all her fresh and youthful beauty. On the fields, the sprouting crops were stained green. The freshly planted seedlings were golden green while the stalks transplanted earlier showed a verdant shade of their own. The luxuriant leaves of the banyan tree and the clustering leaves of the peepal tree displayed their varying hues of green, along with the enchanting green of lush lotus leaves

* The Tamizh month from mid-October to mid-November.

spreading across the pool's surface, the dazzling green of the plantain trees, the ivory green of tender palm fronds, and the viridescent green of fresh grass. Green frogs leapt to and fro on the green-tinted waters of the brook.

Here and there, the white water lilies and red lotuses highlighted the prismatic greens of nature's attire.

Vandiyatevan drank in the ambient beauty as he rode on, ruminating on the differences from what he had seen when he travelled eight weeks ago along the same route in the month of *Aadi*,* when the fresh floods were swelling in froth and foam. Now, their raging speed had slowed down, the red tints were gone and the crystal clear waters flowed blithely along. Back then, the roar of the floods, the din of the high winds assaulting the branches and the merry songs of a thousand birds had generated a huge and festive furore. But now, the rustle of leaves in the gentle breeze, of water gushing into the sluices, and the discordant notes of frogs croaking as they awaited the rains, merged into mother Nature's plaintive symphony.

An indefinable sense of woe pervaded Vandiyatevan's heart. Though he tried hard, he could find no valid reason for it. The truth was that he had several reasons to feel excessively jaunty. All the fantasies he wove as he travelled along this route two months earlier had come true. Unattainable ambitions had been fulfilled. He had obtained an audience with Emperor Sundara Chozha. He had visited the great cities of Tanjavur, Pazhaiyarai, Mathottam and Anuradhapuram. He had found an opportunity to assist Ponniyin Selvan, the prince who was doted upon by the Chozha realm, and win his

* The fourth month in the Tamil calendar that falls between mid-July and mid-August.

friendship. It was a privilege to have a mere glimpse of Princess Kundavai Devi, the goddess of beauty in the Tamizh lands and the treasure of the Chozha clan. What overwhelming good fortune was his to have won the love of her pure heart! But this proud elation was not left untouched by unease. Did he truly deserve that good fortune? Would it last? How many barriers stood in the way of their union?

'Ah! Any dearth of stumbling blocks in a world filled with sirens like Nandini, traitors like the Pazhuvettaraiyars, betrayers like Kandamaran and Partibhendran, madcaps like Vanathi and Poonkuzhali, Vaishnava spies, Kalamukha ascetics, fire-breathing phantoms and unfathomable quagmires! God! Somehow, I have managed to escape from each and every one of them. And now the chief minister has given me the most perilous task of all. On the one hand, there is Aditta Karikalan who is easily roused to a maniacal frenzy. On the other, a bewitching seductress who manipulates Pazhuvettaraiyar like a puppet on a string. I am to bar them from carrying out their game plan! Is this at all possible? Who knows what Brahmarayar really has in mind? All he may have wanted was to separate me from the princess. Both said that Azhvarkadiyan would join me on the way. No sign of him yet. Whatever he may be, until now the man has not harmed but helped me several times. As a travelling companion, his cheerful banter will keep tedium at bay. Where will he join me now? How long do I have to restrain the horse for him to catch up with me? Ah! A copse of trees with roots lying in the waters like crocodiles! This was where I threw my spear at the stuffed crocodile. It was here that Varini and Taraka, Sentiru and Mandakini, laughed at my "heroic" deed! This was where the princess pitied me and reprimanded those girls. Let me halt here for a moment . . .'

Vandiyatevan dismounted near the river and gazed at the clear waters swirling round and round the roots. Ah! A face in the eddies . . . the radiant, winsome face of the princess, Kundavai . . .

A voice sang out, 'I see, I see, I see what pleases the eye.' Startled, Vandiyatevan looked up. Azhvarkadiyan was sitting on the topmost branch of a tall tree.

'Oho! And do I make such a pleasant sight for your eyes? Come down! Let me also take a good look at you.'

Azhvarkadiyan said as he descended, 'My dear man, I did not mean you. Sword on hip and spear in hand, don't you make a fearsome sight?'

'Then, whom did you mean?'

'When the primal lord Vishnu raised his leg to measure the sky, in your Siva's eyes, he appeared to be–'

'Stop! O Vaishnava! Stop demeaning Siva. If you don't, you invite danger.'

'Danger? Dear man, who can harm me so long as the lord's discus–which slew the crocodile and saved the elephant–stands by?'

'I have had my say. Now, it is up to you!'

'What is that danger which threatens me?'

'Remember the tumultuous crowds storming into the palace courtyard? That was when I overheard a few Kalamukhas talking to one another.'

'What did they say?'

'They said that the swelling hordes of Vaishnavas in the Chozha realm must be sacrificed to the great goddess

Kali so that they may dance in bliss on their skulls heaped together.'

Azhvarkadiyan rubbed his head and said, 'Well, this head is strong enough to endure the dance of the Kalamukhas.'

'And today, all along the way, Kalamukhas have been wandering with tridents and skulls. It would be best for you to change your outfit, shave off your tuft and call out to Siva,' Vandiyatevan suggested.

'No good fellow, I can't.'

'Can't what?'

'I can change my guise but can't say the name you mentioned. I can say Vishnu's name alone,' Azhvarkadiyan said, and added 'Look there!'

A palanquin was being carried on the path by the river. Even though they could make out that it was occupied by a woman, they could not recognize her. But she had to belong to some royal household. Who could she be? Surely . . . not the princess herself? A maid was accompanying the palanquin on foot.

'Vaishnava, do you know who that woman may be?' Vandiyatevan asked.

'Tambi, listen to me. Haven't you invited enough trouble by poking your nose into things that don't concern you? So many people pass by. How does it matter to you? Mount your horse and ride away,' Azhvarkadiyan said.

'Oho! So that's how it is! The Vaishnava has become a man of detachment. Have you forgotten Veeranarayanapuram? Didn't you ask me to take a letter to a woman in a palanquin?'

'Why bring up that old story now?'

'Never mind. They said you would join me along the way. I had slowed down just for you. Are you or are you not coming with me?'

'You are on horseback, I am on foot. How can we travel together? Go and wait for me beside the Kollidam. I will join you there.'

Vandiyatevan realized that Azhvarkadiyan was engaged in some secret task and that was why he would not go with him. 'All right, as you please,' said he and jumped on his horse. When he looked in the direction he was taking, he saw dark clouds gathering in the northeast.

'Will it rain today?' he asked.

'Am I an astrologer? The month of Aippasi has begun. It might rain. In any case, get going and fast. See if you can find an inn for the night.'

Vandiyatevan did as he was bid. Azhvarkadiyan's question reminded Vandiyatevan of the Kudantai astrologer. His house was on his way. He thought, 'Why not look in? Who will prove to be lucky among those who wish to ascend the Chozha throne? Hadn't the Kudantai astrologer described Ponniyin Selvan as the Pole Star? But the prince refused to take any interest in ruling. How nonchalantly he dismissed the Ilankai throne! What the astrologer said about the dangers the prince would face has come true. Would his predictions about his glory in the future come true?' He thought, and continued to ponder, 'How is it possible . . . ? What about *my* life's dreams coming true? Will I regain the lost kingdom of my ancestors? How successful will my present mission turn out to be? Can I succeed at all in preventing a meeting between Aditta

Karikalan and Nandini? I did manage to escape twice or thrice from Nandini. Can I do it again?'

Vandiyatevan was filled with dread whenever he thought of the Pazhuvur queen. It was absolutely true that she had shown him great kindness and respect. But he could not read her mind. He felt that she had left him free and treated him with so much patience for some important purpose of her own. What could that purpose be?

Vandiyatevan passed the palanquin. This time, he wanted neither to slam into the palanquin nor allow it to slam into his horse. When its curtain did part slightly as the horse went past, Vandiyatevan realized that the woman inside was Vanathi, the Kodumbalur princess. Briefly, he wondered if he should halt but changed his mind and moved on. He remembered what the princess had said about Vanathi. Where was she going now, at a time when threats were looming on all sides? Nor did she have adequate protection. He also noticed something else that was out of the ordinary. Two Kalamukhas were staring at Vanathi's palanquin. Why? Who were they? Weren't they the two ascetics who had stopped to talk about him as he feigned sleep beside the river Harischandra?

Vandiyatevan had little sympathy for Vanathi. He saw her as someone who was trying to appropriate a place in Ponniyin Selvan's heart that should rightfully belong to Poonkuzhali. It made him resent her. Yet, he could not forget that Kundavai Devi had boundless love for her. The princess would be deeply distressed if anything untoward happened to Vanathi. But why should she encounter any danger? Azhvarkadiyan's advice, 'Carry on without poking your nose into things that don't concern you,' was fair enough. But the image of the two hidden Kalamukhas staring at Vanathi as her palanquin went past them continued to recur in his mind.

He reached the Kudantai astrologer's house thinking that he would be the right man to consult in this matter. Oh . . . oh! How did it not strike him that Vanathi Devi too could be coming to the astrologer's house? Excellent! He would finish his consultation before her arrival. Vandiyatevan left his horse at the doorstep and went into the little house.

32

Brahma's Head

When Vandiyatevan stepped into the Kudantai astrologer's house for the second time, his heart was suffused with an unforeseen mood of elation. It was in that little house that he had seen Kundavai Devi for the very first time. He had stood transfixed by her face as lovely as the pink lotus, with her large, dark eyes widened in astonishment. It was there that he had heard her voice sweeter than honey. The surging memories drenched his whole being in ecstasy.

The astrologer was making preparations for the evening puja. As soon as saw Vandiyatevan, he said, 'Welcome young man, welcome. Are you not Vallavaraiyan Vandiyatevan of the Vaanan clan?'

'Yes, ayya. Your predictions may have gone somewhat awry, but your memory is infallible!' Vandiyatevan said.

'Tambi, a good memory is indispensable to the study of astrology. The planets, stars, their periods of ascendancy, their subdivisions and conjunctions have a million different connections. Predictions can be made only when they are all borne in mind for making calculations based on the year, month, day, hour, minute and a hundredth part of a minute. Never mind. You said that my predictions went askew. What does that mean? Did none of them come true?'

'Can't you discover this from your charts?'

'Yes, yes. It can be done. But they must have worked. Otherwise, would you have returned to this little hut?'

'Yes, yes. Your predictions did come true.'

'Now we are getting somewhere! How?'

'Things happened exactly as you said they would. "Your fortunes indicate that your work may or may not get done." I should say that you were more than right. For when the moment came, my fortunes turned tail and took to flight.'

'Tambi, you seem to be a jester.'

'True. But I am also hot-tempered.'

'You should leave your temper outside when you enter this hut.'

'I'd have done that. But your disciple was not at the threshold and I feared that anything left outside might get stolen. Ayya, where is your disciple? I remember how he tried to stop me the last time.'

'Today is the day of the new moon in the month of Aippasi. He would have gone to the Kollidam shore.'

'What is the connection between the full moon and the Kollidam shore?'

'That is where the great convention of the Kalamukhas is taking place tonight. My disciple belongs to the Kalamukha faith.'

'Ayya! I am thinking of giving up the Saiva faith. I want your friend Azhvarkadiyan Nambi . . .'

'You mean Tirumalai?'

'Yes. I want him to initiate me into the Vaishnava creed.'

'But why?'

'I saw some Kalamukha Saivas carrying skulls along the way. It made me want to renounce Siva altogether.'

'Tambi! After having seen so many battles, why should you fear skulls?'

'It is disgust, not fear. Killing the enemy on the battlefield is one thing, wearing a garland of skulls is another.'

'Didn't your master Aditta Karikalan sever the head of Veerapandiyan and take it in a procession?'

'He did it to fulfil an oath he had taken. Later, he regretted it. But even he did not wear skulls round his neck, nor did he roam around with a skull in his hand. Why do the Kalamukhas do it?'

'As a reminder of the transience of life. You and I wear the sacred ash. What is it but a reminder that one day this body will be reduced to cinders?'

'All right, the human body is mortal. It will burn down to ashes and mingle with the earth. But why does the divine Siva carry a skull?'

'Tambi, the skull in Siva's hand symbolizes egotism, to show that everlasting bliss is achieved by eradicating self-conceit. Doesn't Siva dance with a skull in his hand?'

'I don't see how the skull can denote self-conceit.'

'There are many things you don't know. At the moment, you can learn why the skull symbolizes self-conceit. Once, the gods Brahma and Vishnu brawled about who was mightier. It was decided that the first to reach Siva's head or feet would be the victor. Taking the form of a boar, Vishnu delved deep and returned to admit that he had failed. But Brahma flew up as a swan and lied that he had found Siva's head. Siva plucked off one of the five heads of Brahma and continues to hold it as the symbol of arrogance.'

Vandiyatevan broke into thunderous laughter.

'What makes you laugh?' asked the astrologer.

'I thought of something,' Vandiyatevan answered.

'Not a secret, I hope.'

'No. I just thought that if I were to be punished like Brahma, I would require at least ten thousand heads.'

'Have you told so many lies then?'

'Yes, ayya. However, after meeting Ponniyin Selvan, I resolved to speak nothing but the truth. But once, when I did tell an important truth, everyone laughed, no one believed me.'

'Yes, tambi! Times are bad. Nowadays, people don't even believe lies. How will they believe the truth?'

'That seems to apply to your prognostications. Do you remember what you said about Ponniyin Selvan? Did you not say that he was like the Pole Star shining everlastingly in its fixed spot in the northern sky?'

'I did. What of it?'

'Haven't you heard the news about him?'

'How could I not hear it? The entire country is talking about it.'

'Ever heard of the Pole Star drowning in the ocean?'

'No. But, with clouds massing up in the north, you cannot see the Pole Star tonight however hard you may try. Does it mean that the star does not exist?'

'Why, do you have any real news about Ponniyin Selvan?'

'How can I? Rumour has it that it was you who jumped into the sea with him. If at all anyone has any news, it must be you. In fact, I had wanted to ask you about it.'

Wanting to change the subject, Vandiyatevan said, 'Ayya, what about the comet?'

'It appears in the last phase of the night with an exceptionally long trail of light. It is about time for it to start diminishing in size. Any disaster it may portend would have to happen very soon. O my god! Who knows what will befall—and on which person in the royal clan?'

Vandiyatevan's mind raced in different directions. Passing through his mind in quick succession were bedridden Sundara Chozha afflicted by a stroke in Tanjavur, Ponniyin Selvan suffering from the shivering fever in Nagaipattinam, Aditta Karikalan about to meet Nandini in the Kadambur palace, Madhurantakan, who had enraged the people with his lust for the kingdom, and Nandini, who held and caressed a slaughtering sword.

'Let it all go, ayya! Why bother about the royals? Tell me how my present task will fare.'

'I repeat what I told you before. You will encounter any number of perils. You will receive unexpected assistance to overcome them all,' said the astrologer.

Vandiyatevan wondered whether what was approaching the threshold at that moment was peril or assistance. Hearing male and female voices, both men looked at the doorway.

Vanathi Devi entered with her maid.

Vandiyatevan stood up respectfully, and said, 'Devi, pardon me. Had I known that you were visiting, I would not have come here.'

33

Vanathi Seeks Help

'Ayya, why are you so angry with me? What wrong have I done to you?' Vandiyatevan was moved by Vanathi's forlorn tone. Why should he be aggrieved by her? Poonkuzhali flashed through his mind. How was it fair to resent the Kodumbalur princess because of Poonkuzhali?

'Devi, pardon me. I meant no such thing. All I said was, I would have waited outside until you finished consulting the astrologer. I am in no hurry. Even now–'

'There is no need for you to go out. I am happy to know that you are not in a hurry. In fact, I did not come here to consult the astrologer. I have lost all faith in his forecasts.'

'Devi, it is as you will. But one day, you will come to realize the accuracy of my predictions. And you will commend this old man,' the astrologer said.

'When that happens, we will see,' said Vanathi and added to Vandiyatevan, 'Ayya! It was you I came to see. I saw you riding past. I thought you would stop to greet me. But you did not even glance at me. I am not surprised. Why should anyone care about an orphaned girl?'

Vandiyatevan felt tears pricking his eyes. He said, 'Devi! What are you saying? Who will agree that the daughter of the Siriya Velar of Kodumbalur, the foster daughter of General Bhooti Vikramakesari, the intimate companion of Princess Kundavai Devi, is an orphaned girl? I did not stop because I thought it would be discourteous to greet you on the road. If there is anything I can do . . .'

'Yes, ayya! There is. I came to this house to ask you for an important favour . . .'

'Tell me. If there is anything I can do . . .'

'Is there anything you cannot do? I have heard something about what you accomplished on the Ilankai trip. Can you promise to help me now?'

Vandiyatevan said as he tried to temporize, 'It will be good if you can tell me what it is.'

'Yes. I should not inveigle a promise from you. And it is all right if the astrologer too hears this. I have decided to join the Buddha's faith and become a *bhikshuni*, a renunciate.'

'What? *What?*'

'What's this?'

'Never!'

'The world won't take it!'

'Impossible.'

Hearing the astrologer and Vandiyatevan exclaim alternately, Vanathi said, 'Yes. I have decided to become a nun in the Buddha order. Why should you remonstrate so strongly? What is wrong? Haven't many women renounced the world in the ancient Tamizh realm? Didn't Madhavi's daughter Manimekhalai attain divinity as a bhikshuni? But my ambitions are not so high. I tried to end my useless life and failed. It seems to be god's will that I should live on for some time. I would like to spend the rest of my life in a Buddhist monastery, serving all living beings. Surely, you will not hesitate to help me in this endeavour?'

A small suspicion sprouted in Vandiyatevan's mind.

'Devi, I have no right to say that your decision is wrong. It is the elders in your household who should advise you. Your foster father Bhooti Vikramakesari will be returning soon.'

'Ayya, I am not going to wait for anyone or ask for advice. I have made my decision. I request your help.'

'How can I help you in this matter, Devi?'

'I will tell you. I am going to the Chudamani Viharam in Nagaipattinam, hoping to be inducted into the faith by the gurus there. I request you to escort me.'

Vandiyatevan was startled. The Kodumbalur princess was no ingénue. She must have heard something of the conversation he had with the princess and was trying to extract all the information she could from him. She had left for Chudamani Viharam to meet the prince. He could never assist her in such a venture.

'Devi, I am extremely sorry. It is beyond my power to give you the help you require.'

'How strange! Is it really impossible for the man who performed great deeds in Ilankai to escort a helpless woman to Nagaipattinam?'

'Devi, the task is not impossible, but it is one that I cannot undertake now. The chief minister and the princess have ordered me to go to Kanchi at once with the letter they have given me. At any other time . . .'

'Yes, yes. Any number of reasons can be trumped up for unwillingness! Never mind. I had left with the idea of travelling alone. I became a little afraid because I saw groups of Kalamukhas along the way. But god is always duty-bound to protect all living beings. Anyway, who would harm an unimportant person like me who has decided to renounce the world? Ayya, I will take your leave.'

The astrologer followed her and said, 'Devi! Devi! It is getting dark. Moreover, it is the dark night of the new moon. The clouds are billowing in the northeast. Why not stay in my humble home tonight and leave in the morning?'

'No, ayya. Forgive me. I planned to spend the night in Tiruvarur. This man has refused to escort me. Won't I find someone in Tiruvarur? Nor am I over-concerned about my life. Who gains by it, anyway?'

These were the last words heard by Vandiyatevan and the astrologer as Vanathi got into the palanquin waiting outside. The palanquin moved on. The two men went on staring at it until it disappeared from view.

Vandiyatevan said, 'Until recently, the Kodumbalur princess had been extremely timid by nature. Princess Kundavai's companions would tease her about it. They hid a stuffed crocodile in the waters to give her a scare. I too was tricked by it. How did this girl suddenly become so assertive? How strange that she should have started out on a journey all by herself. How did Princess Kundavai allow it?'

'I too am surprised by it. Last time, when this girl was here, she fell into a sudden swoon. And she spoke in faint, mumbling tones. Now I wonder if it was the same Kodumbalur princess. How bold and confident she sounded today!'

'What could have brought about this mental transformation?' Vandiyatevan asked.

'Some important piece of information must have had a powerful impact on her sensibilities.'

'What could it be?'

'Why? Is the news of Ponniyin Selvan drowning not enough? There had been talk of a marriage between this girl and the prince.'

Vandiyatevan pondered, 'What could have staggered her—the news of the prince drowning in the sea, or that he was alive and safe in Nagaipattinam, or the news about Poonkuzhali?' He asked the astrologer, 'Ayya, the Kodumbalur household has followed the Saiva faith for generations. Why should this girl develop a sudden interest in the Buddha's creed?'

'Could be an influence continuing from the previous birth.'

'But why go to the monastery in Nagaipattinam?'

'That's what amazes me.'

'Can't you discover the reason from your astrological treatises?'

'Tambi! How can this be discovered by astrology? This belongs to the discipline of espionage.'

'Is espionage a discipline at all?'

'Why not? Have you not heard the *kural* verses on this subject by the prophetic poet?'

'I recall that there is a book of that name.'

'That book has a chapter called espionage.'

'I see! Do share a couple of good verses from it.'

'All the verses are excellent. Here's one. "A king must learn about those who work under him, his kin as well as foes, by appointing secret agents to gather intelligence about every one of them." Another has it that, "A spy is he who can disguise himself as a monk, feign to be a corpse, never spills secrets even under torture, and works tirelessly." The poet also tells you, "A king must employ a spy to investigate and verify the surveillance work done by every other spy." Are you telling me that you have never heard any of these verses?'

Vandiyatevan was left astounded by the genius of a poet who could come up with such insights a thousand years ago. He decided to read the whole book as soon as he got some free time.

They talked a little more. 'I will come again and be your guest,' Vandiyatevan said as he rejected the astrologer's invitation to spend the night in his house.

'When you come again, you will see that my forecasts have come true,' the astrologer said.

'Ayya! How can they come true when you made no forecasts at all!' laughed Vandiyatevan as he mounted the horse and left.

From the astrologer's house, he found that he had to take the straight path where he would have to follow the palanquin. Soon, the road split into two. One went north to the Kollidam. The other went southeast to Tiruvarur, where Vandiyatevan sighted the palanquin in the distance. He was shaken by a momentary dilemma.

He felt rueful about refusing to accede to Vanathi's request. What if she really needed his assistance? What if he were to hear later that she had encountered some danger on the way? Could he ever forgive himself? Would he regret not having escorted her? But what could he do? He had strict orders from the chief minister and the princess. He had faced difficulties enough in getting sidetracked into concerns that were no part of his business. Azhvarkadiyan too had cautioned him. Besides, he could not even dream of taking Vanathi to the Chudamani Viharam.

Arriving at this decision, just as Vandiyatevan directed his horse on to the road towards the Kollidam, he thought he heard a faint shriek from a woman. He turned to look. The palanquin was not to be seen. It could have taken a turn on the road. Vandiyatevan made a split-second decision to investigate. The delay would be insignificant. The horse leapt into a gallop and reached the turning in no time at all. What he saw there made his heart stop. A woman had been gagged and bound to a tree. It had become dark by then, but as he went nearer, he recognized Vanathi's maid moaning and trying to free herself. Vandiyatevan jumped down from the horse, ran to remove the gag and untie her while registering that she was not badly hurt.

'Girl! What happened? Tell me quickly. Where's the palanquin? Your mistress?'

The maid gabbled her answer. When the palanquin turned the corner, seven or eight men came running from behind the trees. Some had tridents and skulls in their hands. Two of them hit the maid, threw her down and gagged her. Meanwhile, the others said something terrifying to the palanquin bearers who left the road and began to run with the palanquin into another path. The men ran with them.

Vanathi's voice could not be heard at all. The maid pointed to the path they had taken.

'Girl, go and wait in the Kudantai astrologer's house. I will see if I can find your mistress,' said Vandiyatevan and leapt on the horse. The horse swivelled from the highway onto the crosscut and galloped across mound and ditch, bush and wood.

34

The Torch is Put Out

It was the early part of the new moon night. Darkness had swept in. The black clouds rising in the north had spread across the whole sky. Not a single star twinkled in the sky. In the dim light of the fireflies hovering over bushes and trees, Vandiyatevan guided his horse without any clarity about why and where he was going. Kundavai's dear friend was in peril. It was his duty to try to save her. The rest was up to god.

Half an hour's riding brought him no nearer the palanquin. As Vandiyatevan wondered if he had embarked on a wild goose chase, he heard the sound of hoofs. From one horse or many, he could not determine. Perhaps they belonged to the palanquin guards. He had to be wary of stumbling unexpectedly into a big company. It would be of no use to Vanathi, and his work would suffer.

He moved slowly until he decided that it was a single horse. In a little while, it looked as though that horse was trotting upwards on a slope. As he followed, he looked around to see if he could find a place to remain unseen and unnoticed.

An old, dilapidated pavilion stood close by. He rode to hide behind one of its broken walls. His eyes began to ache with his intense focus on staring at the horse ahead, which had now climbed on a mound.

'Who's there?' The voice startled Vandiyatevan. It sounded familiar.

'Your majesty! It's I, your slave,' another voice replied.

Momentarily, a man holding a burning torch could be seen coming from behind a tree. The horse and rider became visible, confirming that the rider was indeed Madhurantakan.

The horse had been standing on the bank of a wide canal. But as the man raised the torch, the horse took fright, lifted its front legs, swivelled to spring up suddenly and began to gallop until it leapt into the waters.

The torchbearer shouted, 'Your majesty!' and jumped into the waters too, only to stumble. The torch fell with him and was extinguished.

Pitch blackness swept in. It began to drizzle.

The voices shouting for help mingled with the unrelieved cacophony of the trees rocking in the winds, the sound of rain and the dry croaks of the frogs.

Vandiyatevan knew that Prince Madhurantakan was not exactly well known for his courage. He was shaken by the thought of the prince having met with an accident. His horse could have run helter-skelter with the prince still on its back, thrown him into the flowing canal or on the ground.

Could the torchbearer save him? But he himself had tumbled into the canal!

What should Vandiyatevan do? Search for Vanathi? Help Madhurantakan?

He did not know where Vanathi was, but Madhurantakan had met with an accident in front of his eyes. It would be easy to find him and help him. After that, he could still go to seek Vanathi. God! What about the resolve he had taken at the start of the journey to avoid all distractions? Vandiyatevan rode out from behind the wall. It was by instinct that he went through the drizzle and the darkness to find the place where the horse had jumped into the canal. But he could see nothing there. All he could hear were indistinct sounds in the distance.

He crossed the canal and climbed over the bank, only to see paddy fields everywhere. It would be impossible to take the horse through the crops on the squelchy ground. He would have to ride along the bank.

But the bank was a tangle of plants, creepers and thorny bushes. Vandiyatevan followed a footpath cutting through them. He had rain coming from above, slippery slush below, the canal on one side, paddy fields on the other and thorny bushes all around.

The horse made very slow progress.

Each minute passed like an age.

The darkness was getting more intense.

Vandiyatevan's mind was immersed in thoughts.

Why was Madhurantaka Tevar riding alone? Where was he going? Who was the man who approached him?

Was there any connection between Vanathi's abduction and this event?

What had happened to Vanathi?

Why should he get involved in these baffling problems?

He could get on with his job. He could find the highway and make for Kanchi.

But how was that even possible in this darkness and rain?

How could he decide that these matters were of no concern to him?

In the Kadambur palace, how useful did his intrusion into affairs of no personal concern later turn out to be?

But on this dark night, riding beside the bank was going to serve no purpose except that of getting thoroughly drenched. If the horse were to slip and break its leg, the whole journey would have to be abandoned.

He would have to return to that ruined mandapam and resume his journey after the rains stopped.

A sudden streak of lightning flashed directly on what seemed to be a horse standing on the elevated threshing floor.

Having come thus far, why not go a little further and take a look? he thought. Lending the endangered Madhurantakan a helping hand could prove to be advantageous to his mission in several ways.

Vandiyatevan descended from the canal bank into the little dyke in the field and rode towards the threshing floor where he thought he had spotted the horse. On closer view, it appeared to be a big, black phantom.

Another flash showed the standing horse for a split second. Vandiyatevan saw that it was riderless.

Thunder crashed. Terrified, the horse bolted away. It would be pointless to follow it.

Vandiyatevan tried calling out several times. 'Who's there?' His voice rose above the battering rain only to set echoes rebounding from many directions.

The downpour increased. The ferocious winds turned the downpour into an angled assault. The horse shook itself.

Vandiyatevan began to shiver under the pelting rain and chilling cold.

Realizing that there was no point in lingering, Vandiyatevan cursed his own stupidity as he turned his horse back. Never again should he get into such silly situations, but stick to his own business.

The horse found its way back by instinct and neighed when it reached the dark mandapam. Vandiyatevan returned from his ruminations to the real world and dismounted. His clothes were dripping wet and had to be dried. He looked to see if there was any dry spot in the mandapam for him to spend the night with his horse.

Suddenly, he leapt up as though flames were scorching his feet under the deluge. What made him jump was no ghost or ghoul, but the voice of a little child calling, 'Amma! Amma!'

How could he be sure that it was no ghost or ghoul? How could a child's voice be heard in that mandapam, and at that time? Chee! Chee! Ghosts and ghouls were nothing but the fancies of terrified fools. It was only a child's voice. 'Amma! Amma! Mhmm . . . Mhmm . . .' They were the frightened wails of a human child separated from its mother, coming from the darker side of the mandapam.

Was it just a child? And no one else?

'Amma! Amma! Hmm . . . Hmm . . .'

Vandiyatevan approached the voice and asked, 'Who's there?'

The child echoed him, 'Who's there?'

'It is me. Who are you? What are you doing in the dark? Come out!'

'It is raining outside.'

'It has stopped raining. Come out.'

'Where's my mother?'

'Your mother has gone to fetch milk for you.'

'No. You are lying.'

'Will you come out? Or shall I come in?'

'I have a sword in my hand. If you come, I will stab you.'

'O my goodness! You seem to be a mighty warrior. Why don't you come out and stab me?'

'Who are you? You are not a tiger, are you?'

'I am not a tiger, I am a horse,' Vandiyatevan said.

'You are lying. Can a horse talk?'

'Can a tiger talk?'

'Mother said that there was a tiger outside and it would pounce on me if I came out.'

'I am no tiger. I won't pounce on you. Come, don't be afraid.'

'Afraid? Why should I be afraid?' said a small child as it came out of the mandapam.

By this time, the rain had stopped completely. The clouds had parted, a few stars could be seen.

Vandiyatevan looked at the child under the starlight.

He could have been four years old. A very good-looking child, wearing a silken garment and a chain of rubies. He had to belong to some aristocratic household. Who was his mother? Why did she come here, and why did she leave the child here?

The child too had taken a good look at Vandiyatevan. He said, 'You are no horse. You look like a man.'

'There is a horse too, see!' Vandiyatevan said.

The child looked at the horse.

'So you brought it for me? But they said that a palanquin would come for me.'

The child's response gave rise to conflicting thoughts in Vandiyatevan's mind. Who was this child? Why was he alone? Such a small child and so unafraid–was it not amazing? Who told him that a palanquin would be sent for him? Why had it not arrived? Who was the mother who had left him here? Where could she have gone?

'Child, why has your mother left you?' he asked.

'She did not leave me. It was I who left her,' the child answered.

'Why did you leave her?'

'A horse came galloping by. I said that we should catch it and I would ride on it. Mother said no. I ran after the horse without her knowing. Is this the same horse?'

'No. This is a different one. But how did you come here?'

'I couldn't find the horse. Mother too was not to be seen. It began to rain heavily and I came into this mandapam.'

'Are you not afraid to be alone in the dark?'

'Why? I live like this every day.'

'Are you not even afraid of the tiger?'

'Mother is afraid, not me. I am a fish. I will swallow the tiger.'

'Hey! Can a fish swallow a tiger?'

'I am no ordinary fish. I am a gigantic fish, a whale. I can swallow lion, tiger, elephant, everything.'

Vandiyatevan was troubled by a host of ideas. A marvellous fish that swallows a tiger! Who would have taught such a thing to the child?

'What's that noise?' asked the boy.

Vandiyatevan saw a group of people approaching from a distance. Some held flares. A palanquin could be seen in their midst. Everyone was running excitedly with a woman among them. There were perturbed shouts of 'There!' and 'Here!'

One of them pointed to the dilapidated mandapam. It was the signal for everyone to run pell-mell towards it.

'There they come! With a palanquin. I don't want the palanquin. Will you take me on your horse?' the boy asked.

Vandiyatevan was charmed by the boy's face, appearance and speech. He wanted to hug the child and hold him in his arms. At the same time, something stirred within to stop him.

'I'm in a hurry, I have work to do,' he replied.

'Where are you going?'

'To Kanchi.'

'Kanchi? That's where my principal enemy happens to be.'

Vandiyatevan was stunned. He thought that even to stand beside that child was the wrong thing to do. But the crowd had come too near for him to mount the horse and ride away. It would invite suspicion. Vandiyatevan was also curious to know what was about to happen. He moved into the darkness beside the broken wall.

'Here I am,' said the boy and went forward.

The woman was the first to reach him. Ignoring her own breathlessness, she grabbed him in an embrace and said, 'Pandya! Why did you do this?'

Ravidasan, who came next, said, 'Your majesty! Should you give us such a fright?'

'I *will* give you a fright. I asked for a horse. But you have brought a palanquin!' said the boy.

Now Soman Sambavan, Idumbankari, Tevaralan and others surrounded the boy.

'Your majesty! We will bring you a thousand, ten thousand horses. But for today, please get into the palanquin,' Soman Sambavan said.

'No. I will ride on that horse,' said the boy and pointed to the horse standing behind the broken wall.

It was then that they noticed the horse and Vandiyatevan who was standing beside it.

Ravidasan's face was aflame with astonishment, dread and rage.

Taking two steps forward, he asked, 'Blackguard! How did you land up here?'

'Ghoul! How did you get here from Kodikkarai?' Vandiyatevan asked him.

Ravidasan howled in laughter. 'Did you really think I was a ghoul?'

Vandiyatevan replied, 'Some people turn into ghouls after death. You are a living ghoul.'

The boy said, 'Don't fight with him. I like him a lot. He protected me in the dark. He said he would kill any tiger that came by. Let him come with us.'

Ravidasan said to the boy, 'Your majesty! We will certainly take him with us. Please get into the palanquin just for today.'

The boy walked to the palanquin.

Ravidasan faced Vandiyatevan and asked, 'Now what are you going to do?'

'Is it not you who must tell me?'

'Join us. You knew quite a lot about our secret before. Now you know even more. We cannot let you go. Come with us.'

'If I refuse?'

'I know that you are a dauntless warrior. But we are twenty men. You cannot escape from us.'

'You are saying that I cannot escape alive.'

'You are a young man. You have not experienced the pleasures of life. Why should you lose your life unnecessarily?'

'Who will want to do that? You are asking me to accompany you. To which place? Where are you going?'

'Ask me that and I will tell you. We are going to the young queen of Pazhuvur.'

'That's what I thought. Where is she?'

'The young queen would have reached Tirupurampiyam by now. Are you or are you not coming with us?'

'I have to go that way. I was thinking about engaging a guide. Good thing you turned up. Come. Let us go,' Vandiyatevan said.

By this time, the boy was in the palanquin. It started moving. The men surrounded it and walked along, holding flares in their hands and shouting slogans.

Vandiyatevan followed them with various thoughts flailing in his mind.

What had happened to Vanathi? He didn't know. What was his plight going to be on that night? He didn't know that either.

There was no doubt at all that he was going to gain first-hand knowledge of a conspiracy many times more terrifying than the one he had witnessed in the Kadambur palace. To that extent, what had happened to him would be fruitful. But after that? Would these men allow him to escape with his life? They would certainly compel him to join them. If he refused, they would sacrifice him. Perhaps, Nandini might help him out . . .

Vandiyatevan reappraised the alacrity with which he agreed to follow the men the moment Ravidasan mentioned the Pazhuvur queen's name. It astounded him. Is this what the elders described as 'delusion' and 'desire'? He knew only too well the ghastly nature of the conspiracy she was involved in. Despite that, his heart yielded to a fervent and irrepressible desire to avail of any opportunity to meet her. His mouth had said 'Yes' before his mind could reflect. But did he have any other recourse? As Ravidasan said, it would not have been possible to fight them all. But perhaps he could find a way to escape. Before that, he could gain greater clarity about the conspirators and their intentions.

Vandiyatevan kept on recalling the little child lisping, 'Kanchi? That's where my principal enemy happens to be.' Who was that child? Why did they call him 'Your Majesty'? Whom did that boy mean when he said 'principal enemy'? The answers kept flashing in his mind only to increase his dread. God! When would all this end? A voice within told him, 'Very soon'.

The bizarre procession progressed through fields, canals, mounds and woods without an instant's pause or halt. Finally, it crossed the gushing the river Manni and reached the outskirts of Tirupurampiyam. It pushed through the forest tangled thickly around the *pallipadai* tomb.

35

The Time Has Come

We have seen the pallipadai memorial shrine once before. Built a hundred years ago, it was now dilapidated and forested all around. It was here that Azhvarkadiyan had hidden himself to glean information about Ravidasan and his collusions. Now, Vandiyatevan and the others reached the same spot.

They took Vandiyatevan and his horse to one of the walls of the tumbledown shrine.

Ravidasan said, 'Stay here. We will call you if needed. Don't even dream of escaping. No one who is not familiar with this forest can get in or out of it. You will lose your life if you try.'

'Enchanter! If I try to find my way out, you will cast a spell to kill me, right?' Vandiyatevan laughed.

'Laugh! Laugh! Go on, laugh as much as you like,' said Ravidasan as he too broke into guffaws.

A jackal howled in the distance. It set off an owl to whimper nearby.

Vandiyatevan's body quivered. Not because it was cold—even the breezes seemed to be afraid to penetrate the dense forest. Nor had it received much rain. On the forest floor, only a few spots were moistened with raindrops. The windless wood was so warm that Vandiyatevan's garments had dried by the time he reached the place. Only the sash around his waist was still damp, which he unrolled and spread out on a rock lying beside him. He sat on the edge of the same rock and leaned against the wall. Only one man stayed back to guard him.

The sepulchral shrine had become the meeting place for the cabal. The men sat in a circle in a clearing further down. One of them brought an old throne from the shrine for the boy they addressed as 'Your Majesty'. Smoke rose and spread as they extinguished the flares, keeping only two alive.

'The queen is still not here,' said one.

'She has to find the right time. I have asked her to come during the second phase of the night. Until then, one of you may sing of the glories of the Pandya clan,' Soman Sambavan said.

Idumbankari pulled out an *udukku* drum and tapped it gently. Tevaralan began a song.

Vandiyatevan saw and heard all this from where he was sitting. The song sounded like a dirge. The plaintive notes and the resonant drumming touched his heart. He could hear only a few words, but they made him recall the great war that had taken place on that very spot a hundred years ago.

Yes, it was right there that a savage war was fought for three days between Varaguna Pandya and Aparajita Pallava.

Prithvipati of the Ganga dynasty had come to the Pallava king's aid. He fell dead on the battlefield along with a hundred thousand soldiers.

After the death of the Ganga king, the scattered Pallava forces began to flee. The Pandya troops seemed poised to win. That was when the Chozha troops came to support the Pallavas. That army was led by Vijayalaya Chozha, famed for his ninety-six battle scars. The old king had already lost his legs. Two men carried him into the war field. Twirling two swords, one in each hand, he plunged into the ranks of the Pandya foes. Wherever he went, Pandya warriors fell dead on both sides. He left a mountainous pile of bodies in his wake.

The fleeing Pallava soldiers began to return. Ten thousand spears flashed back and forth from both sides.

Swords and spears clashed together and glittered in the setting sun.

Heads went rolling everywhere in their thousands and ten thousands.

Lifeless bodies dropped down in their thousands and ten thousands.

Horses neighed as they fell dead.

Elephants trumpeted as they slumped to death.

Corpses of men and beasts floated in the flooding blood.

Twenty thousand kites circled and soared to cover the sky with their wings outspread.

Thirty thousand jackals howled as they came running to surround the battlefield.

Fifty thousand groaning voices rose together, *Ayyyyyo-o-o-o-o-o-o!*

A hundred thousand voices bellowed, '*Catch! Grab! Chase! Stab! Punch!*'

Ten thousand drums reverberated, *Doom! Doom! Doom! Doom!*

Twenty thousand conches went, *Boom! Boom! Boom! Boom!*

Sixty thousand ghouls hollered, *Ha! Ha! Ha! Ha! Ha! Ha!*

Vandiyatevan was jolted out of his snooze. He gaped in all directions. He realized that he had drowsed off leaning against the wall of the shrine. He recalled the gruesome nightmare he had endured. Was it just a dream? No. The descriptions of the battle in Tevaralan's saga—synchronized with the drum beats—must have turned into visuals in his mind.

At that moment, Tevaralan was singing about the Pallava and the Ganga troops fleeing from the Pandya army. The gloating laughter of the listeners, sounding like the cackling of a thousand ghouls, must have shaken Vandiyatevan awake.

The drumming ceased. So did Tevaralan.

The torch lights came closer and closer. A palanquin followed. The bearers put it down, the curtains parted. A woman emerged. Yes, it was Nandini, the young queen of Pazhuvur. When Vandiyatevan had seen her earlier, she had appeared to be an enchantress, decked in splendid ornaments from head to toe. Now, with her open tresses billowing around her, she appeared to be a mighty goddess in a rage.

To see her in this form was to be filled with dread. Vandiyatevan's body began to shake.

As soon as she got out of the palanquin, Nandini directed her gaze at the boy on the throne. She began to walk with her eyes fixed on him.

The boy too had eyes only for her. The others were looking at both of them.

The woman who had been addressed by the child as 'mother' stood behind the throne.

As soon as she came up close to the child, Nandini stretched out both her arms.

The boy looked alternately at Nandini and the woman behind him.

'Aren't you–and not she–who is my mother?' he asked.

'Yes, darling.'

'Why does she say that she is my mother?'

'She is the mother who raised you.'

'Why did you not raise me? Why couldn't you have me with you? Why is she keeping me hidden in a mountain cave far away?'

'Darling! Only to fulfil your father's wish. To avenge your father's murder.'

'Yes. I know,' said the boy as he got up and came to Nandini.

Nandini hugged him with both her arms. She kissed his forehead. The boy too hugged her tight, as though to prevent her from leaving him ever again.

But the scene could not be prolonged. Nandini removed his arms forcibly and freed herself. She made him sit on the throne again and returned to the palanquin to take a sword from it. At a sign from her, the bearers carried the palanquin further away and sat down where they were hidden from view.

Nandini returned to place the sword crosswise on the throne.

Staring at the sword with inestimable ardour, the boy asked, 'May I hold it?'

'Wait, darling,' Nandini replied.

Then, starting with Ravidasan, she looked hard at everyone in turn.

'Anyone here except those who have taken the oath?' she enquired.

'None, Devi!' said Soman Sambavan.

Looking at Ravidasan, Nandini began with, 'General . . . !'

Ravidasan laughed.

'You find it funny today. Who knows how things may be on the same day in the following month?'

'Devi! We have been waiting for ever so long for that day to come.'

'Ayya! We are but few in number. Our emperor is a small child. The Chozha empire is mighty. The strength of the Chozha army is measureless. Haste would have ruined our endeavour. Maintaining patience has brought us close to the moment of mission fulfilment. Ravidasan! Anything you want to say? Is there anyone here who has anything to say?'

Ravidasan looked at each face one after the other. Everyone seemed to have taken a vow of silence.

'Devi! We have nothing to add. It is you who must speak to us. You said that we have come close to the hour of oath fulfilment. Please let us know where, how and by whom this deed is to be accomplished.'

'I will. I came here for this very purpose. That is why I insisted that everyone should be present and had our emperor brought here,' Nandini said.

Everyone, including the child on the throne, was gazing at Nandini's face. She continued, 'Some of you were in a hurry. Some of you wondered if I had forgotten the oath I had taken. Such a doubt is unforgivable. I have more reason than all of you to remember it constantly. In the last three years, I had no other thought, by day or by night. I did not think of anything except finding the right time and opportunity, the means and strategies. Wherever I went, whatever I did and whomever I spoke to, all I could think of was about how best I could make use of them to accomplish our mission. Now, the time and the opportunity have arrived. The feudal lords and high-ranking officials of the Chozha realm are divided into two factions. Pazhuvettaraiyar, Sambuvaraiyar and their cronies have decided to crown Madhurantakan. Bhooti Vikramakesari of Kodumbalur and Malayaman of Tirukovilur oppose them. I hear that Bhooti Vikramakesari is marching to Tanjavur with the southern contingents of the army. I understand that Malayaman is gathering his troops. War may break out at any moment.'

'Devi, I hear that you are making tremendous efforts to stop this war. We understand that talks of settlement are to be held in Sambuvaraiyar's palace in Kadambur.'

'Yes. It was I who arranged it. But can you not guess the reason for it?'

'No, queen. The elders have said that even god in all his omniscience cannot fathom the depths of a woman's heart. How can we do it?'

'Yes, it would be something beyond you. I will explain it so that you may understand. We cannot gauge the consequences of any internal strife in the Chozha land, should it break out before our oath is fulfilled. Sundara Chozha is still alive. So is Aniruddha Brahmarayar. They may succeed in suppressing both factions. Moreover, our goal would become unattainable should one faction lose and another establish its supremacy. That is why I have launched these settlement talks. We must accomplish our goal before the fight begins. Then the war between the feudatories will never end but continue until both sides are wiped out. Now do you understand the reason for promoting accord?'

Zeal and wonder were manifest on every face in the gathering. Among themselves, the men shared their enthusiastic appreciation of the Pazhuvur queen's astuteness in hushed tones. Ravidasan too could not withhold his astonishment.

'Devi! We are amazed by your singular foresight. We have grasped the reasons for the settlement talks. But you said that the day was approaching for us to fulfil our oaths. Who is to accomplish it? How? When?'

'I have devised a strategy to serve that purpose as well. An invitation has been sent to our prime foe to come to the Kadambur palace under the guise of peace talks. He *will* come. It is there that we must fulfil our oath. O men of Veerapandiyan's emergency squad! The day of revenge will soon be at hand. Today is Saturday. Our oath will be accomplished before next Saturday.'

All the twenty men who were present raised shouts in unison.

Some sprang up in excitement.

The drummer banged the drum twice in his excitement.

Owls sleeping in tree holes snarled as they awoke and flew to other branches.

Bats flapped their wings noisily and zoomed away.

Vandiyatevan's horse shook itself.

Vandiyatevan looked up. All he could observe was that Nandini was saying something that excited the others. He could not hear her words.

Ravidasan calmed everyone with a gesture and told Nandini, 'Devi! Your last words have brought us boundless joy. We are delighted that our revenge is imminent. But who is to have the privilege of performing that deed?'

'It is natural for all of us to compete for that honour. I asked our king of kings, the royal son of Veerapandiyan, to be brought here for the sake of solving that issue without any grievance among us. Veerapandiyan's sword is here too. The person to whom this little child hands the sword must perform the deed of vengeance. The others must remain close by, ready to render assistance. If the chosen person should happen to fail, others must come forward to complete the task. I will be in the Kadambur palace. Idumbankari is one of the fort's guards. We will enable the chosen man to enter the palace. Are these arrangements acceptable to all of you?'

Members of the emergency squad looked at each other eagerly. Everyone seemed content with the arrangements.

Ravidasan said, 'The arrangements you outlined are good. We agree to abide by them. But there is one more thing. We must also decide that everyone must follow the lead of the person to whom the task is assigned. Additionally, everyone must agree that until our emperor comes of age, they will, without question, abide by all the rules stipulated by the man who fulfils the oath.'

A smile appeared on Nandini's face. 'Does this include me?' she asked.

'Yes, Devi. No exceptions can be made.'

'Good. Do you all agree with Ravidasan?'

The men looked at one another doubtfully. Some of them seemed to disagree with that plan.

Soman Sambavan asked, 'How is that fair? How can our Devi, who has been assisting us in every way, be subjected to this general rule?'

'Don't worry about me. I have continued to live only for the sake of taking revenge for Veerapandiyan's gruesome murder. I am ready to be the slave of anyone who succeeds in avenging it,' Nandini said and looked at the little child who had been listening to them without fully comprehending their exchanges. 'My darling!' she said. 'This great sword belonged to your father. Raise it in your tender hands and hand it over to the person whom you like best among us.'

Ravidasan came closer and said, 'Your Majesty! Look at each one of us carefully. Give this great sword of the Pandya clan to the man you believe to be the most valiant and the most courageous among us.'

The child emperor seated on the throne looked around.

Everyone was looking at the emperor's face with irrepressible excitement and anticipation. The eyes of each bore the expression of supplication, pleading, 'Give it to me!'

Ravidasan's face and eyes alone conveyed the intimidating, authoritative command, 'Give it to me!'

After looking at them twice or thrice, the child picked up the sword and raised it with great difficulty.

The fever reached its peak.

Swiftly, the boy turned to Nandini. 'Amma! It is you whom I like more than anyone else. It is you who must rule the kingdom for me until I reach the right age,' said he and gave her the sword.

36

A Figure in the Dark

Nandini took the sword handed to her by the boy addressed as 'emperor'. She placed it on her breast and embraced it. Then she picked up the child and hugged him close. Tears continued to stream down from her eyes.

Transfixed, the others looked on.

Ravidasan recovered first and said, 'His Majesty has not understood our request. That is why he has given the sword to you. We must explain again in detail . . .'

Nandini stopped him. In a voice quivering with charged emotions, she said, 'No, ayya, no. His Majesty grasped it all as he gave me the sword. Don't be perturbed by my tears. Elation makes me weep for having obtained the privilege of avenging Emperor Veerapandiyan's assassination.'

'Devi! Consider this! When so many of us in the emergency squad are still alive . . .' Nandini stopped Soman Sambavan from continuing. 'No need,' she said. 'That responsibility is mine. It is not that you have no work to do. Half of you must take His Majesty to safety in the Pancha Pandava hills. The rest must come to Kadambur. Those who cannot gain entry into the palace must stay outside with fleet horses, in all readiness. Once the job is accomplished, should we not try to escape with our lives intact?'

Ravidasan came forward to say, 'Devi! There's something that I forgot to tell you. Please permit me to do so.'

'Tell me quickly, ayya. Pazhuvettaraiyar has gone to the Kalamukha convention by the river Kollidam. I must reach the palace before he returns.'

'Did you not say that our prime foe, Aditta Karikalan, will come to Kadambur? It is by no means certain that he will.'

'What makes you say that?'

'I have a sound reason to say so. A message is being sent to Karikalan asking him not to go to Kadambur for any reason whatsoever. The Pazhaiyarai princess and the chief minister have sent it.'

'Did you think I did not know this?'

'Do you still expect him to come to Kadambur?'

'Yes. I certainly do. That Pazhaiyarai snake woman does not know Aditta Karikalan's true nature. Nor does that monster, Brahmarayar of Anbil. With all your expertise in magic and mantra, you too remain in ignorance. Aditta Karikalan will do the very thing that anyone attempts to stop him from doing. I know it with absolute certainty. He is not like Arulmozhi Varman, who toes the line. Nor is he a cowardly simpleton like Madhurantakan. He will certainly make it to Kadambur precisely because his sister and the chief minister have asked him not to go,' Nandini said.

'Devi, you don't have to depend on this alone. Their message will not reach Kanchi,' said Ravidasan.

'What are you saying, ayya? Please explain,' Nandini said.

'Devi, do you know through whom the message has been sent to Aditta Karikalan?'

'Not with certainty. But I can make a guess.'

'Well, there is no need for guesswork. Actually, we have captured him. He was in the mandapam where His Majesty took shelter in the rain. He knows all our secrets. Letting him go once again would be tantamount to destroying ourselves by design. Idumbankari! Bring that spy,' Ravidasan ordered.

Idumbankari went to the pallipadai shrine. Two others went with him. Nandini began to stare in their direction. Her face had borne a fierce expression until then, but now it sported an enchanting smile.

Idumbankari and the two other men pounced on a fatigued and half-asleep Vandiyatevan. He wondered if he should wrestle with them, but changed his mind and remained passive to see what would happen. The trio bound his hands to his body with a long rope and then steered him by the shoulders until he stood in front of Nandini.

Vandiyatevan smiled when he saw her.

Nandini's face remained unchanged. Calmness pervaded it.

'Ayya! Once again–' she began.

Vandiyatevan cut in with, 'Yes, Devi! I am here again. But not by choice.' He looked at the men.

The child beside Nandini said, 'Amma! This is the man who saved me from being swallowed by a ghoul in the dark. Why is he all tied up?'

Vandiyatevan said to the boy, 'Child, keep quiet. You must not open your mouth when the elders are talking or the tiger will gobble you up.'

'I will gobble up the tiger,' said the boy.

'Can a fish swallow a tiger?' Vandiyatevan asked.

A macabre growl rose from the throats of the men standing around. For an instant, even Vandiyatevan was terrified by it.

Ravidasan said in a loud voice, 'Devi! Hear him? He cannot be allowed to get away with his life. At your word, twice before did we allow him to go free. Not any more.'

Vandiyatevan said, 'Sorcerer! How can you lie so blatantly? Was it *you* who allowed me to get away? Was it not *I* who let you escape? Devi! Take a good look at this man and tell me if he is truly Ravidasan or Ravidasan's spirit.'

Ravidasan laughed hideously and said, 'Yes. I am a ghost. I am going to drink your blood today.'

Once again, terrifying growls rose from the throats of the men standing around.

The child said, 'Amma! He has a fine horse. Ask him to give it to me.'

'Child, come with me. I will take you on my horse,' said Vandiyatevan.

Ravidasan glared horribly at Vandiyatevan and said, 'Shut your mouth!' To Nandini, he said, 'Devi! Give the order quickly.'

Nandini asked calmly, 'How did he come here? When?'

'This spy tried to make away with our emperor who had taken shelter in a dark mandapam. We stopped him at the right time. A second's delay could have been disastrous,' Ravidasan said.

'Ayya, is this true?' Nandini asked Vandiyatevan.

'It is you, and not I, who will know whether your men speak the truth or not,' Vandiyatevan said.

The smile on Nandini's face vanished at lightning speed. She told Ravidasan, 'Please stand aside, all of you. I must learn certain things from him in private.'

'Devi, it is getting late, danger approaches . . .'

Before Ravidasan could go on, Nandini said in a scathing voice, 'Remember the resolution we took just a while ago. Stand aside. Take the emperor with you.' To the child, she whispered, 'Son, go with them. I will get his horse for you.'

Without any further ado, Ravidasan and the others moved away, taking the child with them.

With her eyes boring into him in the faint torchlight, Nandini said, 'Ayya! You and I seem to have some kind of bond.'

'Devi, that bond seems to be as nasty as it is strong. It holds my hands and body in a tight grip,' Vandiyatevan said.

'Put a stop to your wisecracks. Did you come here by design? Or by chance?'

'Neither. Your men dragged me here by force. If not, by this time, I would have reached the banks of the Kollidam.'

'I see how vexatious it is for you to meet me and how eager you are to get away from me.'

'I have no problem at all in meeting you, and I am truly unhappy to leave you. You are trapped by the doddering Pazhuvettaraiyar on one side and these loathsome sorcerers on the other. Give me the word. I will free you from their clutches and take you away.'

'Where would you take me?'

'I will take you to your mother who is roaming in the forests of Ilankai like one bereft.'

Nandini released a long sigh of disappointment.

'Would you like to see me in the same state, wandering around like an abandoned orphan? When such a time comes, I will certainly seek your help to find my mother. But before that, you must help me fulfil my ambition.'

'Devi, how can I promise to help you unless I know what is in your mind?' Vandiyatevan said.

'No one who has genuine affection will give this answer. They will come forward to help even without knowing anything about what was required of them.'

'Devi, those who are impelled by affection will also give a timely warning to prevent harm. These conniving scoundrels have enmeshed you in great peril. They are exploiting you to accomplish their mission.'

'You are wrong. Know that it is I who is exploiting them to fulfil my mission.'

'They have caught hold of some child from the wilderness to deceive you.'

'Do you know who he is?'

'He is to be placed on the Pandya throne and crowned king.'

'Wrong again. Not to be placed on the Pandya throne, but on the throne of the Chozha empire spreading from the river Tungabhadra to the Ilankai island.'

'Ammamma! Who is to assist you in accomplishing this stupendous task? These men standing around us like a pack of jackals? Will you be able to defeat the mammoth Chozha army of two million warriors with these ten or twelve jackals who hide in their holes all day to emerge only at night?'

'I have not placed all my dependence on them. I trust the sword in my hand. It is with its help that I will fulfil the wish of my heart.'

'Devi! You are never going to use that sword. You do not have the strength in your arms or your heart.'

'Why do you say that?'

'I said what came to my mind.'

'Right now, right here, I can prove that you are totally wrong.'

'If that is the case, I am fortunate indeed. Would I not be privileged to be killed by your blessed hands?' said Vandiyatevan, bending his head down, as though ready to be slain.

'Do you wish to be slain and not crowned by my hands?' Nandini asked.

Raising his head, Vandiyatevan enquired, 'On how many heads will you place the crown you possess?'

'That is up to me. I will place it on the head of the person I finally choose to crown.'

'What about this young boy then?'

'Is it not my wish that decides to crown him or not?'

'Devi! Give the crown to the person of your choice. Not to me.'

'Why?'

'My winsome curls have been widely admired. I don't want to ruin their appeal by wearing a crown.'

'You will not give up your wisecracks. All right,' said Nandini and continued with a sudden change of tracks. 'Was the princess extremely distressed when she heard the news of her brother's death by drowning?'

Overcoming his momentary discomposure, Vandiyatevan said, 'How could she not be distressed? Are all women heartless?'

'Is it true that the Kodumbalur girl fell into the stream intending to give up her life? Who pulled her out to save her?'

Vandiyatevan recalled the disaster that had overtaken Vanathi. He did not answer, lost as he was in thinking about her plight.

Nandini hardened her voice as she said, 'All right. I know that you will not tell me about those things. Are you going to stop Aditta Karikalan from coming to the Kadambur palace?'

'I will try to stop him,' Vandiyatevan replied.

'I say that you cannot do it.'

'I too am not saying that I can, Devi. All I said was that I would try. Once the prince makes up his mind, it is not easy to make him change it.'

'You have understood Aditta Karikalan's nature very well.'

'You know more about it than I do.'

'Well, all my persuasions cannot make you join my side. You will remain in my enemies' camp. Isn't that so?'

'Devi, who is your enemy?'

'My enemy? The Pazhaiyarai princess. Who else?'

'That is a figment of your imagination. Devi, I want to tell you an important truth.'

Bristling with animosity, Nandini said, 'Enough! Enough! Don't I know that when you start speaking the truth it ends in arrant falsehood? You may keep your truth to yourself.'

When she clapped her hands, Ravidasan and the others hastened towards them. Vandiyatevan realized that he had wasted a god-given opportunity. The demoness was certainly going to order them to kill him. God! What a death! Could he not die on the battlefield fighting with foes? Was this to be his fate?

Ravidasan and his group surrounded him, growling like wolves approaching their prey.

'Queen! However much you try, I know that he will not allow himself to be swayed. You may leave at once. We will sacrifice him on this sacred ground before we go,' Ravidasan said.

'Sorcerer! Beware! That is not my wish. None of you must harm him in any way. With this sword will I kill any man who touches him,' Nandini roared.

The men fell back in astonishment.

'I have many things to be done by him. Understand? I am leaving now. You may leave too. Let him go wherever he wants. No need to bar his way.'

Ravidasan said, 'Devi! A request. We are ready to follow your orders. But consider that he has a horse. Would it be wise to let him go before we do?'

'All right. Tie him to the pillar in the pallipadai shrine. It will take him some time to free himself. You would have crossed the forest by then,' she said.

Vandiyatevan was tied to the pillar and his horse was tethered to a tree close by.

Nandini left on the palanquin.

Two men took the throne away.

Ravidasan and the others left with the child.

The torch they carried dimmed slowly before it vanished.

The scenes that had occurred a little while ago seemed to be a dream.

Pitch-black darkness enveloped Vandiyatevan all around.

Giant bats flapped their wings.

Owls snarled.

Jackals took turns to howl hideously. Vandiyatevan felt them advancing towards him, howling still.

Indistinguishable shapes moved in the dark forest.

He remembered his nightmare in the Kadambur palace. He shivered at the thought of a thousand jackals surrounding him to tear his flesh and devour him.

He tried hard to untie himself, but the knots could not be loosened easily.

Had there been light, it would have been easier. But there was no sign of any light, not even of lightning or fireflies.

Nor was there any possibility of starlight penetrating the forest, even if the clouds had dispersed.

Ah! What was that sound?

No surprise. After all, so many creatures moved in the forest.

No, it sounded like human footsteps.

The horse neighed softly and moved its feet in discomfort. An approaching tiger . . .

Vandiyatevan struggled with his knots without success.

There! A shape . . . like a silhouette in the deep darkness. A human form? Or . . . what else could it be?

It came nearer, and nearer.

Vandiyatevan mustered all his mental prowess.

He gave a powerful kick.

Eeeeee, screamed the figure and jumped back.

A ringing crash . . . it must have banged against the shrine's door.

The figure stood there for some time, perhaps leaning against the wall.

Vandiyatevan had the sensation of being stared at even though he could see nothing.

Once again, he made hurried attempts to untie himself. Those demons had made such strong knots! The next time he saw Ravidasan, he would teach him a lesson.

The figure moved as though it was entering the shrine.

A little later, there came sounds of pebbles striking one another.

Flintstones . . . ? For there was a light in front of the shrine.

There! The figure was coming out of the shrine, holding a torch.

It was approaching him.

It was the figure of a Kalamukha ascetic. A terrifying figure with a long beard, matted locks and a garland of skulls.

Coming up close to Vandiyatevan, the figure loomed over him, raised the torch and gave him a hard stare.

37

Unmasked!

Encountering the grotesque figure of the Kalamukha Saiva in that place and at that time left Vandiyatevan momentarily terror-stricken. But his inborn courage drove the fears away. A vague sense of familiarity made him wonder where he had seen the man before. Didn't two men glare at him while he was feigning sleep under a tree by the river Harischandra? This was one of them. Had he seen him only once? Hadn't he seen these penetrating eyes elsewhere?

The Kalamukha stared at him and laughed aloud. That voice . . . sounded familiar . . .

'Chee! Is it you? Was it for you that I made such a tremendous effort to be here at midnight?' As he spoke, the Kalamukha gave the impression of trying to disguise his voice.

'Whom did you come for?' Vandiyatevan asked.

'I came in search of the prince,' said the Kalamukha.

'Which prince?'

'What do you care? Why do you ask?'

'I am a prince too. That is why.'

'You, a prince! With a face like yours?

'What's wrong with my face, ayya? Would I look charming only if I grow a beard and matted locks like you and wear bones?'

'Try it! Then you will know.'

'How long will the beard and dreadlocks take to grow?'

'No big deal. A day . . . an hour . . .'

'That's what I thought.'

'What did you think?'

'Nothing. Untie me. I will join your cult.'

'Enough! Enough! There are spies like you in our group already. That is why our great convention ended as it did.'

'How did it end?'

'We waited for the prince. He was to appoint our *Mahaguru** as the royal preceptor as soon as he ascended the throne. The prince never did come.'

'Untie me. I will tell you why the prince did not turn up.'

'Which prince?'

'Who else but Madhurantaka Tevar, the son of Gandaraditta.'

'I guessed right.'

'What did you guess?'

'I guessed that you were a spy.'

'How?'

'When I came searching for the prince, I saw some people coming out of this forest. I know who they are. They must

* Highest-ranking guru.

have left you all tied up because they recognized you for a spy. Only, I cannot imagine why they left you alive.'

'Untie me. I will tell you.'

'No need. Nor will I untie you. If you swear to do what I say . . .'

'Do what?'

'A hundred and eight sit-ups, promising that you'll never interfere in things that don't concern you.'

'Is that so?' asked Vandiyatevan. His hands had not been idle during the conversation. They undid the last knot just as the Kalamukha mentioned sit-ups. Vandiyatevan jumped up to pounce on the Kalamukha and struck him down. The Kalamukha's torch fell to the ground but was not completely put out.

Vandiyatevan sat on the Kalamukha's chest and shook his beard until it came off. The Kalamukha pushed Vandiyatevan off and stood up.

Vandiyatevan picked up the dying torch and held it high.

Shorn of beard and dreadlocks, the Kalamukha turned into Azhvarkadiyan.

The two men looked at each other and began to laugh.

'Vaishnava! Didn't you advise me to stop butting into matters that did not concern me? What about you?' Vandiyatevan asked.

'But I did not bump into danger like you, my man! If I had not turned up here . . .'

'So you think it was you who freed me from my bonds?'

'Even if you had freed yourself, you cannot get out of this wilderness without my help. You would have become the jackals' prey.'

'Forget the jackals. If you had seen the conjuring jackals who had gathered here some time ago . . . Great luck to have escaped from *them*.'

'I know those sorcerers. Anyone else?'

'A little fish. A strange little fish wanting to devour the tiger.'

'Ah! Tell me! Tell me! Who were they? What happened? Tell me everything in detail.'

'Why did you adopt this disguise? Where were you this evening? What happened there? If you tell me everything, I will tell you what happened here.'

'I don't have much to tell. The great convention of the Kalamukhas was to be held early in the night beside the Kollidam shore. I wore this costume to check on it before meeting you at the Kollidam jetty. The convention was held. Periya Pazhuvettaraiyar attended it. The Mahaguru of the Kalamukhas was also present. But the most anxiously awaited guest did not arrive at all.'

'Was it not Prince Madhurantakan?'

'Yes. But how did you know that?'

'This kingdom will be brilliantly governed if Madhurantakan ascends the throne.'

'Why do you say that?'

'He was not even able to control a recalcitrant horse! How would he manage feudal lords like the Pazhuvettaraiyars, insurgent Kalamukhas and belligerent Vaishnavas?'

Azhvarkadiyan laughed and said, 'Did you see Madhurantakan on the way? Do you know what happened to him?'

Vandiyatevan gave an account of seeing Madhurantakan's horse taking fright and bolting when it saw the torch, searching for the prince and finding only the horse standing on the threshing mound. 'Ayyo, poor man! Who knows where the horse toppled him? His life could have been endangered. That is why he did not come to your great convention. Shall we go and search for him?'

'Good grief! What is it to us? Let us go about our business. Come on. We must be at the Kollidam jetty before the day breaks,' said Azhvarkadiyan.

'What if Madhurantakan is lying dead in the canal or dyke? Would you still say it is a matter of no concern to us?'

'That would not have happened. Aniruddha Brahmarayar would have taken care of it.'

'The chief minister? What would he know of this?'

'Ah! Nowhere in this kingdom can anything happen without Anbil Aniruddha Brahmarayar's knowledge.'

'Oho! So he knows about the Kadambur conspiracy too?'

'Remember how both of us watched the Pazhuvur queen's palanquin passing by during the festivities in Veeranarayanapuram?

'Yes. I remember how excited you became when the curtain parted. You asked me if I would deliver a letter to the young queen of Pazhuvur.'

'Believing that I was sending a love letter you replied, "Chee! Chee! What kind of a job is that?" All I wanted to do was to send a warning to Madhurantakan not to trust the conspirators, as ordered by the chief minister.'

'Did you know that Madhurantakan was in that palanquin?'

'It was suspicion at first. The curtain parted, the truth was out. You are extremely close-mouthed. All my probing could not make you disclose that it was Madhurantakan and not the Pazhuvur queen.'

'What about you? You refused to tell me where you were going this evening.'

'If I had, you would have insisted on butting in. See how you got into difficulties despite that! From now onwards . . .'

'Did the chief minister know about the Kalamukha convention and Madhurantakan's intention to attend it?'

'Why would he send me there if he didn't? At the same time, he had also arranged for Madhurantakan not to get there. The man who held up the torch must have been the chief minister's man. He would have deliberately provoked the horse to bolt. Someone would have picked up the fallen prince and taken care of him. Right now, they may be going to Tanjavur by palanquin or chariot. Come on, let us go our way.'

'Vaishnava! I cannot come.'

'What is this? What about the job you agreed to perform? I hear that Prince Aditta Karikalan has left Kanchi. Only if we fly like the wind can we . . .'

'You can hand over the letter to Aditta Karikalan. Unlike Madhurantakan, he will neither be disguised as a woman nor travel furtively in the night.'

'What will you do?'

'Honestly speaking, I did not start out this evening to follow Madhurantakan. I saw him by chance as I was following someone else.'

'I will make a prediction. It was a woman.'

'You are a wicked man. One day, I am going to crack your skull before I do anything else.'

'It is a task beyond you. I have already pledged my skull to a Kalamukha. Never mind. Who was the woman you started following in Kudantai?'

'The princess of Kodumbalur had come to the Kudantai astrologer's house. She left in a palanquin all by herself. I did not start with any intention of following that crazy girl. Her palanquin happened to be travelling on the same road. Suddenly, a few men attacked the palanquin. They bound her maid to a tree and took Vanathi away. I don't want to come with you without discovering what happened to her.'

'Why are you so worried about that girl?'

'What do you mean? Is she not the daughter of Siriya Velar who lost his life in Ilankai? The dear friend of Princess Kundavai? Moreover, was there not some talk of getting her married to Ponniyin Selvan?'

'My dear fellow, Ponniyin Selvan fell into the sea and passed away! Why bother about his marriage now?'

'How is it certain that he did die? Pure guesswork.'

'So you think he is alive?'

'Vaishnava, if it is your intention to trick me into spilling my guts . . . forget it!'

'All right, all right. I know how tight-lipped you can be. But there is no need for you to worry about Vanathi Devi. You know how extremely dear she is to the princess.'

'That is why I am worried. The princess may not know that Vanathi is in danger.'

'If not today, she will know by tomorrow.'

'What is the use of knowing it tomorrow? What if the Kalamukhas sacrifice the girl tonight?'

'Did you say that the Kalamukhas abducted Vanathi?'

'That is what I thought. Vanathi's maid said the same thing to me.'

'If that is true, there is absolutely nothing to worry about. The Kodumbalur clan is affiliated with the Kalamukhas. When they learn that Vanathi is the princess of Kodumbalur, they will shower her with royal honours.'

'Oh! I didn't know!'

'That is why the Kalamukhas oppose Madhurantakan.'

'How does it matter if these skull-toting monks oppose him?'

'You don't know. All the high-ranking clans are affiliated with the Kalamukhas. They have many adherents in the army as well. That is why Pazhuvettaraiyar had made arrangements to gain the Kalamukhas' support for Madhurantaka Tevar. The attempt failed due to the recalcitrance of a horse. Get started! Are you coming with me or should I go on my own?'

Vandiyatevan got up reluctantly and took the reins in his hands. They found a path to push through the forest in a single file and made their exit.

'Look!' said Azhvarkadiyan, pointing to the sky.

Vandiyatevan saw the comet, larger than ever, occupying half the sky.

Cold breezes blew. A shiver ran through Vandiyatevan's body.

In the distance, a village dog wailed dismally.

38

Vanathi's Plight

The sun had set and darkness enveloped all sides as Vanathi travelled in her palanquin from Kudantai to Tiruvarur. Her mind was in a state of chaos. She was desperate to reach the Chudamani Viharam in Nagaipattinam and nurse the sick prince. But how was that possible? With mounting dismay, she wondered if she would be allowed to enter the monastery at all, and whether it would be feasible for her to see the prince. Even if she did, would she be allowed to serve him?

The thought of journeying to Nagaipattinam all alone filled her with an unease that she tried to replace with courage. After all, could any major endeavour in the world be performed so easily? How hard did some people struggle to complete the mission they had undertaken? How brave-hearted that boatwoman must be, to sail a boat on the sea, alone? How courageous she must be to have rowed through the mammoth waves and saved the prince? How silly of her to be scared of such a short journey. It did not matter if she could not enter the Chudamani Viharam. It would be enough to see the boatwoman. Yes, that was the right thing to do. If Vanathi could somehow contact her, it might be possible to see the prince with her assistance. Vanathi felt that she had to prove to the prince that her love for him was not motivated by expectations of personal gain. After that, she could give up her life. Or she could join the Buddha faith and become a nun.

When Vanathi parted the palanquin's curtains to ask when they would reach Nagaipattinam, she thought she saw some figures hiding beside the path behind the trees. She stared harder and realized that they were men of the Kalamukha faith. This did not worry her at all. The Kalamukhas had been frequent visitors to the Kodumbalur palace where she was raised. Her uncle Bhooti Vikramakesari had made grants to several temples for feeding the Kalamukhas. They would speak to her uncle and accept whatever they needed. Once, the Mahaguru of the Kalamukhas had himself visited the Kodumbalur palace to be worshipped and honoured. Therefore, the Kalamukhas would not harm her. They might even help her. Vanathi also knew that their big convention was to be held on that day. She had seen groups of Kalamukhas along the way from Pazhaiyarai to Kudantai. And yet, why were they lurking behind trees? They could harm her if they mistook her for someone else . . .

The hidden figures ran out swiftly and surrounded the palanquin. Vanathi was still not perturbed. But before she could identify herself to them, she saw two men binding her maid to a tree. Involuntarily, she let out a terrified screech.

One of the Kalamukhas pointed his trident at her face and said, 'Girl! Don't scream! We won't harm you. But if you make an outcry, we will kill you with this trident.'

Vanathi regained her courage. Intending to speak imperiously, she demanded, 'Do you know who I am? I am the daughter of the Kodumbalur Velar. If you touch me, you will be utterly destroyed.' Vanathi's voice did tremble, though she wished to appear confident.

The Kalamukha said, 'We know it all and that is why we waited for you. Keep quiet. If you don't . . .'

At the same time, the sharp sounds of swishing whips and cries of 'Ayyo!' were also heard. Vanathi knew that the voices belonged to the palanquin bearers. Infuriated by this injury to her men, she tried to get out of the palanquin. But before she could, the bearers had begun to run with the palanquin. Vanathi realized that her cries would be in vain as the Kalamukhas were shouting horribly as they ran alongside. Jumping out of the moving palanquin would merely land her among those monsters. She also felt a sporadic urge to know where and why they were taking her.

Half an hour's running brought them to a Durga temple hidden by the trees. It had become dark by then. One of the men brought a lamp from the shrine and held it close to Vanathi's face. Looking hard at her, he said, 'Girl! Give us the information we require and we will leave you unscathed. We can also take you safely to wherever you wish to go.'

Vanathi was now assailed by an unforeseen suspicion. 'What information do I have? What are you going to ask me?'

'Girl! Did you not start on this journey all by yourself for a clandestine meeting? Whom did you wish to meet?'

Vanathi's suspicion grew stronger. In an instant, a remarkable change took place within her. The timid doe turned into a fearless lioness.

'What is it to you? Who are you to question me? I will not tell you.'

The Kalamukha laughed.

'You don't have to tell us. We know it all too well. You are going to meet Prince Arulmozhi Varman. Tell us where he is hiding. We will not touch you.'

'Do whatever you like. You cannot get anything from me,' Vanathi said firmly and clearly.

'You won't dare say "do whatever you like" if you know what we could do.'

'What will you do? Go on, tell me.'

'First, we will burn one of your lovely flowerlike hands in this flame. Then we will burn the other one. We will set fire to your dark tresses . . .'

'Go ahead. Do it. Here's my hand. Bring the torch closer,' Vanathi said.

Vanathi knew all about the intrigues and collusions in the kingdom. She thought, 'These scoundrels must be the conspirators' henchmen. They are trying to find the prince, undoubtedly intending to harm him. What greater fortune can I have than to undergo these brutal tortures for his sake?' The thought gave her immense courage.

'Girl! Think again. Don't be stubborn. You will regret it. You will remain blind all your life.'

'Burn me inch by inch. Cut my flesh bit by bit. You will get nothing from me.'

'All right, we will. Bring the torch here!' the Kalamukha said to his disciple.

Vanathi's attention was caught by something in the distance. She saw a long cavalcade with elephants, horses, palanquins and foot soldiers. By god's grace, she was going to receive unexpected help.

'Look! Beware!' She pointed. The Kalamukha laughed.

'Do you know who is coming?' he asked.

'It looks like the chief minister. If I shout, they will hear me. Beware. Leave me. Run! Otherwise . . .'

'Yes, my girl, it *is* Aniruddha Brahmarayar. It is on his orders that we have seized you,' said the Kalamukha.

Vanathi was once again filled with dread. Her throat emitted a terrified shriek. She tried to cover her mouth to stifle it.

39

Deliverance

Vanathi had been inside the palanquin all this while, which was now placed on the ground. When she came out to look at the approaching procession, the Kalamukhas were also looking in the same direction. Frogs croaked in the water-filled fields, branches crackled in the chilly winds.

The thought of running away did not enter Vanathi's mind. She knew it was impossible. While clever tactics might have helped in getting her away from the Kalamukhas, not even in dreams was an escape from Anbil Aniruddha Brahmarayar a possibility. His intellectual brilliance, his diplomatic guile and artfulness were world-famous. The world also knew his great influence over the emperor. Women in the Pazhaiyarai palace gossiped about other office holders and feudal chieftains, but never about Aniruddha Brahmarayar, afraid that even the softest whisper in the innermost chambers would reach his ears. Everyone knew that whatever the emperor may overlook, he would never forgive any slander of the chief minister who claimed his affection and esteem.

Knowing that Princess Kundavai held him in great respect, Vanathi too expected to get his help and protection. But what the Kalamukhas had said shattered her confidence. Why should he have ordered the capture of an orphaned girl? Perhaps the men were lying. It could be the Pazhuvettaraiyars or Prince Madhurantakan who were approaching. One thing was certain—whoever it may be, whatever the consequences may be, even at the cost of her life, she must never disclose anything about the prince. This thought made her regain her confidence. She would establish the fact that she belonged to the valiant tribe of Kodumbalur. She would show them that she was the intimate companion of Princess Kundavai.

The procession came to a halt. A single palanquin came forward and was placed on the ground near Vanathi. Chief Minister Aniruddha Brahmarayar emerged from it.

At a sign from him, the palanquin bearers and the Kalamukhas stood aside.

With his glance raking Vanathi from head to toe, he said, 'How strange! Is this a dream? Is it not the Kodumbalur Princess who stands before me? Is it not Vanathi, the beloved daughter of Siriya Velar who died on the Ilankai battlefield?'

'Yes. But ayya! Is this a dream? Is it not Anbil Aniruddha Brahmarayar, who inspires awe and reverence from the people of the Chozha realm that stands before me? The chief minister held in intimate regard by the emperor?'

'Amma! I am happy that you recognize me. This makes my job easy. Nor would I have to give you much trouble.'

'Ah! Please do not regard it. I will not mind enduring any trouble for a minister like you. In fact, I will not consider it trouble at all.'

'Your words give me great satisfaction. I don't wish to bother you. I am going to ask you one or two questions. It will be enough if you answer them. After that . . .'

'Ayya! Before you question me, I have a few questions to ask.'

'Ask me, amma, don't hesitate. I am like a father to you. A few days ago, I met your uncle Bhooti Vikramakesari in Mathottam. He asked me to treat you as my daughter. I promised to do so.'

'Father, I thank you! I lost my father when I was a child. Once, the emperor promised to be a father to me. Now you have given me the same assurance. What more do I need?'

'Be quick with your questions, amma. The sky is turning black, darkness surrounds us. It looks like rain.'

'Father, was it you who had these Kalamukhas seize me on the road and bring me here by force? Was it you who ordered the hands of a helpless girl be torched? These terrible men made this accusation. I did not believe them.'

'Child, what they said is true. It was I who gave them that order. If that was a crime, it is I who am responsible for it.'

'Ayya! You astonish me when you say, "If that was a crime". You are renowned in the three worlds as the chief minister of the Chozha empire. You are learned in all the sacred treatises of law and justice. You bear the responsibility of maintaining law and order in the Chozha empire. You have the right to censure the emperor himself should he act unjustly, and demand that he follow the rules of justice. Who is to determine if an act is right or wrong if you cannot do it? If you don't know whether it is right or wrong to forcibly abduct a girl travelling on the road and threaten her with torture, who else can provide that information? I had heard that wayfarers had nothing to fear under Sundara Chozha's rule. I had also heard that there were severe punishments for miscreants who harassed women. Is it not astonishing that you should wonder whether what happened to me was—or was not—a crime?'

Vanathi's barrage left the chief minister staggered. He did attempt to stem the tide once or twice but without success. Now, he hardened his tone to say, 'Girl! Stop! You don't have to display all your eloquence. It is not without reason that I doubted whether it was, or was not a crime. It depends on your answer. I heard that a girl who knew an important state secret was travelling on the Nagaipattinam highway. I ordered my men to stop that girl. They have carried out what they thought was my order. They could have erred. Instead of the girl involved in state intrigue, they might have seized you as you were returning after consulting the Kudantai astrologer. Daughter, tell me, is it your intention to return to Pazhaiyarai? Did the palanquin bearers take you towards Nagaipattinam by mistake? If you can prove that you were not going to Nagaipattinam to meet a man involved in machinations against the state, what they did would be a crime. And I would have played my part in it. What do you say? I will make it clearer for you. You are not going to a clandestine meeting with Prince Arulmozhi Varman in Nagaipattinam, are you?'

The princess was flabbergasted. Her wrath made her want to set the chief minister on fire. But she realized that anger would serve no purpose. And suddenly, the demure girl somehow acquired new skills in deliberation and guile. Instead of giving a plain answer, she said, 'Ayya! What are you saying? Are you accusing Prince Arulmozhi Varman of scheming against the state? Is it not a crime to speak in this manner about the emperor's beloved son? Is it not a conspiracy against the Chozha clan? Ah! Princess Kundavai must be informed about this at once.'

'Please do! Amma, if you answer my question, you won't have to endure even a moment's delay. I will myself make arrangements for you to reach the princess safely.'

'And if I don't . . .'

'There is no "don't". Amma, it is not so easy to escape from this old man. You will *have* to answer my question.'

'Chief Minister! You are all-powerful. But helpless and powerless as I am, you will not learn anything about the prince from me. Not even if my hands are to be burnt as these hellhounds threatened just now.'

'You are certainly a true daughter of the valiant Kodumbalur clan. I appreciate your strength of mind. However, what you have said is not quite true. You have already given me some information. You won't lose much by adding one more detail. It will make my job easier.'

Vanathi was startled again. Shaken, almost choking, she wondered if she had unwittingly revealed anything in her confused state. She mustered some courage by reassuring herself, 'No, the old man is trying to trick me.'

'Ayya! Should you lie with the tongue that chants the scriptures? Should Sundara Chozha's chief minister indulge in fabrications? I said nothing about the prince. But you insist I did!'

'Think, amma, think about it. It is a great mistake to believe that it is impossible to give details about things left unmentioned. Let me explain. Listen! The whole world is talking about Prince Arulmozhi Varman's death by drowning. You know it too. Citizens, officials and all others are plunged in sorrow. And yet, when I asked you about the prince, you refused to give me any information about him. From this, it can be deduced that you know that the prince is not dead. Nor did you deny that you were going to Nagaipattinam to meet him. You did not counter me with, "How can I go to see the dead prince?" Nor did you say, "I am going somewhere else." Therefore, you have already disclosed that the prince is alive and you are going to see him. There are only two details left. You must tell me where the prince is staying in Nagaipattinam and how you came to know of it. Then there will be no necessity for you to continue to talk to this old man. You can go wherever you like without an instant's delay.'

Vanathi was now completely undone. The chief minister was right. In her ignorance, she had indeed exposed the prince. Was there any atonement for her crime? Never. All she could do was give up her life.

'Ayya! You said that you were my uncle's close friend. You claimed me as a daughter. I make a request to you. I don't want to go to Nagaipattinam or Pazhaiyarai.'

'You wish to go to Kodumbalur? Fair enough. I will ensure that you reach it safely.'

'No, ayya! Not Kodumbalur. I wish to go to the other world. Please tell your men to sacrifice me on that altar over there. I am ready for it,' she said.

'Amma! I promised to fulfil your wish. If it is to the other world that you want to go, I can send you there. But before that, you will have to answer my questions.'

'Ayya! Don't torment me. I am not going to answer any questions. If you meant it when you said you see me as a daughter . . .'

'Undoubtedly. I do see you as my own daughter. You may not know how close your family is to me. Your uncle and I have been friends for forty years. But there are no considerations of family and friendship in matters of state, nor of father and daughter. Why, look at the emperor's actions. Did he not order the arrest of his own son when the son plotted against the state?'

'Ayya! Why do you talk about Ponniyin Selvan in this manner? How did he conspire against the state?'

'Oh! So you don't know! Ponniyin Selvan went to Ilankai to wage war. When our brave armies defeated the Ilankai forces, our prince made use of that opportunity to grab the Ilankai throne. Was that not a conspiracy against the state? Learning of this, the emperor ordered his arrest. The prince resisted the order and jumped into the sea to spread the false rumour of his death. He reached the shore and hid himself. You must have refused to speak because you were unaware of these details. It would be a great crime if you tried to help such a traitor to the state. Now, tell me all.'

All the rage that Vanathi had suppressed until then now welled up and exploded in an outburst. Unable to bear Ponniyin Selvan being vilified, the meek girl turned into the personification of fury as she railed at him. 'Ayya! There is no truth at all in anything you say. You have cast unjust aspersions on the prince. Our disheartened troops recouped their energy and fought bravely only because the prince joined them. The whole world knows that Ponniyin Selvan was the cause of our victory in Ilankai. The people of Ilankai grew to love him for his valour and other great personal attributes. When their king slunk away from the war to hide, they wanted to replace him with the prince. You have slandered a man of integrity who rejected the throne offered to him by the monks of the Buddha order. When he learnt about his father's order, the prince willingly started for Tanjavur. He did not jump into the sea for any other reason than to save his dear friend's life. Nor did he conspire against the emperor. I don't know why my ears are so unfortunate as to be forced to hear these insults.'

Aniruddha Brahmaryar chuckled as he remarked, 'Girl! Do you know, those who heard your passionate defence of the prince would conclude that you were lovers.'

'Ayya! What you said is half true. I have lost my heart to him. I don't wish to hide this from you. But there is no reason for him to have any feelings for an orphaned girl like me. The anril bird may fall in love with the moon shining in the sky. But the moon would not even know of the bird's existence.'

'Ah! I had not known that my dear friend's daughter was such a connoisseur of poetry. After all, are you not the intimate companion of Princess Kundavai?'

'Enough. Enough. No compliments, please! Either let me go on my way or call your men and give them the order.'

'Wait, girl. You know so many details about Ponniyin Selvan. Therefore, you must certainly know where he is now. Give me just that bit of information. I will send you to your uncle at once. He is returning from Ilankai. By now, he must be in Madurai.'

'Ayya! My uncle is no friend of someone so full of malevolence. I spoke only of what everyone knows about the prince. You can't extract anything more from me. Don't waste any more time.'

'I shouldn't. Looks like a downpour is imminent.'

'Downpour? People like you would draw thunder, lightning and the apocalyptic floods.'

In accordance with Vanathi's statement, a long and dazzling streak of lightning leapt from one corner of the sky to the other. As soon as it vanished and the darkness plunged in, thunder resounded in a stupendous burst that shook the heavenly bodies in the cosmos.

'Girl, you will not tell me the whereabouts of Ponniyin Selvan?'

'No.'

'My guess has been confirmed. You are going to deliver a secret message to him. True or false?'

'Ayya, you are wasting time. I will not answer you.'

'In that case, there is no option but to give you the punishment reserved for those who conspire against the state.'

'I am waiting to accept that punishment. I can place my head on the sacrificial altar at your command.'

'Chee! Chee! You are the daughter of the Kodumbalur clan. You cannot be given such a trifling punishment. There! Do you see the elephant?'

Vanathi looked at where he pointed. An elephant stood there like a black hill, shaped out of black rock and painted with black ink. Two white tusks, long and curved, highlighted its blackness.

'Girl! Have you not heard the story of the elephant's salvation? Hearing the elephant's cry for help, lord Vishnu came rushing to kill the crocodile and liberate the beast. In return, this elephant has brought deliverance to any number of people by sending them to the world where Vishnu dwells. Did you not say that you wished to leave this world and move to the next? This elephant will fulfil your wish in the blink of an eye. If it picks you up with its trunk and flings you, you will go straight up to land in the higher world,' said Chief Minister Aniruddha Brahmarayar and ended with a laugh. That laugh left Vanathi horrified. She thought that the minister was not a man at all, he was the devil incarnate.

He spoke again, 'Girl! I am asking you for the last time. Will you tell me about Ponniyin Selvan or should this elephant send you to the higher world?'

'Ayya! Will the elephant come to me or should I go to him?' asked Vanathi in a peremptory tone.

The chief minister made a sign and said something in a language that Vanathi could not understand. The earth shook under the elephant's stride. It came to Vanathi, twisted its trunk around her soft, flowerlike body and raised it above the ground.

In those few seconds, several thoughts rushed through Vanathi's mind. She was astonished by her own courage. Princess Kundavai used to often call her timid and cowardly. How surprised she would be if she could see Vanathi now! Surely, one day she would learn about this incident, about how Vanathi died fearlessly for Ponniyin Selvan. She would certainly tell the prince about it. What would the prince think of her then? Would it make him realize that the daughter of Kodumbalur Velar was braver than the boatwoman?

The elephant's trunk rose very, very slowly. Vanathi rose with it. 'What that demon of a minister said was true,' she told herself. 'This elephant is going to send me straight to the other world. In the next moment, it is going to toss me. I don't know how far I will be thrown but I will not be conscious when I fall. I would have lost my life.'

Now Vanathi was above the elephant's head. She closed her eyes. The elephant raised its trunk. At that moment, by god's grace, Vanathi lost consciousness.

40

Anaimangalam

One of our heroines has the habit of frequently falling into a swoon. We plead with our readers to forgive her just this once, for her cure is almost at hand.

When Vanathi regained consciousness, she wondered if she was swaying on a swing or drifting in the vast firmament. She heard the resonant tapping of the raindrops. Puffs of cool breeze blew over her body, making it tremble. It was dark all around. Lightning flashed intermittently. 'Well,' she thought, 'I am soaring into the sky through the clouds.'

She faintly recalled the chief minister telling her about the elephant's deliverance and then its trunk twisting around her. So, his words had come true. Her life on earth was over. She was going to the other world to see gods and goddesses.

But she would not find the god of her heart among them. How pointless to reach a world so unpleasing?

What was this swaying movement? Her body was being bumped up and down, but her head rested on something soft and cosy, like a mother's lap. Why, it was like the lap of the princess who gave her more than a mother's love. What would Kundavai Devi be doing in Pazhaiyarai? Would she have received news of Vanathi by now?

It was good to journey to the other world across the sky and through the clouds. But what was the mode of travel? *Pushpaka vimanam*, the aerial chariot of the heavens? Or the *Airavata* elephant of Indra, king of the gods? O my god! The very word 'elephant' evoked trepidation. The elephant and its waving trunk! How powerful it was! But all that was over now. Why fear it any more? Or worry?

But what was this, as soft as silk, that her head was resting on? It was too dark to see. When Vanathi moved her hand, she touched something that felt like a slightly wet silken curtain.

What was that? Who was touching her cheeks with hands as tender as jasmine blossoms?

'Vanathi! Vanathi!'

'Akka! Is it you?'

'Yes, who else can it be?'

'Are you also coming with me to the world above?'

'What's the hurry? Have you become sick of this world so soon?'

'Then where are we going?'

'Have you forgotten it already? Don't you know that we are going to Anaimangalam?'

'Where? Say it again!'

'This is too much! We are riding on an elephant to Anaimangalam.'

'Ayyo! Elephant?'

'Crazy girl! Why are you trembling? Has the very word "elephant" started frightening you?'

'Akka, did I fall asleep some time ago?'

'Yes, yes. The luxury of travelling on the elephant's back made you fall blissfully asleep.'

'Bliss? No, Akka. I had nightmares.'

'That's what I thought. You babbled quite a bit.'

'What did I babble about?'

'*Kalamukha*, *sacrifice*, *elephant*, *elephant's trunk*, you said! Then you cursed the chief minister soundly. He certainly deserves it. He would lose many nights' sleep if he heard you hurling curses at him.'

'Akka, was it all really a dream?'

'Real dream? False dream? What do I know about your dreams?'

'The Kalamukhas seized me. The chief minister asked me about the prince. I refused to tell him. He commanded the elephant to throw me to my death. I remained resolute and undaunted. Akka! I thought of you and wished you could have seen me making a courageous stand.'

'Well, I am happy you were brave, at least in your dreams.'

After some moments of silence, Vanathi said, 'I can't believe it.'

'What?'

'That what I saw was a dream.'

'Some dreams are like that. They appear to be real. I have had such dreams, several times.'

'Like what? Please tell me.'

'My brother often appears in my dreams. So many months have passed since he left for Ilankai. But at night, when I close my eyes, he stands there, exactly as though he was with me, in the flesh.'

'You are lucky, Akka!'

'Well, it is you who will have to rejoice in my luck. You don't know how my heart is writhing from the moment we had news of him jumping into the ocean.'

'Is it not a nightmare? Is this news really true?'

'How wonderful it would be if it were a nightmare! But it is true, Vanathi! The man who witnessed it came to tell us about it. How can it be disbelieved?'

'You mean the warrior of the Vaanan clan. Did he not say something else about the prince? Something about a boatwoman and the Chudamani Viharam at Nagaipattinam?'

'You must have dreamt it all. Yes, you did babble about the Chudamani Viharam and the boatwoman Poonkuzhali. You even declared that you were going to become a Buddhist nun. Why have you developed such an early aversion to life? Why should you renounce the world?'

'Akka! Don't you know my heart? What kind of life do I have in this world after hearing that the sea has taken him? I wish the elephant had really flung me to my death as it did in my dream.'

'Wretch! What about my plight if you too were to die?'

'Your case is different, Akka, you . . .'

'Yes, your love for Arulmozhi is greater than mine!'

'Akka! That's not what I'm saying. I don't have your mental strength. After his death . . .'

'Chee chee! What are you saying? Why should you say he is dead? Do you know it for certain? The Pazhuvettaraiyars, the Pazhuvur queen and that simpleton Madhurantakan will exult in saying so. Why should you and I say it, or even think it?'

'Then, what are you saying? What else could happen after jumping into the sea during the cyclone? Would he not be here by now if he had survived?'

'Crazy girl! Does jumping into the sea mean drowning?'

'After all these days, wouldn't we have known if he had reached the shore?'

'Do you know what happened to my father? In his youth, his whereabouts remained unknown for months. Relentless searches led to his being found and brought back to be installed as the crown prince. My grandfather, Arinjaya Chozha, disappeared after the war in Takkolam. Only after several years was he rediscovered. Listen to me, Vanathi. Once, mother Kaveri saved my brother's life. This time too, the sea king would have taken him to the shore. There are many small islands between Ilankai and our shores. Arulmozhi could have taken shelter in one of them. I started on this journey with you only to motivate people to make a thorough search for him. You seem to remember nothing of this matter. Not your fault. Your mind is addled since we had news of the prince. Only now have you started speaking a little more coherently.'

After a pause, Vanathi said, 'Akka, to which town are we going?'

'Anaimangalam.'

'Where is it?'

'On the seashore, close to Nagaipattinam. The Chudamani Viharam that you blabbered about as you were dreaming is at a short distance from Anaimangalam. Convenient, if you should want to become a Buddhist nun. But don't be in a hurry. You can decide after we get some definite news about Ponniyin Selvan,' Kundavai said and gave a small laugh.

'Akka! How do you manage to laugh? How do you have the heart to laugh? Are you convinced that the prince is alive?'

'Would I look like this if I didn't? Vanathi, all the predictions I have looked into will not turn out to be false. The lines tracing the conch and discus on my brother's palms will not prove to be meaningless. Everything has turned out well until now.'

'What has turned out well? I don't understand.'

'How will you understand? Your mind is becoming unhinged. The predictions of disasters overtaking Arulmozhi in his youth have come true. The rest must follow.'

'Rest . . . ?'

'I have said it many times. You have heard it all. Why do you ask me to repeat it? Go to sleep. Let's see what the morning brings.'

Vanathi was lost in thought. Then she asked, 'Are we going to travel on this elephant all night long? Why, Akka?'

'Don't you remember? If we travel during the day, the people will surround us and ask, "Where is Ponniyin Selvan? Where is the precious son of the Chozha land?" They will accuse the Pazhuvettaraiyars, curse the Pazhuvur queen. They may even blame the emperor. Why should we hear all those allegations? The Pazhuvettaraiyars may even say that it was I who instigated the people. That is why I started in the night.

I told you this even before we left Pazhaiyarai. But you are asking me again. You have certainly lost control of your mind! We must consult the monks in the Chudamani Viharam to find a way to cure your madness. Never mind. Go to sleep now. I am feeling sleepy. Tonight, we will have to sleep on this swaying hillock.'

Vanathi decided to stop talking. Her mind was in a state of confusion. One by one, she recalled every incident that had occurred on that day. They seemed to have really taken place. She thought, 'I am not mad, it is Akka who is trying to drive me mad.' Despite her recurrent attempts, she could not remember what happened after the elephant began to raise her with its trunk. Her Akka must have come to save her when her life had been in danger. The chief minister must have been terrified to see the princess. And yet, was it so easy to save someone entwined in an elephant's trunk? Perhaps . . . could it be . . . Was this the elephant that had lifted her? Though it had been dark, she had seen the seat on its back. The princess could have been seated behind the curtain. Instead of flinging her away, the elephant could have deposited her on the seat. Vanathi had seen elephants being trained to do this many times. Had the chief minister and the princess conspired to do this? Why? To prevent her from travelling alone. The princess could have done this to test Vanathi's courage. Earlier, had she not tested Vanathi with a stuffed crocodile?

Vanathi decided to let it be. Her starting on a journey by herself was a big mistake. How soothing it was to rest her head on Akka's lap! Akka's words restored her zest and courage. There was no doubt at all that Ponniyin Selvan was safe somewhere. Would she perhaps meet him at the end of the journey? The thought triggered boundless excitement in Vanathi's heart. Ardour enveloped her, in stark contrast to her earlier apathy.

The elephant ambled on in all its majesty.

The seat on its back swayed to and fro.

A posse of guards marched before and behind the beast.

The rain dwindled to a drizzle and stopped altogether.

The clouds in the sky scattered and dispersed.

The stars peeped out.

Vanathi looked at the stars above.

She wondered whether there could be anything to connect the stars wandering in the sky with the lives that people led on earth.

Could there be any truth in what the astrologers said about the compatibility of the stars' ascendant at the time of Ponniyin Selvan's birth and her own?

As predicted by stargazers and believed by the princess, could the son to be born from her womb rule the three worlds?

Would the popular belief that the comet was the harbinger of bad tidings turn out to be true?

In what way? Was it Ponniyin Selvan getting drowned?

Would he return as Akka believed he would?

In that case, what other disaster was likely to occur?

After mulling over such speculations for a long while, Vanathi dropped into a light doze.

The day broke when she opened her eyes.

Birds sang morning melodies.

The princess was awake. Drawing the silk curtain, she looked out and announced, 'We have reached Anaimangalam. We are at the entrance of the Chozha palace.'

Both princesses dismounted and entered the palace with the maids waiting to conduct them. Finally, they came to the lower level to stand under the ornamental arch from where they looked at the waterway flowing into the sea.

'Akka, you said you were going to intensify the search for the prince. What have you done about it?' asked the Kodumbalur princess.

'Yes, Vanathi. The search has begun. Look there! A boat! Those who are in it may bring some news.'

Vanathi turned to see a small boat that was approaching through the overhanging branches. It had two people in it.

'Akka, who is on that boat?' Vanathi asked.

'The man who is rowing is Sendan Amudan, whom we released from the Tanjavur dungeons on that day. The person seated is Poonkuzhali.'

Vanathi's body quivered.

'Akka! I don't want to see that girl. I am going in.'

'Why are you so scared of her? Will she swallow you whole? I will take care of it. Stay, and don't be afraid.'

The boat was coming closer.

* * *

How did Vanathi escape from the elephant's trunk? Her second surmise was the correct one. The elephant did not lift her to throw her but to place her gently on the seat on its back. Kundavai, who had been waiting behind the curtain, received Vanathi in her arms and put her on her lap.

Then the chief minister too got into his palanquin. 'Devi, may I take my leave? May your journey and its end be pleasant.'

'Ayya, many thanks for all your help,' Kundavai answered.

'You called the Kodumbalur girl a coward. I have never seen anyone with a stronger will.'

'She had been quite a coward. It is only recently that she has acquired courage.'

'It must be your training. The girl will think of me as a barbarian. Never mind. So many people have their own impressions of me. I don't worry about it. Go on your way, amma.'

Accompanied by four guards, the chief minister's palanquin went westward. The elephant, horses and other members of the entourage started moving towards the east.

* * *

It started raining. Unmindful of the rain, the chief minister's retinue continued to march.

The rains decreased and the drizzling stopped. The palanquin came to a sudden halt.

'Why have you stopped?' the chief minister asked.

'Swami! Looks like someone is lying under that tree,' said the guard in front.

The chief minister stared hard at the spot to which he pointed. There was a sudden flash of lightning.

'Yes, someone seems to be lying there. Let me see,' the minister said.

When he got out of the palanquin and approached the man, he could hear him groaning.

'Who are you?' Aniruddha Brahmarayar demanded.

A faint voice asked, 'Chief minister?'

'Yes, but who are you?'

'Ayya, can't you see? It is me, Madhurantakan.'

'Prince! What is this? How did you get here? What happened?' asked the chief minister in agitation as he tried to prop him up.

41

Madhurantakan's Gratitude

Madhurantakan screamed the moment the chief minister touched him. 'Ayyo! I am dead. Don't touch me. My legs! Gone! Gone!'

The minister stopped trying to raise him. He asked anxiously, 'Prince, what has happened to you? Your leg?'

'My legs are broken. I can't walk. I can't stand up!'

The chief minister gave the order, 'Bring the palanquin here.' To the prince, he said, 'Ayya! How did you get into this accident? What is the reason for you to be lying here, alone, in the rain? Where are the guards who accompanied you? How dare they leave you alone and go away? No punishment would be sufficient for them.'

'Chief minister, don't punish anyone. It's not anyone's fault. It was I who started out in the evening on my horse, alone. I was riding by the riverbank. Suddenly it started raining. There was a huge lightning flash followed by thunder.

The horse took fright and bolted. I got caught in a branch and fell down. The horse got away. I don't know if my leg has been broken or sprained by the fall. Fortunately, you came by.'

'It is due to the good deeds done by your father, the great soul Gandaraditta, that I happened to be here. Please grit your teeth and bear the pain as I put you into the palanquin. I will ask you more about this when we reach my house in Nathan Koil,' Aniruddha Brahmarayar said.

The palanquin was brought closer and the chief minister raised the prince slowly and made him recline inside. He ordered the bearers to carry the palanquin gently and steadily as he walked beside it.

In a short while, they reached the chief minister's mansion beside the temple. Madhurantakan was carried in and laid on a bed. Under the light of a lamp, it became clear that the leg had suffered a sprain, not a fracture.

The prince's fears too were somewhat allayed.

Both ate the offerings from the Vishnu temple.

Then the chief minister said, 'Prince, sleep in peace. Let us take whatever steps you find appropriate in the morning. I am going to Tanjavur. If you come with me, I will make sure that you reach Tanjavur safely.'

'Ayya, you have done me all kinds of harm. But you have atoned for them and I will never forget your coming to my aid today. I will always show my gratitude to you. If I ascend the Chozha throne, I will retain you as my chief minister,' Madhurantakan said.

Feigning astonishment, Aniruddha Brahmarayar replied, 'Prince! I am duty-bound to serve the Chozha empire. It is my job to counsel and help as far as I can all those who belong to the Chozha clan. Therefore, there is no need for you to convey any personal gratitude to me. But I don't understand what you mean when you mention my doing you some kind of harm. I don't remember having harmed you intentionally. However, suitable atonement can be made if you graciously let me know more about it.'

'Ayya, the world knows you as an extremely clever man, an expert in diplomacy. But you don't have to show off your skills to me. Don't think that I do not know how brutally you have harmed me. I am going to forget about it in the light of the help you rendered today. Tell me how I can show my gratitude. Tell me if there is anything I can do in return.'

Aniruddha Brahmarayar smiled and said, 'Yes, prince. There *is* a boon that this old man would crave from you. Do not go riding alone ever again. Take a chariot, with your retinue around you. And then, perhaps, a palanquin would serve you best. The times are bad. The people are seething. You saw this in Pazhaiyarai today. Therefore, a curtained palanquin would be a good choice. It would be particularly wise to use the Pazhuvur queen's palanquin.'

Madhurantakan was dumbfounded. Once again, his face showed traces of fear. After taking a little time to overcome it, he said, 'Chief minister, what did you say? What do you mean by asking me to travel in the Pazhuvur queen's palanquin? Do you intend to insult me?'

'Prince, I did not know that you considered travelling by the Pazhuvur queen's palanquin to be shameful. Since when have you started feeling this way? You have used it frequently before. You must have come to this well-founded decision after the last time you journeyed to Kadambur.'

Madhurantakan experienced a greater dread. His face was shadowed by fear.

'Chief minister! I . . . I . . . Kadambur . . .' he stammered.

'Prince, did you not take the Pazhuvur queen's palanquin to and fro when you went to the Kadambur palace on the eighteenth day in the month of Aadi? True, I did not like it much. Palanquins are good for old men like me. It would be more appropriate for youngsters like you to ride a horse or an elephant. But proper training is required to develop equestrian skills. I will make arrangements for your lessons as soon as you recover.'

'Chief minister! Beware! Your slights offend me more and more. You have concluded that I know nothing of horsemanship merely because I had an accident today. You say that I always take the palanquin just because I used it once. I have decided to overlook this in consideration of your age and the assistance you gave me today.'

'Prince! Your patience delights me. The adage has it that "those who are patient shall rule the earth". What does the great Tamizh poet say? "The earth not only continues to bear those who delve deep but offers them crystal clear water." Those who wish to rule must possess this quality of the earth. You must show forbearance to old codgers like me even when we make inappropriate remarks.'

Madhurantakan's fear was transformed into rage. With twitching lips and knitted eyebrows, he asked, 'Ayya, what are you saying? Are you accusing me of wanting to rule the Chozha kingdom?'

But the chief minister remained unfazed. 'Prince! Why do you say that I am 'accusing' you? How can it be a crime for you to wish to rule this kingdom? You are the descendant of Vijayalaya, the warrior of warriors, you are the son of the great-souled Gandaraditta. You have every right to ascend the Chozha throne. Don't believe anyone who advises you to get involved in clandestine deals and conspiratorial efforts to claim this right. Prince! Please deign to listen to this old man. Your parents had a certain plan. You had accepted it and immersed yourself in piety. Now you have changed your mind. No one has the right to blame you for that. You can claim your right openly. You can tell the emperor about your wish. There is no need at all to go to the Kollidam banks all alone in the dark night of the new moon, in a petty attempt to petition the Kalamukha group for support. Nor is there any need to hold a meeting in Sambuvaraiyar's palace in the middle of the night as burglars do, to engage in intrigues. Please understand that people who give you such counsel are your worst enemies.'

Madhurantakan was bewildered and amazed to learn that the chief minister knew of all these affairs. At the same time, he was terrified, and that terror fuelled a growing anger.

'Ayya! How did you come to know all these things? Which traitor has acted like a friend and disclosed all this to you?'

'It would be useless for you to try to discover this. I have eyes and ears everywhere. Nothing can happen in this vast kingdom without my knowledge.'

'Does it mean that the emperor too knows it all?'

'No. He doesn't. Any number of secrets brought to me by these eyes and ears remain buried in my heart. Urgent necessity alone would bring them out into the open.'

'Yes, yes. There are so many hair-raising secrets buried in your heart. Won't the entire Chozha kingdom quake if they should come out into the open?' Madhurantakan remarked. His voice refracted more duplicity and malice than before.

The chief minister spoke as though he had not noted these shifts in Madhurantakan's tone, 'The emperor is an intimate friend of mine. But there are secrets in my heart that even he does not know. Sundara Chozha is afflicted by a grim ailment. There are many reasons for him to have been hurt already. I don't wish to wound him further by disclosing the conspiracies of the feudal chieftains. Nor has there been any need to do so. Prince, rest assured that I will never reveal anything about your activities to him.'

'Ayya! Anbil Aniruddha Brahmarayar! Why this sudden concern for poor Madhurantakan?'

'Prince, I have not developed any sudden concern for you. I have always had the same interest in you that I have for the sons of Sundara Chozha. But there had been no opportunity to show it until now.'

'Today, you had that opportunity because I fell from my horse and broke my leg. And yet, if this had happened some time ago, you would have squeezed my neck and strangled me there and then under that tree.'

'Narayana! Narayana!'

'Ayya! You need not think that I am totally ignorant. Nor need you think that I am such a simpleton as to believe everything I am told. You started plotting against me from the time I was in my mother's womb. You arranged for me to be killed the moment I was born. There! You look surprised! You cannot figure out how I came to know this. Don't imagine that you are the only man in the Chozha kingdom who knows shocking secrets.'

The chief minister's face presented a singular sight, registering expressions that changed rapidly from moment to moment. Finally, forcing himself to smile, he said, 'Yes, prince. It is true that I took pride in that conviction. Today, that pride has been shattered. But how did you survive when such an infanticide had been arranged? I will be grateful if you can reveal that secret.'

'You are testing me to see how much I know! All right. I will tell you. You had made arrangements for an infanticide. They took the newborn away in great haste without checking to see if it was a boy or a girl. When you were told that it was a girl, you decided to let it live and gave it away to be raised by a temple priest. Half an hour later, I was born. You did not expect it at all. My stars were powerful. I survived. When your plan backfired, you schemed to prevent me from ascending the throne. You arranged for me to be raised as a man of piety, in other words, a madman. Even there, you missed the mark. I did not become entirely mad. Ayya! Why are you taking this quietly? Why don't you insist that all this is untrue?'

The chief minister remained frozen. Then, managing somehow to recover his powers of speech, he said, 'Prince, what is the use of trying to prove that it is untrue when you have so many details?'

'Yes, it is useless indeed. I also know why you have developed this sudden empathy for me. You don't like Aditta Karikalan. You wanted to put Arulmozhi Varman on the Chozha throne. You have become sympathetic to me because he has drowned in the sea. And yet, I am going to forget all the harm you had done to me before. I will also show my gratitude for your help today. If you promise to be on my side, I would like to retain you as my chief minister,' Madhurantakan said.

'Prince! Your words thrill me beyond measure,' said Anbil Aniruddha Brahmarayar.

42

The Fever Subsides

Ponniyin Selvan was lying on the wooden bedstead in the chamber adjacent to the chief monk's room in the Chudamani Viharam. For three days, he had suffered from a high fever and remained mostly unconscious. He was nursed with the utmost care by the monks, who ensured his regular intake of medicines and water.

During the short spells when he was half-awake, the prince tried to find out where he was. The mural on the wall before him attracted his attention. It showed a scene that seemed palpable. It had gods and goddesses, some holding musical instruments, others bearing gleaming white whisks and state umbrellas, or trays of many-hued flowers. After viewing them over and over again, Ponniyin Selvan came to believe that he had reached the land of the heavenly beings. He also thought that the *deva, yaksha* and *kinnara* beings had assembled to welcome him. How did he reach the heavens? Through a stream flanked on both sides by dense bushes filled with golden screw pine flowers. He could recall their fragrance. He had a faint impression of having been taken into a boat and rowed across by a young god and goddess. The young god sang sweet tevaram songs. The young goddess? She did not sing. But she had looked at him with ardour and affection. The few words she spoke now and then sounded like the music of the spheres.

Where were they both now?

Monks of the Buddha faith seemed to occupy a special place in the land of the gods, guarding the pot of heavenly nectar. A monk frequently approached the prince to pour a little nectar into his mouth. The comforts of heaven did not dispel his great thirst. Why couldn't the monk give him some more to drink? Why such niggardliness even in paradise?

Perhaps nectar could not be taken in large quantities. But was it nectar at all? Or some kind of liquor? Chee chee! Would monks touch liquor? Or pour it into his mouth? But why did he feel so groggy? Why did he become unconscious soon after drinking it?

After three days of oscillating between the world of the gods and the world of oblivion, Ponniyin Selvan fully recovered his mental faculties on the fourth day, as though awakening from slumber. His body was enfeebled. But the mind was crystal clear. He realized that the figures on the wall were painted images. He knew that the deva-yaksha-kinnara beings were not waiting for him but to welcome the Buddha as he entered the heavens. On another wall, he saw lord Buddha ascending in the cloud-filled expanse of the sky. He understood that he was lying in a Buddha monastery. As he wondered which one it could be and where, he remembered the sequence of events from the time he left Ilankai. He could recall how he and Vandiyatevan were buffeted by the billowing sea and drained of all their strength. But things became inchoate after that.

Cup in hand, a monk entered his room as usual. The prince took the cup and examined its contents. He made sure that it was not nectar but a potion, perhaps mixed with milk. He asked the monk, 'Swami, what place is this? How long have I been lying here?'

The monk left without answering. The prince heard him go to the adjacent room and say, 'Acharya! The fever has gone. He is fully conscious.'

In a short time, an elderly monk came into Ponniyin Selvan's room and looked intently at the prince. Then he said with a bright face, 'Ponniyin Selvan! You are in the Chudamani Viharam in Nagaipattinam. It has been three days since you arrived here with a high fever. We were privileged to serve you.'

'I too am fortunate. I had been eager to see this Chudamani Viharam. I glimpsed it some time ago when I came to the port in this town. A blessing to be here now. Swami! Can you tell me how I happen to be here?'

'Prince, please drink the medicine. I will tell you what I know,' said the monk.

The prince swallowed the medicine and said, 'This is no potion, it is nectar from the heavens. You have taken enormous pains to nurse me. But I am not going to thank you for that.'

The chief monk smiled and said, 'Prince, nor is there any necessity for you to show gratitude. The Buddha has said that serving the sick is the greatest dharma. The Buddha's faith commands that even sick animals are to be nursed. Nursing you is nothing special. We are deeply indebted to the Chozha clan. Your father, Emperor Sundara Chozha, and your sister, Princess Kundavai, have given great support to the Buddha's creed. We also know how you have organized the renovation of our monasteries in Anuradhapuram. We don't expect any thanks from you for the small service we have rendered.'

'Acharya! I did not mean quite that when I spoke of gratitude. I have realized how severe my ailment has been. I have seen the plight of those who had this fever. In fact, by now I should have been in the world above where deva, yaksha and kinnara beings may have welcomed me. Today, I might have been blissfully drinking nectar with the gods and goddesses. I don't think you have done me any good by bringing me back from the threshold of heaven into this world of misery. That is why I refused to give you thanks.'

The acharya's face brightened even more as he said, 'Ponniyin Selva, when the time comes for you to go to the world above, all the gods will appear on their aerial mounts to welcome you with flowers and dundubhi drums. But that moment is still far away. There are many great deeds for you to perform on earth. Only after completing them can you consider departing to the other world.'

Ponniyin Selvan had been reclining until then. Now he sat up. A singular radiance lit up his face. Light beamed from his wide eyes and filled the entire chamber with effulgence.

'What you say is true, acharya! I do wish to accomplish great and marvellous deeds in the terrestrial world. I have seen this monastery from the outside. I am going to renovate this

Chudamani Viharam along the massive lines of the Abhayagiri Viharam in Anuradhapuram. I am going to see statues of the Buddha built here to rival the huge figures found in that city. Having seen the monuments in Anuradhapuram, even thinking of the temples in this land makes me cringe in body and mind. I am going to renovate the Siva temples in this Chozha land modelled on those monuments. I am going to build a magnificent temple in Tanjavur with a tower reaching the sky. I will make Mahadeva, its reigning deity, match it in size. The domes of the Buddha faith and the towers of the Siva temples are going to compete with each other as they rise through the clouds. Thousands of years later, our descendants born in this sacred Tamizh realm will see them and stand transfixed in wonder.'

After speaking passionately as though in a trance, the prince sank back in bed, as his body had not wholly recovered its physical strength. The chief monk supported him and slowly made him lie down again.

'Prince, in time, you will fulfil all the great work that you aspire to accomplish. But now you must stay calm and get well.'

43

The Nandi Mandapam

The acharya came to see Ponniyin Selvan the next afternoon. The prince was desperate for information. His efforts to get answers from the younger monk had not worked. The only reply he got was, 'Ayya! *Gurudeva*[*] will tell you everything.'

As soon as the acharya came, he asked the prince, 'How are you feeling now?'

'Ayya! My body is giving me a great deal of trouble, asking, "Why do you laze in bed? Get up! Run! Mount a horse! Dive into the river! Swim! Fight with the elephant! Don't take it easy!" The stomach is extremely active. The food brought by the young monk is not sufficient for its needs. Acharya! I cannot believe that I was lying unconscious and with a high fever for so many days. Your medicines have brought amazing results,' Ponniyin Selvan said.

[*] A term that equates the guru with god.

'Ayya, you must not believe everything that the body says. That is how one feels after the fever breaks. It could be fatal if the fever recurs.'

'Gurudeva, I don't care much about any danger to my life.'

'You may not. But do you know how distressed millions of people in the Chozha land have been in the past four or five days? The entire country is in a state of uproar. From little children to senior citizens, everyone has been shedding tears.'

'Ayya, I don't understand. Why should the people be distressed? Is it because they think that I will not recover from this fever? Why should they worry when they know that I am receiving medical treatment in this Chudamani Viharam?'

'Prince, no one knows this. How can peace prevail in this monastery if the townspeople knew that you fell ill and are being nursed here? They would have smashed the walls and rushed inside to see you. If you could have heard their laments on the day we had news of your having drowned in the sea . . . Why, there was none even within the viharam who did not sob and shed tears!'

Ponniyin Selvan sat up in bed. 'Gurudeva! What are you saying? I am all at sea! You had news of my drowning? When? Who brought such terrible news? Why?' he asked.

'I don't know who brought the news. One morning, it was all over town that the ship which brought you from Ilankai sank into the sea during the cyclone. The news spread everywhere that you must have drowned because your body could not be recovered despite Pazhuvettaraiyar's exhaustive search. I too was mourning when a monk informed me that a boat had arrived in the canal behind the monastery. I went to look into the matter and saw that it was you. We nursed you for three days. It was only yesterday that you gained consciousness.'

'Acharya, who brought me? Can you tell me?'

'A young man and woman.'

'Yes, yes, I remember it like a dream. Do you know them? Was the young man Vandiyatevan of the Vaanan tribe?'

'No, ayya. He said his name was Sendan Amudan. He looked like a devout follower of Siva. I did not learn the girl's name. She is someone who has physical and mental stamina.'

'I can guess her name. She is the boatwoman Poonkuzhali. Tyagavitankar's daughter. Did they not tell you why they brought me here?'

'No, prince. Nor did I ask them.'

'Did you not let anyone know that I am safe here?'

'No, ayya. Those who brought you told me not to make it public. Considering the state of your health, I too thought it best.'

'Acharya! There has been some conniving here. My father, the king, had ordered my arrest. That was why I left Ilankai. Several incidents took place along the way. This one seems to have been manoeuvred to accuse me of rebelling against my father's command. They have also fabricated the story of my drowning in the sea. Acharya! Sheltering me would be an act of sedition. Keeping me here any longer would be a major crime. Send me to Tanjavur at once.'

'Prince, I will joyfully welcome any punishment for having sheltered you, even if it is the battering down of this ancient Chudamani Viharam.'

'I appreciate your kindness. But, gurudeva, how did you take me in without making any enquiries from the people who brought me?'

'Where was the need for any enquiry? What higher duty could there be for monks like me than to nurse you when you had a high fever? Moreover, your elder sister, Princess Kundavai, had informed me earlier that you might come to stay here for a few days.'

'Oh! Is that so? The princess sent a message to you? When?'

'A few days before you arrived. Sendan Amudan who brought you here also said that it was the princess' wish.'

'Gurudeva! Did those who brought me here leave immediately? Would it be possible to locate them? I must get more details from them.'

'Ayya, don't get flustered. They are both still in town. They come once a day to enquire about your condition. Somehow they have not been here today, until now.'

The young monk entered and made a sign to the master, who went out with him after assuring the prince that he would return soon. When he returned in a short while, he saw that the prince's excitement had mounted.

'Acharya! I cannot stay here a moment longer. I don't want to hide and shoulder the blame for disobeying the king's command. Nor do I wish any harm to come to this ancient Chudamani Viharam because of me.'

The elderly monk said with a beaming face, 'Truly, I too cannot shoulder such a huge responsibility any more. Not for a moment do I wish to keep you here against your will. You can leave at once. The boat is waiting in the stream.'

'And go where?'

'That is something you must decide. The two people who left you here have come to take you.'

The prince hung back for a moment. The mysterious smile on the acharya's face made him wonder if there was some deception involved.

'So both are back? Did they not tell you why they are here?'

'Yes. At half an hour's distance, there is a Nandi mandapam, the pavilion of the bull, beside the stream. Two women are waiting for you there.'

The prince sprang out of bed. 'Acharya! Take me to the boat at once. So much time has been wasted already.'

The acharya supported the prince as he took him to the stream, but there was nothing in the prince's stride to indicate that he had been sick and bedridden for four days. Sendan Amudan and Poonkuzhali were elated to see Ponniyin Selvan's majestic strides as he approached them.

As soon as the prince was seated on the boat, the acharya said, 'Ayya, all the monks of the Chudamani Viharam would deem it their great fortune to serve you. It would be wise for you to return and stay for another week to regain your strength.'

'Gurudeva, I too feel that I will return. Otherwise, I would not be leaving in such a hurry, without taking leave of all the monks,' said the prince.

When the boat started to move, Ponniyin Selvan said to Sendan Amudan and Poonkuzhali, 'When you brought me through this channel, I thought that you two belonged to the world of gods and were taking me there. Instead, you deceived me and left me in a monastery. Never mind. I must ask you about everything that transpired from the time I got exhausted in battling with the waves. But first, tell me who is waiting for me in the Nandi mandapam.'

Though Arulmozhi Varman addressed his question to both, Poonkuzhali did not open her mouth. It was Sendan Amudan who explained that Kundavai Devi and the Kodumbalur princess had come to Anaimangalam and were waiting at the pavilion.

'Ah! Why has the princess brought the girl who faints in fits and starts?'

Sendan Amudan replied, 'Ayya, a new fever is spreading among the girls in the Tamizh country. They are talking about abandoning the Saiva cult to join the Buddha's creed and turn into nuns.'

'Who are they?'

'The Kodumbalur princess. This wonderful lass as well.'

'Amuda! Just two? No loss to the Saiva faith. I know several nunneries in Ilankai where women lead lives of penance. If they like, I can get them admitted there.' Ponniyin Selvan's words made Sendan Amudan chuckle.

Then he recounted everything he knew from the time Vandiyatevan and the prince reached the shore. Ponniyin Selvan listened eagerly, comparing his memories with Amudan's account.

'There! The Nandi mandapam!' said Poonkuzhali. The prince looked at where she pointed.

44

The Nandi Grows

The boat was making its way between the banks that were high on both sides when Poonkuzhali pointed to the pavilion with a flight of steps. Two sculpted figures of Nandi, the sacred bull, stood on either side of the topmost step, so exquisitely carved and lifelike that they could be gazed at all day. The pavilion was named after them. Once a year, during the spring festival, when the temple deities Kayarohana and Nilayadakshi were showcased in the pavilion, the people came in droves to witness the festivities and picnicked there by moonlight. Located at some distance from the town, the pavilion did not attract visitors at other times.

The boat approached the pavilion. Once he saw the two women there, the prince had no eyes for anything else.

The princess came down to the lowest step while Vanathi stood behind a pillar, half-hidden.

The boat stopped at the steps. Sendan Amudan and the princess helped the prince get out of the boat.

Sendan Amudan and Poonkuzhali took the boat to wait at a short distance.

Tenderly, in a voice moistened with tears, Kundavai said, 'Tambi! You have become so thin!'

Ponniyin Selvan said, 'Never mind my health. Akka, your face blooms like a flower when you see me. Why is it drooping now? Why is it clouded? Why are your eyes welling up with tears? Many painful things must have occurred to wound you to the core. Otherwise, you would not have sent me that letter in such haste.'

Kundavai said, 'Yes, tambi! So many things to share with you and learn from you, and quickly. I know you have rejected the Ilankai throne, but please do occupy this throne of stone for now.'

Ponniyin Selvan touched his sister's feet with his hands and placed them over his eyes before taking his seat. Her eyes brimming with more tears, Kundavai placed her hand on his head and kissed his forehead.

Both had seated themselves before Kundavai said, 'Tambi! I should not have had you brought here today. The head monk of the Chudamani Viharam sent word that you had recovered completely. That is not true. The fever has drained you. But I could not wait. After reaching Anaimangalam, every moment seemed like an age.'

'Akka, don't regret bringing me here. Had you not sent the boat today, I would have left for Pazhaiyarai. Even when I had a high fever, it was your letter that distressed me. I have never seen anyone as audacious as that warrior of the Vaanan clan who brought it to me. I tested him in different ways. He passed every one of them. Where is he, Akka?'

Some of the shadows left Kundavai's face. Her rosy lips parted in a gleaming smile. 'Tambi, why should you bother about him now, when there are so many other things to worry about?' she asked.

'Why do you say that, Akka? Did he do anything to displease you?'

'No, no. Why should I be displeased? He promised to bring you to me. He kept his word.'

'I am astonished to think of all the tricks and subterfuges he deployed to achieve that. Where is he, Akka? I thought he would have accompanied you. Instead, this great lady who faints at every opportunity is here.'

'Tambi, you don't know how brave she has become. Yesterday, our elephant picked her up with its trunk and threw her. True, I was seated on the elephant and it threw her into my lap. But she didn't know that. If you had seen her courage at that moment . . .'

'Enough! Stop singing your friend's praises. Tell me about *my* friend.'

'What can I say about him? His work was over. He has returned to Aditta Karikalan, his master.'

'If that is so, he has broken his word. Did he not say that he would remain in the Chozha country and not go back to Kanchi?'

'How is that possible? What can he do here? Even those who belong to the Chozha country are uncertain about their future. If you are so fond of him, it may be possible to tell the emperor to give him the domain ruled by his ancestors.'

'What will the great warrior do with such a paltry domain?'

'He will do what all the feudal lords do. You think he would reject it as you rejected the Ilankai kingdom?'

With a little smile, the prince said, 'Akka, I rejected the Ilankai kingdom before witnesses. And yet, father has accused me and ordered my arrest.'

'No such order would have been issued had you accepted the kingdom. You would have become an independent king. Then who could arrest you?'

'Should I have done it against my father's wishes?'

'Ponniyin Selva! Father would have been happy if you had done it. He would have found peace in dividing the rest of the kingdom between your brother and Madhurantakan. Even now, efforts are being made to create two kingdoms, one to the north and the other to the south of the river Kollidam. Father believes that you would be of help in achieving this partition. He ordered your arrest only because you did not come when summoned earlier. The emperor knows very well that you rejected the Ilankai kingdom.'

'Never will I help to partition the kingdom. There is no greater crime than that. It would be better to give the whole to Uncle Madhurantakan.'

'That means you and the chief minister are of the same opinion.'

'Yes. He came to Ilankai only to discuss it with me. Shall I tell you the true reason for refusing the Ilankai kingdom?'

'Tambi! With whom can you share it, if not me?'

'Yes, there is no one else with whom I may share my inmost thoughts. Akka, I had this inflated impression about the magnitude of the Ilankai kingdom. Only when I went there did I realize what a small country it is. You can go from east to west, right across the kingdom, in a single day, by horse or elephant.'

'Is the Chozha kingdom any bigger? Is it not possible to cross it on horseback in a single day?'

'The Chozha country is small too. That is why I will say no to the Chozha crown if someone should offer it to me. Those who divided this sacred Tamizh land into Chozha, Chera and Pandya dominions committed a great crime. That is why, though great men of valour have been born here, this land has not achieved greatness. In the north, emperors like Chandragupta, Asoka, Vikramaditya and Harshavardhana ruled over vast empires. Has anyone established such a huge empire in the Tamil realm? The Pallava dynasty of Kanchi did produce Mahendra and Mamalla, after which the clan became enfeebled. Akka, if I were to rule, it would not be over a tiny kingdom. I will rule over a kingdom that is deep-rooted and wide-ranged, spreading from the Ilankai island to the river Ganga. I will be seated on the throne of a magnificent Chozha empire with the tiger flag flying in lands far away, including islands like the Maldives and Java. I am sure you think I am raving mad.'

'No, Arulmozhi! I am delighted to find that you are just like me in spinning dreams and building castles in the air. If you are insane, I am even more insane. I know that our grandfather, Emperor Parantaka, had indulged in such flights of fancy. They did not wholly come true in his time. But I am going to see it fulfilled in my lifetime. I am going to die only after seeing the Chozha kingdom expanding from Ilankai to the Ganga, from the Maldives to Java. I thought this ambition of mine would be fulfilled by my elder brother, Aditta Karikalan. No longer. Aditta Karikalan is a mighty warrior, but he cannot accomplish great things because he does not possess the power to keep his mind under control. However, I continue to nourish the hope of fulfilling my ambition through you. If that fails, I will still not despair. I am determined that it will be realized by your son. I will take your son the day he is born and raise him to become an indomitable warrior, with the kind of valour hitherto unknown to the world. I will turn him into a lionheart who remains undistracted by petty desires and performs miracles.'

'Akka! You must be crazier than me. I have absolutely no intention of getting married. And here you are, talking about my son yet to be born. If one of your pampered companions has fancies of wearing the crown and sitting on the throne by marrying me, well, it is never going to happen. Please tell them so, squarely and clearly.' As Ponniyin Selvan spoke, he glanced at Vanathi for a split second as she stood behind the pillar. The next instant, he turned his face away to look at the bull sculpture in front of him.

'Akka, here's the thing. Though Ilankai may be a small kingdom, its past rulers were great men with large hearts. They made mammoth plans and accomplished stupendous tasks. To honour the Buddha, they built monuments that reached the clouds. They constructed shrines with thousand, two thousand chambers. They put up pavilions with ten thousand pillars. To manifest his inordinate glory, they created figures of the Buddha as tall as the coconut tree you see there! But look at the bull before us. How small it is! Would Nandi, the mount of a measureless god, be so tiny? How can the divine bull standing guard at the gates, control Siva's retinue of spooks and goblins if he is so small in size? Akka! Look! Right now, this Nandi grows before my eyes! It rises higher and higher and higher until it becomes a gigantic figure whose head bumps into the pavilion's ceiling and breaks through. The whole roof is gone now. Nandi fills the skies. The ghouls and goblins arrive. Awestruck, they stand in reverence before the divine bull and beg for an audience with Siva. With so colossal a Nandi, how vast must be the temple that houses his master? Should it not tower like Meru mountain of the south? Should it not have corridors in proportion to that size? The temples of Siva in the Chozha kingdom today are perfect for the dwarf sage Agastya, not lord Siva. I don't want territories and kingdoms. I will request whoever sits on the throne to appoint me as the officer in charge of the temple development board.'

'Tambi! We might as well compete with each other to see who is more insane. The Chozha land is surrounded by great perils. It is threatened by foes within and without, and by foes who pretend to be friends. I have been having recurrent nightmares for some time now. A sharp, dazzling, lethal sword appears before my inner eye. It is going to fall on someone . . . on whom, I don't know . . . I cannot figure out if someone belonging to the Chozha race is going to be its prey or whether the sword will cut this Chozha kingdom into two. You and I must give thought to this, and make efforts to avert this catastrophe,' said the princess.

'Yes, Akka! Vandiyatevan's disclosures make me agree with you. You know from whom the worst danger to the Chozha clan is to be expected, don't you?' asked the prince.

'Tambi, don't you mean the young queen of Pazhuvur?'

'Yes, Akka. You know who she really is . . .'

'I learnt it from the details Vandiyatevan gave me. That is why I made such haste to come and see you,' said Kundavai.

45

Vanathi in Peril

'Akka! Do you remember my falling into the Kaveri when I was five years old? Do you remember mother Kaveri saving me before she disappeared?' Arulmozhi Varman asked.

'What a question, tambi! How could I have forgotten it? It is that incident which led to your being celebrated as "Ponniyin Selvan",' Kundavai said.

'In Ilankai, I saw mother Kaveri who had saved me . . . Akka! Why don't you say something? Aren't you surprised?'

'Not surprised, tambi, but eager to know more. Tell me all about her.'

'I cannot tell you everything in a single day. But I will share the most important details. She not only saved me from the Kaveri floods but several times in Ilankai as well. Saving my life is not such a big thing. So many people save others' lives by chance. However, her love for me is unequalled. Why, even the love you have for me comes second.'

'You need not hesitate to say that. My love for you is not so pure after all. Tambi, I will admit that it is motivated by self-interest. I will confess that the glory of the Chozha empire comes first for me. My affection for you is contingent upon your serving that cause. My love may turn to hate if you hinder me in achieving that goal. But that mute woman's love is of a different kind altogether. She has showered on you all the love that had been surging in her heart for our father, for over twenty years. Nothing in any world can equal that.'

'How did you know this, Akka?'

'Know what, tambi?'

'That she is our stepmother.'

'I deduced it from what my father and Vandiyatevan told me. Tambi, does she think you are her own son or the son of a co-wife?'

'Why should you make this distinction when such a thought has never occurred to her or to me?'

'Tambi, our mother sits on the throne that she should have occupied. Would it not be exceptional if she loved you despite being aware of it?'

'She must know that I am not the child of her womb. Would she not know that I was born some years after she had given birth to her child? She cannot speak, she cannot say what is in her heart. I learnt what I could from the pictures she drew. Never mind the love she bears me. My heart melts when I think of her love for our father. Akka, did father resemble me when he was young?'

'No, tambi, no. At your age, our father was so good-looking that they say the god of love paled in comparison. The Chozha clan is famous for valour, not beauty. Our grandfather Arinjaya married the peerless Kalyani of the Vaidumbarayar clan. She seemed to be made of unblemished gold, her face was as lustrous as the full moon and her loveliness enthralled the world. You have seen how beautiful grandmother Kalyani is, even now, at this age. That was the reason why our father came to be called "Sundara", the "handsome" Chozha. We are like our mother. The descendants of the Malayaman clan scorn physical beauty. They believe that beauty diminishes valour.'

'I don't know anything about the connection between beauty and valour. But I know that there is no connection at all between beauty and love. Otherwise–'

'–Otherwise, why is this girl Vanathi gazing at you unblinkingly from behind the pillar? And there in that boat, why is Sendan Amudan staring at Poonkuzhali rapturously?'

The prince smiled as he said, 'Now you have gone completely off track! I was talking about my foster mother's love for me. Never mind. Akka, is it possible for someone in this world to look exactly like another?'

'Why not? It is possible among twins. Mother and daughter may look alike at a certain age. Besides, it is possible for creation to occasionally come up with someone who looks exactly like another, totally unconnected person.'

'Can what Vandiyatevan says about the Pazhuvur queen and our foster mother looking exactly alike be true? I saw Nandini when she was a little girl, but not too often after she became the Pazhuvur queen. What do you think?'

'I have seen only the Pazhuvur queen, not our stepmother. But what Vandiyatevan said must be true. I thought so from what my father recounted to me.'

'Did father himself tell you about it? What did he say? When?'

'Vanathi and I had gone to Tanjavur a few days ago. That was when he told me about the incident in his youth. He told me about getting stranded on a little island near Ilankai and the affection shown by a mute girl there. He also spoke about King Parantaka sending men to bring him home, and how, on the day he was made crown prince, he saw her in the crowd outside the palace. In the next instant, she had vanished. He sent the chief minister to bring her back, but he returned to say that the girl had jumped to her death from the top of the lighthouse. This incident has haunted and tormented father for twenty years. He thinks of her as dead. He believes that she was so shattered by his betrayal that she killed herself. Tambi, setting aside all our fantasies for the Chozha kingdom, there is something that you and I must do for our father. You must somehow bring that lady to Tanjavur and prove to him that she is still alive. If not, our father will find no peace in this lifetime, nor hereafter.'

'Akka! I have recently been at death's door two or three times. Do you know what I thought in those moments? I regretted having to die before taking our stepmother to father. Akka! Whenever I think of her, I become greatly agitated. If she could speak, she could find solace by sharing her anguish. If she could hear, she might overcome her sorrows with words of consolation from others. Think of the plight of a woman who cannot speak nor hear! She would have to suppress all her love, ardour, grief, angst, rage and yearning. Do I need to describe the mental condition of someone whose hopes have been shattered? What is surprising then that she should be wandering in the Ilankai forests like a mad woman? Thinking about it makes me feel as though my heart would explode. I am eager to take her to father. But do you think father would like it?'

'Whether he likes it or not, it is our duty to do so. Our father screams at night believing that the spirit of that dead woman comes to torment him. That is why his condition does not improve.'

'How do you know that, Akka? Did he tell you?'

'He did, and so did my friend Vanathi.'

'Vanathi? How is she concerned in this matter? Did you tell her?'

'No, no. I will ask her to tell you in her own words about what she saw in the Tanjavur palace. But you have become very inconsiderate, tambi. You have forgotten all about the traditions of courtesy in the Chozha clan. You have not spoken a single word to the Kodumbalur princess. You haven't even enquired about her well-being. Is this the respect you give to the daughter of the noble Siriya Velar? Well!'

'Akka, why should I worry about Vanathi or enquire about her when she is under your care?'

'Very good! Just keep quiet for some time! Vanathi, come here. The prince wants to take a good look at you.'

Vanathi approached as though she was oblivious to the prince and said in a voice soft as silk, 'Akka! Why do you imagine things? Your brother doesn't want to look at me. His glances are confined to the boat on the stream. He seems to want to return quickly.' Perhaps she had Poonkuzhali in mind when she mentioned the boat.

The prince said with a chuckle, 'Akka! Your friend actually speaks! I thought she was mute, like some members of our family.'

'Akka! Whenever I look at him, I begin to fear that I have indeed turned dumb.'

The prince said, 'That's a very good thing. There's a man in Kodikkarai, Poonkuzhali's elder brother. He manages to stutter and stammer to others but turns dumb when he sees his wife. His family members now consider him to be truly mute.'

'This Kodumbalur girl is a bit like that. There was a time when she never could stop talking even when we begged her to do so. But since you left for Ilankai, she speaks but little. She goes off by herself and gets lost in her thoughts. Never mind. Vanathi, tell the prince everything that happened in the Tanjavur palace on that night.'

'Let the Kodumbalur princess sit before she starts speaking, Akka! Her uncle would melt to see her standing for such a long time. The general would go on enquiring about her whenever he saw me. But since you sent no information about her at all, I had to struggle to answer him.'

'I sent you a detailed message about her through the Vaanan warrior. Didn't he tell you?'

'He would have, Akka. But it would not have fallen on his ears. He has so many things to think about,' Vanathi said.

'True enough. Akka, after seeing your letter, my mind refused to attend to anything else. My hearing too has become somewhat impaired after this fever. Ask your friend to speak louder,' said Arulmozhi Varman.

Vanathi then proceeded to recount how she went up for a stroll after Kundavai left for the Durga temple and heard the emperor's cry for help. She spoke of what she saw when she looked down. However, whenever she happened to look up at the prince's face, Vanathi became too enthralled to speak. Each time that happened, the princess had to goad her to continue.

After listening to everything with great interest, the prince remarked, 'Akka, your friend seems to have left out a crucial detail. Surely, after seeing all this, she must have fallen into a swoon!'

Kundavai laughed. Vanathi bowed her head bashfully.

Looking at her affectionately, Kundavai told her, 'Vanathi! Go for a stroll by the stream. Or go and join the others inside. Arulmozhi will be here for a few days. You can meet him again.'

'Yes, Akka,' said Vanathi and skipped away, overcome by an inexplicable mood of glee.

Looking at Vanathi as she left with a bright face and wide eyes, Arulmozhi Varman said, 'Akka, I see why father cried out. But what do you think of the scene he witnessed? What did he see? Was it some hallucination? In that case, how could your friend have had the same hallucination?'

'What father saw was no hallucination. Nor did Vanathi see anything illusory. It was a midnight drama in which the young Pazhuvur queen, Nandini, played the main character. I had guessed as much there and then. It was confirmed later by the information that came from you and Vandiyatevan.'

'But why the drama? Why should the Pazhuvur queen play that role, Akka?'

'Nandini has suspicions about her birth. She knew that the emperor had swooned once before when he saw her. After that, she never came into his presence. She thought that this drama may make some kind of truth emerge.'

'Would she have deduced anything from this?'

'I don't know. Not even the god who created Nandini would know what is in her mind. I pity Pazhuvettaraiyar when I think of how she torments him. Tambi, we were talking about beauty. It is Nandini who is the real beauty, the rest of us are as dust at her feet. Any man who sees her becomes her slave at once. Pazhuvettaraiyar, Madhurantakan, Tirumalai, Kandamaran, and last of all, Partibhendran. Terrified of her beauty, Chief Minister Aniruddhar never goes anywhere near her. She is the reason why Aditta Karikalan does not come to Tanjavur. Tambi, only one person remained unalarmed by Nandini's beauty, and unvanquished by it, to return intact.'

'You mean the warrior of the Vaanan clan.'

'Yes, it is he. That is why I have sent him to Aditta Karikalan in Kanchi.'

'Why?'

'The Pazhuvur queen has sent word to our brother, inviting him to the Kadambur palace. I have sent the Vaanan warrior to prevent that meeting and any disaster that may spring from it. Karikalan does not know that Nandini is our elder sister. Nor do I know whether Nandini has discovered our kinship.'

'Is it certain that Nandini *is* our sister?'

'How can it be doubted? Tambi, I have changed my mind completely from the time I learnt this. When we were children, I loathed Nandini and humiliated her. I was jealous of her beauty. I was determined that you and Karikalan should not even talk to her. My envy and aversion persisted even after her departure to the Pandya country. When she returned as the wife of the Pazhuvur lord, I shamed and ridiculed her. Now I am determined to atone for it all.'

'How, Akka? What kind of atonement?'

'Next time I see her, I will fall at her feet and beg forgiveness for all my sins. I will accept any punishment she may deem fit.'

'I will stop you. You have not committed any sin. Nor is there any need for you to ask anyone to forgive you. There is no one in the whole world who can punish you. You did not feel jealous of the Pazhuvur queen. It was she who was jealous of you. It was she who hated you.'

'Tambi! You told me that your heart was convulsed whenever you thought about our stepmother roaming like a lunatic in Ilankai. I feel my heart would break when I think of how Nandini, who should have lived in the palace with every luxury and comfort, went through all the sufferings that she did in her life. Because of a mistake committed by someone, sometime, long ago, the sister born before me had to marry the old man Pazhuvettaraiyar.'

'Akka! Have you any inkling of how these things could have happened? Why does our father believe our stepmother to be dead? What is the reason for Nandini to have been raised like an orphan in some stranger's house, and to be in this situation?'

'I think about this day and night but am unable to discover answers with any certainty. There are two people we know, who will know these secrets. Our great aunt Sembiyan Mahadevi knows something. Chief Minister Aniruddha Brahmarayar probably knows everything. But we can never learn anything from them. Azhvarkadiyan too must know something about it, at least in part. But he is more tight-lipped than his guru. Tambi! There is no urgent need to discover these secrets. What is important now is to prevent the catastrophe or dishonour that may befall our clan through Nandini. My heart has been thrown into turmoil from the time I heard Vandiyatevan saying, "The Pazhuvur queen is paying homage to a sword as refulgent as lightning, marked with the sign of the fish." I fear that she may take some wrong step, ignorant as she is about her birth in the Chozha clan.'

'Why not tell her everything?'

'I'm not sure if it would serve any purpose. Her rage against us may increase. But we must do our duty.'

'You were right to send Vandiyatevan for that purpose. But should we not tell father as well? Why should he suffer in mind as he does in body? Can we leave for Tanjavur at once?'

'Not at all, tambi. I am leaving for Tanjavur in two days. But *you* must stay in the Chudamani Viharam for some time.'

'Why do you say that? Are you asking me to break father's command and stay in hiding here?'

'Yes. If you came to Tanjavur now, the whole country would be plunged into an uproar. The people are furious with Madhurantakan and the Pazhuvettaraiyars. They are angry with the emperor too for having ordered your arrest. If the people see you now, they will explode in fury. The consequences would be incalculable. The people may lay siege to the Tanjavur palace and fort, and start demanding that you should be crowned at once. Father would be more pained than he is now. Tambi! It was for the sake of the country's welfare that I sent you the missive I did, asking you to come here. For the very same reason, I now think that it would be better for you to go back to Ilankai.'

'Akka! That's impossible. I won't return without seeing our father. If you think it would be better for me to make a secret visit to Tanjavur, I will do so. But I will have to see the emperor. I must tell him about mother Kaveri who rescued me.'

'I can do all that at the opportune moment. Do you *have* to come?'

'Father will be convinced only if I, who had seen it all, tell him about it. I too will gain solace. I will also obtain his permission to bring our stepmother . . .'

'Arulmozhi, I will not oppose your wish. But please stay in the Chudamani Viharam for another week. I will go to Tanjavur, tell father about your arrival and send word to you. Tambi! I came here not only to see you but also to beg you for a boon. If you grant it, I will trouble you no more. Tambi, men should undergo perils. I do want you to gain fame as a fearless and invincible warrior. But you must yield to my entreaty before you get yourself into dangerous situations again.'

'Akka, why this long preamble? Have I ever refused to do your bidding?'

'No, you have not. It is with that faith that I ask you this. Aditta Karikalan did not marry. Nor does it look as though he *will* marry. The lineage of Sundara Chozha must be continued through you. You must fulfil my wishes . . .'

'If I fulfil your wish, you will consent to my marrying the girl of my choice, won't you?'

'Why do you ask this question? Our wishes have not run counter to one another for twenty years. Why do you ask for my consent in this particular instance alone?'

'Akka, there *is* a reason for this. The girl I marry must be someone who will support me in fulfilling my ambitions.'

'Tambi, do you wish to fulfil your ambitions with a girl's support?'

A cry for help broke through that moment. 'Ayyo! Ayyo! Akka! Akka!'

It was Vanathi's voice.

46

Vanathi Laughed

As the prince and Kundavai Devi were conversing in the Nandi mandapam, with Vanathi listening from behind the pillar, an important exchange was taking place between Poonkuzhali and Sendan Amudan.

'Amuda! I am going to ask you something. Will you answer me truthfully?' Poonkuzhali asked.

'Poonkuzhali, I can speak nothing but the truth. That is why I have avoided talking to anyone in the last four days,' Amudan answered her.

'There are some people whose tongues are unable to speak anything approaching the truth. Vandiyatevan, who took the missive to the prince, is one of them.'

'But he is a good man. He has never lied to harm others.'

'He said something about you. I wish to know whether it is true or false.'

'There is no need for him to say anything untrue about me. But tell me what he said.'

'He said that you heaped praise on me.'

'Completely true.'

'He said that you loved me and wanted to marry me.'

'Did he really say that?'

'Yes, Amuda!'

'I must express my gratitude to him.'

'Why?'

'On my own, I would not have had the courage to open my heart to you. I must thank him for speaking to you for me.'

'Does this mean that what he said was true?'

'Yes, Poonkuzhali, no doubt about it.'

'Why do you love me?'

'Must love have a reason?'

'Think about it and tell me. There would have to be *some* reason for it.'

'Poonkuzhali! Until now, no one in the world has discovered the "why" and "how" of love.'

'Don't people begin to love because they are impressed by each other's good looks?'

'Yes, they do. They can get infatuated with beauty. But it cannot be called true love, nor does it last long. You mentioned Vandiyatevan. He became my friend the moment he saw me. I was ready to give my life for him. Did he become my friend because I am handsome?'

'But didn't he talk a great deal about my beauty?'

'Yes. He did. But he was not enamoured of you. He described the beauty of the Pazhuvur queen a hundred times more. But he did not fall in love with her.'

'I know the reason.'

'What is it?'

'It is because that warrior's heart is with the princess who is talking to the prince over there.'

'Doesn't this prove that love has nothing to do with beauty?'

'What do you mean? Are you saying that I am more beautiful than Princess Kundavai?'

'Of course. How can there be any doubt in this matter, Poonkuzhali? You are many times more beautiful than the Pazhaiyarai princess and that princess of Kodumbalur who is now hiding behind the pillar. Even the beauty of the young queen of Pazhuvur, who is supposed to be as bewitching as the divine seductress Mohini, cannot equal yours. But this beauty of yours is my enemy. That is why I am unable to express the love raging in my heart. I fear that you, who may be sought by the gods in the heavens and the kings of this world, may never be attainable.'

After a short period of reflection, Poonkuzhali said, 'Amuda, what will you do if I say that I don't care for you?'

'I will be patient for a while to see if you change your mind.'

'How can it change?'

'The human mind can be strange. Sometimes, we are unable to understand what lies deep in the heart. External circumstances may cloud our minds. We know our true mind when these delusions are cleared.'

'All right, so you will wait. But what if my mind does not change?'

'I will try to get over my love for you.'

'Is it possible?'

'It is, if you try. It is possible if you direct your mind towards the almighty. Our elders controlled the mind by their devotion to god.'

'Amuda! I don't think that what you feel for me is true love.'

'Why do you say so? What is true love?'

'If you have genuine love for me, you should want to kill me when I reject you. Your rage should boil over if you come to know that I love another, not you.'

'Poonkuzhali, I spoke of love divine, with the attributes of goodness and serenity. The love you are talking about is demonic and could be called monstrous love.'

'I know nothing of divinity or monstrosity. All I know is human nature. Love must generate joy. What if it produces pain instead? If someone we love does not return that love, why should we put up with betrayal? Is it not human nature to take revenge?'

'No, Poonkuzhali, taking revenge is not a human instinct. It is demonic in nature. If we truly love someone, that person's happiness must fill us with joy. Even if rejection is painful at first, if we endure it and respond with acts of goodness, we will experience a tenfold increase in joy.'

'What you describe is not human nature at all. Nor is it an attitude that is at all possible for human beings to possess. A physician's son accompanied Vandiyatevan. As soon as he saw me, he became enamoured of me. When he realized that it was in vain, imagining Vandiyatevan to be standing in the way, he betrayed Vandiyatevan to the Pazhuvur men. He would have tried to kill me too.'

'In that case, he doesn't belong to the human race but to the tribe of demons.'

'There stands the Kodumbalur princess. She has lost her heart to Ponniyin Selvan. What would she do if Ponniyin Selvan did not accept her? Certainly, she would try to poison him and kill him. If she knew of any other woman who had captivated his heart, she would try to kill her too.'

'Poonkuzhali! Not for a moment do I think so. Vanathi, who is all goodness, would never try to do that.'

'Maybe. But that is what I would do.'

'I would pray for you to be forgiven and saved by the lord.'

'Who is god to forgive me? It is I who should forgive god.'

'God will forgive your blasphemy too.'

'Amuda! You are noble. You have inherited our older aunt's nature.'

'What's that? You are saying something new . . .'

'Haven't the people in our family been saying that our older aunt is dead?'

'Do you mean your father's and my mother's elder sister?'

'Yes. She is not really dead.'

'I had heard about it, vaguely.'

'Even now, she is wandering like a madwoman in the wilderness of Ilankai.'

'Who can do anything about a family curse?'

'But a family curse is not the sole reason for her madness. The real reason is the betrayal of a Chozha prince.'

'What? What?'

'When she was young, our aunt lived on a little island near Ilankai. A Chozha prince pretended to be in love with her. She believed him. He spurned her when he was crowned.'

'How did you learn all this, Poonkuzhali?'

'Through my mute aunt's language of signs. Listen, I will tell you something else too. Some time ago, some men from the Pandya country had come here. They asked for my help to take revenge on the Chozha race for what had happened to my aunt. My blood was boiling after hearing her story. I decided to join them. That was when I learnt about my aunt's outlook. Not only had she forgiven the man who betrayed her, but she saved the life of his son, born to him through another wife. I gave up my idea of joining the Pandya men. My aunt's love is indeed divine, as you have described it. But I won't be like her.'

'What will you do?'

'If any prince betrays me, I will exact my vengeance. I will kill him and the woman who stole his heart, and then I will stab myself to death.'

'Good god! What horrible things you say!'

'Amuda! You do not know how my heart has been burning for the last two years. That is why you are advising me to be calm.'

'Why should your heart burn when your aunt's does not?'

'That is my aunt's business, this is mine.'

'Yours? Poonkuzhali, is it true? Reflect before you speak.'

'Yes, Amuda. Is there anything to distinguish the blood in my veins from Vanathi's blood if you should compare them?'

'No.'

'Is she in any way superior to me in beauty, brains or skills?'

'No. You were raised on the billowing ocean, she grew up in the palace. You kill wild animals with your bare hands, row your boat through harsh whirlwinds and save people from drowning. Vanathi would be too scared even to look at the waves of the sea; she would scream when she sees a housecat, and faint if she gets bad news.'

'If that is so, what is the reason for the princess to treat me with scorn? Why does she coddle and cosset Vanathi?'

'Poonkuzhali, you are blaming the princess without any cause. Vanathi is her long-term friend. She has just met you. Did she not express overwhelming gratitude to you for having rescued the prince from the sea?'

'Yes, but who wants that palace lady's gratitude? Let her keep it. Amuda, if the prince has to be taken back to the Chudamani Viharam, you may row the boat on your own. I may deliberately overturn the boat.'

'Never will you do such a thing, Poonkuzhali. What crime did the prince commit for you to overturn his boat?'

'Amuda? I have gone mad. My mind is not under my control. I may sink the boat thinking about the way his father betrayed my aunt. Handle the boat by yourself.'

'All right. I will take the prince back. What will you do?'

'I will follow Vanathi and drop a stone on her head.' So saying, Poonkuzhali bent down and picked up a pebble on the canal bank. At the same time, a majestic bull came out of the palm grove by the shore. In a spurt of anger, Poonkuzhali threw the pebble at the bull.

The pebble hit the regal beast on the head. It shook itself once and stared in the direction from which it was thrown.

'Ayyo! Poonkuzhali! What have you done? Should you throw a stone at an animal?'

'Why not?'

'It is a creature that cannot speak or protect itself.'

'There was a mute woman in my family. What about those who hurt her? Was it not because she didn't know how to protect herself that a prince cheated her and ruined her life?'

'What can this bull do about the injustice done to your aunt by someone else?'

'This animal is not such a helpless creature. It has sharp horns that it can ram into the attackers. What can a poor woman who cannot speak or hear do? I will not easily let go of any prince who behaves like that with me.'

'You will not let him go easily. You will throw a stone on a bull and from a boat which it cannot reach to attack you.'

'If it cannot attack me, let it go and butt someone else.'

'That would be just like the way you made this bull the target of your rage against somebody else.'

The bull could not comprehend their argument, but it did end up doing more or less what Poonkuzhali had suggested.

Unable to get down into the canal and attack Poonkuzhali, the bull turned around and went leaping forward.

On the other side of the palm grove, Vanathi was walking by herself with her heart skipping in glee. At first, this glee increased when she saw the bull leaping before her. But she started to feel afraid when she saw the animal running at her with its head lowered, horns pointed and tail raised high. She had no other option but to turn around and run towards the canal bank as she tried to reach the Nandi pavilion. By that time, the bull had come very close to her. All she could do now was to go backwards and fall headlong into the stream. That was when she shrieked, 'Ayyo! Ayyo! Akka! Akka!'

Vanathi's cry for help reached Ponniyin Selvan and Kundavai Devi.

Startled, they turned to look at where it came from. At a short distance from the pavilion, Vanathi appeared on the high bank, with her back to the canal, casting a look of terror at something in front of her. The next instant revealed what had terrified her. A king among bulls stood before her, bellowing in all his majesty, 'Mmmmmaaaaaaa!'

One step back and Vanathi would be in the stream. She had no option but to take that backward step. Gauging the situation in an instant, Arulmozhi Varman jumped into the canal from the flight of steps and rushed with the speed of lightning. The timing of his reaching Vanathi from below coincided perfectly with her fall from the canal bank. He caught and held her with both his arms, preventing her from falling upside down into the canal.

For a split second, Kundavai was shaken by the danger about to overtake Vanathi. The next instant, she was plunged in delight on seeing Arulmozhi Varman catching her in his arms.

Arulmozhi came to Kundavai with Vanathi lying like a creeper in his mighty arms–arms steeled by spear throw and swordplay.

'Akka, take your friend. I can't imagine how this girl came to be born in the dauntless clan of Kodumbalur,' he said.

'Tambi! What on earth have you done? How can you touch a young, unmarried virgin?'

'God! Is that a crime now? Are you saying that she should have tumbled down into the stream? Good thing she doesn't know that I caught her. She fainted when she fell. Here, take her.'

Vanathi broke into a peal of laughter. Still laughing, she got out of his arms and jumped to the ground.

'You imp! So you were fully conscious!' Kundavai exclaimed.

Ponniyin Selvan said, 'Akka, ask her why she closed her eyes and pretended to have swooned.'

'It was no pretence, Akka. When he touched me, I closed my eyes in embarrassment.'

'How do I know that? I thought it was your friend's habitual fainting,' said Arulmozhi Varman.

'I will never faint again, and certainly not in his presence. Akka, he must never forget the great good turn I did him today.'

'What? What? *She* did *me* a good turn? This is fantastic!' the prince exclaimed.

Kundavai too looked at Vanathi with some surprise and said, 'Are you saying that you will never forget the good turn my brother did to you?'

'Not at all. Akka, it was I who did a great big favour to your brother. And it is he who must never forget it.'

'I should thank her for saving her from falling into the canal? Does your friend have any mental disorder, Akka?' Ponniyin Selvan asked.

'I am in my right mind, certainly. It is he who is confused. I will explain. You told me that, as a child, he fell into the Kaveri. A woman saved him. He was struggling in the sea. A boatwoman rescued him. Obviously, getting saved by women has become a habit with him. It was I who helped him overcome this loss of face. Have I not made him acquire all the fame of saving a girl from falling into the canal? Should he not therefore show his gratitude to me?' said Vanathi and laughed. Kundavai joined her in laughter. After failing in all his attempts to suppress it, Ponniyin Selvan too exploded into full-throated laughter.

The sounds of their mingled laughter crossed the pavilion and rose to echo from the sky.

Those in the boat heard that laughter. 'Amuda! Do you hear those three madcaps laughing?' asked Poonkuzhali as she too broke into laughter. Amudan began to laugh with her.

Birds dwelling in the palm grove released their tinkling laughter.

Standing regally all the while on the high bank, the bull bellowed with laughter.

The waves of the sea laughed in all their majesty.

The cool breezes blowing from the sea laughed softly, tenderly.

End of Part 3

To be continued . . .

Scan QR code to access the
Penguin Random House India website